"Benderson is the most original thinker I have ever known. . . .
He has the aggressive verbal and analytic style of the Talmudic
tradition, combined with the hipster slant of modern urban
bohemia."   —Camille Paglia, in *Vamps and Tramps*

"Mesmerizing . . . compelling . . . raw, naked, full of
unshielded candor . . . tossing poignant logs on the fire that
makes the best of the book burn into readers' memories."
                                  —*Orlando Sun Sentinel*

"A near perfect piece of writing. . . . An extremely
accomplished and moving book, scary, frequently beautiful,
wonderfully exact in its gloomy poetry and dark humor, and
tempered on every page by compassion."   —*Out*

"Filled with unforgettable characters . . . shines a spotlight into
a corner of society most people never see. . . . The power of
Benderson's work is that it speaks for people whose voices are
never heard, and it reminds us that every one of these living
shadows is a human being."   —*Boston Phoenix*

"Will knock your blinders off. . . . Benderson's work is not
only brilliant fiction, it is also a dispatch from the rawest edge
of experience."   —*San Francisco Bay Area Reporter*

BRUCE BENDERSON is the author of one previous novel, *The
United Nations of Times Square*, and a short story collection, *Pretending to Say No*. His work has appeared in numerous literary
magazines and anthologies, including *The Portable Lower East Side*,
Between C & D, and *Men on Men 3*. He lives in New York City,
where one of his short stories is currently being made into a
movie, and where he is also involved in interactive computer
culture.

Bruce Benderson

U S E R

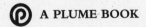 A PLUME BOOK

PLUME
Published by the Penguin Group
Penguin Books USA Inc., 375 Hudson Street,
New York, New York 10014, U.S.A.
Penguin Books Ltd, 27 Wrights Lane, London W8 5TZ, England
Penguin Books Australia Ltd, Ringwood, Victoria, Australia
Penguin Books Canada Ltd, 10 Alcorn Avenue,
Toronto, Ontario, Canada M4V 3B2
Penguin Books (N.Z.) Ltd, 182–190 Wairau Road, Auckland 10, New Zealand

Penguin Books Ltd, Registered Offices:
Harmondsworth, Middlesex, England

Published by Plume, an imprint of Dutton Signet,
a division of Penguin Books USA Inc.
Previously published in a Dutton edition.

First Plume Printing, August, 1995
10 9 8 7 6 5 4 3 2

ⓟ REGISTERED TRADEMARK—MARCA REGISTRADA

The Library of Congress has catalogued the Dutton edition as follows:
Benderson, Bruce.
User / Bruce Benderson.
p.   cm.
ISBN 0-525-93722-6 (hc.)
ISBN 0-452-27461-3 (pbk.)
1. Drug abuse—Fiction. 2. Prostitution, Male—Fiction.
I. Title.
PS3552.E5386U82   1994
813'.54—dc20   93–45807
                                                    CIP

Printed in the United States of America

Original hardcover design by Steven N. Stathakis

PUBLISHER'S NOTE

My thanks to Ursule Molinaro, Kevin Mulroy, and Matthew Carnicelli for their advice on this manuscript.

To Anthony Colon, for his quiet courage and wisdom.

My gratitude to Joey P'tail, Kathy, Mayler, and the staff at T.'s.

He clasped a corpse: a body so cold that it froze him. . . .

—Là-bas, J.-K. HUYSMANS

I

Mrs. BUSTER HUXTON III, FIRST NAME SOFIA, AN eighty-six-year-old Portuguese, still maintains an elegant triplex over her porno theater on Eighth Avenue. The discovery of her world lies beyond a musty, rubber-backed velvet curtain that must be swept aside upon entering. As the eyes slowly adapt to darkness, sweating walls become visible. You fumble down the aisle, using the sticky top edges of the leather seats as a guide, then slide into a row, your shoe likely to make an imprint in some viscous liquid.

In the second row are men with thinning hair and defeated shoulders, about to watch a dancer, whose name is Apollo, mount the stage in black posing strap. Lit only by footlights, the room is orangey dark, and the lone silhouettes of the scattered spectators punctuate the gloom. In a moment the music will blast through scratchy speakers; the dancer, a pale-skinned mulatto with a mournful mouth, will leap barefoot onto the stage and lithely slip in and out of a few geometric poses. Then he will drop back onto the stale carpet and zigzag down the aisle to those few stranded men, to ask each under the cover of the blaring music if he might like a private show.

Call me Apollo—that dancer you watched in the shadows and said was mulatto—and you, my date, are somebody in the theater I was lucky or pushy enough to talk into a private show. Thirty's the price I told you, but that will only get me two or three bags of dope this time of night. I only got one foil of crushed-up Dilaudid that I got from a doctor I tricked with. But what about cigarettes and a quart of beer for later?

I already know how to play you into coughing up another twenty. At just the moment when I say I don't got enough to get back to Connecticut will be when you feel most off-guard. Right after you've shot your load, in other words. At this moment I imagine you being as high as I am. There is no explanation for this. Maybe it's just being so close to your face. It's that weird feeling of my eyes about to roll back as the Dilaudid races through my veins to begin the lick at my brain.

In a room below the stage, in the basement, a head keeps bobbing between Apollo's splayed thighs, the taste of rubber blocking out the smell of sweat, mixed with the odor of mildew and cracking vinyl. Up and down the lips and tongue glide, while the bridge of the nose butts dully against him. Each dark, sparkling wave of Dilaudid hitting his brain, reversed by the teasing tongue on body parts.

This must be cozy as Mrs. Huxton feels in her high-class apartment above the theater. I saw it one time. It's all carpet. There's a silver tea service on the first floor in the sitting room. Polished sparkling furniture in the chandelier light and her lifting the control to that cable television . . . Nothing in this four-story building on Eighth Avenue except the theater and the basement, topped by Mrs. Hux-

ton's three luxury floors. Her middle-aged kids are begging her to sell out and move somewhere safe. But seems keeping up her husband's business, which started as a tiny striptease joint on this very block in the 1930s, and can't pull in much now but is worth several million in real estate, became her thing. They told me the evening he finally croaked and the corpse had to be carried down the stairs past the entrance, they switched the lights on and told guys with their pants down to leave, gave rain checks. It was years before I was even born . . .

Outside this room, in the dank corridor lit by one bulb, a fat man in pale clothes lurches by the entrance to a dingy lavatory. His sulfur gaze fixes on a dancer in a stretched-out jock strap hoisting a granite leg to the sink to wash off a thick foot, the calf of the other leg bulging in a big knot. In the faint, purplish light, dark hollows of muscle cleave his bending back. He lifts his head to gaze in a dull come-on at the fat man fumbling toward him and parting his lips in a soft popping sound like some marine creature.

Farther away, where the corridor rises in two steps leading to a fire door, crouches a boy shakily trying to light a match. The head of the first match disengages and sparks into the darkness, giving a glimpse of a bristling red crew cut, waxy skin. Then another match flares, revealing an opaline glass stem phosphorescent with smoke, pursing lips, and pinched features. He sucks in his breath as the end of the pipe glows brighter and the match fades.

In the dressing room, in front of a decrepit dressing mirror that is missing bulbs, sits a downy-lipped teenager with large, shiny curls and grimy hands, squinting almost as if in performance in the dim light at the open math book in his lap.

Meanwhile, in the room with the so-called mulatto, the grunts of arousal have become more manifest. The gentleman's hand jerks at the wan penis that sticks out from the open zipper of his pants, groanings occur, and an ejaculation hits the black wall. The lips spasm around the half-erect member of the drugged dancer and then loosen. He sits up and clears his throat, then wipes his mouth with the back of his hand; he tucks in his shirt and zips up, buckles his belt, and fishes into his pocket for the thirty dollars he had ready . . .

. . . My cock shrinking from the peeled bag that I toss on the floor with the others, speaking quick but soft so as not to ruin the mood, going heavy with the lingo of the street that puts the fear in some of you, and putting myself between you and the door, your only means of escape:

"You took too long, daddy, I got to take a cab to the station . . . man. I got to hit New Haven tonight on that last bus. Come on, I said, now pass me another twenty!"

I'll go on and on without budging. The Dilaudid's a drug for cancer patients that kills pain and tranquilizes, but I can get chatty and speedy from its rushes. I know that this must sound very flipped for a john who has come and now wants out of this little room with me blocking the door. But nobody'll probably hear should you call out . . . And believe me, in Mrs. Huxton's world scenes like this can turn into a bad dream. Even a big guy who is outraged will think twice before pushing this situation to the max. There might be an argument as you fumble too long in another pocket for more money . . . But even if you decide to stand up to me in the tiny room, I won't take my eyes off your face. The Dilaudid gives me a strange kind of courage as you flip back and forth between decisions.

No one else is there to witness the standoff. The fat man wandering in the hallway and the dancer at the lavatory sink had disappeared together into another stall. At the sounds of agitation, the crack smoker and the curly-haired boy with the math book took the stairs two at a time. But perhaps in a room three floors above, sequestered from Eighth Avenue

4

by concrete grillwork and ventilation ducts, an old woman shifts quaveringly in her sleep.

The so-called live show is over now. A tepid fantasy film colors the screen: the bedroom of a tract house somewhere in Southern California, an acrylic painting of a sunset seascape color-coordinated to the violet bedspread upon which loll two scraggly-haired teenagers whose locked limbs are at odds with the overlay of frantic disco music . . .

In the back by the curtained entrance, Casio, an ex– gang member who's been the bouncer in this place ever since he got out of jail the second time, raises a brow over a dark-circled eye at the sound of the dull thuds coming from the private rooms. *What was that crash?* It could be that one of the boys is giving a trick some trouble. And with all the new construction changing the neighborhood, things have become hot; the authorities are waiting for an excuse to come in and shake the place down. By habit, the bouncer pricks up his vigilant, nocturnal ears, unconsciously compresses into an animal crouch . . . perches inwardly on the shot of dope that he did earlier to muster what remains of his old machismo.

But maybe the noise was just a seat slapping into position. Or a middle-aged trick stumbling on a stair. He strains to hear. All he can make out is the synthesized disco of the porno film, an occasional sigh or intake of breath. Then again, the unmistakable sound of a body thudding against a thin wall.

He moves toward the stairs but pauses. He's reluctant to go down there before he decides: which of the five kids going out and coming in high and going out again and coming back in is it?

Carlos is no problem. He's so doped up he don't want no trouble —a papi-*crazy faggot who comes off like a barrio homeboy and'll always back down. And white-one-what's-his-face, Red? Even if*

*thirsted out for rockets he'll crumble up the minute he see my face,
'cause of the time I found him doing that queen behind the movie
screen for a toke.*

*But the half-breed nigger always talking crap about that Miss
Huxton owns this place and inviting him to teas? Wacky enough
to go the whole mile! . . . Oreo cookies're like that. I just might end
up having to nix his ass.*

He marches grimly down the stairs with a sense of ailing
authority. But the trick with the thinning hair has already
dodged Apollo after being pushed against the wall by him,
has fled the private room and ducked behind the stairwell.

Out of the private room stumbles the stoned dancer,
looking for the vanished green. And what conspires next
takes place only in Apollo's mind. For only he could explain
what happened in the stairwell: how running into the prematurely aged Casio with his glaring eyes and permanent
scowl threw him into a rage—back to the South and shorts
and a blackberry patch where he'd had the same feeling of
being mistrusted for no good reason . . . had picked up a
thorny branch lying on the dirt path and started swinging
it . . .

Why the bouncer's snide rictus smile filled him with
spite at merely being a serf in the empire of Mrs. Huxton . . .

Until Casio's eye exploded under Apollo's scarred fist.
The bouncer careened on his heels and fell back, tipped
forward again to regain his balance, then fell back off the
stairwell for good. His spine struck the floor in a wet smack,
and he lay there with his back askew, while the trick
crouched in his hiding place in fascination and dread.

Then Casio's eyes rolled up, back, and his mouth dangled
wide open. And he couldn't stop hearing his ears ringing.

Apollo the attacker ran down the sweltering street, his fist bleeding and pulsing. A dim shiver must have crept along his sweaty spine as he wondered how badly he had hurt Casio. He headed for a haven from revenge—the transvestite lounge just a few blocks up the avenue.

Tina, the drag-queen owner, was slipping her shoulders out of her three-quarter mink, which she wore to offset her expensive green pants suit, despite the summer heat. It fell into the hands of one of her waiters, who hastily locked it in the storeroom downstairs. At the same time, Tina's index finger swept from the center of her siliconed chest to the door, like a sultan in a low-budget movie banishing a subversive subject. Standing near the door was the shirtless and breathless Apollo, who had no I.D. and whose knuckles showed congealed gashes in the orange light.

With glowering eyes, he held his ground until Tina took a step forward. Then he skulked into the street. Tina's pointing hand unfurled into a flattened palm, which daintily patted her extravagant but provincial coiffure.

"Love the little ones," she quipped, " 'cause they're real easy to push around."

The embarrassed fugitive was bumped back into the no man's land of Eighth Avenue, his mind seething with the indignity of being kicked out by an authority-figure queen. He headed north with his clotting fist. But the more he ran, the more his anxiety about what had happened diminished . . . Soon he let off steam by kicking over a box. It still held the three bottle caps and the pea that he had set up earlier as a betting game to dupe some German tourists. Leaping shirtless through the polluted, copper-colored mists, he became a smaller and smaller dot. For him, the dot of himself was shrinking so fast that it seemed as obscure as one of tonight's tricks. His high dwindled as he dwindled, and he'd need another shot soon. Especially tonight, after what had happened.

As he moved from block to block, he passed other exiles barred from Tina's, such as Angelo, a tall, rotten-toothed adolescent whose speech was permanently slurred by the ridged jaw of constant crack use, and whose bare toes poked from ripped sneakers. Angelo tried to lure him farther west, promising to get him a deal on a hit, but Apollo kept going, past big Cubby, also bare-chested, covered with tattoos that he claimed told the story of his life in stages, like stations of the cross, and who spit out wisecracks about Apollo's butt and alternately pleaded for a dollar.

A shiny limousine caught up with Apollo and seemed to slow down to his pace. In his mind, it must have been Mrs. Huxton's driver, whom she used for her rare outings or for transports of human and other cargo. For him, Mrs. Huxton was the principle of order in all this chaos, the final authority, even beyond Tina and the cops. She stood with the means and the schedules for things. Her high principles even seemed to regulate the ritual of taking dope, a revolving door she watched him go round and round in. If she'd ordained that he be brought in and punished for what had happened, then maybe he'd have to go; but the limo picked up speed again.

The air made his lungs smart. Tonight the street stank of something worse than the bar or the theater. They had smelled like bug spray and filthy toilets and stale beer, but the street was perfumed by polluted river water or clothing rotting. He gasped for breath and slouched against a trash can.

The trick from the theater—the cocksucker with thinning hair and defeated shoulders—hadn't given him more money after being knocked against the wall but had pushed past him out of the room with a weird smile on his lips. What was worse was that the money Apollo did get must have fallen out of his posing strap when he pulled his pants on after wasting Casio. There was nothing stuffed in the posing strap or in his pants pockets but a folded square of paper with a pinch of the Dilaudid he'd gotten from the doctor, a freaky M.D. who came straight from the emergency room to the theater during breaks from a nearby hospital. This and the Percodan he sometimes picked up from his friend who had AIDS were Apollo's only pharmaceutical sources of downers.

He surveyed the spacious avenue, which made him feel like a sitting duck. Anybody who didn't keep moving on this strip was obviously hooking, dealing, or looking to cop. Bobbing toward him on scrawny legs like a diseased chicken was Gloves (*Georgie Golden Gloves, was that his name?*), now and then almost losing his balance to shadowboxing. He was the angel-dust head who always carried around a frayed picture of himself losing a Golden Gloves tournament.

Apollo stomped into the middle of the sidewalk, and Georgie collided with him.

"Listen! I got a problem, I gotta get outta here, lemme stay with a couple dollars," Apollo muttered as Georgie fumbled against him.

Apollo crashed against him again with more force, throwing his shoulders into it. But Georgie was numb and answered from the fantasy world of angel dust in the voice of Al Pacino's Scarface:

"I took a little on the side, but I never fucked you, Frank."

"Then gimme a stogie," was how Apollo countered the non sequitur.

But Georgie Golden Gloves was already bobbing up the block.

An aftershock of Dilaudid, jammed in some capillary until now, troughed out a wave of high, and Apollo concentrated on riding it. He let the memory of the theater wash away by thinking of this morning's clever evasion of arrest. It had a shiny coating of triumph from this high perspective.

There he was in "Dark Park" in the Bronx at 5:00 A.M. this morning, trying to cop with no I.D., when the cops stopped him, carrying his blade and his works,

. . . the two white cops saying we don't want 'em, and the P.R. cop saying give 'em to me, I'll take his ass.

So they ran up a warrant check on me, but even though the name was right, the D.O.B. (that stands for date of birth, dork) was wrong. What are you, a black or a Hispanic? I got kids, I sobbed. So they just hit me with a D.A.T.—a desk appearance ticket. And let me go. So where does all the good luck come from, you're wondering? People loving you, praying for you . . .

He crashed off the doctored memory with the realization that he was reciting it to himself as if he were telling it to somebody important. *Getting ready to tell it is all!* he caught himself philosophizing through the high. But then the departed wave of Dilaudid dropped him on his ass again, and pride about the incident deflated. He yawned and peered with fierce vigilance through the copper light of dilapidated Eighth Avenue.

Mercedes was flouncing across the street. The black transvestite, in an outrageous gold lamé outfit, had halted at the curb and yanked up her top to pop out her breasts, grabbing and squeezing them for him. In the shimmering pollution and from a distance, the image took on an idealized quality.

Glancing quickly both ways, she pulled her miniskirt up and panties down, kept her cock pressed between her dark, sinewy legs, and mimed a pussy dance just for him. The astonished passengers of an Oldsmobile stopped at a red light—theatergoers—clicked shut the locks of their car and lurched forward. Apollo delightedly mimed a jerking-off motion to the queen. It was only for a split second that a collapsed version of what had happened maybe two months—a year?—ago flared up in his mind. He'd been her boyfriend then.

Kind of. But well, then, one night I needed—something—
from her purse . . .

All right! It was fix money, and when she found out, well . . .

She'd come looking for him on Ninth Avenue . . . And he'd
had the bad luck of being in the act of rapping to another
queen when she spotted him . . . *"Mercedes, really, I woulda*
asked you."

"I'll fucking cut you, you son of a bitch!" reaching into her
purse.

"No, come on now, put that shit away, there's cops around."

Mercedes's big hand with its inch-long fingernails was
whipping the gleaming blade from side to side. First it
slashed open his shirt, then made some long cuts across his
chest. She kept reaching for his face, but he fended her off,
let her cut his forearm instead.

Winded, she let the knife drop to her side, her eyes
streaming with tears, running the mascara. Her straightened
hair had come undone and was plastered by sweat to her
Nubian-boned face.

It wasn't so much being cut by a queen in public but
noticing that one silicone-plumped cheek had fallen slightly
below her prominent cheekbone that curled his fingers into
a hard fist. It hit the cheek and her mouth, chipped part of
a front tooth out . . .

"Is this guy giving you trouble, little lady?"

"Yes, officer, he tried to rape me." Her head was bowed, her
hand clasping her bloody mouth. She was sobbing.

"Against the wall! Put your arms up!"

"Can't you see it's a guy, officer! That's no lady!"

"Keep your mouth shut!"

The cop found his works and a bag right away, so he
was sent to Rikers, bleeding like a pig, and waited three
months without bail.

The queen was gone. The space where she had appeared
across the street was now a dull blot of dirty air, tinged with

red neon from the porno marquee above it. With the sensual certainty of still being a little high, Apollo reassured himself he no longer had feelings for her, or anybody else on the street. The thought itself was anesthetic, so he slipped hypnotically into it, probing the dimensions of that lack of feeling.

He remembered a conversation about johns with another hustler from Tina's. The hustler moved his out-turned palm up and down the length of an imaginary wall as if he were lathing it. The wall permanently divided "them" with the money from "us" out here. *They're fake*, he kept repeating about the johns. *They don't exist*, he kept saying. *But us, we're out here, we're down by law . . .*

A sentimental image of the boy—ripped jeans, big ass, blue tank top—flashed into Apollo's stoned head. A white boy who was also hustling and doing dope. And then one night—

What happened? Oh, yeah. I ended up in bed with my buddy's john. Hee, hee, hee.

A tiny smirk crossed Apollo's lips. He marveled at his wispishness. He complacently pictured his own naturally lithe body and imagined steamy breath, those hungry caresses.

I didn't plan to get over on ole buddy like that. But let's face it that the drug acts like a wild aphrodisiac sometimes. People who say that you don't like sex on dope don't know their ass from their elbow. I can really turn a trick out some days when I'm high. So the john kicked him loose. And then moved me in.

A burst of breaking glass! Apollo and the john leaping out of bed in the middle of the night. The tank top and the ripped jeans! Apollo's old, good buddy (who'd gotten skinny, lost his big ass) had shattered the kitchen window, was crouched by it.

Yeah, but had I already moved my things into the john's house by then? Yeah, that must be how I lost that jacket . . .

Apollo's thoughts flipped back once again to the guy's

working tongue, his inner thighs tensing and relaxing with wetness, before—crash! . . . *My ole buddy has him facing the refrigerator and is trying to tie him to it. The john's looking at me over the turns of rope with pleading eyes, like why don't I help him? What the fuck am I supposed to do? You don't treat a hustler like that to make him your favorite boy and then dump him for another. "Just don't hurt him," I told my ole buddy. But I had to let him lie in the bed he made . . .*

After the john dropped Apollo for not protecting him, Apollo shortchanged the same hustler by buying him a bundle—ten bags of dope—and then cutting it with talc and baby laxative. Then he made a vow to fly solo, which he'd kept to this day. It was an obvious mistake to trust anybody in this world of sudden calamities and quick solutions. As if in confirmation of this idea, he saw Angelo, that crackhead he'd passed earlier, lurching out of the all-night fruit-and-vegetable store across the street with a bag-sheathed quart of beer. A tall, dead-faced guy in a stocking cap stumbled next to him.

Apollo squinted at them through the copper light, which seemed suddenly to have thickened, making everything look distorted, as if through gelatin. The cap had a shimmering white *X* on it, but it was too hot for a hat. *So this guy is obviously worried about his hair looking nappy.*

Through the rubbery light, Apollo watched Angelo snake a brotherly arm around the guy's shoulder. *But that's the dude Angelo said killed his cousin!*

Apollo momentarily wondered how Angelo could hang with a guy that murdered relatives. Then that thought too began to shimmer like gelatin. *Something about Angelo's cousin doing codeine that night? And Angelo said the guy slipped eye drops in his cousin's drink that put him over the edge. A dude who always wears a big stocking cap that said X.*

He squinted again. The *X*-cap was passing a few bills to Angelo, who palmed them quickly.

But is that really the one he said's the murderer?

Either the guy seemed like somebody Angelo imagined had killed his cousin—and he'd probably imagined it when he was high—or the guy really was the killer. But now that Angelo was high he didn't remember it. Or maybe wasn't thinking about it. If you asked him about it now, his eyes would dim, he'd say, "Hey, you know why I know it wasn't him? 'Cause I was with them all that night!" 'Cause the guy with the *X*-cap was his buddy, kicking in bucks toward another bag of rockets.

Apollo considered bolting across the street and trying to pry one of the bills out of Angelo. But he wondered how the *X*-cap guy would take it. That's the way things worked out here. One minute you slithered your arm around a shoulder, the next you vowed to off somebody.

What's a friend anyway but he gives you something? What a fool you are to give that to somebody. And knowing he does it makes you feel please don't deny me 'cause I'm so hungry! It makes you feel low so you just grab for it, it shows more balls. 'Cause both of 'em are games, pretending I care, pretending I . . . don't care . . .

Apollo condescendingly watched the unholy couple moving up the block until they too were swallowed by the gelatinous light. His thoughts strayed to the one time he'd admitted having feelings for somebody and had gone to jail for it. It was a man who'd been to college. He supposed the guy had been well-meaning—in a white sort of way. In fact, now—just a year later—they were speaking again, the poor dude was sick with HIV symptoms. It was him Apollo got Percs from now and then.

Back then they'd kept tricking over and over. The guy had even wanted to help Apollo kick dope and get rehabilitated.

. . . So he buys me bags of dope and feeds 'em to me, trying to cut down the dose little by little. "I'm in love with you," he keeps promising . . .

Until Apollo believed it was true. But whenever he tried to act appreciative it was the worst—he got goose flesh. He felt a force field of depression forming around him, pressing in and keeping everything out. It fed on the need for the dope and sucked everything good he had seen in the john out of him . . .

One night in the sex theater Apollo started to get the shakes because he needed more dope. The guy wouldn't pass him any money.

I guess he was from a spoiled background and didn't have the balls to keep up with my habit and turned into kind of an asshole.

Words started to shout in Apollo's bursting head. He was sweating and puking.

Saying you care when you leave me here with diarrhea in the dirty toilet . . .

Apollo stalked him out of the theater to the street to try to explain things better . . . *"Don't leave me without a penny to my name when I told you plain and clear that I just needed help this very last time . . ."*

. . . traipsed faster after the bright spot of money getting into a cab, pushed past the pain of his cramping legs to catch him before he got that taxi, rage at what had suddenly diminished to a retreating piece of green taking hold of him . . .

The guy was lying on the pavement, and Apollo was kicking him convulsively.

I didn't really attack my friend, my withdrawal went into spasms.

Connecting with the guy, joining his pain to him with the toe of his boot . . .

So the man pressed charges, and Apollo went back to jail.

———

Some of the cons in jail had put ads in gay papers, about being lonely and needing a gay they could write to and call collect. After that you were supposed to write about your big dick until the guy cracked. You'd talk about all the things that would happen when you got out, and then hit him up for money and cigarettes.

For some, the person on the outside started to do all kinds of favors. He'd send cigarettes, books, commissary money, call relatives for you. Occasionally, the locked-up one got strung-out, so that the other's generosity took on strange, impossible significations. Sexual identity stretched like a rubber band . . .

It was just Apollo's luck yet again to attract one who wanted more than anything else to be a nice guy. This weird type kept popping up. *"Don't write me sexual letters. Let's be honest with each other."* A series of "spiritual" letters passed between them, discussing third-world liberation and the prison system, which he'd learned about from his first white sugar daddy. The guy complimenting his intelligence. There was sensitive talk about relationships, the meaning of friendship, and dreams Apollo had had.

"May upon the arrival of this letter, it will find you in the best of health . . ." Apollo always began each letter, cursing the fact that his perpetual, damning, and desperate need always had to rear its ugly head again. *"I sincerely hope that you . . ." "Please forgive my asking but . . ." "Hope you are well and by the way could you . . ." "I'm sorry we got to know each other under such bad circumstances for me but if you could . . ."*

This time it was worse. When you're alone in your cell after lights out, anguish might settle in. The loneliness seems limitless. You're tempted to think that this guy could . . . Later it will seem absurd.

Nightmares of torture and sadism, witchcraft being performed on and by him. He felt, as he sat bolt upright in the bunk in the middle of the night, that it was only fair to warn his pen pal with whom he was dealing. *"I've got to admit to you right off the bat that I'm not a very trusting person." "I hate to say it but I'm full of bitterness and rage."* He even told him why he was doing time—for stomping the only guy he'd ever liked outside a sex theater.

But the admissions backfired. *"I'll take the chance . . . I can handle it"* were the guy's responses. An avalanche of feelings piling up. An intolerable need to believe that the guy really might understand everything. Ferocious hate about the better possibility that he would not. He wrestled with it and pushed it away.

"Dear Comrade . . ." But it was too late. The mark had already marked him.

There were sweet moments, his weakest, when he sank into the dream of a friend and protector who was taking care of everything. A kind of Frankenstein patchwork of a buddy-father-brother with a strange, scary erotic aspect. It intoxicated him like the dope. Coming off it was worse. The sense of injustice riddled him, made him feel murderous.

"This will be our last letter. For both our sakes, I think it better we stop communicating. I'll never be able to make you happy."

But the guy kept writing. Was he the con artist of the century? It had almost lulled Apollo into what seemed like a passive, infantile state. A desperate, intolerable need leaking with sexuality. It felt like incest. There he was daydreaming about lying in his arms like some kind of woman. He'd turn into jail pussy if he wasn't careful . . .

Then on Christmas came the pair of Nikes he'd been asking for. And with it the letter that set his teeth on edge. *"This should finally prove to you that I'm really thinking about you in the best possible way."*

What exactly was that supposed to mean? A man who needs shoes on his feet like anyone else having to bow down and suck the dick of the one who provides them? He wrote a grateful-sounding letter, but he had the gnawing sense that every word of it stoked the guy's ego.

A month later the guy came to visit. Apollo was saving the expensive sneakers for when he got out and never thought of wearing them. Not thinking that the guy would not understand the communal nature of prison, he borrowed new sneakers from buddies to dress up for him. Traded a pack of cigarettes for hair gel, got a pressed shirt, and even some stolen cologne. He cleaned his teeth . . .

Sitting in the visitors' room surrounded by couples with their tongues in each other's mouth or hands up skirts, a sinking feeling as he tried to imagine what he would do when he got out to please his benefactor—*the guy's hairy arms, his schoolteacherlike clothes.* He pushed it out of his mind, courageously promising himself not to let his benefactor down.

The guy is staring at my sneakers!

"I thought you said you desperately needed sneakers."

"I did. I borrowed these from somebody."

The guy is giving me a doubtful look! It made him feel lucky to be locked up, because all he wanted to do was slash up the guy's face and hurl the sneakers into the wounds. Everything he'd suspected had come true in one overwhelming wave.

By accepting the sneakers he had branded himself a user, coated himself with slime. And all of it had been ordained by the other person, who was always in power.

But for the guy it had obviously been no big deal. He kept up the sweetish letters, spelling out high ideals, forging a high-class image.

Apollo's emotions like hot coals put all his strength into playing along, waiting for the chance to strike.

The guy's letters and calls had a plaintive element now, because his father was dying. Apollo mimed the right sentiments.

I told him I was there for him . . . Until the guy wrote that his father had finally passed away. Then Apollo went right to work. *"May upon the arrival of this letter, it find you in the best of health . . . I've got to admit what I think of you . . . Sad, lonely gay guy who likes to fantasize that he can control other people . . . felt sorry for you and appreciated what you did for me, I was willing to make some sacrifices for you when I got out—sacrifices, if you know what I mean!"*

Gleefully, but with gritted teeth, he took his punishment as cigarettes, commissary money, books, and promises of lodging stopped abruptly. The rejection was exhilarating, as the reins fell back into his hands. The bitterness reinstated its bulwarks, and life became simple again . . .

Until his time was up. He was back on the streets with no place to live and no sponsor. Within a few days he was combing the sex theater with a needle in his coat pocket. It was almost as if time had stood still.

So still that here he stood: in the spot he had been hundreds of times before, a couple blocks from Tina's bar. No money and a gnawing yen to get high. Eighty-sixed from his only source of money, the sex theater, for wasting that used-up bouncer Casio—who'd fallen half a flight and landed on his back with a wet smack.

II

A MIDDLE-AGED GUY WITH A SAD, DROOPY LOOK TO his shoulders, thinning hair, came loping up the street, almost as if he were heading for the spot in which Apollo was stuck. The dirty sneakers were appropriate for his Caucasian look.

It took Apollo a couple of seconds to place him, even though they had had sex at the theater less than an hour before. It was the john who'd dodged past him and out of the room after he'd pushed him.

Using the instinct-radar of being high, Apollo tried hard to place the nerd. It was obvious that the guy liked taking the tightrope walk between this world and the namby-pamby world he'd been born into. That's why he was still out here cruising the streets, long after scoring and being threatened. Neither world was probably enough for him, only some war between the two. In a way he reminded Apollo of his HIV-positive buddy with the Percs: the well-meaning one he'd shamefully stomped outside the bar a long time ago. Apollo knew he had an instinct for attracting the do-gooders. But a closer look revealed something different, opposite, about this new guy.

When the guy was just about to pass, Apollo leapt into the middle of the sidewalk and spread both arms as if greeting a long-lost friend. The man stopped and reared slightly.

"Remember me?" Apollo beamed, fixing eager, lap-dog eyes on the man's startled face. Hidden within Apollo's puppy eyes was the fang of a threat. He was hoping for a chance to play on the guy's fear, or even guilt feelings about their sleazy hit-and-run sex an hour ago.

Just as he'd figured, the man lapsed into a white-bread reaction. Apollo, who had a white mother, congratulated himself on his instinct. The man simply did not have the skills to brush off the street greeting for what it was. After all, he'd just sucked his dick, even if Apollo had gotten a little rowdy afterward. The well-brought-up man felt he owed him a stiff, sheepish handshake. Apollo slapped it with a confident high-five.

The man's eyes swam eerily under Apollo's bold, dead glance. He looked at Apollo's bare chest but was too tongue-tied to question where his shirt was. It was at this moment that Apollo realized again there was something he didn't understand about him. Like most people who ended up here, there was some flaw . . .

With windup-toy jerkiness the guy resumed his walking, but Apollo caught up to him and stepped up the conviviality. Unable to break the white-bread streak, the guy made some pleasantries but quickened his pace. Apollo matched him step for step, looking for an opening. He decided to go for broke. He apologized about his behavior in the sex room and launched into some big offers that couldn't be refused. He promised the man he'd show him the kind of time he'd never had. Now that he was stuck in the city for

the night, he explained, and couldn't get back to Connecticut—though he didn't blame the guy for it—there'd be
plenty of time to make up for too short a session earlier. If
the guy wanted, they could even get it on when they woke
up in the morning.

A cab had stopped for a light at the corner they were
passing, so Apollo boldly yanked the door open. It was
somewhat to his surprise that the man climbed in without
hesitation and mumbled an address to the driver. The taxi
lurched from light to light as Apollo searched for the
rhythm of the man's breathing. He let his knee fall casually
against the man's thigh and tried to tune his mind toward
his occasional mute gaze. Still, he felt something unfathomable, even the weird hunch that they had something in
common.

What he didn't know was that two years and two months
had passed since this white-collar worker had touched a
crack pipe. Self-help had gotten him to a level where he
could be without drugs, yet strangely enough still craved
atmospheres where they were illegally taken.

Even the most insignificant word or image could start
a tantalizing chain of associations going—a synaptic series
with a will all its own. "Smoke," "match," "rock," or the
sight of a wire hanger like the ones he had used to dig out
his stem, certain odors not uncommon in urban settings—
all had special meanings. Gashed knuckles and sullen expressions like Apollo's could draw him back to the past as
well: the air of a sealed-off room, a young hustler-addict,
and occasional voiceovers from a porno tape that had contributed to the heightened atmosphere of crack smoking
and sexual chance-taking.

Apollo slouched nonchalantly against the door and
sensed the guy's sporadic glances dive-bomb his body like
insects. With that detached flow of consciousness of the constantly at risk, he idly wondered what he could be in for.
But the man's face in the gloom was charged with thoughts

that were unreadable, and, with the wisdom of those who know that almost any decision may be their last, Apollo decided not to worry about it.

With his next nervous glance, the man drank in the two creases showing in the skin over Apollo's brown stomach. He may have had sex with him in the gloomy theater, but now he could get a different perspective on the leanness of that kind of stomach that had nothing to do with the gym. Those creases reminded him of the thrill about to come, in former times, as he rode with some wiry adolescent or other back to his house, his pocket filled with little plastic vials.

Their taxi cruised on past the theater where they'd met, from which a sheet-covered stretcher was now being carried. Though the man was fairly certain that Apollo didn't know he'd seen what had happened in the theater, dread mixed with eerie satisfaction began to trickle through him. He imagined a finger poised on a button that could blow up their world, then promised himself he wouldn't do it . . .

Next to the ambulance in front of the theater, a man in a chauffeur's cap lounged against a gleaming black limousine. He was talking to the fat, greasy theater cashier, who wore an obvious toupee. The chauffeur gawked at the stretcher being hoisted into the ambulance as the cashier undoubtedly held forth about what was supposed to have happened. His four stubby fingers sliced by rings flew up into the light from the garish marquee to make a point.

Apollo ducked below the cab window and eyed his companion warily. The man noticed that in the gloom of the taxi the whites of his big, panicked eyes seemed to glow like two golf balls. The shadows had reduced Apollo's chest to the two pointed black dots of his nipples.

"Wonder what all the ruckus near the theater is?" the man ventured in a neutral tone.

Apollo glanced nervously at the man's battered sneakers. Then his eyes darted to the thinning hair as he shook the question off. "You got to watch out around here, but not with me!"

"You sure?"

"I'm not sitting on my ass all day like these other guys. I'm going to go to junior college. You can search me if you don't believe me."

A cone of light illuminated the man's swank yet sterile, disordered bedroom. Apollo didn't even bother looking around. His face sank into the junkie's lunar passivity and showed no interest in the sparse furnishings, books, or jumble of papers on the table. He imagined a clarified version of his real face floating above it, leaving behind a dimension. This made him feel handsome in a posed sort of way. At this point he had stopped strategizing. All he wanted was to do up the Dilaudid and feel high.

His bare, sinuous arms snaked apart to shove both battered hands beneath his black jeans. The jeans popped open and slid down his hips so he could knead his pubic hair. Then a knife tumbled out of his pocket and clattered to the floor.

"You aren't going to need that here," said the man in a tight voice.

Apollo's large, downturned mouth made a show of resenting not being trusted. He picked up the knife and placed it gently on a table. In sullen defense of himself, he began listing the magazines and TV programs of an educational nature that he chose to read and watch in preference to comics or karate movies—something that distinguished him from all the other hustlers. They were one reason a person needed to carry something to defend himself out there. He told the man about his white, college-educated mother, who was now into New Age. But the man mugged large indifference to the calculated harangue and held out his arms in a conciliatory gesture. Apollo wetted his lips with a little spittle and parted them in a grimace of gratitude for being understood.

Against the man's mouth, Apollo's lips tasted like to-
bacco. In the man's arms it was as if the body were fading
in and out of the approximate picture of itself. The boy's
skin smelled cloying yet phosphorescent, like the scent of
those moments the man had seen time telescope into a jag-
ged series of arousals and climaxes, coming impossibly close
to a perpetual state of orgasmic disintegration . . .

Such continual stimulation, aided at times by an erotic
videotape, had been fueled by frequent passes of the pipe
between the man and his partner for the night . . . And only
when the last rock had melted into smoke did the nightmare of groveling for more life-substance descend upon
him with any reality. Then consciousness was compacted
into a ghoulish struggle, and each gesture was fraught with
imminent failure, as life slipped through his fingers like
sand through the hand of a skeleton . . .

"Got any porno with girls too?"

The man firmly shook his head.

Apollo stared dully at the tangle of limbs for a few seconds before pressing Stop.

"What kind of work you do?"

"Research."

"Use me as a guinea pig and you better make sure I
get something out of it."

The man had noticed the bilge color intensifying on
the surface of Apollo's skin as his eyes clouded with impo-
tent annoyance. Frustration was trickling into those eyes as
the drugs drained out of the membranes of his nervous
cells. He slumped onto the bed and his cigarette dropped
out of his hand. Patiently the man stood up and put it in
the ashtray.

"I don't understand why you would pick up guys
around where we met," Apollo mumbled from script.
"They're all about getting high."

"____"

"Some of these men pick up guys to get high to have

25

sex with. Next you're gonna tell me you get high and that you smoke crack? I don't like to be around that shit."

"Don't worry."

"I mean, I smoke a little reefer or drink a beer. You got a beer?"

"Unh-uh."

"I don't know if you know they got some really wack people working in that theater I work at."

The man threw him a blank, noncommittal look.

"This one guy, the bouncer or what you call it, he's really fucked-up, man, been a junkie for years."

"Oh?"

"Casio? You ever heard of him?"

The man shook his head.

"These other guys got no control. It's okay to get high from time to time, but you got to have discipline."

"Some chemicals don't even respect discipline."

"You sound like one of those N.A. people. Like sometimes I have done dope but I have never gotten hooked on it."

"Keep doing it and you will."

"I appreciate your concern. Listen, I'm going to do some dope tonight. Not really dope. It's pharmaceutical Dilaudid. I got a doctor friend gave me some. That doesn't bother you, does it?"

"Well . . ."

"No. Don't worry. The guy's a doctor."

The man's face turned even more poker-blank. "Can I put you in the alley when you overdose on me?"

"A man with your high morals wouldn't do that to me, I know, and besides, it won't happen!"

The mixture in the bottle cap bubbled over the flame of the lighter that Apollo had asked the man to hold. Apollo's unzipped pants had fallen farther off his hips, revealing the swell of his ass cheeks. In one hand he held the bottle cap. In the other he balanced a needle and a wad of cotton.

Apollo moved the cap away from the flame and dropped in the cotton, which soaked up the whitish liquid immediately. Then he inserted the point of the needle into the cotton and slowly drew back the plunger. The point sucked the liquid silently.

Once the spike was in his arm, a little blood gushed out of the punctured vein around the point of the needle; then it mixed with the liquid in the syringe as he drew the plunger back. In small taps he eased the solution back into the vein.

The man's face began to mimic Apollo's pasty glow. For some reason he too had lost his color. Witnessing penetration into the taut striation of muscle under velvety bruised skin must have thrilled him with the possibility of entrance to the pain swirling inside, about to be extinguished in a flash.

The image of a functioning body began to dissolve as Apollo fell out of the cone of light and sank onto the bed, coughing, and consciousness flowing out of the large, fluid eyes.

One arm snaked about the man's neck and he pulled him toward him. He lit a cigarette and inhaled.

"You liked watching that."

"I was afraid you'd O.D."

"Not with that, it's pharmaceutical, I know how much to do."

"Really? Where did you get your training?"

"See, I'm smarter than the others you probably go with."

Emboldened by his high, Apollo made another wild stab at credibility. "I got this friend—well she's kind of a friend—name of Mrs. Huxton, who owns the whole neighborhood we just came from and can see I'm not exactly like the others, so she kind of has me keep an eye on her theater for her—you know, where I work. She wanted to keep me from getting into trouble, see . . . and offered me this apprenticeship with a friend of hers. It's a school."

"What kind of school?"

Apollo fumbled for an answer. "Technician's school."

"What kind of technician?"

"Guard-dog training," he blurted out.

"You train dogs?"

"Sure."

"How do you train them?"

"Well you have to make sure the dog isn't distracted. So you get all in white—dogs don't react to white—and you take the dog in a white room all lit up white. Nothing in the room but you and the dog. Now you're whispering and the dog has to listen, because you're the only stimulus."

"What do you tell the dog?"

"To attack things . . ."

The voice trailed off as the man's eyes moved more hungrily over the body. The pants had slipped all the way down and been kicked to the floor. Apollo fell back in a slump against the wall. His chin was down; his eyes rolled back into his skull, then reappeared as consciousness came and fled. One naked arm rose and floated through the air. Then it lay dangling over the edge of the bed, a raised, shiny purple scar showing on the soft side of the forearm. There were several light, crisscrossed scars on the chest.

Farther up the arm, in shadow, the man could see lightly festered holes, ringed in black at the beginning of tracks that seemed to fade away in their journey along the skin. The boy was sleeping or had fallen into a deep nod, for the breathing seemed incredibly slow and heavy, the soles of the feet curling into faint spasms.

On the TV screen the image of the stretcher and theater and even the gesticulating cashier appeared, so that later the man would wonder whether he had actually seen it on the street or only on television. Then a commentator talking, it seemed, about an attack, a man in critical condition holding on to life by a thread.

The kaleidoscopic light of the TV enveloped Apollo's body as if it were a cloud of incense. It used all its colors to baptize him a "perpetrator," from whom all consideration or empathy was now supposed to be automatically withdrawn. Yet at moments, the man suspected that a sixth sense was making the perpetrator aware of the television or of being watched. He would stir suddenly as if ready to second-guess, flee, or defend himself at the slightest sign.

The tension of harboring him was suddenly excruciating, intolerable. So the man shook him awake.

"Let's play guard dog."

"Huh?"

"What about your education? Who's going to be the dog, you or me?"

Apollo shrugged in perplexity, then began to nod out again, the lids heavy and convex.

The guy got down on his hands and knees. He opened his mouth and stuck his tongue out. He started licking me all over like he was starving, gobbling my nipples and armpits, licking and kissing my balls and legs and toes while I fell in and out of my nods . . .

Then anguish opened the man like a ravine. He slapped Apollo awake and told him to get dressed fast, gave him money, and ushered him out. He rinsed out the filthy glass of blood-tinted water with hydrogen peroxide . . . after picking up his cordless phone to call the police to report the whereabouts of the fugitive.

III

CASIO LAY IN THE AMBULANCE, UNABLE TO STOP
hearing the ringing in his ears. It was like rubber striking
steel; originally, the early-morning sound of the guard
checking for contraband in every pipe of the common
room, in a section of the prison known as House of the
Dead.

This echo from the Joint was a sound as real as that
which a person who has tried everything to stop still hears
perpetually—until he finally throws himself under the protection of a head-shrink or hypnotist or drugs. Razor blades,
spikes, joints, condoms, or other contraband stuffed inside
the hollow of steel, so that when the corrections officer had
finally struck that spot with his mallet, it rang out with a
duller tone.

That day eleven years ago when the corrections officer had struck his fatal blow against the radiator pipe, the very young Casio had managed to stuff a shank through the steam-valve socket into the radiator. The shank was some strip of metal a member of his crew had been able to lay his hands on, stroking it over and over against fixed metal until it got razor sharp, then wrapping it with cloth and string to make a handle.

It was long enough to go through two thicknesses of guys—or through one guy and half a foot out the other end. Dangerous enough to cause big trouble for the one caught holding or hiding it.

Behind the Wall, new beautiful fish like wiry-limbed Casio, whose then-angular face had boasted a lush mouth and whose skin was like satin, sometimes sought security by running in a rat pack or posse whose actions they'd try to "perpetrate." But once you were down with a particular crew, there'd come a vulture who was a member trying to make you out to be his happy-butt or siphoning every cigarette off you.

When this vulture stuck another con over a stupid dis, zooming in on him from behind so the shank slipped between his ribs and came out wet the other side, Casio had the rotten luck of being in the vicinity, and the attacker passed the shank to Casio, telling him to stash it as the C.O.s came charging.

"And for months now 'cause of that, this ringing shit in my ears driving me fucking nuts, Doc, reminding me how's I got glazed by a brother and took his rap and got tossed into the Box for this vulture for ninety days. It's the same fuckin' sound all the time— when the C.O.s come in and hit everything with this rubber mallet that tells 'em ifs you was holding contraband."

The Box is Solitary, where the only light comes from the small grate at the top of the wall facing the corridor. And when the light in the corridor is off, it is total blackness.

Though he tried to keep his muscles toned with endless calisthenics, there was no way to mark time or the passage of days. His mind began wandering. The ringing sound was something flying in the dark: an insect or bird getting closer and becoming louder. But when he swiped at the blackness, his hand closed on nothing.

At times the sound swelled: into absurd laughter when he ate those *chiba* cookies with Tito and started to trip in class on the white teacher's wack hair; or spinning on his back on a piece of cardboard when the crew used to break. Or it got evil, swooping into replays of past wrongs and imagined revenges. Like the bird or insect, his mind zoomed closer to panoramas of primal scenes.

That bitch playing virgin on my ass and then shacked up next day with one of my boys. Or that shithead calls himself a father raising his hand to her again . . .

It was hard to tell whether you were dreaming or not in this blackness as you slipped in and out of consciousness, thinking once that he held his great-grandmother's two front teeth in the palm of his hand, after that time they'd been knocked out by her boyfriend and he'd watched them roll across the pavement like dice . . .

I had to pick up drunken Abuela a little bag of bones—like some bird wrapped in her shawl, and go up six flights to lay her on the bed . . .

Out of Solitary and back on the street, the sound got louder. It was the same ringing; he was out, but the city seemed to keep up jail-thinking. *Once you been up river you find it . . . wherever.* Each nonwhite guy on the subway seemed to have honor to protect. *You got to control where you let your eyes rest.* The eyes of homeboys never met your glance but for a transaction or a challenge. How he moved was being judged with contempt or fear—in other words, respect. One arm

32

stretched behind your back, the palm resting upturned on a buttock, meant "ready to cop." Thumb hooked in front pocket, fingers splayed across thighs, meant "My dick is king" and/or "I got a weapon."

Don't pull your knees together pussy-style somebody sits down next to you. Let the bastard scrunch up. The rush of the train accompanying the building rush of insult . . . and always, always this shrill ringing in his ears.

Though a dose of heroin would smooth it out sometimes. But because of Casio's enormous stamina for suffering, he shot it only when he could take the ringing not a second longer. Then he went chasing after a bag and did it up with borrowed works, but so infrequently that his habit was spun out over a couple of years before it began to interfere with his routines.

He was still lean and smooth-skinned, with big, liquid, stoned eyes, working the door to Tina's, the transvestite lounge. An old gang member named Sugar Bear had risen to temporary prominence by hooking his giant dick up with Tina, the queen performer. She was half-owner—with strings attached to some old Portuguese lady. The dude had not forgotten Casio but gave him the afternoon post, which paid minimum. It was mostly just a security job, since almost nobody but a few queens came in during the day. Casio could nod out and put himself on automatic.

Nighttime he'd stick around and sneak some drinks at the circular bar or catch the show, always half in Spanish. He liked fielding the sex quips of the queens who worked as hookers, some of whom were not half that bad-looking. And then finally, the party for someone's birthday, where there'd be food—a mountain of chili and rice or a sidewalk of lasagna or franks and beans. And here, how you lined up for the food told them who you were. Everybody made a big show about not being that hungry, they were used to better. No one wanted to turn the atmosphere of the club into the Salvation Army. *"Shit, I don't know, I got sick on that kind a stuff once, but I'll try a bite . . . let me have some a that lasagna—no, man, none a that lettuce shit! I don't eat rabbit food . . ."* Grudgingly taking your first chomp on the hand-out while you boasted about the kind of class food you were used to and your stomach rumbled with anticipation.

Because who was he unless he was hooked up with his own place and own meals? So one day he paid a surprise visit on East 111th to sharp-tongued, diminutive Monica, his son's nineteen-year-old mother. She kept the chain on the door, but he could see she looked good these days: her coffee-colored face framed by comb-studded, bleached-blond hair. Not doing bad at all, she boasted across the chain lock. Getting my beautician's license at night and gonna work part-time in a salon. And as for his getting busted and going to jail one month before the baby was born, I don't blame it on you, I blame it on myself, she answered.

But as she tried to shut the door on him, he forced it and snapped the chain. Brought the bag of reefer and bottle of rum from his hip pocket to the table. He even had an electronic minigame for the kid. Monica's warm eyes widened. "Come out here and say hello to your father!" A cool four-year-old appeared and appraised Casio with hooded eyes, then grabbed for the game like it had just fallen from the sky. *"Where do stuff come from? You just gets it when you gets it."*

Now everybody's happy, so Mom and Pops light up, take a couple shots of Bacardi; Junior wanders away, transfixed by his game. Casio and Monica go into her bedroom to do the Wild Thing. His fingers slip under her lavender sweater and remember her taut body.

With no bodacious ta-ta's, just little titties, a little Yard Bird body. I always got off on her little butt, a chico-butt I calls it, and nice honey skin. That little twitching birdie lying underneath me . . .

They stayed in bed until the next afternoon, when he had to go back to work at Tina's. Then Casio returned with more weed and ate her *pernil* and avocado and they smoked again and went back to bed. Afterward Monica pulled out her beautician's kit and began to practice a style on his shiny longish hair, rollers and all. Casio had begun talking about the queens, and, stoned as he was, with the rollers in his hair, he found himself doing right-on imitations that made Monica bust a gut. Her nymphlike naked body rolling on the bed in hysterical birdlike laughter, sending some curlers flying to the floor, as Casio with the sheet wrapped around him bumped and ground in a baroque imitation of a queen imitating a woman . . . The boy came in to watch with eyes unblinking, his poker mouth giving him a bored, sophisticated look . . .

It took a while for Casio's son to really worship him. Casio dubbed him "Baby Pop." And eventually Baby Pop began following him around the apartment all the time, kicking at the closed door when Casio went to the head. Casio put a lock on the bathroom door. At least there he could do some up in peace when he had to stop the ringing in his ears.

By now the boy was five, surprising everyone with his precocious head for math. Casio would walk him through the projects to Central Park on the weekend, taking normal strides on purpose, with the kid huffing and puffing to keep up with him. It gave Casio some satisfaction to see his son's mettle proven—*the way a green member of a gang will go through all kinds of shit to keep up with the rest.* But on this particular day Casio's brain was stabbed by a memory of a pain in his own side as he tried to keep pace with his own father, the year he was twelve, which was the only year they had spent together.

They were running to a vacant lot trying to get there quick, before dawn, when it would be too late to cop. Running beside him, Casio got a horrible pain in his side. And then his *papi* got there just in time; he copped, the dealers took off, and his father went deeper into the lot behind a burned-out building to do it up, and suddenly began sinking down . . . down into the rubble . . . because he'd O.D.'d.

Casio pushed the image down. Dwelling on it had nothing to do with surviving. In point of fact, nobody was doing anything else, and, more than food in the mouth and a bed to sleep in, this meant medicate pain. In his case, with the ringing suddenly there and the phantom hurt in his side, the border between physical pain and mental anguish grew fuzzy. The more medication he took, the more the two merged. The more he needed not to feel bad before he couldn't stand it anymore.

He later swore to a drag queen named Angelita that he honestly never thought things would turn out this way. He wasn't getting high often enough to take responsibility for Monica developing a habit. She knew about his, and sometimes they shared a needle, but most of the time she liked to make love to him when only he was high.

She'd watch him naked and tieing up. Then it took a long time for him to get a "dope stick," but when his woody was up, it stayed, all the blood was stuck inside, and he could turn her out for hours while their son slept soundly in the living room. Monica always kept one ear cocked for any gasping, since Baby Pop had developed asthma.

He couldn't put his finger on the time when Monica's cooking stopped and the naked shoot-ups grew more frequent and the house started to go seedy. *But for sure that I'm not gonna take a fall for this one. For one thing, she'd been making drops to support the kid while I was locked up. Associating with dealers, may the truth be known. Her first mistake was Wrong People. Though yeah she was still clean at the beginning. When I come out she was only doing a little bit a mopping, for mascara and stuff from Woolworth's. Seein' that I'm from the old school, I wasn't no way letting her go off on me . . .*

But then Monica started to park the boy with her father—to

*come to Tina's instead of to beauty school, hustling free drinks and
rubbing shoulders with the queens. When she toots she'd get this
squeaky little machine-gun mouth—"Hands off, honey, these tetas
be real, you can play with the plastic over there." "You dissin' me,
bitch? When your man touch 'em I bet he think they feels as real as
them little avocados you got." "At least you can take a bite outta
'em, girl, without gettin' a mouthful a silicone," etcetera.*

*When was it, some time or other, when me and her gets locked
out of her place for a couple weeks? She who don't never pay the
rent on time, so up coming the landlord with a toolbox and changing the lock. Next these friends a hers, these high-class junkies in
Brooklyn Heights fixing up a brownstone, tells us, you and the kid
can sleep here ifs you bring us a bag a night. Word! Nice black
schoolteachers with money from parents to renovate a house carrying
on like street junkies! They'd get zombied right in front of the kid,
lose all their money, and go to buy loose stogies from the bodega.*

By the time Casio and Monica got back inside the apartment, they'd spent a few days in shelters, and one freezing
night in the street. It was clear Monica had let go of beautician's school, but Casio made a rule that she had to take
back the kid from her parents and start staying home evenings. He'd tie her to the kitchen table and shoot her up
before he went to work if he had to. He kept all their money
together and portioned out enough for dope and food.

*'Cept for this female is the kind knows how to play men real close
to get everything she want. We'd do dope one night, and she's getting up tomorrow and saying she needs bazooka to get through the
day. Then sometimes a speedball on the weekends. You don't go
back and forth that way without payin' for it. It was gonna do no
good cutting her off 'cause she started feeding her father bouncers.
Her habits usin' up Daddy's whole account. Stealin' the key to his
mailbox to grab the mail from the bank and burning it 'fore he
would see. Papi got played by her over and over but came back for
more, being she was his only daughter.*

Then finally that she starts getting too live on me. Real loca.

37

All day locked up in the bathroom, staring at her hands. Her arms up in front of her face when I walk in, like I'm going to fuck her up, and saying I was a hypnotist to control her mind. She even got afraid being in the room with our Baby Pop, saying that witchcraft was gonna make him suddenly stop breathing. Went to see a bruja. *But what's bugged is she wasn't doing too much drugs, really.*

IV

It was a month later, in that golden age of Times Square's sleaze empire, that a Latin queen named Angelita strolled into Tina's Lounge and eyed the still-young Casio slouched at the entrance, in black from his old days as an outlaw—a black exclamation point of machismo that had drooped into a question mark now that Monica had thrown him out.

She took in his sulky death's head and big vacant eyes and wondered what it would be like to put her tongue between the formerly lush lips, now stretched into a mute speak-no-evil.

As she slinked up to him, he silently took in her body, blooming from hormone injections. She asked him for the key to the ladies' room and he held it out indulgently. It was still afternoon outside, but in the darkness and orange lights from the bar, her pale, dusky skin took on a matte glow.

Casio had never noticed whom she hustled, and he himself had never been with a drag queen. Yet when she returned with the key in her hand, her thank-you soft-spoken and breathy, it occurred to him that he had nowhere to stay that night, and he caught himself rejoicing at the look sullenly glinting in her black eyes.

Her body came close enough so that her breasts grazed his face. As she stepped away, he let his hand glide gently up her skirt to stroke her buttocks.

That night Casio and Angelita took the PATH train to her Jersey City apartment. He dropped onto her bed as the queen sashayed across a real Oriental rug to a lacquered Chinese screen. Turning on one side, he studied his face and body in her gilt-trimmed mirror, which was turned sideways to give a full view of the bed. He focused on his hollowed-out cheeks and broad forehead, convincing himself that he didn't look half that bad for a guy of twenty-two.

The queen was behind the screen slipping out of her skirt and pantyhose and into a blood-red kimono. Pale as she was, the red kimono made the skin of her downy, frail forearms look olive, and she mentally blessed the new body cream she had boosted from an East Side perfumery because she knew it would make her skin feel silky-soft to the touch. Angelita slowly unraveled her thick chignon and shook out her long black hair. When she strode out, she put the "Quiet Storm" on the radio and swiveled back to him across her prize rug.

His blunt splayed fingers combed through her hair, making her shiver as she eyed their mirror image: a babe and her shadowy, wiry master—who looked like a pimp—framed by gilded carvings.

It was an image that reminded her of the framed picture on the flowered wallpaper of her sick mother's bedroom in Puerto Rico, when she had been a little boy. There was a woman in a pageboy hairdo, wearing a beret and violet angora sweater, being pushed backward in strict Apache dance formation by a gangster in a pin-striped suit, one eye concealed by a black patch. In imitation of the couple, she and her cousin had choreographed an Apache dance for her bedridden mother, which climaxed in him dragging Angelita across the floor by one of her mother's wigs, as she held it to her seven-year-old head by pulling in the opposite direction.

Suddenly, as if the picture had come to life, Casio was holding her real hair like a shank in his fist. He lowered her head roughly to his crotch and shoved. The violent gesture left a lipstick smear along his fly as she resisted, but then she used her tapered, lacquered fingernails to unbutton his black jeans.

Nothing happened. It didn't go up.

Angelita sat up and sighed. She smoothed her hair in the mirror as her cat wrestled under Casio's callused palm, and he used his forearm to pin it against the bed until it played dead and he could stroke its vulnerable stomach.

Her eyes sought the gold-bordered bower of the mirror for an answer and saw that the image had not lost any of its allure. Lean and crouched, Casio still sat on the bed with all the romantic defeat and weary nobility of the degraded macho. And this couldn't mean that he wasn't the man—the pimp, the Apache dancer, the gangster—she'd conceived him to be in the mirror.

The cat, who was female and in heat, had squirmed away from his big hand, and Angelita tried to stand up to feed it. When an arm snaked about her waist and pulled her back to the bed, she gave in willingly, then lay trapped that way and moaning while her mind raced.

The man's hard biceps creased her waist, and she could feel the bones of his lean chest gnawing into her. As he reclined, his breathing was as tense and determined as the breath of a man used to taking his rest in jail. It was best not to think about the motives of men, because the true man never revealed his ultimate strategy. She would now concentrate on waiting like a mirror lake for his will to break through the surface, or until she fell asleep.

And from then, he just stayed there. Under the fur blanket, they'd sleep with the cat on top of them. He'd fondle her breasts and with his lips and teeth nip at her neck and ear-lobes, sometimes leaving purple marks as a kind of branding. A week later he gave her some of his pay and joked that he'd kill her if he ever caught her hustling.

When Angelita stayed home to sew, some of the other queens came over by train to practice lip-synch routines with her cassette player, while Casio grew restless, drank Olde English, and paced. He boasted about his sexual prowess and told jokes.

"There was this king a long time ago said he'd give a million to somebody could make his horse laugh. But couldn't nobody until this Puerto Rican comes, says let me behind a curtain with him. All of a sudden the horse starts to laughing hee-haw. So then a year later the king gets tired of a horse laughing hee-haw all the time, says I'll give a million anybody can make this horse stop laughing and start crying, and the Puerto Rican comes back, says let me behind a curtain with him. All of a sudden the horse starts to crying.

"Okay, here's your million, but tell me for chrissakes how you did it. Well the first time, says the Puerto Rican, I went behind the curtain and whispers in the horse's ear my dick is bigger than yours. And the second time I shows it to him."

"And what 'bout you, Cas, how you measure up to dat hoss?"

" 'Bout the only competition to me round here might

be what you got strapped up under that pantyhose, Negrita."

Negrita didn't like him. And privately she began hinting to Angelita that if Casio wouldn't have sex with her he was holding out—or worse, a faggot. She was a fool to have him in her house and not to demand what was rightfully hers in the relationship.

So Casio tried to imagine sex with Angelita. But how could he think about more than one female at a time? Monica was still on his mind. And anyway, Angie was just a drag queen.

Sometimes her chest felt the worst sense of leaden dread. Her thoughts sorted through the fantasies she had built about true love as she did her makeup at the vanity table and bright mirror for her Wednesday-night shows at Tina's.

Casio lay behind her on the bed. To maintain the fragile formula that kept her female, certain conditions had to be repeatedly fulfilled at all costs, as regularly as the doses of estrogen. But in the mirror she saw the eyes of this husband who was not a husband running up and down her naked back.

She'd gathered her hair loosely at the top of her head, which revealed her shoulders. She intuited his glance grazing the shoulders and being put off by them. But then maybe it moved to the hormonal swellings of her buttocks perched upon the velvet vanity bench with its claw-foot legs and had a different feeling? Lying near the bench on the Persian rug were piles of fashion magazines of the classiest sort, as well as cassettes of the singers she impersonated. Perhaps his eyes were now scanning the cassette covers and imagining the breasts, thighs, and asses of these real women.

She finally agreed that they get a bag for the very first time since he had moved in with her. Angelita didn't get high very often—almost never, in fact. And he'd cut way down.

But maybe doing this together one time would create a new atmosphere, and things would happen differently.

He tied her arm up and did her, then himself. Because he'd been off it for a while, the rush overwhelmed him. He couldn't sit up. He fell back onto the pillow, but it was as if his body were levitating.

Angelita stayed sitting up because her body took in the drug differently; she was stoned to the tits, but it just intensified her stillness; she hovered above him like a cumulus cloud, her hand gliding toward his black T-shirt, which floated off under her touch. It was all slow-motion. His arms were dropping over his head, and a sound like a gas jet was in his ears . . . open red lips teethed his nipples, stretched taut by his flung arms.

I putted my cherry suckers on his tits to find out the kind a man he was being and then the tip of my tongue along his blade scar to prove it . . .

The real secret in getting hard was letting her take control. He let her invent the smooth cock that would penetrate as if it were hers. Lips licking from the base of the shaft to nip at its ruffle of foreskin, until it unsheathed gradually along the lean thigh.

Now if I can slip careful out a this kimono and keep my legs all pressed together. Then she tipped back with raised knees trembling and an open palm shielding what he must not see while a current of the drug picked him up and he suddenly swooped over her.

The dope decreed no taking or giving, just one body quivering. Casio entered her soft body differently than he had with bonier Monica—sinking deep into a source of energy, while the dope made time for everything in the backs of his thighs, heading toward his cock and balls into more dope spiraling inside of her.

Much later, in the morning, he found it easy to reclaim his cock, to hop out of bed like an athlete and resume the ascendant role. Dark eyes still smoldering, with a touch of irony, Angelita asked him in almost a parody of meekness for a few dollars. Before she went out, while he drank beer and watched a porno tape, she shivered blushingly but triumphantly under his soft, muttered threats as he warned her to keep away from other guys.

"And what you going to do about it?"

Nothing. The longed-for homeostasis had been established. They had to get high every time they had sex. And this time there were no recriminations as to whose fault the growing habit of each was.

The infinite expansions taking hold most nights gave birth to bright pictures more intense than he'd found in Solitary. Angelita's breasts and warm thighs were becoming luminous clouds, the levitating feeling dissolving into an even higher wave of high. Nausea that came during a reach for a pack of cigarettes by the bed was accompanied by bright specks falling through air. Breathing was sand. Then pictures were cut off by dozes on top of her body.

All of a sudden it was the sick urgent morning: a total environment of the kind where dope is making sex into rubber people who merge into a world without conflict, and only Angelita's voice becoming more and more insistent . . .

See, I'm talking to you, Cas, remember that God is good, baby, I prayed for someone to love, and look, He putted us together. But you ain't gonna fool Him or nobody to thinking that you treat me this way. Everybody does know, papito. So why you's always telling I'm your bitch, you gonna teach me a lesson tonight? Lyin' that you got ahold a me and got me workin' for you and bringin' in mucho money. Where is my girlfriends seeing the act you be putting on?

I ain't gonna let you dig a hole in my head wid dat same boolshit no more just to look good. For you I gave up dreamin' of a man who understands my shoes and dresses costs money. 'Cepting now I got to go out with the same ratty dress and nothing in my pockets. Tell me how we go about getting some respect in this world with habits like we got and scroungin' the way we been. We gotta get more money, and ain't neither of us doin' a thing about it but playin' ourselves.

Her voice came slashing through his high with a man's deep-voiced, urgent authority: *COME CORRECT, CASIO! MAKE THE MASTER PLAN WHAT'S NEEDED!*

V

O'HARA:

See, way back when ten years ago, even though the drug addicts and scammers had took over, the old Portuguese lady still owned every joint on this block. You could still find people who were what they said they were. You could drink your money's worth at my place: O'Hara's. It stood right over there next her theater, plain as the gin-tinted noses on my guzzlers' faces. Neither wasn't it breathing foul odors like the joints on the block today. 'Cause it'd been scrubbed with ammonia by my own hands and sparkled like the pasties on one of the old Portuguese lady's naked hootchy-kootchy dancers—when that place catered to men who liked missies.

In those days, middays was slow. Only a straggler or two managed to crawl into the bar between 10:00 A.M. and 2:00 P.M.—after the hard-core A.M.-ers had come in to swill down their morning pick-me-ups at seven.

And then came that day when the big lady-and-a-half with hair down to her bottom waltzed right in.

These were the end of the sweet good-old-days, mind you, before things really took a turn for the worse. Before the Devil claimed this neighborhood but didn't come in person to lay his claim. He sent his emissary in the form of a lady-and-a-half with seal-sleek skin and lips like rubies to put an end to those days. She walked right through that door over there into my saloon at the stroke of noon and slinked up to the bar. Then she let her head drop on it.

"What's weighin' on you, Missy?" I says. I poured her a stiff one and leaned my elbows on the bar. I'd be lying if I said I didn't give a glance at them two cabbages spilling out of her dress before I went back quick to my business of wiping the mugs. Wary as I was of types like this one, who show off their jugs like prizes at a county show, I still got a shameful kick by eyeing some of the big-boobed trollops of the neighborhood.

"Don't pay me no mind," is what I think she mumbled, "for it ain't you nor nobody can help me now."

"God be with you then," I shot back to her. And true that I'd gone back to my business, still could I not resist one peek at those melons in my mirror. The glance made a flush pass over the big girl's raised face, and she tucked back the cabbages and lowered her round eyes back to the counter.

"I know what you take me for," she complained at my lascivious looking. "But only had you seen me just three months ago in Puerto Rico, you would've had a different opinion of me then."

"Of what might I have been thinkin' if I'd have met you, Miss?"

"But how could you've?" shoots she right back, "it being such a strict order, and them only allowin' visits from relatives."

I'll have to admit that the remark turned me red as a schoolboy. As a Catholic I could not find the voice to comfort the lady for having lost the cloth and turned into what I saw. So leaving her in the shame that colored both our faces, I went downstairs to curse the world and bring up a case of beer, and then knelt in penitential silence by the cooler, putting away the brew. Still, I could not help wondering how she'd managed to grow so quickly that mane of hair of hers. Neither could I shake the feeling of the lost girl's presence behind me.

"Miss, are you sayin' you've come out from a convent?" I dared not look directly but spoke my words to the mirror.

"Would it weren't true," says she sadly, though I'm sure she phrased it differently, in her own Spanglish. "For if it weren't for my brother's visit I would still be there today."

I was lost in the mean-spirited grip of curiosity now, and filled with pity and doubt at the same time. So coming as close to the large, sad lady as I dared, but keeping the bar between the cabbages and my manhood, I fully coaxed her story out of her.

"You were tellin' me you left the nunnery and followed your brother to America, lass?"

"What choice had I," she tosses back, fixing her eyes straight on mine, "what with me carryin' his baby?"

The rest of her song of woe was more loathsome than the darkest ballad. About a man had made his own sister his whore and brought her to this country like a slave to pay his drug bills. He had her in a death grip that if it weren't for the baby, she would have killed him and then herself.

The girl was sobbing and heaving so helplessly that the cabbages had slipped from their sacks all the way to the brown aureoles. In comfort I reached out a gentle hand to stroke her silky arm, just when an angry bloke burst into the bar. I known it was him right off 'cause the lady screeches and slides off the barstool. She rushes for the door as the cur's big hand reaches out for her and yanks her back with a snarl by the hair.

The lady falls, but he won't let go. And by that hair itself, he drags her from one end of the room to another!

I won't tell what he then started to do, it not being fit to describe. But leave it that I saw more of the lady than any stranger should.

Armed with my shillelagh, which I keep for such emergencies, I shot out from behind the bar. I may be no hero, but I did what any decent man with two arms and two legs needs to have done. "Leave her alone, by God," raising the shillelagh in the air, "or I'll use your skull as a doorjamb!"

49

Leaving that safe station and not grabbing the revolver I keep at it for such emergencies was my fatal mistake. For before I can bean the scoundrel, he lets go of her—and puts his own gun right up to my skull.

"Don't you make a move, Mick, or I'll blow you to pieces!"

And suddenly our sad sister became full of merry giggles. And sashaying to the cash register without a care in the world, she begins to stuff the bills between those cabbages.

It's not until that moment that I see I'm wearing the crown of the King of Fools. Though I suppose her come-hither act, mane of hair, and phony tale of incest would 'ave laid a trap the same for any red-blooded man. With her as lookout he marched me right downstairs to the safe and relieved me of a few thousand.

Next thing I know I'm lyin' right there where they found me —with this horrible pain between my two ears. The bloke must 'ave beaned me with my own shillelagh.

VI

THE MYSTERIOUS DARK LADY DISAPPEARED LIKE AN apparition. Look as they might, the police could have discovered no closer resemblance to her than a crew-cut, soft-featured boy. He went back to a long-ago name before breasts and hormones.

Angel.

Under the clipped hair, the eyebrows were still tweezed, but somehow the eyes had lost their smoldering gleam. In the pocket of his baggy shirt he copped the daily fixes with O'Hara's money and brought them back home to the man who'd held the gun and who now stayed inside, drugged or sick, looking for new veins.

Sex had lost all interest for Angel and his onetime paramour. Casio's mind floated instead back to the days before Monica and his son Baby Pop, to his outlaw days, those all-for-one-and-one-for-all times in the Bronx before he even went to jail. Angel's mind was uprooted from the fantasies that had made him Angelita and that revolved around the mirror. Reverting to the shadow of his original biological self, which had long ceased to be an identity and now became only a shabby alias, he grew emaciated and pale.

One afternoon, without any desire to be near Casio, Angel crept from the bed to the floor and lay beneath the large blowup photos of a queen in her prime. Above him reigned his former self, besequined and high-heeled, holding a microphone. He rolled up a sleeve and felt among the scar tissue for a vein, but it was no-go.

Across the room, Casio was spread out on the unsheeted mattress, his bent arms and legs flung apart like a swastika. At moments his half-closed lids twitched convulsively while the eyes rolled upward. Suddenly he would come to with a start, and then sink back into his stupor.

The ghost of the propriety of their old relationship made Angel want to be certain that Casio wouldn't be watching. Checking sporadically to be sure that Casio was unaware, he unbuttoned his pants and cupped a blunt penis in his hand. He stretched back a fold of skin lying over a blue vein and delicately inserted the point of the needle. The rush relaxed his back into a curve, and his breasts drooped into loose cones, but he held on to his senses with all his might until he could stuff the member back into his clothing.

Detective Juan Pargero, with his buzz cut and hawk face, was no stranger to cases like this. He knew Times Square inside and out; and his career, first as a beat cop on the street and then as a detective, had involved him in the full spectrum of exchanges between the down-and-out and the not-so. Pargero was a racial mixture and a strange hybrid of tough cookie and sentimental slob, a middle-aged cynic but weirdly goodhearted. A certain fondness for queens had raised some eyebrows in the neighborhood but perhaps gave his investigations a personal touch.

Still, Pargero knew when and where to turn the screw. It had taken an intimidating interrogation of some of the dealers who frequented Tina's and verification with Mrs. Huxton for O'Hara's study of male mug shots to bear fruit. But identification of the female accompanying the gunman had not come to pass.

Weeks later, the search for the gunman led to a rickety two-family house in Jersey City, at the end of a dreary street overlooking the tunnel of the PATH train. Detective Pargero tramped quickly up the creaking staircase with a signed warrant and two overweight policemen to do the grunt work. The cops drew their guns before bursting through the unlocked door, but they stopped in amazement at the sight of the effeminate-looking boy passed out underneath the drag photos. The detective had once watched the lip-synch routines of stunning Angelita at Tina's. Yet the skeletal Latino beneath the posters had journeyed so far from his queenish image that even the detective, who thought himself a connoisseur of female illusion, did not make the connection.

His thoughts were distracted by the heavy slosh of water coming from the bathroom. Inside, the stockier of the two grunts was grumbling about the fact that his uniform was splattered with water. He bent toward the tub and once more yanked at wet wrists, but they slipped through his fingers like eels. The naked body of Casio flopped back into the tub, sending another swell of water onto the floor and forcing the cops to hop backward.

The other cop removed his jacket and rolled up his sleeves to fish in the water for the ankles. His drenched shirt stuck to his stomach, showing the crease of the navel. "I'm surprised the sucker didn't drown," he sneered.

"So maybe we saved his life," answered the other with mock concern.

In the tub, Casio's lids had opened halfway. The thick,

dark lashes fluttered effeminately. Casio's fingers twitched once before they fell back into the water, making a tiny splash, followed by a low moan. The voice of the perpetrator won the attention of the detective, who had been gazing at the drag posters with an expression that seemed wistful yet wily, a squeamish yet lewd smile characteristic of some law enforcers.

Creeping to the bathroom door, he stepped over the puddle forming outside and peeked in. His blue eyes proprietorially caressed the flagrant disorder of the squandered body of Casio, lying shamelessly naked and unconscious in the tub.

Detective Pargero was capable of the kind of hardnosed voyeurism that feeds investigations. However, at moments like this a drop of humanity tinged his voice with soft resignation.

"Get the landlord," he commanded in a whisper.

Not that Pargero liked the looks of the colicky and stony-faced landlord who appeared hesitantly at the threshold. Potbellied and wearing a bathrobe and slippers, he lingered there resentfully until the detective impatiently waved him into the room. When the man saw the flooded floor caused by the cops, his expression blackened. He followed Detective Pargero into the bathroom with lips compressed.

"Who's this?" barked the detective, gesturing with his chin to the naked body in the tub. The cop was holding the head by the hair to keep it from sinking under. The mouth drooped and wheezed. The other cop was fishing in the tub for the plug, but he couldn't find it and began cursing under his breath.

"How should I know?" answered the landlord, averting his face.

"This isn't your tenant?"

"She is." The landlord pointed toward the other room.

She? The cop's raw face clouded over only for a second, before he made the connection between the fragile boy out there and the missing voluptuous accomplice. But the re-alization tread on a weak spot and brought out the fantasist in him. A tight swallow made his Adam's apple bob. "Does this guy"—the detective pointed to the tub—"is he the one that's involved with . . . her?"

"Why you asking me?" said the landlord, looking point-edly at the flooded floor. "I stay out of people's business—unless they cause me a problem."

Breaking off the conversation with a laconic snort, the detective strode authoritatively from the room. Each foot plopped into the puddles. The landlord followed gingerly and hesitated, then crept toward the stairs and disappeared.

The detective had made a decision. Angelita—but only she—would be spared.

When the burly redheaded man and the fireplug blond woman in tight white pants arrived with a stretcher, they made straight for the waxy-skinned boy collapsed beneath the drag posters. But almost betraying a protective instinct, the detective motioned them toward the bathroom.

"Not him—the one in the bathtub. And wake him just enough to verify his name and read him his rights. Don't give him too much, 'cause he'll probably go into withdrawal, right?"

The medics nodded in grim obedience.

"And that would be awful messy," clucked the detec-tive.

When the medics had disappeared inside the bath-room, he walked quietly over to the boy on the floor and nudged him gently with the tip of his shoe. But there was no reaction.

In the bathroom, the female medic pulled one of the arms out of the water and pressed it firmly against the tub wall, while her partner, wearing rubber gloves, readied the injection. Avoiding the reddish, white-ringed hole near the wrist that seemed to be festering, he plunged the needle into the muscle tissue of the forearm near a swarm of scars and bruises. The detective and the two cops peered in from the doorway. This time the detective's face maintained a mask of cold determination.

A barely audible moan came from the submerged form, and it squirmed weakly. The moan increased to a howl as the female medic reddened and struggled to keep a grip on the arm and avoid the sloshing water.

Now the body began to writhe more violently. The male medic backed toward the door, but his partner stuck grimly to her post. Her white blouse was drenched, the form of her bra appearing through it; and one cop nudged the other with a sly smile.

"What the fuck?" Casio's eyes were wide open and red with misery. "What the fuck?"

"Theodoro G. Rodriguez, also known as Casio?" said the detective.

"What the fuck you want a me?"

"You have the right to remain silent. Anything you now say can, and will, be used against you."

Casio struggled against the medic's grasp, while his already wet, pale face streamed with tears and his legs thrashed jerkily. "My legs! I'm dying, you're gonna kill me!" he chanted.

The fatter cop tiptoed in. The water on the floor welled up over the toes of his shoes.

He bent to take Casio's free arm, but it flew into the air, spewing water in his face. The other cop leapt into the bathroom, landing on the flooded floor with a sharp splat as the medic gritted her teeth and tightened her hold on the arm.

Casio was shrieking like a baby. An enormous convulsion arched his back and jerked his head so far back that it disappeared below the surface of the water. The fatter cop grabbed him by the hair and yanked the head above the surface. As Casio gulped for air, the cop and the medic wrenched him forward and yanked his arms behind him to slip on the cuffs.

The body was hoisted from the tub onto the stretcher, and a blanket was thrown over its nakedness. Then the stretcher was eased out the doorway and hoisted laboriously down the stairs, while a singsong moaning spiraled up the staircase and through the open door.

But the detective lingered, staring down at the fragile form that he had pardoned. His face faded in and out of expressions like trick photography: desolate and tender, guilty and knowing, sentimental but resigned.

It was his discreet departing footsteps that finally woke the figure sprawled under the blown-up photos. Angel squinted dazedly at the open doorway and shakily rose to his knees. He peered around the room for Casio. Then he danced to the sheetless mattress and fell out again.

VII

It was the night he wasted that out-of-it, over-the-hill, sometime-junkie Casio, and soon after the bugged-out trick told him to leave, that Apollo copped some dope with the money he'd earned and jumped the number six train. He was still high and shirtless. And his lucent skin over its compact musculature was stained with dirty rivulets of sweat.

Anyone who wanted to look closely could have seen and studied the tracks, bruises, and punctures that covered his shapely arms, which seemed as perfectly formed, and moved as jerkily, as an automaton's. Paled by fatigue, liver toxins, and the stresses of sex, his ovoid face looked lit and open, yet dazed and numbed.

First he straddled two cars to do up the new bag. A white guy would have said it was like cross-country skiing:

balancing the sway with one foot on each car as the train zigzagged around curves while he cooked up in a bottle cap. The vibrations of the train caused the spike to jiggle in his hand, so he quickly found a vein by using the same festered hole. And as the stuff seeped into him, even the sparking steel wheels on their unrepaired track giddied out into a long, smooth rush. Then he went inside one of the cars and stretched out on a seat, feeling relaxed and justified, a hard day of work like anybody.

Against his nodding eyelids, a secret dream resurfaced of the bedroom he had just vacated. He saw the stripes on a sheet and had the sensation of sinking down to it as the guy's breath tinged his nostrils while his nipples hardened. *Dog training.* But what did that have to do with it all? A cynical delight trickled through him at the thought of the tense, eerily restrained middle-aged man who'd ended up gobbling his toes like a dog. Then laughter chortled out of him and woke him up, causing a glance from a startled passenger, which was itself suddenly cut off by the next dope nod . . .

The train clanged along on a powerful dream or fantasy (or had it happened?) of laying on a now nameless trick under TV light a tale about Mrs. Huxton sending him to dog-training school. Then all of a sudden there he was: back in front of her building again.

The theater marquee with its missing letters—OPEN TIL AWN—was still lit. Above it, Mrs. Huxton's windows shut out its light and Eighth Avenue with thick stucco grillwork in the shape of arabesques, like a harem. Just a little light would filter in during the day, it occurred to him. A view of Eighth Avenue even in the daytime was just not classy enough for her.

Next to the building was her public parking lot, stark in its salmon-colored mercury-vapor light. It was empty at 4:00 A.M. And it occurred to him what a stupid thing it was to do: drifting back to the theater when the cops must be looking for him by now. Anybody could have dropped a dime on him by calling 911. But still his feet remained rooted to her sidewalk, his head thrown back and eyes fixed numbly on her sequestered windows.

Slowly but surely, a vulnerable rage was melting some tender core in his narcotized brain. It concerned the fact that the lady would be disappointed in him. How especially painful, since he knew about that soft spot for him in her leathery old heart. What did he have to go through to please her, anyway?

Shuffling like a subterranean, will-less denizen of Mrs. Huxton's squalid realm, he edged into the harshly lit parking lot. He hid in the shadow thrown by her mysterious building. Gulping at the night's rank air, he pressed his naked shoulder against the cool brick, feeling for life in the building. But there was no give-and-take; it wasn't breathing. Inside it was the secret reason for his stupid crime—an illogical rage that had left the bouncer lying on a sweating cement floor. Meanwhile, a dumbass junkie with the high-class name of Apollo who didn't even know where he'd left his shirt cowered animal-like in the next-door parking lot. It was no wonder Mrs. Huxton stayed above in her air-conditioned rooms as he and other nonentities waded through the murky lagoon of her theater. He'd been programmed to let her down; it had been ordained the moment she set eyes on him. So as usual he was just playing a part of some higher power's agenda that didn't give a shit about him.

Mrs. Huxton probably rose early and would soon be opening her closet to dress. Apollo's mind ferreted among the veiled hats and whisperings of taffeta she had preserved there since the forties, for accouterments of a darker, more masculine cast.

The revolver slipped within a stack of lingerie might have a pearl handle, but the blackjack that had always been carried by her husband, Buster, would be blunt, ugly, scarred. Just as uninviting, but arousing because of the respect it elicited, was the leather-covered address book of the payment distributors and intermediaries—all the profiles of all those thugs-cum-chauffeurs she used to palm-grease the politicians or protect her from the smut peddlers.

If only he could be granted an audience with her to explain things, he began thinking. That haughty and slow-moving higher-up in her Colonial-style armchair would offer him a seat and a cup of tea, maybe even a brandy. But he'd be sitting with naked tits and new scabs on his knuckles and a tied tongue, hoping that his sweat-drenched jeans wouldn't leave behind stains on the bone-colored couch upholstery when he stood to be sentenced.

Yet what was the big hurry about standing up, anyway? She hadn't bargained for the fact that he was an ace bullshit artist who could spit out alibis faster than an Uzi could shoot slugs. And maybe they weren't even alibis. A class act like her would have to recognize that he and she were two of a kind. Both of them were trapped in the same sewer by circumstances, yet both saw a myriad of worlds beyond. Both of them were plagued by dummies and deadheads too low class to grasp the heartbreaking insights that he and she shared . . .

The sparkling gray eyes under white hair peppered his plea with her cynicism. Did he really think they were in the same league?

Okay, maybe he *hadn't* had the luck—all right, the smarts—to latch on to the high life like she had. But certainly things had not gotten too cushy for her to see through the grime to his active brain and aching heart. Let's face it: she needed the streets as much as he. And—no offense—but he imagined she'd probably had to make some of the very same compromises when she was his age . . .

———

61

In the ticket booth to the theater, the bloated cashier spent this last hour dozing in a bent-forward position. Even on nights of unusual violence like this, his forehead would end up on the ticket counter, the askew hairpiece pressed against the filmy glass.

Apollo's mind was too focused on Mrs. Huxton's unfair judgments to analyze the seduction of being able to sneak past him, back into the theater to turn one more trick.

The musty, rubber-backed curtain caressed his face like the familiar hand of an aged relative as he fell past it. Inside the darkness, he let the thrill of defying the menace of being at the scene of the crime swirl around him and mix with the smell of the sex. It was that unhinged moment when the wildest of plans is a success precisely for its foolhardiness, a moment he had experienced before only during the best of highs.

The seat cushion into which he was sinking sighed with expelled air as a Charlie McCarthy puppet-head rotated toward him. "Want a private show?" Apollo whispered close to the carved wooden ear.

As if the man had been absorbed into his high, they floated toward a door next to the movie screen that led to the other side of it, Apollo's mind still flip-flopping through his defense to Mrs. Huxton. Had she forgotten that up to now he'd been one of the more discreet employees, who never sneaked tricks off the street past the box office like some of the other hustlers did? And maybe she'd like to know about her reliable bouncer, Casio, holding on to cuts from every night's take. . . .

On the other side of the screen, the porno film was visible in mirror image and as if seen through gauze. There was, he decided, no big necessity for a condom, as he planned to let the guy suck him only for a few, without coming. It would, he knew, take hours to get a woody when he was this high.

The man had unbuckled Apollo's pants and pushed

them and the posing strap down. Suddenly Apollo's stoned attention corkscrewed into those spastic rhythms. *The guy's plastered!* He took in the suit in late-for-the-train-to-Westchester dishevelment before shutting it out and forcing him down by the shoulders. He felt the dribbling mouth burrow eagerly into his groin. The hands spidered over his chest and forearms, creating a focus that recrystallized his train of thought.

The drugs? Okay, but he was working on that, for her (Mrs. Huxton's) information. It just wasn't that easy after all these years, but someday. Anyway, up until now, like her, he'd never let this Times Square atmosphere come between him and his work.

Where would even she be without wizards like me who know, when johns stumble into this stinking place, how to reel them in against the odds?

But her jewel-cut eyes only reflected his low opinion of himself. Hers was the glance of somebody who'd written the whole book, and even the words that were coming out of his mouth.

Apollo pulled back, and his balls slid away from the man's mouth. He stuffed them back into his pants and zipped.

Ruefully, the man stood up to fumble in his pockets for money, and Apollo impatiently grabbed the twenty from his hand. Now it was time for the boldest part of his experiment, and his sense of fate expanded to it. This revisit to the theater had become a kind of reparation for earlier this evening. As he stumbled down the steps to the basement, he half expected to trip against the body of Casio, put back where he'd left it. But instead he found Casio's fourteen-year-old son, called Baby Pop, sitting at the old makeup table, with its missing light bulbs. The kid was gazing through big uncut curls into the dimmed mirror, his knapsack dangling from the back of the metal chair.

From time to time the kid, whom Apollo found spooky, dipped into the theater and snuck through the shadows in hopes of locating his father and hitting him up for a few bucks. Or he tried to hustle outside the theater. "You seen my Casio?" he asked, as he had many times before, looking at Apollo's face by way of the mirror.

Apollo shook his head. "You know where I can get me a bag right now?"

Still gazing into the mirror, the boy answered with a nod through the obscuring curls. "You don't even got to leave the theater. The Big Man sent Carlos in here to get rid of a bundle. I'll get you one."

Apollo pressed the twenty into the boy's hand. Sending him up there in his place was a good idea, given the fact that they were probably looking for his ass at this point.

"Get me a bag for ten and gimme back eight," he ordered. "Stay with the two dollars."

The boy took the stairs two at a time. Apollo sat in his place at the dressing table but avoided the mirror. For some reason he feared he would see Mrs. Huxton in it. Not looking into the mirror caused their tête-à-tête to fade into the darkness, replaced by an imageless, shimmery gray . . .

In what seemed no time at all (was it an hour?), the Baby Pop kid was back. With showy efficiency, he pressed the bag and the change into Apollo's hand.

As Apollo was making the vow to save the stuff until later, he noticed the belt of his old terry-cloth bathrobe lying on the dressing table. Then he saw himself pick up the belt and use it to tie up. He took the bottle cap out of his pocket, filled it with stuff and a little water, and held it over a match.

Why was the rush from this injection steeper than the one earlier? Either he was already too high or the dope was better. He became aware of the boy's hooded eyes watching him unblinkingly, the affect concealed, the way a cat watches a TV screen. Then he was zoomed back to his trial before Mrs. Huxton, the dope inflating her living room to massive, cruelly lit proportions.

The only thing to do was to throw himself at her feet, on the plush, suddenly bristling, carpet, his nose squashed against the squeaky-clean mahogany table leg. For nothing hurt more than being kicked out of this world into nothingness again. There wasn't anything crueler than worrying about how he was going to get high without the lady's help . . .

Mercedes the queen in her improbable costume—a foot-high beehive wig, gold lamé halter with heavy-duty cleavage, black leather miniskirt, stiletto ankle-strap pumps with gold metal heels—stopped short at the parking lot to gawk at nodding Apollo rocking back and forth on bent knees in full sight of traffic.

After what he perpetrated tonight and here he is nodding out right at the scene of the crime, was all the transvestite could think. She scrutinized him. The tip of her numbed tongue lightly probed the space where her complete front tooth had been before he broke it a few years back. Her ideas somersaulted on a dainty toke of crack she'd had a few minutes ago. She didn't know why, but every time she saw him, a wash of sentimentality overtook her. Despite everything, words spilled out.

"Parkin' your zonked ass right here of all places on the choppin' block? After you's stupid enough to waste Casio what everybody's talkin' about!"

Apollo's head jerked in astonishment at the sight of the gigantic, mascaraed eyes of the lover from the past not more than two inches from his face.

"I know what I'm doing."

"If you don't do the bird, you're in the meat cooler 'fore you know it."

But shirtless Apollo's eyelids sank and he teetered again into Mrs. Huxton's world, swaying on bent knees.

He's clockin' nods with the law out lookin' for him, reflected Mercedes. *Now ain't that the be-all and end-all of irresponsibility? And he sunk so low into the nod that he won't know he's in the bullpen till the runs set in or he feels a woody up his butt. Well, I'm gonna put on my nurse's cap and feed this sucker some a the devil's dick.*

Mercedes hiked up her miniskirt as she had earlier, but this time it was to pull out a crack stem nestled inside her panties, next to the burn scars caused by stashing it when the cops went by. She took a small plastic bag from her cleavage and pulled out a vial, yanked off the top with her side teeth, and quickly dumped the rock into the stem.

"Suck on this," she hissed nervously, shoving the stem between his lips and holding a flame to the other end. As Apollo inhaled, a numbing stream of vitality seemed to coat his mucous membranes like molasses. It straightened him up.

It was like being in a barrel going over the falls as the toke melded with the downer of dope and shifted him into smooth fall. Mercedes, looking elongated and Egyptian under her foot-high wig, surged into his plane of consciousness with hyperreality, and he found himself swooning into her fragrant arms.

"Baby, whatever happened to us," he mumbled, nuzzling her breasts and probing for the nipples with his open mouth.

Mercedes rode a lower wave of crack high. She felt the tears rising as she fainted into their mutual myth but was able to pull herself out of it. She yanked his head away from her tits but kept her arms around him.

"Walk now, away from the scene of the crime and into sanctuary."

Apollo moved down the street with her as if he were skating—but no, it was more like a conveyer belt. The murky facades of buildings slid by as he floated on Mercedes's marshmallows, hovering in a royal stillness, a most wonderful high.

"I really should visit my mom, I haven't seen her in a while," he lisped with ingenuous sentimentality.

"Your white momma?" said Mercedes. "Why don't you chill with her till the heat's off." They were approaching the entrance to a subway and she nudged him toward it. Lying on the railing was a black string T-shirt. Mercedes copped it and pulled it over Apollo's head. "My baby's all dressed to go home now. Make yourself scarce 'fore a rat drops a dime on you." They stood at the top of the stairs, melting into each other. "They can't do me none," said Apollo with jerky bravado. Once again she felt as if she were falling into the old fable; but simultaneously, a drop down from her own high suddenly called for crack in her head. Almost gratefully, she twisted out of the trap of his arms to heed the call.

"You ain't in condition to be wagin' tonight, and no wildcattin', neither."

"What you mean, I know what time it is."

He realized that he was slurring this to nobody in particular, as at some point Mercedes had left (had she ever been there?), and he was stupidly facing one of the barred exit doors next to the turnstile. A blast from the token-booth speaker shot through him.

"Are you buying or crying? Drop a token or get out of here!"

The corrections-facility-sounding voice, mechanized by the speaker, gushed fear through him. Suddenly he began conjecturing what had happened to Casio, from the moment the body was lying on the floor of the theater basement. Even Mercedes had heard about it, though that Baby Pop son obviously hadn't.

Had Casio merely come to and reported Apollo to the cops? Or had he cracked his skull and gone out of this world for good? Apollo remembered the strange crunching sound and the way Casio's eyes rolled up into his skull. "I'm scared they're going to charge me with a one eighty-seven," he said into the air, playing out the fate of a murder charge in his head. The crescendo of the train rush, an unbearable rattling in his ears, cut off any imagined answer and summoned an unusual athleticism. Apollo vaulted over the turnstile and hopped onboard. He knew just what he should do and who would take him in. Only the friend who gave him Percodans, whom he'd once bashed outside the theater, was the one to trust now.

The train rattled its way downtown as nausea from the previous dose strained through Apollo. It tightened his esophagus and screwed up his face as he dropped into the nearest seat. Next to him, a large woman, a night worker on her way home to another borough, tightened her grip on the shopping bag in her dark hands. She glared at the shame of his condition but stubbornly remained in the adjoining seat. Her expression convinced him of the continuing injustices toward him, radiating from the wicked entrepreneur Huxton. Simultaneously, the air conditioning in the car tightened his nipples, reminding him that his new shirt was only made of net.

He checked his reflection in the swallowing blackness of the window opposite. To his relief, he found that the shirt set off his muscles and looked good against his skin. The reflection confirmed his narcissistic pleasure in his own body and the excitement some hands found in running over it and consequently buying it dope. In a deep, sensual nod, he began to fantasize the friendly touch of the man who gave him Percodan and whom he was on his way to see.

Apollo let his thoughts play over the mystery of this man, whom he usually took for granted, because it was so much easier that way. He was the only person Apollo knew who broke all the rules in this down-and-out context to which Mrs. Huxton had condemned them all. Some people thought he gave Apollo Percs so he could take advantage of him. But when he gave them, it was because Apollo asked, and that seemed to be the only reason. Others took the guy for an easy mark, but Apollo knew he was more than that. The minute you thought you'd played him, you realized the con hadn't even been necessary.

But there was something else about him, too . . . And Apollo's mind only strayed to it when it was feeling most defended by dope: something about the man's sickness, the fact that he had HIV. Because ever since he'd been diagnosed, he seemed to fit into Apollo's world better. This was no mean feat, since he'd been to college—to a fancy Ivy League school, even.

Apollo sat up and winced at the realization. Big disadvantage was the top credential for ending up here. All of them—johns, hustlers, retards, and sick Ph.D.s—were fellow citizens of this Land of the Doomed. And this guy's outsider attitude—wry, ironic, bitter, a little above-it-all—was exactly what brought him and Apollo together again and again.

Apollo's mind strayed back to the months when they'd lived together, until Apollo blew it by stomping on him during withdrawal one day outside the sex theater. And then he had gone to jail as a result and come out and they were cold strangers.

When Mercedes cut him, he went to jail again. The seasons changed; he came out again and was drawn toward the guy like a tack to a magnet.

Two nights ago, the guy had willingly parted with half his supply of Percodan, which his doctor gave him by the hundreds for the pain and numbness in his legs and feet. What was it like to be beat up, to have somebody arrested for it, and then to forgive him a year or so later? At this moment, Apollo's imagination couldn't make the stretch. The closest he could come to what it was like was the time he'd been very high and got caught trying to rob a midtown office by security guards. The guards kept whacking him with their nightsticks. Apollo fell and somersaulted, rolled down the corridor, and stood again, grinning.

But his white friend with AIDS couldn't be hanging around him for the same reason: that dead kick of turning off to life's bashers. Suddenly his friendship with Apollo— his secret reasons for identification—formed an alibi for the nausea drowning Apollo's body . . .

It was obvious that the friendship felt much too sticky. Whom he sometimes referred to as his only friend appeared in a harsher, nauseating light. His ailing flesh fastened its suckers to Apollo and was tugging at his naked skin.

Apollo irately felt the sensation of being dragged into the heap with the losers. In the safety of an evil high, he considered paying his slick little buddy a visit. House the rest of the Percs? The guy could always go to the emergency room if he needed painkillers, couldn't he? He had AIDS.

But it wouldn't be enough to scoop up the Percodan; if the guy wanted to take care of him, maybe he wouldn't mind if Apollo borrowed a bunch of CDs and the little VCR that only played, not recorded. For when you really thought about it, this gay guy, by the presumption of being different—by choosing to slum, even sick and in this context where everybody was reduced to the same level—was just playing him. He would probably savor a nice lesson from the sick, mean junkie that pretty-faced Apollo knew he was.

The train jiggled Apollo awake. And in the bright light the image of the guy rotated suddenly. There was an almost grotesque shift, in which the ailing friend became sacrificing and enveloping. Against his will, as the next nod took hold, Apollo was plunged again into the motherly arms and their transcendent familiarity with death.

He was whisked away from the petty plane of street deals and fleeting highs and bitter resentments of the last nod into the smarting ether of real friendship, as painful as it could be.

Mrs. Huxton's world-weary realm of condemnation withdrew in reverse zoom, an aerial view of the building roofs and water towers of her seedy empire growing ever more distant, as he and his buddy sped into pain like astronauts in a heart-rending free fall.

Out here, there were comets and great wakes of stars that shot through you for loving; it was like coming, but obviously quite sexless, and painful. So above natural laws were they that Percodan, CDs, and the VCR sitting in the apartment were now perfectly okay to take. Even the black lady glaring at him had a right and a reason to feel pain. Life was a tragic banquet free of ownership at which everybody wept and kissed. The woman did a double take as he flashed her a sudden loving smile.

Happy, he hopped off the train at his good buddy's stop, confident that a firm pressure on the doorbell would gain him entrance into his brave utopia. He saw the guy's gentle smile as he tipped the vial of Percodan into his pocket, apologetically borrowed a shirt and socks, and unhooked the VCR. The smile filled him with such gratitude that he wanted to come back as soon as he could with a present: a book the guy wanted to read, flowers, a cake.

But nobody was answering that buzzer. Apollo leaned on it with all his weight. The fleeting realization that it was past 4:00 A.M. only inspired him with contempt for those who were not free enough and big enough to be there when he needed them. So he walked backward from the building and looked up at the darkened windows on the third floor. He opened his mouth and let sound spill out.

"Yo! Yo! Yooooo!"

The street was silent. Then, in the wrong window, a light switched on. He saw a curtain part and furious eyes peek out at him.

"Yo, you know my friend? The guy in three A?"

The curtain closed.

The nausea began to well back up. And like last time,

it was attached to a feeling. The drama of the friend whom he'd thought of ripping off, who'd then suddenly become a super friend, shrunk. All that had the petty status of a hallucination. It was replaced by a cold sweat in the real air of predawn: the feeling of being a fugitive, the reality of the crime at the theater. He just wasn't high enough to avoid it now.

Everything bore down on him: the cops looking for him, the cold public light from the street lamps, the closed and darkened buildings; his exhausted, stale body.

If he didn't chill out, get some sleep where it was safe, the rock and the hard place moving in on him would crush him. On weary feet he began the nineteen-block walk to his white mother's home, whom he pictured with contempt about ready to rise, climb into sweatpants, and begin chanting for abstract love before eating her vegetarian breakfast. A bubble of energy forced a bitter laugh out of him at the thought of her rent-controlled apartment and her lunar calendar, the jars of grain on a shelf above the stove.

Day was just beginning to break as he tiptoed up the stairs to her roof. As usual, he had no intention of going down to her apartment to see her. On the roof, the air felt fresh and hopeful for the first time.

He stretched out on the tarpaper next to the bag of bread he'd brought up there a few days ago. Inside was a small crust, which he chewed before lying back with his mouth open.

A pigeon winged through the air, dirty and on the loose, curtailed by the world of tar-covered water towers and sparse trees of the stinking city. It looped up and then dove for him. He felt its claws on his face. Its head dipped into his mouth and sucked some chewed bread out of it. Then the bird lifted back into the air.

Mouth fallen open like a baby bird's, with the remainder of the chewed bread in it, soft-skinned Apollo fell into a deep, long-term nod. It relaxed the muscles of his face like a coma and took years off it.

VIII

"You stinking black bitch, you're a fake. There's no such thing as a lady in our world. You either got to be a bitch or a faggot in drag."

—ICEBERG SLIM, *Pimp*

THIS IS DETECTIVE JUAN PARGERO SPEAKING *through your thoughts. Seems an employee of the Ecstasy Male Theater has been badly beaten and may be crippled. Turns out it's the same pincushion junkie I arrested for armed robbery of O'Hara's place almost a decade ago. That time we had to hoist him out of a bathtub, he was so high.*

Once more I go undercover. The kind of places I got to go, you get the goods quick when you blend in with the crowd. The best snitches about the sucker who attacked Theodoro G. Rodriguez, a.k.a. Casio, I figured, would be at Tina's. Believe it or not, the queen is an old pal of mine.

We go back. Seem funny to you? Being how she has chosen to represent herself. I mean, her crotch suppressor and all? Then think again. A dick like me runs into all kinds of people. Some are a helluva pain in the butt. But Tina is kosher. She's square with the guys in blue. She knows how one person's hand wipes another's ass. And none of them come up smelling like 4711.

I first bumped into Tina undercover as a john on a missing person's case. The brother of a certain V.I.P. had evaporated into thin air two months back. Rumor had it he was a love slave. Some queen was keeping him in vials in a midtown hotel room.

His daddy's will was waiting to be distributed, and all that they needed was a signature. The brother wanted him found fast, before the papers did. Somebody contacted Buster Huxton's widow. She said the transvestite bar was a good place to start the investigation.

"Looking for female company?"

This was way before she owned the place. Just a skinny queen squeezing up to the bar to get in next to me. I could smell Muguet des Bois coming from her armpits. Her bony knees pinned one of my thighs between them. I felt her fingers snake along my pants and slide in my pocket hunting for some green.

"I found the family jewels, honey, but no bucks."

So I took my wallet out of my breast pocket.

"Doubles?" she suggested, testing her luck, and at the word, Ethel Girl, that mop-headed bartender, who might have been a botched transsexual, came running with a bottle of vodka from the B shelf, her lips parted to reveal a rotten-toothed smile.

Miss T played the lady, pressing fingers to her mouth while she waited for Ethel Girl to stop pouring and for me to pick up the tab. Then she grabbed her glass and managed to hook her arm through mine. We raised our drinks in a toast, Latin-style: arms linked and eyes glued to each other.

A quiver passed through those bare shoulders, jiggling the falsies into action (it would be years before she went the silicone route). Her polyester curls bobbed up and down. She poked a finger under my belt to tug me closer. But an alarm must have gone off when she felt my piece through the jacket making a dent in the falsies.

74

"When a man's carrying it means one of two things. Somebody's looking for him. Or he's looking for somebody."

"All I'm looking for is a little information."

"Why not let your fingers do the walking?" Miss T placed my hand on her buns.

Our research continued upstairs. A week later she'd become my eyes and my ears for everybody that came in that bar.

Ten days later, we had found our man.

Those were the old days, when Tina was just a bit player. Now she owns the whole shebang—second only to Mrs. Huxton in controlling the block. The night the attempted murder happened, an anonymous call came in about a certain Apollo Nelson. The unidentified caller dubbed him the perpetrator, named the theater where the bouncer had been nixed, indicated whereabouts of the suspect somewhat below Fourteenth Street, and gave us dial tone. We put a qui vive on the area, but to no avail.

Mrs. Huxton, being very perturbed about the incident in her establishment, had arranged for her driver to pick me up near my digs in Jersey and drop me in front of Tina's around 4:00 A.M. It was gonna be Sunday morning, and Mom was looking forward to the usual game of gin, but the good woman has adjusted to my operations over the years.

The after-hours crowd had packed the place to busting. Tina was in back counting up the loot from the legit take. A member of the force was parked discreetly outside, keeping the blue laws at arm's length.

She'd already heard about the trouble at the theater and had laid out my first move. So she took her cigarillo out of her mouth and blew me a kiss, poked aside the backroom curtain, and pointed at a black queen with a yard-high beehive in gold lamé.

"Name's Mercedes. Used to go with one of the boys from the theater—'fore he broke her jaw and she sliced him up. A junkie, name of Apollo? He's the one you want, if my grapevine honked me right."

"Tina, love o' my life, what would I have done without you these years? If I'd the time, I'd—"

75

"Shovel the manure for that queen over there, handsome. You're gonna need plenty of it."

And right she was: Mercedes was the proverbial brick shithouse, with nails longer than the switchblade between her luscious chocolate tits. Under her yardstick 'do, her black eyes shone like tacks, ready to nail the first sucker that came along. A sweet smile parted over a broken coconut-sliver of a tooth. Except what was the diva palming? A little plastic squeeze bottle. A homeboy she called Fierce One whispered like the devil into her wig.

I snuck in nearby and pricked up my ears. Seems he was training her for a long con. A milquetoast john in an undertaker's suit was their mark-to-be.

"That's the best way to get the sucker, sweetheart," Fierce One wheedled. "Pour the whole bottle a this in his drink. I boosted it from an eye doctor. After a couple sips he won't remember nothing and starts walking bad. Shitting in his pants before he gets to the corner. You just follow him at a distance, is all."

"Eye drops'll do it?" says the queen.

"Sure will, baby. He'll be hallucinatin'."

"You ain't shitting me, Fierce One? If so, I'd be snappin' mad."

"Baby, read my lips. The Love Bandit don't never lie. I'm into crowd control. Now bus it, 'fore the john leaves."

Her homeboy raised a blunt finger to test the torque on his gold cap. He tapped the queen on the ass toward the john.

She tucked the bottle between her silicone knockers and slinked forward, but it slipped down and fell out of her halter as she walked.

I dived for it, and watched her play the john for broke. She moved like an expert, and I had to admire it. He bought them fresh drinks. Then she went for the eye drops and found they were gone.

Five minutes later she was back at the bar. Fierce One had already moved on to one of his other girls. The queen was in a dither, furious about missing the mark.

Up came my line. "Buy you a drink?"

"A couple, if you want."

I paid for the drink and palmed the eye drops. Gave her five dollars for the jukebox, told her to "play our song."

I'm an all-round sport, a good-time guy. All's fair in love and war. Sometimes a man's work takes precedence, so I emptied that bottle of eye drops right into little Miss Mercedes's drink.

She came back and put her two-inch nails around it, stuck her lips to the edge, and took a swig, then ran the tip of her tongue across her top lip, not knowing she was windshield-wiping an optometrist's cocktail.

"Out-of-town?" she asked.

"On it."

"A live wire."

"I got plenty of juice."

"AC or DC?"

"Why?"

"I carry an extension cord, if ya want me to unstrap it."

"I got all the length we'll ever need."

"One prong at a time, baby."

"You got my motor humming."

"Let's go upstairs and git some grease 'fore it burns out."

Not one to take a man's word, she grabbed hold of my coil for verification. It unwound for her, and we steered it upstairs.

Watching her hunched on a cheap mattress in the seedy hotel sent a clammy feeling creeping through me. This was no Madonna, but my heart went out. At least the diarrhea was over. The eye drops had had the effect of pulling everything liquid out of her, and they raced her nervous system like an overdose of not-so-good speed.

Her problems got worse when I pulled out my badge. She was too weak to stand and too wigged to clam up. Words came pouring out of her like the other stuff had. She jump-cut from one memory to another.

"Apollo? . . . Now where that sweet piece been chillin'? Strange fancies, that butch queen. Could never go nowhere without singing to his Mercedes. Ain't that the truth, baby, every day of the week?"

She rode the memory of their love affair like it was the Concorde *instead of the Coney Island roller coaster it was. But I got to say: she took the swells without a barf bag.*

"Them days with Apollo! I was runnin' through some crazy money! The nigga's be payin' me stupid dollars! 'Cause I was pullin' 'em in 'fore they had a doubt. Even so, that nigga had no business dipping in my purse! And catching the sucker on Ninth Avenue conversatin' with another female finished it for me! I'd been faded by the punk too many a time.

"So I told him, listen, you know, you got no respect. That why if you don't hand back my loot, I'm gonna cut you. But the dough was already in his veins. And so was the Budweiser. You know, Mister, if you haves a lot of alcohol in you, the blood is thin. It really flows out. So I was sorry I opened him up. The cops come along, but my pantyhose saved me. Then I lost my man to Riker's when they found the works on him. Now it's history."

She got off the ride to the past quick, a dazed stare at a broken press-on nail. Catching sight of it, she snapped. She put her head in her hands and started bawling. She wailed for Apollo and for lost love. The room was hot, so I unpinned her wig and laid it on the night table. Then I put a finger on her cheek to wipe the tears away.

"You got heart, Lieutenant."

"Why would a pro like you let a guy like that use you in his Monopoly game?"

"I started early. Everybody made me eat it raw when I should a been on formula."

"Sure, kid. Rough."

"You end up feelin' at home in any bed, 'cause you know you'll never be in any bed you can call home. You got a rag?"

I tossed her my clean handkerchief, and she blew her nose.

"You got no idea where I can find the punk?" I asked her straight out.

"You're askin' me to snitch on my man?"

"You just got finished telling me he was history."

The queen began to bawl again. "But he was no more'n fifteen when I first meets him. Just a nose junkie, and where was he? Oh my me, let's see. Cock blockin', I think? In front a the head down-*

stairs. You know? Reelin' in the johns comin' to the head before the other hustlers can get to 'em by flippin' out your dick. Turnin' heads that way. The guy that guards the head was clockin' z's and didn't notice no thing! But what was the line he feeds me? Something like, I saw you on a deck of cards. Ha ha.

"Right about then I get interrupted. Some stooge thinks he can get the better of me tellin' me I need gaffer's tape to keep my meat from showin' through the panty line. I can see it, says he. See it, suh? You've sucked it, you no-account! I'm twice the woman you'll ever get, and twice the man you'll ever be!

"The dude's about to bean me when Prince Apollo steps in and drops him. Real fineass sucker back then! Fierce. Say what you'll be sayin' 'fore anybody can. Kinda educated, like almost white. Although he gots a black daddy. A smile like survival. He was the boy who would a never touched ground, if it wasn't for that habit a his . . . Made him shady. He put it down to the neighborhood and the way things lay. Take some responsibility! says I.

"And I'm here to see that he does."

She couldn't turn off her waterworks. "But seeing that I was the cause of our boy bein' incarcerated . . . Shit that hits the fan there maybe set the stage for what was to come tonight. 'Cause Ocifer, he come down river again kind a violent. He got that scar on his soul when he was new fish at Riker's, some older boy tryin' to make a female outta him, come-here-I-want-you-to-do-my-laundry, that kind a stuff, and hold-my-dick-for-me-while-I-pee."

"Don't ya see? His card was drawn long ago."

Mercedes finally stopped crying and honked into the handkerchief. "Okay. You can try the alphabets. His white momma lives there. Over on B and Seventh. Look. My dress's all fucked up. I ain't got no other. How'm I gonna work?"

"I'm sorry, baby."

"You couldn't help me out, Lieutenant?"

"Sure. Come on over to Paramus and my mother'll cook dinner." I handed her my card. "Oh. And maybe she's got a couple designer duds she was looking to get rid of."

The queen sobered up immediately. "You think she's my size?"

I nodded.
"You're cool, Detective."
I was only doing my job.

Pargero's job took him to the computer at the precinct, then toward the building where Apollo's mother lived. To get there, he and his two cops cruised past Mrs. Huxton's block and through the several trillion dollars of real estate that made up their now-deserted midtown precinct, then down the wide avenue still empty in the very early light of morning.

They headed east leisurely, past the 24-hour fast-food stores, with their high-watt fluorescents still fighting the previous night, and turned onto the avenue, where they entered one of the most eclectic neighborhoods in the world, overcharged with races and religions, art students and almost-artists, gay subculturals and squatters, rebellious rockers, adjunct professors, sixties leftovers, window trimmers, illegal aliens, Rastas, welfare families, jazz singers, restaurateurs, numbers takers, pot sellers, permanent outcasts, and transients.

They cruised past ancient bars that had stood in the same spots since the turn of the century, next to silver-painted clubs that had been thrown up yesterday. They passed a mangled, velvet-upholstered chair that someone had tried to spray-paint orange and whose stuffing was scattered all over the sidewalk; they dodged an overturned carton of books and a crutch lying in the street.

They turned down a street from which an unbroken string of building facades was reflected on their window against the hatchet silhouette of Pargero—looking like the figurehead of a ship—its harsh, eclectic, city-made expression fading in and out as images were superimposed on it.

Pargero was thinking about the perpetrator and mulling over the question of race. In the last file dealing with

Apollo's previous incarceration, notes still remained about the character-witness appearance of his white mother, as well as the letter she had later written, eloquently but somewhat bizarrely petitioning the Board of Corrections for his early release, using as an excuse the sad fate of his father.

Each of these documents was haunted with the eery tension of what Pargero sometimes jokingly called miscegenation. And Pargero himself was a product of it. For Pargero's mother was an Anglo, whereas his father had been from Paraguay. And Paraguay had been revealed as that haven for international criminals who . . . Suffice it to say that when alibis of mixed race came to the fore, another of the detective's fetishes was stimulated.

His overloaded brain began trying to sort through these thousands of mismatched neighbors, these heaps of lives that defied categorization or surveillance. Normally he would have seen it as just another neighborhood. But as he came closer to the race-scarred mother who had given the testimony and written the letter, he found himself entering some of the buildings in fantasy.

In this part of the city, he had seen countless fauna and numerous habitats, from pierced-nose Caucasian gay boys living tripled up since none could afford to pay the rent singly, to lonely Polish newcomers whose chests had been systematically disfigured during interrogation by the knives of anti-Solidarność police, to university film students in spacious two-bedroom apartments who papered their bathrooms with tin foil and painted each room a different daring fluorescent color. He had entered buildings with all Italian tenants, whose hallways were oil-painted and adorned with the figure of a saint at each landing, and who could be awakened at a moment's notice when irregular noises filtered under their black doors with their peepholes, protected by police locks extending into kitchens with tubs, and windows giving onto air shafts.

He had even encountered a commune of Syrian fundamentalists, who would already be rising to fry the chickpeas for the falafels that would be served at the restaurant on that corner, as well as at the nearby mosque, before each climbed into a limo to drive his twelve-hour shift, as well as an astrologer and satanist Pargero had once seen on a bust, who had painted the century-old floorboards of her kitchen with a six-pointed star, and below whom lived the forgotten black Beat painter who had been the girlfriend of some of the most illustrious abstract expressionists but had put on more than a hundred pounds after years of antidepressants and antipsychotic drugs.

As they neared the next avenue, Pargero remembered the middle-aged Dominican man who had been born in this neighborhood, and now lived in its streets and shelters, whom Pargero had discovered in a hallway interlocked in coitus with his deaf-mute lover, also homeless, an empty bottle of Night Train by their side. And all the possible crimes being committed at that moment began to parade through Pargero's mind, drawing from the petty and not so petty busts of his career. Perhaps a white law student in that apartment facing the street was cooking up his second batch of free-base cocaine; or that Israeli exterminator who lived over there had again broken his wife's nose while the children surrounded them in a sobbing circle; or Midwestern squatters in those two adjoining buildings had just crashed out after an evening of mushrooms and garage-band records; or a solitary Vietnam vet was up and cleaning his cache of weapons; or the Ukrainian-speaking homeless woman was now squatting once more in a hallway with a broken doorlock where she'd once been caught peeing; or some Austrian accountant had been up all night falsifying papers for a small business; or a black real estate broker was coming home from moonlighting as an elegant uptown call girl, which she'd started to do ever since property values went down.

And now they passed that block and broke into the sunlit avenue, where there was a hyphen of space from the chaotic crush of humanity packed into the buildings, so that

Pargero could clear his head before another parade began: the peroxided performance-artist junkie from the South who played with gender, alternatingly ruing his gangly body and savoring the next club date; the bewildered and sullen Swiss dancer who was studying with a New York master and who'd become the girlfriend of a coke dealer; the heavily snoring Puerto Rican super whose son, on summer break from medical school, had been murdered; the Panamanian sex-change and the rehabilitated Irish killer who were living on welfare; the Connecticut gay actor who worked in the cookie shop and once got beaten and robbed by a pickup; the Wisconsin-born missionary who'd lost part of her liver function through a stomach parasite she'd caught working in the city shelters; two black people very sick from HIV and some whites panicking about it whom Pargero had seen in the middle of the night waiting in the emergency room of the nearby hospital.

Until they were so close to Apollo's building that if Apollo had woken up and walked to the edge of the roof, he would have seen the loathsome blue-and-white vehicle pulling up to it. Felt the rush of enzymes in Pargero's brain unable to organize the quirky stew of humanity. Heard the doorbell ringing and the buzzer opening it.

Feared the entrance of the law enforcers, who called no neighborhood home.

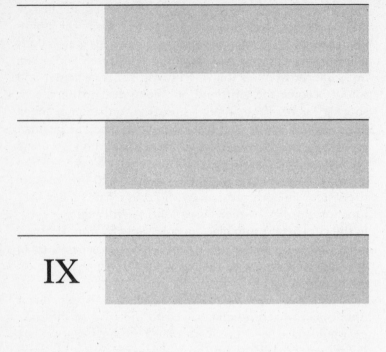

IX

Casio's son baby pop lay on a piece of cardboard among the summer homeless at World Trade Center Plaza, his famous and valuable shiny curls poking from a found bandanna.

"You be tellin' me my father is askin' for me?" said the fourteen-year-old. He sat up abruptly on the piece of cardboard and blinked disorientedly, rubbing his eyes with grimy fingers, as if the information had come from a dream.

Angelo, the rotten-toothed crackhead who'd come to find him, ground his big jaw trying to spit out the words.

"Me and Manny, the guy always wears the hat with the big X, was conversating 'bout—"

"But ain't that the dude who nixed your cousin?"

"That's bullshit. My cousin was just takin' too much codeine."

"Yeah?"

"And so Manny says to me, you knowing about that my sister's a nurse's aide over at the hospital on Ninth? Well she's telling to me that they got *Casio* over there!"

"My father?"

"They was getting ready that he was goin' to die!"

"He O.D.'d?"

"No man, some motherfucker wasted him! He was in a coma and shit but he come to and be askin' for you!" Angelo sat down on the cardboard with a sigh and looked at Baby Pop expectantly, like a dog that has performed a trick watches for the biscuit about to be tossed.

"Who?" said Baby Pop. "Who wasted him?"

Angelo shook his head and gave a bewildered shrug. Baby Pop reached into his pocket and took out four quarters, flicking them one by one into Angelo's hand. Immediately the crackhead bought a toke off a nearby smoker, grabbed his blackened stem, and inhaled.

Ten minutes later, Baby Pop had hopped the D train. In his duffel bag he carried a pair of dirty socks, his asthma inhaler, a bible, an algebra book, a Stephen King novel, and a pair of jeans. The socks would be traded for clean ones at the very next opportunity. The bible and the Stephen King book got him through the hours as he sat in a stall in the men's room of Port Authority waiting for it to be late enough to go to sleep at World Trade Center. The algebra book was, in his mind, preparation for college.

Up until his last year in school, which was seventh grade, Baby Pop had proved an astoundingly brilliant student, excelling in math. More than anything he wanted to return to that arena and the adulation that had been poured upon him. But from the time he had run away from the group home—where he'd been placed after being taken from his mother, Monica—he'd had to rely for survival on his lustrous curls, his satiny olive skin, his enormous dark eyes with their curly lashes, his elongated, almost girlish limbs, and his serene, passive charm.

He stripped off his T-shirt to expose another, and then took that one off, so he was down to his tank top. Despite the heat, he'd been wearing three layers on top and four—undershorts, shorts, sweatpants, and pants—below. The layers worked more or less like a walking closet, to which he made additions and subtractions at the homes of tricks.

Circulating through his brain at this moment was a simple thought. It was the impulse to "be there" for his father. The fact that Baby Pop had a father was one of the few palpable proofs that he himself was somebody. This fact needed periodic manifestation, though at other times Baby Pop's perception of Casio was numbed, and Casio seemed like just another street person who worked at the theater that Baby Pop himself sometimes stood outside of when he tried to hustle.

As a hustler, Baby Pop was tops but problematic. His serene detachment pricked some potentially long-term johns with adoration but gave others a sense of inferiority that led to their unloading him. And then, of course, his status as a minor didn't help. His nearly photographic recall of names, addresses, and conversations gave him an edge over others, but his other intellectual powers could also perplex or threaten the typical customer.

The train screeched to a halt, and Baby Pop leapt from his seat and out the door. As he passed a man who had exited another car, he caught the guy eyeing his slender arm muscles. The guy looked like a *bugarrón*—a butch—but Baby Pop looked back. The moment of attention was a sign of good luck for the day. Attracting the male gaze did not make Baby Pop think he was gay. On the contrary, it set off his interest in the asses of both sexes and the possibility of ruling over them.

It was the active role he normally took as a hustler, unless forced, or tempted by large sums, to get fucked. Because of this, he preferred a *loca*, an effeminate party-type who liked clubs and discos, as customer. However, he'd had enough experience to realize that a *loca*'s flightiness and fickleness couldn't be depended upon, and ultimately he was looking for a *casera*, a homebody, to move in with for a while. These types spent their time cooking or making the house look good and usually had a nest egg. But because they were not promiscuous, they were hard to find. They were looking for real husbands and usually saw through you when you played them.

There were other types, like the *bugarrón*—a male gay who liked to fuck—who were okay, provided they were white. Blacks and Hispanics might force you, but whites could usually be talked into just a suckfest, and it wasn't embarrassing to go to the movies or dinner with them, because they usually weren't effeminate. But to be avoided at all costs were the *cafres*—the freaks—especially the white ones, because they got high on drugs or could get violent or give you strange diseases.

Baby Pop's hustler skills all dated back to seven years ago—two years after Casio moved out—when Monica began looking for ways of increasing the drug flow into the apartment. Cubby, who was the whiteboy leader of a rat pack of dustheads and hustlers, had begun visiting with his crew and had become Monica's man. Monica would get zonked on rock and dust and party down with Cubby while Baby Pop looked after his own asthma medication and kept up his schoolwork, leaving the apartment each morning neatly dressed, his homework meticulously packaged in a plastic briefcase, with a glance of cool contempt at the others passed out on the bed and floor.

One night Baby Pop found himself alone with Cubby while the clique and Monica partied down in the bedroom. Cubby began to tell Baby Pop the story of each of the tattoos on his body, which represented landmark occurrences in his life. He would take Baby Pop's finger and trace the blue-and-red outlines of the Executioner, the Bat, or the Devil on his skin stretched taut by muscle. Then he recommended that Baby Pop get a tattoo with a shining light bulb that said "Genius" and told him to strip off his shirt so that he could scratch the light bulb and its rays into his skin with a razor blade and some shoe polish.

Baby Pop stripped off his shirt and Cubby got playful, tickling him as his fingers moved over each part of his skinny chest, belly, and arms, describing how it might hurt to get a tattoo there or there. Then he insisted that Baby Pop's ass was the best place, it being their secret only, and got him to slip out of his pants.

The boy lay facedown on the bed, gritting his teeth but not crying as Cubby traced a light bulb and rays with the edge of the razor blade. He blotted up the blood with a T-shirt, then worked bits of shoe polish into the cut with the tip of the blade. When it was over, Baby Pop stayed naked, on his stomach, until it clotted. But when the cut had congealed, Cubby pinned him to the bed, squeezed two fingers inside him, and entered him.

When Baby Pop reached the hospital, Father Kraus was feeding Casio breakfast. The bouncer had been moved from intensive care to a regular room when his vital signs improved. He lay propped up in bed with his head wrapped in a bandage like a turban.

Father Kraus greeted Baby Pop with a sweetened, dentured smile. The old face floated in Baby Pop's gaze like the easy food and lodging and limp moral advice it had always represented. One of his first memories was watching Father Kraus officiate at the funeral of Casio's old friend Chino. They'd laid Chino in an open casket spray-painted with the graffiti tag of every member of their already defunct gang. He was wearing all his colors and had two bandannas tied above each knee. His spanking white-and-green Reeboks stood out against the green satin lining of the coffin, since green had been the gang's color.

Five-year-old Baby Pop had held on to the stiff jeans of

his father and watched the whole show. The bros had marched past the coffin while Father Kraus prayed, and, as in the days of the pharaohs, each placed in it articles that had been dear to the departed: green-and-white packs of Newports, a hookah and a bag of weed, a steel pipe, a 14-carat gold chain with a devil's tail, and a six-pack of Budweiser.

Now the diminutive gray-haired priest hugged Baby Pop, copping a quick feel like a blushing adolescent, simultaneously clearing his throat and swallowing uncomfortably, before letting Baby Pop approach his dad's bed.

"Bendición."

He bent over his father's sallow face and kissed the forehead lightly, taking in the tube coming from his nose and the IV in his already multipunctured arm. One eye was purple and swollen. "What up?" His eyes moved away when he noticed that one of his father's hands was handcuffed to the bed.

Casio tried to speak, but his lips were dry.

"What happened?" Baby Pop asked the Father.

"An accident," Father Kraus opined daintily. "A boy named Apollo who works at the theater apparently got into a disagreement with your dad—"

Apollo? So that was the cabrón! An archaic reflex jerked through Baby Pop so strongly that it bounced his shiny curls. This mental activity was a thing apart from his psychological insights or his superb ability to do math. He pulled his inhaler from the duffel bag and took a couple of tokes. Then he bent over Casio's bed. "You don't have to tell me to waste the *cabrón*, Papi. I'll take care of everything while you heal."

Father Kraus watched this communication primly, with a kind of pained anthropological politeness. Then a doctor strode in. He was a tall man with a thick trunk, a healthy tan, and a shiny bald head.

"Which of you is the nearest of kin?" he boomed cheerily, without bothering to study either.

Casio stirred and winced. He tried to sit up but fell back onto the bed.

Father Kraus smiled a bit unctuously at the doctor. "The young man," he said, and discreetly left the room.

"And what's your name, young fellow?" said the doctor, without even a cursory glance at the boy.

"Ricardo," Baby Pop answered unblinkingly, trying to tune the unreal personage in white from another class out. "Why they got the handcuff?"

"They found a controlled substance in his pocket," said the doctor with casual heartiness. Then he glanced impatiently behind him at the door. "I want someone to get in contact with if anything happens to your father. Could that be you?"

Baby Pop nodded, wondering at the hair sprouting from the guy's forearm and, with a rush from the inhaler, seeing it as if in magnified closeup.

"Give me your phone number, then."

Baby Pop shrugged and kept staring at the hairs.

The doctor blushed. "Well, just leave us a friend's number."

"What happened?"

"What?"

"He gonna be all right?"

"Do you know what nerve tissue is, son?"

"You ain't got to tell me nothing. I'm gonna go to college."

"Fine. Well, your dad damaged a bit of his spinal cord—" The doctor stopped, having accidentally met Baby Pop's eyes for the first time.

As for Baby Pop, he distrusted such sprouts of hair on a white guy's pale forearm. It reminded him of a *cafre*. A *cafre* was the kind who wanted you to get high or to fist-fuck you or piss on you or something. He really hated white guys with hairy forearms like that.

He squinted up to peer at the too-bright bald head and

suddenly remembered the booming voice, as inappropriate in this sickroom as it had been in the bedroom.

Cafre! he thought. It really is him. The freak was a doctor.

This time the doctor's voice cracked. "So we don't know if your father will be able to walk . . ."

Baby Pop stared at the shiny dome with nearly brazen contempt. He remembered the man, when he was drunk, offering him some kind of drug. A self-satisfied look smoldered in Baby Pop's large eyes. The doctor was turning beet-red now.

"But with some physical therapy, there's a good chance . . ."

Father Kraus had come back in from the hallway, and he too was blushing, having caught the twosome staring with naked recognition into each other's eyes. But Baby Pop's intelligent eyes were about to empty into the blank look of the street hustler, realizing the inevitability of it all.

"Listen," he flatly silenced the doctor, using his eyes to indicate his own naked arm muscle, "you couldn't lend me ten dollars?"

Later that day, Casio went through a violent reaction from heroin withdrawal. He had been cranked up in bed eating applesauce when convulsions catapulted the tray toward the ceiling. His body released a flood of diarrhea onto the sheets as he jerked in and out of consciousness.

By the time the nurses came running, he had floated out of it, his wrist scraped raw from the handcuff, looking like a pale pine carving of himself.

A Jamaican nursing assistant muttered curses under her breath while she sponged him off and changed the sheet. Interns immediately put him on an anticonvulsant and methadone to stave off the mess of abrupt withdrawal.

Methadone maintenance would take the edge off the future. Like an abused animal who finally welcomes the containment of a safe, solitary cage, Casio gave in. Abuela, his little great-granny with her wrinkled yellowed face, missing teeth, and gnarled fingers, was bending over his bed in ecstatic gratitude. His eyes locked to hers, because he knew she was no stranger to seizures.

She was his maternal great-grandmother and Baby Pop's great-great-grandmother and was in her seventies, but she had acted as his mother when he was a boy, bringing him up when her daughter fled to Puerto Rico and her daughter's daughter died from an overdose. She had laid yucca slices on his forehead when he had a fever, putting a clean glass of water next to a white candle from the *botánica* near the bed. In those days her room was always moist and warm from the beans cooking on the stove.

The haggard woman bent closer to Casio and announced that she felt no portentous vibrations coming from him. To him she looked like a ghost of a bird now, all skin and bones, but his passive gaze stayed glued to her watery brown eyes. She smoothed the hair away from his perspiring face. In one bony hand she clasped a small piece of folded white paper, an *oración*. She tucked the special prayer under his pillow. As she understood it, her great-grandson's body had been full of venomous fluids, the excretions of spirits. The blow he had received had shaken the poisonous spirits into turmoil. To gain exit, they'd caused convulsions.

Whenever Abuela herself had a seizure, it was preceded by a pressure in the head or the chest or a numbness in one of her extremities. Rather than a demon inside her, it was usually a good spirit's foreboding of something negative happening or about to happen. For example, the night Baby Pop had had a bad attack of asthma and had to be rushed to the hospital, Abuela had been in her SRO hotel room blocks away, had felt pains in her chest, and had palpated the area only to be knocked unconscious by a vision of her great-great-grandson lying in a white room surrounded by white flames.

Abuela began putting the room in order as proof of her profound thankfulness for her great-grandson's release from demons. A merciful sense of relief about her great-grandson spun inside her bony chest and issued from her mouth as a humming sound. Apparently he was now being given a medicine that would keep the bad spirits from re-entering. But she was convinced that to keep the entire room in defense against the evil, everything had to be symmetrical. The vase had to be in the very center of the windowsill. She took the comb and brush and mirror and hair oil she had brought for him and arranged them in straight lines on the dresser. In front of them she arranged the beads of a wooden rosary in a perfect oval. This was the kind of order she demanded in her own home. Even change was stacked into neat columns and never put in a place that would unbalance the surface of the table.

She unwrapped the *rellenos de papa* and the little codfish cakes and set them on the swing tray above the bed. She smoothed the sheet at the foot of the bed and sat down on it, beaming at her great-grandson lying in safety with the room in order around him. Even the sight of the handcuff could not dispel the deep sense of peace she felt at seeing Casio released from the spirits.

Casio hardly had time to bring a bite of the food to his mouth before Abuela leapt to her feet and clasped him desperately to her. *Mi corazón. If the boy that did this to my great-grandson has a mother, may she someday feel this terrible pain*, was a thought that suddenly coursed to her lips like brushfire. Against the white sheet, Casio's brown fingers stood out. Her eyes fixed on the extra cartilage covering his knuckles from the many scrapes he'd been in since the time he was a boy. The image of the fighting fingers sent more sobs seeping through her. Why was her flesh and blood being put through these tests? A horrible monster had attacked her great-grandson for no good reason. The villain had almost taken his life, and her flesh and blood might be crippled forever.

Casio kept his free arm around the sobbing woman until the sounds faded into silent heaving. He knew that she almost never left her room. When she did, it was only for a family emergency or because she had not had a drink for a long time. She couldn't stand being so high up on the fifteenth floor and rarely even went near a window. She was afraid that if she did, she might jump. It was Casio who usually brought her groceries, but now he was no good to her. Getting to the hospital must have been a tremendous calvary. Because she feared the elevator, she'd likely walked down the fifteen flights, and then up several more to see him. Now the prospect of getting back would appear with dread before her.

Abuela's heaving became deep breathing. She stood and took a pint of rum from her purse. The swallow went down as if her throat had been numbed. There was no burning, no taste. But the liquid was a kind of resignation seeping through her. She sat back at the foot of the bed and watched her great-grandson eat. She watched as one watches something on another plane—a cloud, a bird, an insect—with detachment and fascination. A blood tie in a strange bed eating. All her fears were absorbed by the stillness of watching, broken by the intervals of swallowed rum.

But why that handcuff? The sight of it suddenly made her powerless as its meaning was driven home. Her great-grandson was going to prison again. This was a place where there were many evil spirits that caused diseases of the body and mind. One new disease that ruined the body even seemed to be invulnerable to counterspells.

Abuela broke down again, slouched at the foot of the bed, strands of hair doused in tears, the pint brought more and more often to her lips. She still could not taste it, but it began to burn her throat, her gullet. Her tears blurred her eyes so that the image of her great-grandson got more and more vague. Through her tears the light haloed objects. It haloed the blur of her grandson's head and the hand he raised, like the light radiating from a hand in a sacred painting. The whiteness of the sheets pierced her eyes. They burned her great-grandson in a purifying fire. Abuela's body was warm with gratitude, resignation.

God would take care of him.

X

Who dares dose out your tranquilizer?

—ANTONIN ARTAUD

APOLLO'S SITUATION IS BEGINNING TO PENETRATE his numbed mind. At the sound of the cops he'd come to and leapt to another roof. He'd forced a door and run down to the street.

Foremost in his thoughts is the matter of dope. It'll take a bundle—ten bags—to chill out of reach of the law for two or three days. This need shifts his thoughts again to his AIDS-sick friend. He hops the train back to midtown, hoping to find him at Tina's before evening. In his head he's already planning on how to ask him if he can hide out at his apartment. And if he can't get money for a bundle out of him, he'll have to settle for his supply of Percs.

Tina's opens at noon. Because it's daytime, she's not around, so he gets in the bar without any trouble. He buys a beer and takes a sip. Then he begins to nod out for some length he can't calculate. As soon as he opens his eyes, his friend's pale face is in front of them.

In a plaintive voice that Apollo doesn't himself believe, he convinces the wan-looking man to let him stay at his house and to advance him the money for a bundle. He says it's just to take back with them until the heat is off and he can get himself into detox. The moment the guy says yes, a wave of sentimentality washes over Apollo at the merciful kindness of his helper. His mind flits like a colt to a reminder: his helper has AIDS. His thoughts bump suddenly into the time he beat him up and rears in horrendous shame.

He reverses the vector of his feelings: a customary coolness settles in.

The sick friend becomes a thing, a convenience, that he follows to the cash machine, then sits next to as it takes him, holding money, in a cab to 112th to cop. But maybe saying he is a thing is shortchanging, since the feeling of security that comes out of sitting next to the money fills him with a warmth coming close to contentment, swollen at times with riffs of infantile gratitude.

After he cops, they ride back to the apartment. Apollo hears himself chatting glibly, even enthusiastically, with his savior. He tries to keep his mind off the first hints of withdrawal and comes up with the usual jokes about queens and lawyers, hypocritical doctors, politicians, or whores, which the guy likes. But beneath it all is his motivation: the bundle of dope—ten real doses—powerful in his pocket like uranium.

When they get to the apartment, a familiar ritual takes over. Apollo strips down to his briefs, kicking the clothing on the floor next to the bed. In his vision's periphery, his rawboned friend is doing the work of caretaking, bending to scoop up the clothes, hanging up what is salvageable, and tossing the rest into the laundry bag with the dependability of a trusted servant or machine. Then the friend sits down to write in his diary with a fountain pen.

Needle insertion, which represents the netherworld between being about to get high and being high, clefts Apollo's mind to let a shadow-feeling sneak in. It is an image of his friend, who now sits absorbed at his desk, dying in the future, and Apollo losing the best friend he ever had. Although he flinches phobically at the thought, it is also an electric spark that fuels the fantasy of life going on. This is enough proof of being alive to keep pushing the needle and pumping the drug into his bloodstream.

Suffice it to say that shortly afterward, with the needle still hanging from his arm, Apollo finally finds an enormous space opening in his perception of the world. The space is so big that for the first time real characters appear to him with some substantiality. First, of course, he sees his friend who has helped him, in the room, glancing at him from the desk with a defeated, tender look. He rejoices at being in his company and orders the man to sit down on the bed beside him.

Because the drug is making his body feel whole, he suddenly has a strong desire to have that body be made love to. And what better person than the one who has bought him the dope and also has his best interests in mind?

The dope also soothes potential disgust at the gauntness of his friend's body. Instead, lovemaking goes on at a more primal level, in which large fields of intimacy take over the mental screen.

The pleasure of a mouth and hands on a body charged with dope could arguably be worth any pain or complications that are to follow. Time becomes meaningless as a dope-charged body gathers impulses toward a slow climax. He feels the one who had protected him, bought him dope, picked up his clothes, and pressed against his body spinning out the pleasure. Apollo's orgasm comes in slow-motion waves, like the cliché female's. It leaves him hovering in a warm torpor that needs no words or images at all.

The man goes back to writing in his journal. Apollo remains on the bed, and thoughts begin to creep in . . . He's glad they had safe sex. Other real people march across the screen of his mind. To him this is intensely pleasurable, for it's all in 3-D, although he does not realize that this quality is present in the minds of normal people who don't take dope.

He pictures his friend, who is at the desk, still writing. Wonders smilingly how he could possibly have all those thoughts. Then suddenly he sees Casio and realizes that he had very little against him. His mind replays the sight of the bouncer lurching toward him on the stairs and the feel of contacting his eye socket. He sees the body fall, without any fear but with a naked acknowledgment of his responsibility. Then, in clarity, his mind moves to consider his options. He's already heard that the guy almost died from the blow and might be crippled. To Apollo this means he might have to go to jail and wait without bail for an indictment. It would be hell to withdraw in jail, so the point is to get himself to detox as the dope runs out.

The reasoning becomes boring and unnecessary. Instead he lets his mind play tantalizingly with the image of the queer cop, Pargero, whom Tina's bouncer, Easy, says has been looking for him. The stone-faced guy, his lingering glances at queens, always made Apollo smirk. In a kind of game, Apollo tries to imagine Pargero's erratic trail along his tracks—old tricks, drag queens, and Apollo's religious counterculture mother.

Then a weird feeling wins out. In the lovely cradle of the high, he challenges himself to get into Pargero's after-work life. What is it like when Pargero sits down to dinner? Probably with his mom and some queen he's got the hots for? The three of them try on clothes, or gossip about Mrs.

Huxton and about the good old days. He can see it right now. Is that what it's like to have a job and lead a life called normal?

Dear Death Diary,

Apollo's my pain pal. In the first place, he confirms all my theories about drug use. At this point in the game I'm an alienated sonofabitch—always trying to sniff out the hypocrisy of so-called common sense.

Being HIV-positive, I'm lately going through a period where I'm feeling a lot of physical pain. Recently I spent thirty-six hours in one of our city's glorious emergency rooms. I've got an axe to grind with those licensed pill-pushers. It is my opinion that access to ending pain is controlled by a greedy, insensitive bunch.

Why is it that mind-benders become "medicine" only when somebody with an M.D. gives them to you? Seems to me that anybody taking drugs on the street is merely self-medicating. So sorry that they or their suppliers couldn't afford medical school. Which is why I turn over part of my prescription for Percodan for severe peripheral neuropathy to pain pal Apollo. Until anybody with a bigger heart has a better solution for the guy.

Nobody takes drugs just for kicks. Call it, for some, the psychic pain of poverty if you must. Call it what you will. But a bitter type like me considers Apollo a "qualified professional" when it comes to prescribing for himself.

I, too, dread pain, change—the red stuff going bad in you—and want constant, tangible control of it at my fingertips.

I took Apollo to San Juan a couple of years ago. We stumbled into a seaside ghetto made of tin houses known as La Perla and watched a teenage girl in tears jabbing a needle over and over again into a leg that looked gangrened. I flew into a rage against those who cause the pain in league with those who control the painkillers, who could cure the leg and give them away with scrip if they wanted to. Shortly after, Apollo took me to a shooting gallery on 113th Street to pay for a bundle, and I saw old men who had been in this country all their lives but who still spoke no English walking around with needles still sticking in their jugular veins.

"Why are they doing that?" I asked Apollo.

"Just for the kick of drawing the blood in and out," he answered.

I nodded with some kind of recognition.

Apollo saw the look in my eyes.

Later, when we were in bed, he said, "Don't worry." I knew he'd cop something final for me if I was near the end and decided I couldn't stand it.

Lucky that Apollo left the roof as the cops came up, because I'm sure it was his chanting mother who sent them up to get him. From what the boy tells me, his mother's like that. Principled.

Religious people like her are always judgmental. They refuse to play by the pain rules.

He told me he was sleeping on the roof when he heard the cops' shortwaves come up through the open hallway window. The kid's a gazelle. That's how he lost them and made it up to Tina's to find me. It was afternoon, so he could get in. Tina's not there in the afternoon. Almost nobody goes in Tina's in the afternoon, but, just like he figured, I was there. See, Tina's is the only place I don't get my panic attacks. Cognitive dissonance is so big for me at Tina's that I don't expect anything different. I expect to be misunderstood. So I always feel okay.

During my first few dates from the place I marveled at phenomena that now have become commonplace for me. There was the kid who pulled a knife from his sock to cut his steak when I took him to an expensive restaurant, raising the eyebrows of the maître d'. The crackhead coated in grime who refused to remove his T-shirt to have sex because he didn't want to mess his hair. Their shenanigans burrowed a hole into my class parameters. Their language interlaced my identity and sent me into a craving tailspin. Call it the dance of death, but it's still better than being hooked up to a catheter.

I like to watch the new hustlers who come in the bar and don't yet know how to act. Popping gum and fuck all a yous, I don't need you, I know what you are. Then somebody, a brother or a cousin that they came in with, takes them aside and explains how it's done.

You see, they say, if the guy thinks you think you're big shit, he's not going to like you. He has to think you're dying to go with him in particular. Some of them can't even go with you if they can't imagine you're not liking it. It's all a psychology.

Next, the new kid goes to a corner and sulks a little. It takes him a while to get it. But before you know it, he is sidling up to you with a big smile on his face.

Ever get to see a master open a fresh pack of Newports you bought for him? He pulls them out and packs them all upside down—except for one, for good luck—then magnanimously extends the first cigarette as a sign of being a cut above desperation.

If he really is a professional, he'll finger the bulge in his pants as he exhales the first puff and portrays himself as not somebody who goes with just anybody, but a man about town with a respect for health and good eating habits, a playful dude who likes to get high on weed now and then with old friends, and a good sport who likes *chocha* but isn't embarrassed to have sex with a clean man.

He might catalogue a charmed life full of family, love, luck, "good people," worshipful girlfriends, johns who've made him a regular and a son, money down on clothes, watches, or electronic equipment, and a bright eye on the lucrative professions of the future.

He'll talk about his skills: a Grand Master rapper and Fresh M.C., a scientific weight lifter, and an expert trainer of your favorite sporting dog.

Only Selby's books can measure up to the variety of hawkers, hustlers, pimps, and addicts who frequent Tina's and the streets around it. But the low profiles of the slummers, who finance all the operations and then escape back to their normal lives, are the most unnerving. A nearly illiterate, addicted hustler in this city often spends his time with more entitled, creative, eccentric, or rich people than many celebrities do. Sprinkled among the dope-fiend crew and the queens in Tina's Lounge are a congressman and an ex-bishop, a former boxer who once held a world title, a criminal who is the subject of an Oscar-winning documentary. Oh, and then that prince whose finances created a fashion empire.

Apollo never talked important people or hustler shit to me, which is why we became long-term friends. He merely told me he was a junkie, made it clear that he would only hassle me when things were really bad, and came by from time to time to trick.

Call me identityless. Laugh at me for my silly romanticism about the disenfranchised. Friends did laugh at my goatee, or chino, as homeboys call that kind of beard—until it became a fashion for college art students as well.

Even before I was diagnosed with HIV infection and lost all this weight, I had this strange vicarious feeling of solidarity with the outcast types. For me, day-to-day routines always seemed pointless, like endless tasks done only at the injunction of some abstract parent. My apartment was full of all the requisite objects that made it seem as if somebody was living there.

What had stimulated me in my twenties fresh out of college—other cultures, new cities, last exits to someone's heart: the usual fag thrills—had lost their charge long ago. I was at the point where I could no longer fool myself with the initial fascination of the unfamiliar. The rhythms of the day that appear to be so natural and rooted in the path of the sun for everyone else were out of my reach.

Believe it or not, my diagnosis was a reawakening. Having an end seemed to supply me with a beginning. Now the condition of the down-and-out has become a dramatization of all the desperation and defeat that I've been trying to feel. I'm alive through all this street trash. Feeling alive has an allure that can make you the slave to an entire cosmology, which is I guess what happened to me.

Once I left my Weejuns at home and ventured into Tina's, I got funneled into a world of exchanges controlled by a shadowy figure Apollo says is called Mrs. Huxton, who supposedly owns the whole operation. But as close as I've come to her company is a red-haired guy in black chauffeur's cap who's always parking outside the hustler bar and seems to know all the cops, like that detective who comes in to see Tina from time to time, who Apollo says rubs bellies with queens.

When Apollo and I tricked, I suppose his mind was blown by my once-preppy attire which, because of its unfamiliarity, he interpreted as a potential wig in the closet, since he asked with some fascination, "Why does a real man like you talk like some kind of faggot?"

"I don't," I explained. "It's the way a person with a real education talks."

Apollo didn't start watching the William Buckley show. But he initiated a kind of study of me. In a short time he was living here.

When he wasn't high he began ingesting, transforming, discarding my props. The demitasse cups were planted with marijuana seedlings, a real percolator and large mugs appeared in the house, a legless kitchen table from Shaker country that had been leaning against the wall for some months became an ironing board.

He was a regular urban hunter and gatherer, and I was

fascinated by his ruthless expropriation of my unreal world. You make everything come alive, I had thought at the time, but I had the missionary arrogance of hoping to reform him.

That was near the beginning of a period when we stopped speaking. In fact, after he beat me up in front of a porno theater, I pressed charges. And he went to jail for a while. But before that came a period when we stuck together.

Like the time I got sick with a terrible attack of shingles. I couldn't stand a sheet on my body, and when I tried to stand up it was worse.

Apollo was babbling under the pleasure of the heroin. This prompted one of his canny monologues on my character: a rare contribution on his part, since he is someone who normally keeps his observations and affects close to his chest.

"You see a bed of nails in front of your eyes, and you feel you won't be anybody unless you lay on it. But you're so scared to be laying on that bed that you ain't going to try it until you can lay yourself out so careful that every inch of your precious body is only pushing a little bit on each nail."

Most would probably not understand that his words made me feel free, promiscuous. I lay there wanting to absorb all the pain. I lay next to my yogi.

I knew Casio way back, too. All right, I tricked with him once or twice. I've never had a thing against him. Too bad he got wasted.

Apollo's asking me for something important.

Okay then, bro, sleep your sleep of the dead at my place, in my arms, before the Enforcers of Pain catch up with us.

———

105

The sick man stood up. The weight of Apollo's body had been enveloping—warming at first, but then the pressure had begun to bother his arm muscle. What's more, he remembered that he had not taken his medication. He rolled away from the gently snoring boy and struggled to his feet. A wave of dizziness made him teeter for a moment, but then he regained his balance.

He looked down at the bruised and scratched body of his fugitive. He thought about the improbability of the plan of getting him to detox, making the doses he had bought last through the next couple of days. And at detox they kept you waiting as you went into withdrawal. Because it was a hospital, they wouldn't even let you smoke, so you withdrew from both at the same time. Most junkies gave up before they got seen. Even so, he decided to scoop up the other bags and hide them in the microwave. He'd portion them out to Apollo. If Apollo decided to turn the house upside down, he'd never look there.

In the kitchen he took a capsule of AZT from the cabinet and gulped it down with some water cupped in the palm of his hand. He mulled over the next few days for the boy in the other room. From his brief experience as an AIDS activist, he figured there must have been countless effective detox methods that had been lost in the history of medical bureaucracy, special interests, and morality crusades.

The thought ruffled his consciousness and sent him back to the bedroom. He took a book from the shelf and lay back down next to Apollo's drawn-out sleep. He began reading an essay by René Daumal called "A Fundamental Experiment." It told how Daumal sought an exotic remedy for his cold terrors at the thought of the finality of death. Why not work up a certain familiarity with the Grim Reaper, Daumal had reasoned. Make a brief visit to the other shore.

With the help of a handkerchief doused in carbon tetrachloride, Daumal would sink into unconsciousness, coming close to stopping breathing. Then, as he began to faint and the hand holding the handkerchief dropped away from his nose, he would drift back to life, apathetic to things of this world for days afterward.

A few more moments of reading and he closed the book, gazing at the naked boy next to him again. Despite the needle marks and the liverish pallor, the limbs were still lithe. As he slept, his muscles seemed to draw together like a blunt fist.

What a laughable irony that I'm half-dead, anemic, clinging to life with expensive drugs; but he's lusty and brown, crying out for reduced sensibility, trying to curtail the life process. That fucking junkie has everything to fear from the future. Yet he is not plagued by fear, like I am. It would be perverse to say I envy him . . .

How many times have I watched withdrawal creeping into him like a succubus to take over his body while he's still asleep? A puckering of the skin, as if the hairs were standing on end. An increase in facial twitches—or am I imagining it? Being shut up in this place with him is getting hallucinatory.

He dives into a fetal position to hug the pillow: his nose starts to run, chills roll through him like shudders. Has he forgotten that he shot the last bag yesterday? There ain't no more . . .

Since I'm trapped in time with him, we all know what the perpetually repeated ending will be. He's changed his mind about getting detoxed "right now." We'll go back up there again in a cab. The cold drizzle will be hell on the numbness in my legs and feet. It'll live in my bones, and I won't be able to keep my teeth from chattering . . .

The cab driver's eyeing this scene in the mirror with increasing dread. Should I consider myself lucky? Look at Apollo, taken over by shaking and cramps. I myself have never felt that bad.

Here we are: the magic corner, and new life at the thought of his death drug just moments away. Out of the cab he leaps on two suddenly strong legs, the meter ticking and ticking . . . Don't want to look at the cab driver still tensely surveilling me in the mirror. I'll look at my eyes cold-fish white in the black window.

Just as sand trickles through an hourglass, the drug is creeping into the space where I'm waiting. Apollo's drug is seeping through the cab and the street and even the air. His wanting the drug gives unity to everything and ties it together. It's like a spirit that inhabits a tree or a forest, informing the reality of all of us who take part in it. Me, Apollo, the cab driver, a junkie passing by. This anima in the drug is no different from magic—is actual magic, it occurs to me.

If I'm really to believe certain nineteenth-century writings, there are easy, effective detoxes thrown out because nobody made a penny from them. To read Freud on cocaine or old reports of cures, you'd think that drugs produced totally different phenomena in both body and mind back then. What if I tried a cure on Apollo described by a turn-of-the-century junkie named James S. Lee, who claimed that you can get off opiates by mixing them with cocaine and seesawing the doses of both? According to him, if you shoot a combination of cocaine and an opiate, decreasing the cocaine over time will have the same effect as increasing the opiate. The trick is to stagger both down slowly, decreasing the cocaine a little more whenever the opiate withdrawal rears its ugly head . . .

Apollo just fell onto the floor of the cab with a thud. The convulsions again. The cab driver is flipping out. But this time I think I can handle it better. I think it has something to do with heavy doses first leaving the body—he's not really O.D.ing. See, he's coming out of it already.

But he's extremely cocooned in the high, and I admit it: how I like holding him in my arms to share in his temporary fantasy that there is nothing to fear as we ride through darkness. Stranded on our small, idyllic, diminishing ice floe, the wet streets sliding by, neither of us noticing time melt away . . .

. . . I'm ready for you, Apollo. Fortuitous timing. While you were gaga in front of the TV I paid a visit to a freshly departed friend from my old activist days and scooped up all the drugs from his night table. Then I made a little street purchase. We've got enough

Demerol and enough cocaine to do an old-fashioned cure, if Mr. Lee is right:

"Demerol equaling 150 gr morphine distilled and mixed with 60 minims water; cocaine equaling approx 2 gr mixed with equal amounts (60 minims) water; 4 injections of 9 minims each at 8AM, 2PM, 8PM, and 2AM . . . Watch for symptoms and decrease cocaine proportion accordingly, meanwhile slowly decreasing combined dose of both . . ."

10:00 A.M. next morning: *Can it be? Withdrawal symptoms already abating. He even reports a light euphoria, wants to get some sleep but can't.*

10:00 A.M. second morning: *Finally, he's sleeping like a baby.*

Christ, these events are so intense that though I myself am not high, a delirium has set in. I sink against his sleeping body as though into black water. Again that comforting feeling, of death seeping out all around me.

Instead of just inside.

XI

Yo, CUBBY MAN. CAN I TALK TO YOU?

Baby Pops, I'll talk to my sweet bootie any day.

What you be rappin' to me that way, you know I be through with that shit.

I was just fooling around with you, man. How's the studying going?

I'm gonna go to college. Yo, Cubby, you seen Apollo?

Apollo . . . you mean the one who gots a finger missing?

No. That be Andre. I'm talking 'bout the light-skinned nigga got the fade haircut.

You mean the faggot with the fade always wears the earring?

No, that be Jose. Apollo.

Oh, yeah, I seen him like maybe yesterday or something.

Where you seen him?

Why?

He wasted my father, man. I just come from the hospital.

Oh yeah? We got to snuff the motherfucker, then. Come on, Baby Pop, let's look for him, I'll go with you.

Don't call me that no more.

Okay, okay, Genius. Let's go see if he's in the stalls, man, maybe the *pendejo* be holed up smoking a doobie.

I don't like to go in the stalls no more, Cubby man.

Why?

'Cause they got the Five-O there.

Shit, Genius, what's a matter, you don't know how to play that scene? You got to *time* it. If it's a good cocksucker I can shoot the first load in two minutes flat.

But what let's say if the trick say he ain't through?

What do you think I do, junior?

Bust his head?

You better believe it.

He ain't here, man. Smells rank in here.

Yeah, but check out the other smell. That fucked-up pair of Reeboks poking under the door of the stall got to be that bootie boy from Jersey. And you see what he's doing right here in the Port?

Smell like scotty.

Sure as the fuzz on his little sister's hole it is . . . Get your ass in gear, faggot! Haul out of that stall before I fuck you up! What I tell you 'bout smokin' crack in here. I'm a friend of the director of Port Authority and he asked me to keep this place clean. Now empty that shit in my hand, or I'll turn your ass in. Gimme the stem, too.

Shit, Cubby, what you do that for?

I'm on a mission, man. The punk had a rock.

You should stay away from that stuff.

C'mon, gimme some bootie in that stall and I'll let you have a blast of it.

Get your hand off a my ass, man. I told you before!

Okay, okay. Hey, where you going?

Shit, that Cubby motherfucker ain't worth jack shit to find the ca-brón *hurt my father. I'll go around the corner by Forty-first and see what I can find. Come to think, I ain't checked Tina's. If Apollo the* pendejo's *in there peddling ass, I could jump him if he comes out by hisself on the corner . . .*

Psst, Easy!

Get away from that bar door, Baby Pop.

Don't call me that, Easy.

You know if Tina was to see it she'd nix you from the whole block.

She here yet?

No, man, but she comin' in a few minutes, at midnight. Get lost now.

I don't know what Tina got against me.

She ain't got nothing against you, man. You're fourteen years old!

Yo, ain't nobody gotta know that, poppa.

Get lost now.

Just let me in for a minute. I promise I won't let nobody buy me a drink.

All right, but disappear before Tina comes or I'm out of a job.

This place ain't got nothin' but cafres. *Like the motherfucking doctor. Looks like they got food in the back. Ain't nobody gonna care if I help myself to a little noodles . . . And I'm gonna eat the lettuce, too. It's got plenty of vitamins, and they're good for you.*

Nigga ain't here. Word, that don't be Angelita, is it? She don't look half that bad in this light.

———

Hi, baby.

Hi, Baby Pop.

Don't call me that. Oh, what the fuck, you can call me that. You know that nigga calls himself Apollo?

Unh-uh.

You know what the dude did to my father?

Hold on, baby, I closed the door on that a long time ago. I ain't vicious about your *papi*, Baby Pop, but they all does know how he brought me down.

Tonight you ain't lookin' so down. You lookin' fine.

Think so, Baby Pop?

Yeah.

You're a sweetheart.

Mira, muñequita, you don't know no one name of Apollo?

You mean the one gots the bitch from the projects?

No, no, no! That's Shareem.

Oh.

What you drinking?

Amaretto and milk.

You couldn't put some a it in that empty glass?

Sure.

Thanks. It taste good with these here noodles. So what you been doin' lately?

I won't lie to you. I had my tits redone.

Yeah?

Got me them new water sacks 'stead a the silicone. That shit be dangerous.

You taking care of yourself, girl.

Listen, Baby Pop, don't see me wrong I don't want to hear jack shit 'bout your father. But how I'm seein' it what he did, he strategized to get control a me.

Well, he always be a bootie bandit.

No, I mean control of my mind! Now I'm doin' fine.

You're the finest fineass finance bitch on the block.

I shouldn't boast, but I been pullin' 'em in.

Yeah?

Oh yeah. Come over to my place in Jersey City, it's paradise. I got two CD players, another Oriental carpet, a couple a show dogs . . .

What kind?

Shih Tzu. Listen . . . you know, I loved Casio, but he was dissin' me. He had no respect.

At least he took the whole rap for you when you did the stickup. He could a ratted on you and copped a plea.

They just didn't recognize me, baby. They was looking for a real female.

You always knew how to do your shit.

Yeah, but when they took him in I was in bad shape. I wasn't even doing drag no more. I went to a program where they key-locked you in for all but a hour a day.

That shit is vicious.

But when I come out I says to myself, at least the bra's gonna be clean now, at least the dress's gonna be clean. Now I'm workin' here again. You didn't know that?

Unh-uh.

You got to see my routine. I don't do no tired Iris Chacon no more. It's new-wave stuff.

Word. Listen, Angelita, it's cool chillin' wid you, but I got to find this Apollo nigga. You know, somebody could—

Oh, I can't never play you, Baby Pop. Everybody talking 'bout what happened over at the theater. An undercover was in to shake down Mercedes couple nights ago . . . And you know what? I seen the nigger conversatin' on the street with that one in dirty sneakers over there, right after he was supposed to have perpetrated. The one with the droopy shoulders.

El maricón blanco con la mirada de un loco en los ojos?

Sí, con los tennis sucios.

I don't like the looks a him. He look like a user and got a evil look.

Yeah, well, I seen them on the street together. I remember them sneakers. They got into a cab together.

You sure you talkin' about him?

114

Sure am, baby. Listen, I'm sorry 'bout your pop.

They sayin' maybe he won't walk.

He didn't need that, he already begun to be hurt by the time he ain't got.

Take it light, baby.

Bye, Baby Pop. Gimme a kiss.

Looking fine for a female her age. Maybe I should try for a piece a that someday. But naw. Word. Dirty sneakers is fisheyeing my bi-cho. My pockets almost empty, and she says she seen him with Apollo. Maybe I can kill two birds with one stone.

How you doin'?

Steve.

Ricardo.

Hello, Ricardo.

You from Westchester or someplace?

In point of fact, I live in the city.

Listen, if I be bothering you, you just got to tell me.

Not at all.

So maybe I'm gonna sit down here?

I gather that won't lead to any trouble.

I ain't called Trouble. So what you lookin' at me like that for, huh? Maybe you was looking for some fun.

I was just wondering how old you are.

Twenty—I'll be twenty in a couple weeks. But don't tell nobody, I know you got to be twenty-one . . . What you lookin' at?

You're so well preserved.

What's that mean?

Some people think it's a compliment.

So where you live, *papi*?

Downtown.

That's the Village, ain't it?

If you like.

How much it cost to get down there and back here with a cab?

Why do you ask?

You mean we would have to take the subway down there?

What do you mean "we"?

You know you can't hide it, you know you like me.

It's true I was looking at you.

I know.

So you think I fancy you.

What that mean? Listen, what do you do during the day?

Write. And I'm a researcher.

A what? You got to work early tomorrow? Don't worry, we gonna come quick, I ain't gonna stay all night.

You're not?

Oh no, *papi*, but I ain't gonna rush it. I like to have a good time. You got any movies?

I'm halfway through a tape I was watching.

What's it called?

Salo: 120 Days of Sodom. It's by Pasolini.

I never heard a that one. You mind if I ask you a question?

What?

How old are you?

How old do you think I am?

You look like thirty.

Flatterer.

Listen, *papi*, you into drugs?

No. You?

Oh no, I don't do that shit. I ain't crazy.

Good.

Want to hear something funny? When I first saw you and shit, I was thinking you was a user.

What made you think that?

Something about the eyes.

I'm drug-free now.

Good for you. So listen, you want to go with me? What you like to do?

I like to improvise.

Huh?

You're not going to tell me you're studying guard-dog training, are you?

Say what?

Just joking.

Wait a minute, man, there's some stuff I don't do.

It won't be a problem. To be realistic, though, the problem might be getting out of here with someone who looks, uh, as young as you.

That ain't no problem, 'cause I'm gonna walk out first past Easy at the door and be waiting for you on the corner.

Right.

I hope this one ain't a cafre. What he wanna do, I wonder? I'm saying he be a user, a old crackhead, I ain't never wrong 'bout that shit. Here he come now. He probably 'round forty. Them sneakers be pitiful, man. Hope he got a pair a socks to give me that I can handle. Like should I ask does he know Apollo before or after he come?

The encounter with Apollo, and his upright notion of calling the police, meandered like scum on the man's idea flow. He saw the unclean needle piercing one of the holes on the taut, silky skin, caught a flash of nodding eyelids as smooth and swollen as spoons, remembered his greedy excitement when the half-conscious boy moaned under his mouth.

Feigning coolness, he glanced at the new boy at his side. The little hustler's cocky gestures were like alms tossed to an old beggar. He considered slipping the boy twenty for his trouble and asking him to jump out of the cab; but something pulled him on. Maybe it was pride in thinking that he could interpret the gestures and read the mind. Still, he felt himself becoming ill tempered, slipping into a nasty mood.

The boy was talking about his own problems and about his inflated future plans. His bloated bravado snaked through the man's mind and further inflamed his famished emotions. Empathy for the kid's predicament alternated with feelings of contempt. The kick of the potential danger of being with him came in little bursts. But the high needed perpetual reinforcement. He had somehow to swoon under his mouth and touch.

I won't do nothing freaky. And this john going to be real surprised to find out that I don't touch no drugs. I got to live with 'em every day, and even some of the people that I would say I love don't go an hour without that glass dick in their mouth. Yet a man got to deal with that situation whenever it comes along, and for some reason I was put here among the crackheads and dopeheads to make my way in the world.

Tonight I got to do right what the nigger done to my father. Got to use my brain to play for time. If it's slam-bang-thank-you-man I ain't going to find out a thing about that Apollo. But being that this guy's got some kind a head on his shoulders, he might want to psychologize me as part of his thrill.

You got a million books here.

Feel free to take a look at any one you want.

Maybe you'd be surprised if I told you I knew the word intellectual.

Why would I be?

Say, what's the square root of one hundred eighty-six?

I don't know offhand.

Thirteen point six three eight one. Now you know something you didn't know before.

You are a smart aleck.

My name ain't Alex. I'm Ricardo and just smart. Maybe I'm out here on the street now, but I'm planning to go to college. You probably thinks I got a pea brain like some of the other punks you find at Tina's. But I can see into your mind pretty good.

What do you see, smartass?

Off goes them wasted sneakers. What that those look, I better get ready for a very foul odor. But what's this? I don't smell nothing. Ain't that just like a white guy to be wearing the most disgusting kicks and then got feet that don't smell.

I see you got the bucks to get a new pair of sneakers if you wanted to. But maybe they was your cousin's or something and your cousin died or something—you got an attachment to them.

I just find them comfortable, that's all.

Well, all you got to do is wet 'em and shake 'em in a paper bag with a lot of talc powder. The powder sticks to the kicks and they look good as new.

You know, you seem to do fine without a degree.

Listen, why you keeping all of them books?

What do you mean?

Did you write all of 'em?

Sure, one a day.

Don't make fun a me, *papi*!

Of course I didn't write them all. It takes months to research and write a book—sometimes years.

Then I got a cousin must be a genius.

Why?

How many words on a page?

About two fifty, three fifty.

Well, my cousin she can type fifty words in a minute, which means she can type a page in five, seven minutes.

So?

Which means she could type a whole book in a couple days, and you was telling me it could take you years.

Come on, fella, I said write, not type.

What's the difference? You got an idea in your head. You just type it down.

Tell me something, son, what are you planning to study in college?

Oh, I don't know. I'm gonna be a doctor maybe, or a mathematician or a scientist. You might a noticed when I was giving you square roots out of my head that I'm real good at math. I ain't like the other hustlers.

This conversation is dangerously similar to another one I recently had.

Huh? What's a matter? You don't look so good.

I thought you said you could see into my mind. You tell me. In the meantime, why don't you get comfortable.

You mean take off my clothes that you can start drooling for what you might be getting?

More or less like that.

But first I'm gonna look into your mind a little bit more. You know, some people does say that I'm a mind reader. My great-great-grandmother, she got that talent too.

ESP and all that?

No, it's a real psychology.

Give me an example of your psychological insight.

Well, I can see one thing—you want me to get high.

That sounds more like wishful thinking on your part.

Really? Well, suppose I was to tell you that when I get high I get really into having sex. What would you say then?

I'd say that I might enjoy it if you got into having sex. Is that a really bad thing to say?

You doubting yourself again. Did I read your mind right?

Damn if I wasn't right, 'cause the guy looks pale now. Look how he looks toward his pants pocket, like he going to fish out his wallet, all shaky just like if he about to buy the stuff.

Say if I didn't hit the nail right on the head.

Suppose we said I wouldn't mind finding out about things you like to do.

120

So why don't you lay some cash on me. I know I can find something down the block.

He reaching in his pocket, just like I thought, to get a twenty. I'll buy me a bottle from the nigger on the corner, but then maybe he got a surprise coming.

I'll be back in a few, *papi.*
     You promise?

Hello, *papi.* Like I said, I know my way around the neighborhood.
     What did you get?
     I got me a couple rocks.
     So that's your pleasure.
     I knew you'd like what you saw.
     Aren't you going to light up?
     Well, I'm going to pack the pipe for you, *papi.*
     For me?
     There, that's a nice big rock. Now, you got a lighter?
     Here it is.
     So go ahead.
     I don't smoke.
     Come on, *papi.* You forget who you be talking to. Now you take a blast, and then you can pass it to me.
     I think you're a little confused. I told you, I don't smoke.
     But it ain't no fun doing it alone. Tell you what, you just take one toke, just to keep me company.
     You don't understand. You see, I once did this thing, and now I'm recovered.
     Sure I understand. I understand that just one toke ain't going to change all that.

I knew he was going to take it the minute he let me go out for it. What he don't know is that I won't touch that stuff. I just want to get his mind going so I can pump him about Apollo.

Satisfied, *papi*? You feel good? Just lay back there, now. That's right, you can put your hand on my leg. Don't be shy now. What you jumping up for?

It really hit me.

Stop walking back and forth. You ain't no animal in a cage.

Go ahead and take your drag.

Unh-uh.

What do you mean, no?

I can't do it this minute. I got to get in the mood. Now I'm gonna ask you something.

What's going on here?

You know somebody named of Apollo?

Did he tell you about being here?

Now calm down now, sit down. Don't get paranoid on me. Ain't nobody sent me here but myself. I just want you to tell me something about him.

Give me that pipe.

You just relax now. You better wait 'cause, like you said, you ain't smoked the stuff in a long time.

I'm just going to take one more drag.

All right, but be careful now . . . So where he staying now?

Who?

Apollo.

I don't know any Apollo.

Don't shit me, old man. 'Cause you was seen with him. Wait a minute, if this is some kind of shakedown . . .

Now you know better than that. Relax, here. Go ahead, take another blast. Then we got some talking to do . . . There, sit back down now. Let me rub your back for you . . . Feel good?

I shouldn't have done it, I shouldn't have done it.

Done what, *papi*?

My heart, my heart feels funny.

There ain't not a thing wrong with you.

Listen, I want you to leave here.

I ain't going nowhere till you tell me where I can find the nigger.

My heart's pounding from having smoked this stuff. You fed me the stuff, and now you're asking me strange questions. And you, you haven't had any yourself.

Listen to me, you *cafre*. You been associating with a punk wasted my father!

Your father?

Yeah!

I don't know what you're talking about . . . Apollo put you up to this, didn't he? To get back at me for calling the cops.

You called the cops on Apollo?

And I can do it again.

Ha ha. You ain't calling no cops when you high like this. Now tell me, you called the law on Apollo? I hope you did. That was my father he wasted.

Your father?

Yeah, he wasted him in the theater. But he must a told you about it, which being why you called the law.

No, no, I don't know a thing about it!

Then why'd you call the law on him?

He was giving me trouble some other way. He . . . tried to rob me.

What you touching yourself for?

I can't help it, I get that way when I get high. I have to have sex or I can't stand the anxiety. Listen, take off your pants, will you?

All right, all right, I know what I came for.

Hurry, hurry.

Take a look at this big one. So, you want it or what? First you got to tell me where Apollo is.

I swear to you I don't know. He left before I called the police. I'm afraid I'm going to get convulsions or something. I'm feeling really strange.

You swear on the head of your mother you don't know where he is?

I swear.

Go ahead, *papi*. Careful! You're biting it.

This motherfucker is bugging out. I made me a sex freak even freak-ier. He's beginning to scare me. He gobbling me up like there's no tomorrow. I wanna get out of here.

All right, already, that's enough! Come on, you got to pay me.

Just a few more minutes!

No! Now gimme forty!

What about the rocks you bought?

Here, you can have all the goddam shit.

Okay, okay. Take the money.

I ain't even gonna look for hair gel in the bathroom. Much less ask for a pair of socks. This cafre *likely to lose it altogether and come for me. Look at him twitching on the bed, still playing with his little pootie. I'll lace up my kicks outside!*

As the door clicks shut, he leaps from bed to dresser and spills the white rocks of crack out of their tiny blue bag. The door isn't locked. He lunges for the door and turns the deadbolt and whirls back to the dresser. There really were two more rocks left, weren't there? Everything's going to be okay.

He finds the still-hot stem lying on the bed and tips in one of the rocks, which melts and sticks to the edge. Now it won't matter if his shaking hands accidentally tilt the stem down. The rock still won't fall out. The flame held to the stem is already causing the telltale crackling sound. In a fraction of a second this will be smoke. When the smoke fills the lungs, the surge will come almost instantly. Mean-while you must carefully put the hot stem down. On the dresser. It's burned the edge of a forefinger already but the hell with it.

This surge feels like it is growing out of control. There is no way to deal with this except to keep pacing back and forth and pray for a de-escalation. This pulse will never stop racing. It's taking forever to locate that videotape with images of flesh-colored legs entwined and a mouth full of penis radiating from the tangle . . . The boy called Ricardo's smooth adolescent legs, how stiff his cock felt.

His heart is vaulting gratefully into those images. So close is he to the TV screen that his nose bumps into it. So constantly and automatically does his hand pull at his limp but sensitive penis that it is more like a nervous tic than masturbation. The constant reference to this penis is giving continuity.

But this part of the tape is suddenly no good at all. The scene lost energy, and that room they're in—it's so depressing. Their legs look cold because the color's too grayed. He can't remember the feel of Ricardo's skin or its temperature. Instead he thinks of the boy's father whom he saw hurt. Luckily, the other tape on the shelf is waiting like a lifeboat. Trembling rigidly, he pushes in the new tape and waits for it to rewind to the right part. The floor's caving in and the boy is gone: you're really dying.

This one's better than he'd imagined because he'd never noticed the curve of that guy's hamstrings. Thick sex filling up the room's vacuum and the penis sliding in and out of the ass. Pulling at his own dick, which with the subsiding of crack has begun to stiffen. The guy's upcast, masochistic face and moaning mouth. He really should be fucked harder. Since this has begun to happen he is grateful for it. *Remember Ricardo's thighs splayed and the feel of his balls against my chin?* The sense of completeness is hypnotic. The feeling of climax is building up in his own belly and thighs where before everything was caving in. He's got to lie on the bed and pull his knees to his chest to sustain the flow of energy. But as soon as this is done, he's got to jump to his feet. They've come already, and they're only kissing. *If only some real person would press open lips to mine. I wanted a tender moment with the boy but things had to turn out this way.* He knows the next part of the tape is going to start with a street meeting. Hell will freeze over before they get down to it. Tremblingly he presses Stop/Eject and yanks the tape out.

That other tape has the three-guys part somewhere on it. Exactly where is not certain. *I'll have to fast-forward.* Waiting for this is again a reminder of the vacuum and everything collapsing. Emergency measures to stop this entail a frantic rush to the dresser to tip another rock into the stem, but he had not considered it being the very last rock. There used to be two rocks, but there aren't any more. *Only one. When this one goes into the stem they'll be none left on the dresser.* A giant void swallowing the space of the dresser.

Using a fingernail to split that rock in two is suddenly vaporizing this gruesome inevitability. *Now there'll be two rocks.* But the fragment sticking to his nail mustn't be wasted and must be scraped carefully onto the edge of the stem. He can see the hot stem blister his finger as he does this. Then he puts half the rock in the pipe and positions that whole other half on the dresser. What's left of the rock on the dresser really does have a fullness to it. *Marginally.*

He tries to memorize where that other half is as he swings away from the dresser to light the stem. *There was a bottle of cologne in back of it and a comb at the right.* He's got to make sure that this last rock's not swept to the floor by a clumsy gesture. The smoke from the stem to which the lighter is held is funneling into his lungs more thickly than he'd intended. He feels it fisting through his brain cells to bulge his eyes out of their sockets. *I hope I'll go quick when my heart bursts. I hope so.* But why no chest pain? Maybe it's the anesthetic effect of the drug.

His rush to the bedroom window to open it reveals that it already is. So he yanks it open even farther. The crack smoke's eaten up the air in here and the air outside is too stale. Maybe if he turns up the air conditioner and stands right next to it the blast will coax his skin, his lung sacs, into staying alive and not dying. The cold blast of air on his sweating skin makes him wince.

Maybe in the bathroom, if he splashed some cold water onto the back of his neck. It's impossible to keep from racing down the hallway, but at the same time it seems forever until he's standing at the sink. There, the feeling has de-escalated with the lowering of the temperature. The coolness of evaporating water on his neck. *In the mirror I look like I'll be okay.*

But he certainly deserves a little pleasure now, after the kid trying to intimidate him, half withholding sex. That tape's been running on Fast-Forward. There's a good chance it's run past the right section. When he runs to the bedroom and presses Play it's not at the part he wanted. *It isn't. This part comes* after *the three-guys part.* The tape's been fast-forwarding forever. He presses Rewind, then presses Play. *Now the tape's in the middle of the scene.* He feels superstitious about starting here. It's wasting the buildup, which could also be arousing. Then what will happen when there is nothing left? He forces himself to rewind and counts three seconds. Surely this has to be where to start.

The point at which he pressed Play is infused with perfection: right as they are taking their pants off but not before they've started to suck each other's dicks. *Their dicks in each other's mouths might last for an eternity and be like the taste of the young boy's dick in mine.* Everybody's heart's still beating, and everybody has escaped time. *The slick comfort of those balls in my mouth.* As the orgasm is rippling through him he is beginning to realize that there will be an end to what is happening.

———

Warm come on his knuckles. But all his muscles are relaxed for the moment, and he feels completely normal. *Except for this heart that won't stop racing and this dull pounding in my head.* Lying on the bed might rest his heart but blood rushing to his head feels worse. This come's drying uncomfortably damp and cold on his knuckles. But the porno is still there, pumping and hot. They're on and in each other now. *Too exhausted to stand but maybe if I keep stroking my dick while he plunges his cock into the blond's ass.* But then he pictures the other half of rock.

He'd forgotten about it. He rolls off the bed and fights dizziness to reach the dresser. He knows the rock is on the dresser but he can't locate it. The best system is to lock your eyes to the dresser and scan every inch. *It couldn't take that long. The dresser top's not really that big.*

What he's spotted may be just a tiny piece of plaster fallen from the ceiling. He tastes it and it is, melting like the powdery gypsum it is in his mouth.

But there it is, right next to the comb. *Was the last rock really that small?* He raises it to his face to sniff the faint chemical odor. God, it will never get him up to the same level. The best solution would be to unbend a wire hanger and use it to scrape the sides of the stem to bring the leftover, caked crack to the tip.

But all the hangers in the closet are plastic. Wait a minute, the dry cleaning, still covered with a plastic bag. He rips it from the closet and yanks off the bag, tries to pull out one of the hangers but the shirt's buttoned around it. Shakily, he manages to unfasten the top two buttons. Then by squashing the hanger he can slip it out and the clothing falls to the floor.

He untwists the top of the hanger and uses it to scrape the stem. Pushes the thin fragments, like flakes of soap, to the tip. Pushes the screen toward the other end of the stem. The flakes will fall out unless he keeps the stem tilted upward. He puts in the last rock of crack as well. In order not to tip the stem while lighting it, he has to tilt his head way back and hold the lighter above it. He almost falls over. But once it gets crackling it'll stick to the stem without falling out. He can lower his head and draw a big one.

I misjudged again. The charge of smoke is so thick that he's totally invaded. He lets the hot pipe tumble out of his hand and runs in terror toward the bathroom. They'll be no more reprieves this time. His body, the room, the air are a pumping, escalating column of high. Sweating, sticklike fingers running through his hair in anguish. In the mirror his eyes are polished stones and pinholed pupils. *It could be that the convulsions will start anytime within the next few seconds.* He looks at the high-tech bathroom clock.

He turns on the tap and splashes cold water on his face. His skin jumps out to the feeling, proving that he is still alive. *Real for a second.* Except for that horrible feeling of having all your muscles in a vise while they try to throb uncontrollably.

Pacing in the hallway to avoid behaving spasmodically. If the right amount of seconds pass it will mean that the danger of dying has de-escalated. *Of course there's always some chance of a delayed reaction.* He paces back and forth. Looking for something. Life, or an ending.

At the VCR, another endless time passes before the tape pops out. This other one, which he is already clutching in his hand, is hetero. *A big cock fucking the pussy.* The novelty and anatomical fit will pull him back into the life force. *She's just about to finish sucking him now.* And because she's small, she can leap up onto his cupped hands intended to make a seat and wrap her legs around his thighs while he fucks her standing up.

This was no disappointment because in helping that cock enter her pussy he is filled with enormous vitality and assurance. *Was a dick ever so hard before?* He couldn't fuck that pussy without the buddy dick, so maybe if he licks it as it slides in and out things will keep growing to a climax. In fact this orgasm, though the second in the last few minutes, takes over his whole body and proves the reserve of life that is left in it so he can collapse onto the bed like a winded colt onto grass.

Too bad that the dull pounding in his head, the slicing of breath, sight, dissects the flow of life into uncertain jerkings. *Is this the most horrible feeling in the world?* Because the beats are out of synch, death lies between each one. Like a great weight on his face and chest, and the feeling draining out of his legs. Reaching over the bed, he feels along the carpet for the stem he had dropped. Soon a finger touches the rounded edge of the glass.

He picks it up and looks at it. It's blackened but there are a few opalescent streaks of crack coating it. He sits up and reaches for the lighter, which he'd tossed near the pillow. A small amount of smoke is formed but not enough for a full drag.

His eyes scan the floor. There is just a chance that when Ricardo first loaded the pipe a fragment fell out. *If you look hard, you'll see many tiny whitish chunks on the floor.* Plaster, gravel from outside, a tiny piece of paper tilted into the right light, who knows? On his hands and knees with his eyes a couple of inches from the carpet, he searches the nap, tasting a chunk now and then. Dull, unclean tastes. *That horrible gulf opening.* Is there enough time to jump into his clothes and stuff bills into his pocket?

It was bugged out, thinks Baby Pop. He'd stridden down the stairs of the john's apartment building feeling like he owned the world, exultant about the success of his mission. He had some information worth crowing about to his father. One of the johns had already called the law on Apollo the *cabrón.* He, Ricardo, and only he, was the proud bearer of that exclusive story. Now *that* was taking care of family. And he'd gotten paid, too, because he'd had the smarts to carry out two plans at once using subtle psychology.

But all of a sudden, the feeling changed. It was still too early to go to the hospital, and his spirits wilted. That was what was bugged out—how you could feel up one minute and down the next. He didn't really feature having to find a place to chill out this time of night. It was already 4:30, and in less than an hour it would be light. If he fell out now, he wouldn't get much sleep once it was dawn.

Baby Pop headed aimlessly past the black dealer on the corner, who figured he was back for more rockets, but who quit calling out, "What's a matter, man? You lyin' to me if you say you didn't get off on my stuff," when Baby Pop told him he was just looking for a place to crash out. The guy pointed toward the park, and Baby Pop found a bench partly hidden by the broken bough of a tree. Obviously, whoever had used the bench before him had snapped it on purpose, so it would hang down for shelter and privacy. He squeezed underneath. The leaves felt damp on his skin. He took the forty he had gotten from the john out of his pocket and folded it into a small wad. Then he eased it past his waistband and tucked it under his balls.

He lurches down the stairs, his shirt buttoned wrong, no belt, his sockless feet pounding down the backs of the sneakers he slipped halfway into. The luminous dark blue that hits him as he yanks open the door is like colliding with a flatiron, leveling his hopes. *It'll be day in a minute. Every dealer in the neighborhood will be going home by now.* And the effort of taking a breath says that when he finally collapses onto the sidewalk, his back arching in convulsions, it will happen while the street is still deserted.

There is no other choice, however, but to push forward. Past the closed, grilled shops that reflect his askew image, one panel of the shirt hanging out of his waistband, large droplets of sweat on his balding head.

The black guy on the corner who looks like a dealer,

parka open to reveal a naked chest and new hightops, has just passed something to a waiflike black girl and is heading east at a trot in his oversized jeans. He risks coronary arrest in running after him and by some miracle catches up.

"I'm out," says the dealer. "And you don't look so good. Better go on back, my friend. Might have a heart attack or something at your age."

The judgment thuds against his psyche without stopping the rekindled thirst for crack. He spots a thin figure on the next corner in the dawn light: the black girl he saw copping from the dealer. She doesn't look afraid of his speeded-up footsteps and what must be a wild, fixed look in his eyes.

Her eyes are hard and gleaming, too! Her hand's trembling under the thin sleeve of her blouse. Her face is shockingly refined and emaciated from crack.

"Just looking for a toke," he says breathlessly.

A filigree of electrified hair falls loose as she motions toward a stairwell leading to a cellar.

"Just bought some. I slam-dunked the whole thing into my pipe. You got ten?"

He presses the money into her hand. He sticks as close as possible to her as she moves toward the stairwell. When they're crouched in it, she offers the first blast from a real crack pipe, bowl and all, and holds a lighter to it.

Her long, thin legs crease her calf-length slacks. For the first time he notices the bump in her stomach and realizes that she is pregnant. The smoke is filling his lungs once again and begins shoving up his exhausted system. Midstream she yanks the pipe away from his lips and puts it to her own. She inhales as long as she can with the lighter still held to it. She's on her feet and up the stairs, as if she thinks he'll grab the pipe from her hand. She leaves him sitting on the iron step, the crack pushing and insisting, but his body system failing.

Until he gets up, puts one foot in front of another to reach the top of the stairs . . . takes one heavy, rigid step after another along the street, passing a woman and her two young children. Shunning their curiosity and their dread.

The automaton keeps moving with eyes hard as marbles, his abdomen a cramping vacuum that seems to want to suck his whole soul into it. His apartment building is many more blocks away than he had thought. But the duty to survive pulls him onward—a contract made long ago.

He's a good, grim soldier—*hep two three four*—marching obediently toward the big crack lack.

The closing of Baby Pop's eyes brought the customary pictures. In this fatigued state, eye closing often worked like instant dreaming. What he had thought of with his eyes open as real thoughts or feelings now peeled away like a veil, revealing images that began to dance across the screen of his mind. Sometimes he thought about them merely as entertainment, his own private picture show, but other times they were disturbing demons that would not go away.

This time a memory of a nearly forgotten trick surfaced as if it had a life of its own. The man's kick was bland and weird. He had Baby Pop sit in an armchair and close his eyes. This was scary, because with his eyes closed the guy could try anything. Then he began telling Baby Pop to imagine leading the life he was describing. The life was one like you saw on television. There were brothers and sisters and a mother and father and a small basketball court in the back yard. When he got home from summer camp his loving parents bought him his first car. Then there was this girl he met at college and, according to this man, they were supposed to marry. They moved into a nice house with a garden in the front yard.

When the guy finished the story he told Baby Pop to open his eyes and come and lie down on the bed. Baby Pop wondered what kind of action would come next and got ready to ask for a condom for the sex. But instead the guy pulled him close and held him in his arms. He began to cry and held Baby Pop tighter. His tears got all over Baby Pop's neck. The guy began to stroke his hair. In order to do something to earn the money, Baby Pop comforted him. He patted his back and told him everything would be all right. After a few minutes he said he had to go and the guy got up, dried his eyes, and gave him some money.

Now why was he thinking of that? In answer, he saw an unwanted image of the *cafre* he had had to deal with tonight. Like a tape rewinding, he began to review their encounter backwards. First he remembered the guy's vacuum-cleaner mouth on his dick, then the guy's freaky panic when he finally got him high, and finally the cool conversation before. That cool conversation about books began to make him angry. It suddenly occurred to Baby Pop that the guy thought he was a dork when he asked the questions about writing. This suspicion led to another: the guy was lying. He probably knew exactly where Apollo was.

If that was true, he deserved to die. What had seemed like a coup of genius before was painfully diminished by this suspicion. Anger at the guy boiled up in his mind. If he ever saw him again, he'd kill him.

The murder of the guy became the next feature playing on the underside of the boy's eyelids. He saw himself back in the bedroom holding a hammer to the guy's balding head. Blow after blow reduced the scalp to a bloody pulp. Among the shards of bones lay the blood-spattered books the guy said he had written, which Baby Pop had ripped from their shelves, shredded, and scattered on the floor.

Now that he was being questioned by the police about it, he suddenly became a center of TV attention. This was thrilling, and he decided to take it for everything he could get. He told vivid tales to the police and then to TV about his journey of vengeance, and about a shadow world of drugs, cross-dressing, and sex revolving around certain theaters and bars. He gave a string of aliases as his name, ranging from "Baby Pop" to "Genius," but never his real name, to protect the ancestors of his family. He showed the reporters tattoos in places they were forbidden to photograph and described in graphic detail how and in what situations they were scraped into his young flesh. He said, in fact, anything that could explain the downward spiral that had made him a fourteen-year-old murderer, using his brain power to pull as many corrupters, culprits, and abusers as he could muster into his defense.

Finally, he was brought before the chief prosecutor, and it was his turn to show the world how rotten every single player in it was.

Ricardo Rodriguez, also known as Baby Pop? asked the prosecutor.

I seen you before.

You have?

Yeah, I seen you chilling at Tina's.

I don't think you could have seen me at a transvestite bar, son. But what would you yourself have been doing "chilling" in that vicinity?

Looking for the cabrón *hurt my dad.*

And who do you claim as your father, boy?

They calls him Casio.

And what do they call the cabrón?

Nigger name of Apollo.

What made you think you might find this individual at this transvestite bar?

Because, counselor, he is a prostitute.

And how do you know that to be true?

'Cause I seen the sucker with a man's dick in his mouth.

Where would you have seen such a thing?

Behind the smelly curtain of that theater on the Avenue where he got down on his knees and sucked off a whole roomful of guys without bothering with no condom.

What were you doing in that theater?

My father works there.

Doesn't your father know that that's an adult theater and no place for minors like you?

Ain't him who decides who come in and who don't up there. It's a cold, old Portuguese lady never shows her face, from what I heard tell.

And who told you that?

Everybody does know it.

Why don't you tell me what happened tonight, son. Start from the beginning.

Well, seeing that they got my father in the hospital, Angelo was telling me to go see him.

Who's Angelo?

A crackhead. So's I went to this hospital where was the priest molested me when I was no more than this high.

You're accusing this priest of molesting you, son? That's a serious charge. Do you really want to say that?

Yeah.

What's his name?

Father Kraus.

I'm writing this down, you know.

You want me to write it down for you? You know I can write.

I'm sure you can.

So anyway, there I find my father, who used to always be high all the time when I was a little boy, all fucked up in the hospital bed.

What hospital was this?

Over on Ninth. And he's telling to me that this half-nigger name of Apollo wasted him for no good reason.

And then?

What do you mean, and then? I figured I had to do what any son got to do. Nix his ass.

That's all well and good, son. But the man you killed is not Apollo.

You think I don't know that? That's the problem with you people, thinking that you know everything and that I don't know my ass from my elbow.

Then tell me why you attacked that man, son?

That drug addict was trying for my ass.

Hold on, kid. You're saying the man tried to rape you?

Okay.

What do you mean, okay?

Then okay. That's what I'm saying. This is hard for me to say, counselor. I'm sure you understand.

All right, backtrack a little for me. First of all, where were you living at the time?

I lives in Port Authority.

You mean you sleep there?

I sleep at World Trade Center. But I study at Port Authority.

What do you study?

Math. And I read my Stephen King book, too.

So you're a fan of his? Me too.

Well ain't that something.

Now, this guy you say tried to rape you. Did this man invite you to his apartment?

Yeah.

Well, why did you go?

You see, I was looking for the cabrón *hurt my father. And Angelita says the user in the dirty sneakers was a good place to start.*

Who's Angelita?

She be a queen that got them new water sacs now, used to go with my father. You ain't gonna tell me that you don't know who Angelita is.

———

So Angelita says to me—

Where did you see this Angelita?

In Tina's. You know, where they got the queens hustling for loot and a bunch of hustlers, too, trying to get the loot together for a bottle a scotty or a shot.

So what was Angelita doing in there?

What was she doing in there, counselor? Probably hoping to net one of them rich politicians or businessmen comes in from time to time. You might know their names better than I do.

Oh really, and what gives you that idea?

So Angelita points out this white man and says she saw him with Apollo on the night the shit went down. He was like a what-you-call-it.

A witness?

Yeah, a witness.

Well, what did he tell you about this Apollo?

That he was the one dropped my father and sent him to the hospital.

He told you that?

Yeah!

Now back up again. So Angelita points out this man and claims he was with Apollo on the night of the crime?

That's right.

And then what happened?

I went right up and asked him where was he hiding the criminal.

What did he say?

He pretended like, what was I talking about? But I could see, nervous as he was, that he was hiding something.

Why didn't you call us at 911 if you had information that would help your dad?

'Cause, counselor, about a year ago one of your cars picked me up for loitering and the cop pulled up to a dead-end street and made me do all kinds of shit with him.

Watch it, boy, you don't know what you're playing with.

It don't matter, counselor, I ain't got nothing to lose.

Let's stick to what happened that night. You were saying—

How come you stopped writing, counselor, did your pen run out of ink?

I got things much more dangerous than a pen to work with that you wouldn't want to know about.

I bet I do already.

Let me tell you something. How you talk now is going to gravely influence what happens later. So just keep talking. You get your jollies now, because you're going to have to pay for it later.

I'm only telling the truth, counselor.

You seriously think the world cares about your truths? If they did, you wouldn't have been in this situation in the first place.

Yeah, well I care. I ain't the world. I care about protecting my family even if nobody else do, and that's what got me into this fucking mess.

Ha.

What you laughing at, counselor?

Did you know your mother has been in?

No. Why can't I see her?

Well, she didn't really come looking for you. We found her, family man. You see, she was still using your name to collect a child-support check every month.

———

Now that's family for you, isn't it.

Fuck your mother, counselor.

I'm going to overlook that.

But you dudes been overlooking too much, seems to me. How come you ain't caught the Apollo nigger?

This isn't the case we're concerned with now. Our suspect is you.

I wanna talk to the TV again.

You won't talk to anybody else until you sign this confession.

Pass it here, I'll sign it.

The fantasy of signing the confession reinstated the knightly mission. The sacrifice was big enough to set him glowing again, like he'd felt when he'd left the john's house. Baby Pop sat up, pushed away the bough, and began walking with new energy. What he was capable of had to be shared with his father and with Abuela. It could raise their spirits a lot.

He jumped the train and then walked briskly toward the visitors' entrance of the hospital. In another moment he would find out his father was no longer there. During the reverie on the park bench, while Baby Pop became a notorious, outspoken murderer in the name of father, Casio had been unceremoniously transferred to the infirmary at Riker's Island. Abuela, who'd been camping out in the hospital room, had been sent packing.

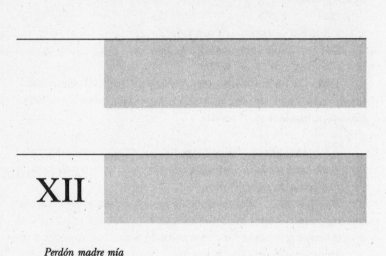

XII

Perdón madre mía

—prison tattoo

Angelita my little angel,

May that this letter I hope finding you in the best of health and spirits. Your Casio be thinking of you even if you think he is a rotten bastard who ruined your whole life and never did you nothing but get you hooked on the needle. But that's in the past, baby, and let's let bygones be bygones. Maybe now when my name come up you don't every time say "I don't want to know about him."

Let me on this occasion now that I be paying once again for any shit I caused you say one thing. Out of all the females that I ever got down with you were the one I did respect. That's why I took the rap for you when we pulled that stickup, Little Angel. If you could find it in your heart to forgive old Casio, maybe that you won't tear this letter up and will listen what I got to say.

It been two months since they shipped me to Riker's. I don't walk so good. I can just hop a few steps on two crutches. Some of the nerves are fucked up in my spine, so they got me in the clinic in protective custody. Most a the other people here got AIDS. I ain't had one visitor save my boy Baby Pop who managed to get out here on the bus a week ago. He told me that Abuela my beautiful little great-grandmother left this world murdered to death by a bum on the sidewalk since she lost her room. That's something I cannot forgive myself, for not being there to take care of granny. When I was around she always had her SRO room.

Angelita Baby I cannot tell you what it's like lying here day after day and watching the AIDS cases die and then to hear news like that about Abuela and I can do nothing about. Making matters worse that they never caught Apollo the *cabrón* did this to me. If it wasn't for him, I would a been out there to help her. I suppose it was stupid the way I came at him fast on the stairway. I'll admit it's caused I never liked niggers. Well one good thing about me is that is changing. Here in jail this time I am getting my education and learning that all us oppressed people got to stick together. Still the lousy jive-ass never had no right coming at me in the theater. So ifs you should see him out there, don't forget what he done to your Casio. And maybe call the Five-O on him? Or better still if you could find a way to get one of our friends to take him down. I'm counting on you, baby.

As for the case who served me right in the hospital, that was none other then Detective Pargera. You know the number. This case must have it in for me lifetime cause according to him he's the one yanked me out that tub in Jersey City so many years ago. That's what he was saying with an evil look in his eyes when he popped me this time. He's a perverted motherfucker who can't leave the queens alone and everybody knows it. What with all the time on my hands,

I lie here all day dreaming about him slipping in the mud someday and getting his badge dirty.

Now I will not hide the fact that Baby Pop had an earful to lay on me about you, *muñequita.* Seem that you got so much going for you now that you don't even have to leave your house to get paid. From what I hear you come a long way from when you was keeping a change of clothes in your bag and working the truck routes in your garters. (Now don't get pissed at me but I knew about that shit all along.) They say you got some big-time sponsors to pay your rent. The line on the street is that you about to go all the way with the surgery cause you got enough loot.

Listen to me, baby. Whatever you want for yourself is what I want, but I always found you fine just the way you are. You always knew how to keep what I shouldn't be seeing out of sight, so why go through all that pain and trouble, justs so you can call yourself a real woman? If you think I'm getting too familiar, just remember all them nights when you felt me inside you. But let's just leave it at whatever you do I'm behind you. (Ha ha.)

I hope you believe me. Cause now I got to ask you one thing and hoping you will find it in your heart not to say no. As you probably know, all they found on me was a couple bags and some works. If it wasn't for my past record and a couple warrants for turnstile jumping they would a dropped the whole thing. So I only got another four to five months here is all. Then I get out.

Problem is, I still don't get around so well. I ain't got much feeling in my legs. If Abuela was alive and still had her room I could chill for a while until physical therapy and shit get me back on my feet. But I already told you what happened to her. All I'm asking of you if you got it in your heart is could I crash with you a couple of months until I get myself together. I'll be getting welfare and so can turn the check over to you.

Baby, if any of the shit that ever went down between us means something to you, I know you won't let me down this one last time. Maybe you could come out here on the bus so that we could at least talk about it? If you did I would never forget your kindness should you be bringing with you a couple packs of Newports or a little money for the commissary?

Don't let me lie by not saying my other reason for asking to see you. Every time I think of that beautiful ass of yours I can't keep from getting hard. Matter of fact, right now it is so stiff and big that I don't know what to do with it. (Believe me, the legs got fucked up but what be hanging between them is still in working order.) Oh baby, I can just feel you taking it all the way down.

It's in my hand now and crying out for you. Hope I can wait to shoot my load until we can be together. It's so hot and stiff that it's a sign you ain't forgot all about the sweet good times. I know you can feel these vibrations and that I'll be creaming in your pretty little ass soon.

Peace,
your lover,
Cas (Theodoro)

Hey, Monica Baby, What's up? Same ole same?

Maybe you wondering to yourself which motherfucker writing to me from jail this time. It's only your old husband, Casio. Yeah, a blast from the past. May that this letter I hope finding you in the best of health.

As for me, things finally turned around this time. Everything's cool! I got no real problems! I'm doing fine! I got my mind together and when I come out I decided to be somebody. Don't get me wrong. I ain't talking that played-out bullshit about having fat cables on your neck and dead presidents* in your pocket, but realistic shit. To study some kind a trade, get it together.

* bills

So how come you ain't been to see me not once, frosty bitch? You really should be ashamed of yourself! You probably find this hard to believe but when a man is in here for a little while and the time don't past you start to thinking bout family. Now I know you must be thinking: it was Casio fucked up the family and my mind when we was doing drugs all the time. Well squash that. You got to take some responsibility.

Oh and woman, I got another bone to pick with you. Baby Pop who was up to visit telling me he ain't seen you since hell freezed over! What kind of shit is that, frosting your own flesh and blood? You his mother, remember?

Oh yeah and listen to me, mamita, I know you must be feeling bad as me about the way that Abuela went out. But we can be glad in our heart she at peace now and together with all the other angels. If you ain't too busy you might want to go over to my aunt's up in the Bronx and see if you could get me a lock a hair they saved from her coffin? I ain't asking you to visit me cause I know now you got your own life and shit. Just to put it in the mail? If you could do me that favor you could tell yourself you done a good deed for somebody. Cause believe it or not, you are the only female that I ever did respect.

Otherwise from that, same ole same ole. Oh yeah, there was one time about six Sundays ago when things was a little cool. My pal Shorty got this fat female comes to see him. She got so much blubber that she could put a pint a Bacardi under one tit and they didn't find nothing in the rolls when they frisked her at security. Then we all sat in the visitors' room with her and him. And she snuck the shit out and poured it under the table in a Coca-Cola can so we could take turns sucking on it. I know that don't much sound like much to you but for us in here it was the MAIN EVENT.

I'm gonna let you go now cause I know you are probably living crazy large with some Herb treating you like a queen. So you can't be wasting time reading letters from old husbands. I'm only asking one more thing, that is could you send me a picture of your legs in them black garters and stockings that I used to like? Or maybe just the titties bare. Don't worry about other cons getting hold of it. I won't let nobody see it, baby. (Promise.) And you ain't gotta show the face in the picture.

Peace and Love,
from,
Your Cas

XIII

APOLLO, NUDE, WAKING UP. THROUGH THE BLINDS
early-autumn sun striates his rising chest and silkscreens his
bare belly. No goose bumps or facial twitches. Just a placid
face. Relaxed muscles.

He rolls onto his stomach and deepens the curve of his
lower back to rear up in a stretch. Dry forehead. No cramping. The heavy-lidded eyes pop open. He swings onto his
side and lets out a healthy yawn.

A touch of ruddiness in the walnut pigment of his skin
has replaced the pallor. Extra weight has added volume to
the calves and thighs to dramatize the taper of his sturdy
legs. This new weight is a thin, soft coating over the old lean
definition. Padding over glass, wrapped in the smooth weave
of skin.

It is shocking how he now looks his age. A teenager

about to enter his twenties. A sheen of black curls that sets off the bloom of skin color. On the otherwise hairless body a faint line of blunt black hairs running from his navel to his thicket of pubic hair. A stiff morning penis half covered by a sheet. Hairless legs. Paler-colored soles of feet, arches high enough to scoop them into shadow.

He's everybody's early morning—that girl's jock boyfriend, that businessman's healthy son, or somebody's hardworking teenage father. Which is to say: unavailable.

Availability went away with the dope he kicked. Now he's turned into somebody staying in a sick friend's apartment. Lying low because the cops are looking for him but feeling healthy. He has to admit he has nothing else to offer the world.

All the colors have appeared in the world and all the shapes are three-dimensional. What to do with all this new stuff? It takes a long time to start having feelings about it. Some of it humbles him by showing him what a fool he was. Parts of it look so awful he can see why he never wanted to see them.

His HIV-positive friend is seated at the nearby desk scribbling in his journal. Just as Apollo's memory cannot recreate the feeling of being high, he can't conceive the memory of having had sex with the man. He feels gratitude for the sad, sweet, sick, human entity. That's all.

It has become obvious to Apollo that he has never had a sex life. He started taking dope too early to fix one onto other people. He still has a sex urge, but for the first time has to admit it has nothing to do with anybody else.

How to explain this rebirth into the ordinary? It's as unmagical as flesh and blood. Life has become a real morning with sunlight that you wake up to. You're supposed to make a comment about how the weather is turning and how fall is coming and then know what you intend to do with the rest of the day. A day without getting high can stretch on endlessly.

Should he turn himself in as soon as possible and try

to make a plea bargain? Should he sign up for a residential drug-treatment program and have them plead his case on the grounds of rehabilitation? Should he say fuck it and get a job and hope they forget about him?

According to his mentor, scribbling away at his desk, these are the tenor of morning decisions that many who are not high often face. But Apollo prefers to spend just a little more time in shadow. A strip of darkness from the blinds is in a perfect position to block the light from his eyes. He shuts them tight and tries to remember . . .

Remember that movie you saw but forgot the ending of? That's what everything that happened before seems like now. There were aimless comings and goings and excuses for not showing up places. You invented things to accomplish on the street. There were power figures like Mrs. Huxton, who held all the good cards in her hand.

Did he ever meet her? All the stories about a rich old lady who owned everything living above the theater. If he ever really did come face-to-face with such a person, it now seems more like a dream.

An old body living in luxury floats above the odors of the theater . . . Then a dream about that fantasy becoming a reason to make up stories . . . a reason to keep taking dope . . . The stories building into a narrative unfolding . . .

You become an actor in it, and your lines flow effortlessly from your mouth. The only unbearable times are when you feel the reason for the story ending. That's called betrayal and is the occasion for more dope. There really was an old lady living up there, wasn't there?

The sick man's fountain pen keeps scribbling. He's trying to deal with the pulsing quandary stretched out behind him in all its luxurious fleshiness on the bed. Now that he's brought Apollo back to life they are "dead on each other"—as the street lingo goes. Meaning there's no sexuality between them. Or, more broadly, no way for them to make use of each other.

What's left has a particularly non-streetish flavor. Milk of human kindness. It's a little hard for this man with just a little life left to admit to himself that he's been making love to dope. It's not easy being Dr. Frankenstein, who succeeded in creating a real entity only to lose control of him. AIDS-sick angst gave birth to a child with perfect limbs and his own will to live. As soon as Apollo became truly desirable, everything about him cut off the flow of desire. But isn't that what friendship is all about?

Dear Dying Diary,

Your pain may live on but mine will be finished by sacrifice. I've got to give though my pen's running dry. It obviously takes sacrifice to convert a zombie into a survivor. But in order to be a saint, there has to be something gravely wrong with you. If I hadn't gotten sick I probably would have spent my entire life crossing the street to avoid people like Apollo.

The ancient rules of the game say I will receive no earthly benefit from this. Apollo is probably so life-oriented now that he would balk at the idea of helping me get something for the final exit. When he was a junkie he would have run out to get a few bags of heroin and let me overdose— if I got to them before he did.

My legacy to the world will be the creation of one more person in favor of self-preservation.

So be it.

Apollo listening. He's tuned the TV to a morning talk show and watches an interviewer ask somebody a question. He notices the movement of the interviewee's eyes and a change in facial musculature that proves the person is listening. He marvels at it. Then he hears the interviewee give an answer based on careful consideration. He marvels again.

His sick friend is speaking now. Apollo can actually hear him. Saying he feels too weak to go out to buy a quart of fresh-squeezed orange juice. Apollo reacts to what's being said. The ebb and flow of Apollo's brain chemicals in reaction to stimuli fill Apollo's buddy with a mournful awe. Feeling Apollo listening is like peering through a microscope and viewing for the first time the cytoplasm of a microorganism flowing. In the wake of this queasy flow are issues from which the two used to be exempt.

What TV program do you want to watch? Is that really the kind of taste you have? Did you really agree with that talk-show host? Do you believe in God? Would you really vote for that president? What did you really think of my unconventional behavior? You mean you never identified with me as an outsider?

The image unattainable—an image of the future—becomes animated. The living boy has stood in reaction to the request for orange juice and is putting on his underwear and pants. Unreal event: Apollo helping out his friend.

At the doorway Apollo hugs his benefactor in brotherly tenderness, pelvis carefully retracted. The man goes back to his journal to jot down a few more lines.

Dear Dead Diary,

Morning brought proof of Apollo's devotion. He went out to get orange juice for me. You, on the other hand, have sapped all the ink out of me you're going to get. One more bloodletting should do it. It's about the irony of the cure I took.

I chased my own sickness like a dog chases its tail and turned the sickness into health to break the circle and die alone . . .

Make something of yourself. After all, you can't be dependent on your sick friend forever.

After getting the orange juice, he changes into clean slacks and turns the ironing of a shirt into a detailed ritual.

Hits the streets and inhales the sensation. It's only mid-morning. *I'm a young, healthy guy looking for work. New kicks, and my feet don't smell. Anything will do for now.* But the future? *Computers, or maybe the nursing profession.*

In the crisp fall sun, people hustle past on their way to appointments. A guy with a briefcase lunges toward a phone booth to make a call. It might all be a cliché, but before it was in shadow. Now the new lighting makes him part of the scene.

Right on cue, the Help Wanted sign appears in the Burger King window. He strides in hyperconscious of the change in atmosphere. His newly sensitive receptors smell work—the oppressive, grease-filled air—and feel squelched immigrants skulking behind the counter and farther back, in the kitchen. He concentrates on certain muscles in his wrist to imagine himself as a hamburger flipper. But the Pakistani manager who hands him the application seems eerily cut off from his potential.

There's always, of course, the garment district. Jaunting by foot to midtown with the fantasy of being an eager young father with mouths to feed waiting at home. In the shadowy depths of stalled trucks he can see the black and Latino faces: some blank with fatigue or boredom, others stilled into clotted rage. They watch him without welcoming eyes as he walks by. He's more competition. Or somebody else you have to worry about trusting. Or another mess with the same depressing life story. He keeps walking west and north.

The old neighborhood makes his heart beat faster. Eighth Avenue, Tina's, the sex theater under bright sunlight. Intuition tells him he was never here—like thumbing through somebody else's photo album. It's not just that the buildings are crumbling in a way he never noticed and that the sidewalk is littered with debris. It's not the stale odor or scaling hands and glazed eyes of the crack ghosts. It's not the half-dressed speed-freak drag queen with smeared mascara and punctured forearms in front of a walkup hotel or the up-all-night junkie dazedly staring at a candy bar in a

151

Korean market. It's the sense of the pettiness of it all. A backwater village. Stupid little bars where no one with any big money comes. Big plans that play over and over like a short tape loop.

Back down toward Port Authority he runs into Cubby, a boosted leather jacket open over his bare chest to show off his tattoo series. Cubby, with his devils and executioner, pirate, Smurf, and crucifixes, who had seemed big and bad and absolutely formidable, now seems small, failing, and poignantly inconsequential.

They still go through the high-five and the bear hug as an eery feeling spreads through Apollo. The guy's tattooed arms are like tentacles with ineffective suckers. Apollo lets them slide off him, but the slime they leave has a catalytic tingle, imparts the hidden urges of the old environment.

Of course Cubby has noticed Apollo's new color, extra weight, and clear eyes and asks a million questions. Apollo is vague, full of shrugs and upturned hands. He plays dumb about knowing that people are looking for him. Where's he been? Chilling out at his mother's to get straight. As a matter of fact he's looking for a job now.

A chance for a hookup sparks Cubby's gray, thwarted-looking eyes. He just happens to know about a job, and maybe Apollo's interested. It seems that Tina's after-hours were nixed by the cops and in retaliation she's opened up a strictly after-hours club way over on Eleventh Avenue, for the wild side of the trade. Cubby's been slapping paint on the walls all morning. It's opening tonight after 4:00 A.M. The cops are paid off; and when it starts to get light you got to get buzzed in, so they need a bouncer.

Apollo's impulses lock like antibodies onto Cubby's offer. This is not the feeling of the Burger King or garment district. *I got a job!* is an immediate, exultant thought. Secret relief at not having to adapt to an alien atmosphere. Cubby agrees to hook him up. All he's got to do is show up around 3:00 A.M. and do Cubby a good one someday in the future.

———

Time—organization—becomes his next hurdle. What to do for the next sixteen hours or so, until work starts? The only answer is to wait it out at McDonald's by slugging back coffee. He doesn't want to discuss this job with his sick friend just yet.

An after-hours job is a good solution for a gig when you're hiding out from the law. It's off the books. They won't bust you unless they decide to bust the whole operation. The atmosphere will be full of all the old posse, but he's planning on handling it drug-free, which he can already see is going to be a bizarre experience.

They slap hands again. Then, in afterthought, Apollo explains that he wants to be known by a new name now. He thinks for a minute, remembers his new sober state, and says: "Perk."

"You mean, like 'Percodan'?" asks Cubby.

"No," says Apollo. "Like 'Perky.' I told you, I'm straight now."

XIV

LOOKIN' LIKE THE NUMBER-ONE GANGSTER HIT PAY dirt!

What's up, Mercedes.

You been locked up, Apollo, ain't you? 'Cause you damn sure been gettin' three squares a day.

I just been lying low for a while.

With some Herb has a full refrigerator, no doubt.

I got a job, Mercedes!

Ain't we gettin' legit. Who you workin' for?

Tina. I'm the bouncer, here.

Here? You still a boofer?*

I ain't with that.

My man been freed! But he come back to hell just to

* addict

154

get a regular paycheck, which is kind a peculiar. 'Bout ten minutes this place gonna be crawling with skin poppers and bazooka suckers.

Well you can't come in, Mercedes. Tina says don't let nobody in high.

Is that so? Ruby Rehab telling me? Lasts times I saw you, you was talking to the subway turnstile.

I don't remember that.

No surprise. You was so zonked you could a made love to the third rail and felt nothing.

I said you can't come in.

You five-dollar trick! I been frontin' for you from get-go! If it wasn' for me that night some snitch likely to call the Man on you! Now I'm stepping into this place, and you gotta deal with it!

Apollo watched her in astonishment. At the door to the bar, she'd showed up weaving in her heels, her platinum wig turned salmon in the streetlight. Her trembling body had made her silver chain-mail dress glitter against her black skin.

When he'd tried to keep her out, rage had contorted her features, like it had when she'd knifed him. Then she'd raised her chain-mail pocketbook and whacked him in the face. With great force she shoved by him.

"Okay, this time only," he called after her. The queen wasn't listening. She'd already trotted into the ladies' room for a blast and would re-emerge even more wound up, more ferocious.

In his unhigh state, he couldn't place the jerky, wiry, belligerent black man in a dress as the syrupy, serpentine queen with whom he used to make love. All he could focus on was the largeness of the fingers sporting clawlike nails and the hard muscle tone.

The impression was drowned out by the great wave of after-hours crowd that began pouring past him. Alert as never before, Apollo cased each and suppressed a sinking feeling. This was not the same crowd that went to Tina's Lounge near Eighth, but a deeper level of exiles. It was full of underage homeboys from New Jersey in oversized clothes and gold chains, petty dealers in nylon parkas and new kicks, and wasted alcoholic johns: trickle-downs from the other bars, now closing, mixed with some of their exhausted staff.

With a new cerebral anxiety that had always been blocked by dope, he was beginning to realize what this job would call for. He'd have to bend or unbend the rules of the game to fit each situation. Anybody had a right to come in high as long as pushiness was balanced against being no real threat. Talks about procedures were so much bullshit. You used them to strike bargains. It was only if Tina came down with a specific sanction that you enforced it to the letter. On the other hand, if he wimped as bouncer in front of comers who thought he held the cards, he'd lose the upper hand pronto.

It dawned on Apollo for the first time—and he couldn't understand why it hadn't before—that he was surrounded by four walls and a ceiling to get high in, after the streets thinned and everywhere else was closed. What might have looked festive to those coming off the all-night streets was denatured in his sober eyes to a moldy bar with a slapped-on coat of paint, some limp paper streamers, and the smell of urinal-deodorizer cake.

With icy wryness he took in the punks with gold teeth and big poorboy caps, looking all mature manhood and lined features, but probably eighteen or under. Skinny bodies made to look big by loose clothing—an old jail trick. Tongue tips that flicked over pursed lips, which he knew was the classic coke tic. One of them, cue in hand, backed away from the pool table into the arms of a sinewy blonde in a pink dress. Look closely: his date was an adolescent drag queen.

In the corner a young mealy-faced gay boy was working

a pickled john who had trouble balancing on the barstool. The boy masturbated him through his leisure pants. He let the guy tongue-kiss him and then asked for a couple of bucks for the "powder room." The guy coughed them up, and the kid disappeared quickly into the head, obviously to buy a beam from a crack pipe. He returned more animated and resumed his job on the old beer-guts.

The images worked on Apollo the way street people work on their marks. They pull you in and grow ugly enough to make you freak a little. Then they try to make you give up everything you have.

A completely pumped Cubby was wedging Apollo against the door frame. His racing pulse vibrated Apollo's breast-bone. The wet heat of his bare skin and his foul odor seeped out of him and began to penetrate Apollo's skin. "I came through for you, Perk," he spit through a crack rictus, "didn't I?" All he wanted was to round out a ten to get high, and he felt Apollo owed him something. "Just six bucks to get me a fried chickens?" he kept whining.

"Away from the fucking door, Cub! You know Tina wants me casing people through the peephole as it gets light!"

Cubby's jaw raised churlishly, and his pinholes glinted menace. He damn well knew that Apollo would already be taking bribes from the few white johns stupid enough to fall for it. He'd be telling them there was a door charge. But Apollo knew how uncool it was to give in to pressure for payoff so early in the game.

The crackhead spun into the street but whirled to face him. "Nigger, I be back in a few, and better you be thinking 'bout me!" He zigzagged east, windmilling threatening arms, past the squadron of homeless camped under the overhang in their cardboard boxes. When he smashed one box with his fist, the woman inside shrieked, "White faggot!" Apollo watched through the peephole of the now-closed door. He saw Cubby taunting the cardboard village, advancing and retreating as the woman flung bottles from her box.

To inaugurate her new club, Miss Tina had decided to make a rare appearance out of female drag. She'd been in the room that held the safe all evening getting her male look together. At the intro to "It's Not Unusual," the crowd was startled into silence as she appeared, her red-lined black opera cape swooping in a great stiff arc behind her, so that homeboys and queens had to lean backward to avoid losing an eyebrow. Under it she wore a loose Tom Jones shirt over bound tits, tuxedo pants, and a cummerbund. She waved a big fake-rhinestone-studded mike in one hand.

The effect was primitive, a great show of dominance, and on either side, Apollo saw drained, drugged faces flinching or straining for her approval: ex-favorites who'd become street people again, essential business associates, drag-queen girlfriends.

He'd seen the fawners hoping to get in Tina's good graces a hundred thousand times before. But what he'd never noticed was Tina's computer-precise assessment of them, glinting sassy acknowledgment at the ones who'd played it fair or the ones who were crucial enough that it didn't matter, sweeping past the others like they were worms.

Worm appeal was the main control factor here. And the wretched often stayed that way to make the powerful all the more so. That the necks of the desperate damned strained like baby birds' was an asset. Usually, they'd made a fatal mistake in the past. They'd broken the rules of this justice system. They'd endangered Tina's business by robbing a paying customer, blabbed secrets, or gotten into an ugly fight.

Hungrily, these scorned beings banned from Tina's other establishment focused their eyes on the spotlight and their second chance. To Apollo, Tina's crucial power was even more obvious in tonight's image as a man—the lined, middle-aged face; thinned businessman's lips; and shrewd, paternal eyes.

No one flinched at the convincingly macho lip-synching of the Tom Jones song. After all, the pope also wore skirts, but did anybody doubt his ability to muster male powers? Then "Woman, Have You Got Cheatin' on Your Mind" came on. Tina lightened up as she parodied its lyrics by scanning the crowd like a schoolteacher looking for pranksters. And a few of the newly redeemed blushed, lowering their eyes in shame.

When the number ended, the mostly coked-up crowd burst into manic applause. At that moment, Apollo noticed the craggy-faced guy near the stage. He looked like a cop, and Apollo's heart skipped a beat. It could have been Pargero, although Apollo couldn't be sure. He'd never caught a glimpse of him when he wasn't high. To the stoned, cops' faces never materialized until the moment of the bust. They were just a fuzzy imago upon which to project your fears and furies. Then, when it was too late, they zoomed in, so that every pore was imprinted on your brain cells. Apollo couldn't be sure if this dream image from his past life was the fey cop or not. Or even if he'd imagined such a creature as one of Mrs. Huxton's fantasy henchmen.

The crisscrossings from bathroom to bar grew to a fever pitch. Gesturing arms flew and tongues wagged at ten times their normal speed. There were outbursts of laughter and then tempers snapped. Rigid-faced users with eyes fixed as coins trembled tensely in corners. Queens on a mission exaggerated their protestations of love or revenge to dealer-boyfriends who held the stuff.

Most disconcerting was the number of outcasts. Some of them hadn't been allowed in any bar in the neighborhood for months. Even Angelo, whose crack career had built him a home in the cardboard village, was there, with his X-cap buddy. But tonight Angelo's bloodshot eyes were bugged out on a crack rush that fixed the X-cap in a deadly stare.

The X-cap raised his arms with the palms upturned as if to shruggingly ask what Angelo wanted of him. Apollo strained his ears toward the danger spot to pick up escalating snatches of gurgled conversation:

"You was wit' him dat night, man . . ."

"What you saying? I was'n even in the vicinity! . . ."

"I'm telling you, man, if I was to find you was the one nixed my cousin . . ."

Suddenly the image blurred, as when two stilled cats with puffed-out fur combine into one snarling ball. The two men hit the floor in a stranglehold.

An erratic wave of action broke throughout the room as some pushed backward and knocked into others, who cursed and got ready to fight. So stoned were they that they had not realized the reason for the sudden movements. The youngest homeboys shoved through the crowd toward the action. They hoped to display their courage by refereeing the altercation. But when they reached it, they hesitated, waiting to see if any weapons would surface from Angelo or the other.

Apollo knew who had to stop the fight, but he too waited for a blade or razor to appear. Then he tightened his buttocks to stiffen his walk and advanced. The X's cap had been pulled off to reveal processed hair standing straight up in stiff sections. One of Angelo's hands was halfway in the mouth of the X-cap, whose jaw he was attempting to dislocate before his fingers were bitten off. Angelo's cheekbone and nose gushed blood as he struggled for his grip.

Apollo froze as Tina appeared in male-to-female transition, wearing her tuxedo pants but with her naked tits unbound. Her Tom Jones ponytail suddenly looked like that of a Connecticut matron, and her irate face was lucent with thick greasepaint. She lunged forward and used the sharp toe of her high heel to kick at the squirming mass until it unlocked. Then she turned toward Apollo and bellowed, "Eighty-six X!"

The X stood up shakily and covered his stiff hair with the cap. Then he swung back toward Angelo and glared. Angelo lunged, but Apollo stepped between them and grabbed the X's arm. Two homeboys restrained Angelo, cooing into his ear like trainers at a boxing match.

"You! Sit down over there!" ordered Tina, pointing to a stool in the back. The two boys led Angelo, whose nose and cheek still gushed blood, to the stool. The X said, "Wasn't me who started it, and I ain't leaving."

But Tina removed one shoe and stood cockeyed on the other. She held it by the tip with the heel pointed toward the X's eye, the finger of her other hand indicating the door.

Stupidly the X lumbered toward her, but Apollo bent and enlaced his waist. He swung him around and propelled him toward the door. The X crashed against it, and the peephole cover dented his forehead. It made a shallow impression that began to dribble blood. As he walked backward in a daze and brought his palm to his head to touch the cut, Apollo swung open the door and shoved him into the street, then slammed the door shut again and quickly bolted it.

Tina bent to put her shoe back on, then stood and folded her arms to cover her naked breasts. She regarded all her gawking customers imperiously and gestured with her chin to Angelo bleeding in the corner. "Clean him up!" she ordered. With a scornful look of nonchalance she marched back into the room with the safe to complete her image transition.

In the toilet, Apollo pressed dampened paper towels to Angelo's bleeding face and breathed the air that was just as thick with crack smoke as he'd imagined. The atmosphere of the toilet was classic after-hours, and it occurred to him that the elation of late-night violence freshly over had often been celebrated with some form of get-high. The tiny, empty blue plastic bags scattered in the urinal, the lighter lying on the floor, and the rolls of toilet paper padlocked on a metal bar against thieves brought everything back. Even the smell of Angelo's blood on wet tan paper towels was an intoxication to which Apollo briefly succumbed.

These images and odors were deeper reminders of the old world than running into any drug buddies could have been. He'd been pressed into some hollow all evening to avoid the seduction of the world he'd been hired to manage. It was as painful as going to a funny movie determined in advance not to laugh or watching a video of a former main squeeze having sex with somebody else.

In such situations everything seemed flat and grotesque at best. Meaninglessness surrounded him, and dying pressed in through the cracks. The feeling had been like walking on a carpet of eyeballs or wall-to-wall corpses. Now this stronger inhalation of death's perfume fired a sudden jolt through him—as when an insect treads upon the sensory hairs of a supposedly inanimate Venus's-flytrap pod. He had to use every cell in his body to stop the hormonal reaction that was about to take place.

Rays of sun crept in around the peephole cover with the smear of congealed blood. A new mood strangled the leftovers in the bar. The butcher paper shutting the window from the outside glowed sallow-brown, like cooked liver. Angelo was dozing in a corner, and the cuts on his face had formed soft globs of scab. Two or three homeboys and a queen were still doing cocaine filibusters—telling jokes or repeating sexual innuendoes. An oily blue haze of cigarette and crack smoke tinged the air above their necks.

Apollo, whom lack of sleep had turned into a robot, lurched around the room, picking up beer bottles, while Tina went through the night's earnings. Cubby had been back and milked a ten-spot out of Apollo. It was almost time to board up the place and go back home with what he had left from tonight's take: twenty-five bucks from Tina, another ten from the white suckers at the door. But first, as instructed, he was to open the door and scope out the block. Tina had indicated that although the Man may have been tolerating the after-hours operation for reasons of his own, he would not appreciate leftovers making morning trouble.

The door swinging open revealed a greasy sidewalk and a grimy street boy, whose razor shoulders poked from a stretched-out red sweatshirt. His oversized jeans were caked with dirt, and his white sneakers discolored by tar.

All that burned in the pinched face were two brown eyes, peeking in passionate rage through the matted curls. They were eyes that seemed to get their energy from some place other than the ravaged-looking body.

"Apollo, *cabrón*," charged the boy.

"My name's Perk," answered Apollo.

"I don't care what you calls yourself now, 'cause it's you wasted my father!"

The boy extracted a large hunting knife from the folds of his pants and stumbled forward. Apollo took one step aside and the hurtling boy fell on his face at the entrance. The knife clattered onto the floor. It struck the leg of a barstool.

Only one thing a man got left is honor. Which is to say, you got to do right by everyone used to cherish you. Honor is what makes the man. Which makes me ask myself how I could ever be giving in to this here Apollo.

And for ten bucks yet. Lasts thing I'm remembering is hitting the doorstep and hoping to myself that the knife's not up under me. And when I come to I thought I was in the interrogation room at the police precinct instead of at Tina's. All I could see was this old Irish face hanging over me asking questions quick. Like what happened to you and why you look so bad and ain't you ate nothing and so forth. It's 'cause I never seen Tina without her makeup and in the light. To me, she was looking like she was Tina's brother if he was a cop.

All right, it ain't no excuse I tell myself! I know. I shouldn't a taken the ten dollars and told Apollo we was square with each other. But nobody understands what's happening to me since I found out I'm HIV-positive. I don't know how it happened and shit. The guy at the hospital where they used to have my father sat me down after I comes to him. I can't keep nothing in my stomach 'cause it leaks out a me. He says, this is something you should a taken care of, but it ain't a death sentence. We got pills, and maybe you'll be taking in food better in no time.

At a moment like this there is no telling what is going to spill out of your mouth. He must a heard a lot of bullshit dealing with people getting the news. But when I says, if I got the AIDS it's that fucking cafre *of a doctor you got working here gave it to me! his mouth really drops open wide.*

I'm gonna put that to rest now. According to this hospital dude, however you got it you would never know 'cause it could a been something happened years back. Well then. It must be that fucking Cubby who was the first and only took my ass. Yet the dude can go on and kill his own self. He is such a crackhead he don't need my help taking him off.

Maybe it's the feeling that no matter what I do to deal I always get smoked from get-go. Inside, my fantasies about my future are stupid large, but out here the leaves are always falling off the trees. The thought was weighing me down when I headed for the after-hours after Cubby tells me they got Apollo working there. Take care of the bastard for me too, he says, before he went to go ho hoppin'. *

When I got to the door I start to feel dizzy and like my stomach was dropping out of its bottom. I'm not the kind of man to let his body get control of him. I'm more like a Ninja master. But I never had this kind of feeling. When I lunges for the nigger with my blade everything turns black. And the next thing I know Tina's asking me them questions.

* robbing prostitutes

What's the only thing I could say to her? Her bouncer is an attempted murderer is what is the plain fucking truth. So she shut the door and comes up close to the table wheres I am lying. She put a hand on my forehead to hush me down.

You know, don't you, that I'm the Queen of the Street, and if a citizen ain't done me no wrong comes to me in trouble, I am always ready to hold out a helping hand. Before you go shootin' your mouth off about my doorman Perk, why you don't tell me why you looking so bad.

I got the AIDS, I told her.

Now nobody must know this, but I think I let go on the waterworks. What am I gonna do? I sobbed. I ain't going to be able to hustle in this condition, 'cause nobody will want me. Tina stepped back from me and I heard her mumble, Stay with me for a while is what you're gonna do. Until you get back on your feet.

I thought I was hallucinatin' when she said that.

Tina's got this big house to herself in Brooklyn. Every hustler on the block is always trying to get a foot in the door. They go in that door as the main man and come back to the block sporting thick gold cables on their neck. They got pockets full of money and drugs and all kinds of new gear.

When they come back out Tina's door for good, like all of 'em do, they are the scum of the earth. They can't get in her lounge no more and sometimes they got wicked habits. That's why it was bugged out Tina deciding to put me through the revolving door looking and feeling like I was. I didn't know if I could a done it.

You got the wrong idea, says she. I said you can stay with me till you get back on your feet. Nobody wants your body chez moi *so squash that idea. It was then I flashed on that maybe I got her wrong all these years. What I thought was evil mean was really just her knowing how things got to stay in proportion. She knows when to be cold and get things done, but also when to be good people.*

So much to say, but that didn't change my mission and how that cabrón *was still standing on two legs out there. Maybe Tina was frontin' for him and thought this was going to get me off his ass. I'm sorry, I says to her, but Apollo, or Perk, or whatever you wants to call him, wasted my father.*

You think I could run this joint without makin' deals with the Man? says she soft. I know all about Apollo being wanted. But I got no reason to drop a dime on him, 'cause I need me a bouncer too careful to be wandering off into street trouble while he's working the door. You see, round about November when elections come along and I already made my bucks, they are then going to shut us down anyways. In the meantime, that nigger out there will stay right where the law want him. When they close this place down, he's going with it. It's all fixed up already. It's a done deal.

That's what Tina is, you see. The word for it is organized. *There be some kind of sweet part to every one of her deals making that it don't matter how bitter they taste on the outside. The only trouble, I knew the nigger would never believe me strolling out there without a word. All that I got left is my honor. I ain't complaining about Tina taking the* cabrón *down for me, but I got to find a way to show him that nobody can mess with Ricardo.*

So I told Tina would she go out there and let him know how she talked me into a settlement? That he got to come in here and satisfy me before I let him off the hook?

So Tina went out to get him, but she closed the door. I could hear the nigger making a fuss with her until my mind began to get floated and my breath short. I took out the asthma inhaler and had a toke. I began to wonder about my stash and whether I should try to pick it up before Tina brought me to her place.

About a month ago I moved into Grand Central, you see. If you go down some stairs and then you go down this hall that looks like it's closed, you come to more stairs. And then you pass through another door and everything's all black, you have to feel your way down some stairs, and you are on old railroad tracks. Then you can go down, and then down agains, and even agains, where it is pitch black, except for a light now and then where they fix the trains. But what it is is a train graveyard. *You can feel your way across miles and miles of them tracks till you come to old silver trains that look like what me and Abuela used to ride to see my father Casio upstate in jail. Sometimes there'll be somebody else living in one of them trains, but sometimes you won't see nothing but a rat or two as you pick your way along.*

And then you come to my place, where I been living since the weather changed. My train that I got hooked up with a radio and even a bed by unscrewing two of the seats and tying them together. I got a quilt and a pillow too. And I got my math book and my bible and my Stephen King book that you can read by the light I grabbed from the electricity of a live rail.

It's so black in there that you ain't got no idea what's happening anywhere else. That air is so black that you could drink it. And when the light's unhooked that black comes pouring back in like syrup. You get the feeling that that train never went nowhere and ain't going nowhere never. It's just stuck in the blackness like a cockroach in Bosco. But it ain't a bad feeling, 'cause all of it belongs to you. There ain't nothing else, just you and all that black night.

It was then, when I be thinking this, the door opens and in walks the nigger Apollo. So I used all my strength to hop up and get ready should he step up to me and act like an asshole. But instead he says to me, I'm awful sorry about what happened with your dad and shit, but the whole thing was an accident. Tina was watching us from behind. And then he holds out ten dollars and says I hope this donation will take care of everything between you and me and fix you up fine.

Apollo was so exhausted that pictures of the night's strenuous conflicts still stagnated on his vision. When he entered the apartment in this condition, he was sorry to find his sick friend awake and white-faced in bed. There was panic in his gaping eyes, as if the ground had been swept from under his feet. His voice sounded strident and fanatic. *Where have you been?* he wanted to know right away. *Working!* Apollo shouted triumphantly. To make his point, he took out the twenty-five bucks and let them rain down on the bed. But the friend swept them to the floor, and before he knew it, they were arguing.

The friend cited all kinds of "recovery" lingo about the

danger of old crowds that Apollo didn't even know he had in his vocabulary. He said he wanted Apollo to work, but not in that environment. He put a bony hand on Apollo's forearm and clutched it like a drowning man. *I'm afraid to lose you,* he kept saying. *I'm afraid you'll get sucked back in.*

Apollo kept pointing at the money and making a big show of it. He portrayed his plans for future independence with the measly sum. He claimed he could now kick in for the rent while he saved to get a place of his own.

But in the glassy gleams coming from his sick friend's troubled, slightly protruding eyes, he could read a jumble of messages. It occurred to him that it might even be his becoming successful, passing beyond the old crowd—and way beyond his friend—that his friend most feared.

Sleep deprivation strangles Apollo's own eyeballs. Now he sees a vision of Baby Pop, outlined against the morning light as he swings open the door. It is lying translucent on his sick friend's drawn face. He hadn't made the connection before. The kid must have AIDS.

He sinks onto the bed and waves his friend away. No matter what he does, ghosts come back to accuse him. With or without dope, he is still a perpetrator. How he wants a shot, a toke, a drink—anything!

Weakened and sullen, the friend gives up and retreats to the other room in shaky silence. On the underside of Apollo's lids ghosts of Tina's first after-hours night continue to snake. Snarls and brittle laughter, smashed bottles, threats, and shameless pleading hammer his ears.

Out of this kaleidoscope a dream begins to form. For the first time since he used to get high, her face reappears. Mrs. Huxton, with a new hairdo, sits a few floors above the squirming mess of Tina's Afterhours, as little interested in the details of what goes on below as someone with a blooming garden thinks about the sex lives of its earthworms.

Leading downward from her is a spiral that ends at the street. Mrs. Huxton picks up the phone and demands Pargero, who's just gotten back from Tina's Afterhours. *He's at the end of the funnel,* she is saying. *Bring a bucket with a lid to pick him up as he pops out.*

But perhaps Pargero is asking for a little more time. Maybe he and his mom will be entertaining tonight.

No, Mom, break out another one. I think that one's just a little too staid . . . Now there's a number for you: the bust's got scarlet tulle with papier-mâché cherries, and the sleeve cuffs are trimmed with sequins. Will it go with her complexion? Well, to be perfectly honest, we're talking about a dark-skinned girl here, sweetheart. Name's Mercedes. But don't get me wrong. She's one of the lookers on Mrs. Huxton's block. Still has plenty of gas left in her. Where'd I meet her? During a routine investigation.

Don't start getting on me about the old days again, Mom. You're better off here in New Jersey, with what's happened to the old stomping grounds. I know you haven't been in the city in years. But you wouldn't recognize the scene anymore. Devil knows why Mrs. Huxton hangs on to that property.

Put that stuff on the chair and give yourself a break, darlin', before the little lady arrives. Whenever I get you pulling out the burlesque stuff, you think you're a young flame again. You know you shouldn't push yourself at your age. You've been cooking all day, and you shouldn't have put yourself to that much trouble.

Where'd I meet this one? I told you, just in the course of some routine work! You know I don't like to talk about the business when I'm off, Mom. No, no, as a matter of fact, this one won't be a murder charge. Assault only. The victim pulled through. Who? Works in the theater right underneath Mrs. Huxton.

No, no, the victim's no lady! That's all I'm telling you about the case, because I don't want to set those wheels spinning.

Yeah, I know where the perpetrator is, and we can thank Tina for that, but now that the victim's pulled through, the case has shifted. I had to put him in the hoosegow. That's all the material for your scrapbook now. Why don't you pull out a pack of cards and we'll play a hand of gin rummy?

All right, well, there was one interesting twist—the perpetra-

tor's got an unusual momma. Interesting in the way that you wouldn't expect, him being a denizen and all. She's white. A religious nut. I guess you'd say she's a hippie.

No, not exactly that kind of hippie. Got some kind of altar in her home for some kind of chanting. And she tried to serve me peppermint tea when I went up there. Course I didn't drink it. What brought a thought like that into your mind?

The father's black. The mom used to be high-class. She's a lawyer's daughter. Says neither she nor her kid have seen his father in years. He's some kind of derelict now, though she says he once had some talent. Her eyes filled up with tears, she didn't want to talk about it.

You got me wrong again, Mom! I'm not trying to put down her mixed marriage. You're always confusing these cases with your own regrets. If you think I'm ashamed of Dad, then you're getting batty in your old age. I know your mother was against it. Don't tell me again how hard he tried to do right by us. But this mother and her marriage . . . If you'd read the letter she wrote to the Board of Corrections like I did, I bet your hair would stand on end.

I was so moved I went up to Mrs. Huxton's to thrash out this one. Better believe she asked about you. She's mummy-ancient, but that mind is still sharp as a tack. Remembers you and how you used to pull 'em in with the feather dance. Misses the old days, too.

What's she still doing there? That's one of the seven mysteries. She's the holdout on that block that's put the whole city to shame. That must give her some sense of pride in her sunset years. Keeps the scene going as if by magic, the way it's thinned out by drugs and disease.

I know she's got a feel for the working kids, Mom, same as always, but that don't explain it. If you saw 'em now it would knock your garters off. Like I said, it isn't what it used to be when you were dancing and Mr. Huxton was alive.

Well, your guess is as good as mine. Does it 'cause she has to, if you ask me. What I'm saying is that she needs them as much as they need her. That's the best-kept secret in history. They go in and out of her clutches, and to them she seems fair and square.

Oh, I don't know, Mom. Start dealing those cards and get

your mind off the past. Of course I know where you came from when she took you in. Of course I know the old man left us without a penny. I'm not trying to dish the lady.

Now cut the tears, beauty. You can't change what's already past. Huxton is doing fine. She'll probably outlive the both of us. What amazes me is the sense of timing the old broad's got. She's got a feel for the exact moment a prospect will turn bad, and bingo! They're out on the street. A boot from her is a sentence to Bumsville, but the minute they get themselves together they're suddenly in her good graces again.

Okay. But family is definitely not the word for it! Don't you think you see the old lady through rose-colored glasses? All the kids know she might need to throw them away in a minute—they just can't blame her for it. It's never supposed to be her fault; it's theirs.

Of course I know that she's got to make a living. That's what holds her and the kids together. She's successful at what they wish they could do. Call it shark love.

I'll prove to you how slippery the old girl can be. The reason I went to see her was to know should I try to work a drop-charges on the victim. He was caught with some drugs when they took him in to the docs. Now he's crippled. He's been her bouncer for years, but since she's thinking of moving anyway she brushed the whole thing off. The guy is in jail now 'cause Huxton wouldn't stick her neck out for him. But as far as she's concerned, he's gone with the wind.

Yeah, she wants to move. Can you believe it? She's got gentrification plans, too. Wants to spruce up the business and upscale the clientele, so she's planning on remodeling the place that used to belong to O'Hara.

What do you mean, you worry about the future, Ma? Nobody can bring the good old days back, but the old girl's sitting on a billion! You mean you worry about the kids, once Mrs. Huxton's gone? Well, you got a point there. But you're doing your best to pitch in.

And just between you and me, neither Huxton nor Tina will come out of this mess without their millions. Why, at this very moment Tina's raking it in at a new after-hours place. That's all you're going to hear. Deal those cards now. But first lay out the dress all pretty on that chair. The little lady should be here at any moment.

Apollo twisted onto his stomach and pressed the pillow to his face. He needed to get a handle on things. Night would turn into day and day into vice versa just as it had in the old times. The realization felt comforting as he drifted awake and then back into sleep.

It's Allhallows eve, but the after-hours has been ruined by a nearly freezing rain. Outside in the big drops, the laws of night cling to the street, indivisible as mud. They chill the bones of the exiled and cut through their highs. At Tina's After the crowd has stabilized. The stabbings have happened, and the eighty-sixes are written in stone. Wearing an orange hat with a jack-'o-lantern face, sullen Perk sits crouched at the door, holding a witch's broom instead of his blackjack. The coffee spiking through him has peaked his eyebrows and compressed his lips. The scars of old tracks on his bulging arms complement the scowling expression for full ghoul effect. Catching his own reflection in the bar mirror doesn't help his mood. He can't believe the hunched and edgy, scowling image he sees. It reminds him of another bouncer with dark-circled eyes, whom he once wasted, in a theater a few months ago.

And like that former bouncer, he's become none too popular. His eighty-sixes have racked up scores on the street. He's got a list of enemies two miles long and has to take special routes to and from the bar.

It's an after-hours evening in which only the desperate will surface in wilted costumes on bad drugs. Even Tina's thrown in the towel and left him manning the post. Tracing circles around him is someone whom he knows considers himself to be his mortal enemy. It's the boy Baby Pop. Tina's overdecorated house in Brooklyn, three squares, and proper medication have put some meat back on the boy's bones. The adolescent face has filled out again, and the clothes are clean and new. Not one to waste resources, Tina has given him some light busing duties a few nights a week. And each night he works he does a bitter toreador dance around Perk perched in his chair. Whenever Perk looks up he finds the boy glowering at him, the eyes miming *cabrón, cabrón.* Which is something he doesn't need.

Nor does he need this feeling that he's in the charnel house again. It was one thing to be part of the zombies on the block trying to hustle a shot. It is another to lurch among the corpses completely straight, like an Igor among snatched bodies. But worst of all is tonight's stranded feeling. Halloween in the rain. At the place nobody wants to be. One thing Apollo never did was hang around a place where there was no action.

Perk the ghoulish bouncer stalks the interior of the bar with a furrowed brow and a snarl on his lips. Among the stoned, he's like a man who's lost his appetite for sweets and fallen into a vat of taffy. From time to time the thought occurs that the best thing to do would be to open his mouth and suck.

As a matter of fact, business has fallen way off. From time to time, the cops come around and make like they're hassling Tina. She cites this as reason to be more stringent about whom they let in. Little by little, she's whittled away at the available population.

Change is in the air, but Apollo can't figure it. He shuts off. He picks up a bottle or two missed by Baby Pop. At least it's something to do. He frowns at the lowest of the low creeping in for shelter. Angelo with a broken arm, his wet cast dissolving. The woman who lives in the cardboard box making an attempt to enter and Apollo leaping into action to stop her at the door. Real heroics. He watches her tramp back to the wet cardboard. There's too much wind tonight

173

for any protection from the overhang. The cardboard shreds as she pulls it around her.

Later a bewildered German tourist steps in to dry off. The only other client, a hook-nosed drag queen, puts herself in his startled face.

By 8:00 A.M. Apollo decides to shut up shop. Not one tip or bribe to supplement Tina's twenty-five bucks waiting with the bartender in a white envelope. Tomorrow is his day off. He puts the five in his pocket for coffee and an egg sandwich and the twenty in his shoe. Better safe than sorry. Out there are all the people stuck in the rain whom he eighty-sixed at one time or another. He begins sloshing east through the rain toward the subway.

Under the pelting rain he considers strategy. This is the third week of work and his friend is still throwing shit fits. He's waiting for Apollo to slip back into the old ways. The rent is due tomorrow, but Apollo hasn't been able to put away any money. He's still a freeloader. What will he do when Daddy gets sicker or dies?

His sneakers inhale the freezing water like a sponge. He can feel the cold, slick twenty-dollar bill caressing his heel like an aged trick's clammy hand.

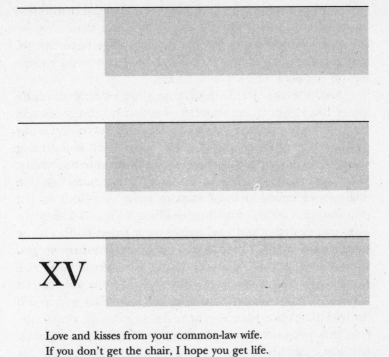

XV

Love and kisses from your common-law wife.
If you don't get the chair, I hope you get life.

—prison toast

LOOK WHO COME OUT OF THE WOODWORK. MY ONE
and only, my first true love, my Casio. Yeah, baby, it's me,
Monica, writing back like you hoped. You'll excuse me, *pap-ito*, for not writing sooner. It's just that I'm not about writing
to cons up river anymore. Surprised, *chulito*? Being that you
always thought I was trash and never would make nothing
of myself anyways.

Well I got news for you, Big Man, I'm moving to Fort
Lauderdale! I got me my beautician's license and a cousin
of Pablo's is opening up a salon. I ain't with the jailbird shit
no more. I decided to keep away from anybody tries to pull
me down.

You know I got two kids from Pablo after you moved

out and I got rid of Cubby and his crew. I'm going to make damn sure that their life is going to be better than mine by the way. Down there in Florida they got cheap apartments and good weather. I don't know nobody come along knocking on my door which is fine by me.

Listen to me, Mr. Jailbird. Don't run off at the mouth about Baby Pop to me. Didn't I give that boy every chance I could? Well a couple months ago me and Pablo find a big garbage bag of clothes against the door. I put it out back with the trash and went to bed. About three in the morning somebody starts banging on the door. It was Baby Pop out of nowhere saying he come back to move in!

Fine and good, I told him, but I got a life too. I'm living with my husband and two babies and I don't think they would want you here. Well you know what? When we got up the next morning there he was in the hallway on top of his garbage bag. Pablo come out and told him you got to leave and Baby started mouthing off bad. He's a chip off the old block and don't want to know nothing about the laws that get normal people through the day. Living with you was sticky black and finally a ray of light is creeping in. Don't take it personal, but you shouldn't be writing to me no more.

Take it light, my Big Bad Homeboy,

EX-wife Monica

P.S. I called up your aunt and said send you the hair. And as for the legs and tits pictures, sorry but my shit ain't available. I put something in with this letter that I know is more your style. I hear she be doing so well that she moved to California.

The sound of lockup in the unit was a pulverizing echo inside Casio's ears. The noise went through him and threatened to grind up his bones. He grasped the corner of the picture that had come with the letter in a shaking hand.

Obviously, it had been ripped out of a porno magazine.

And to get it through prison censors, Monica had felt-tipped out certain body parts.

Angelita looked plump and sensuous in some "Dynasty"-style bedroom, her black hair moussed into a stiff mane. Her naked tits were stretched firm and luscious over their new water sacs. At the edge of one of the felt-tip marks he could make out the tip of her hard erection. It looked about to enter the asshole of the spread-eagled blond man lying half on the satin quilt and half on the broadloom rug. He'd stretched his beefy arms back so that his tanned fingers could spread apart his ass cheeks.

Within his world of the perennial tuning fork, the incarcerated let the picture fall from his white-knuckled fingers. Rather than smash them against the cell wall, he groped as if for a charm under his mattress to find and clasp the lock of wavy hair.

His attacker got home soaked to the bone and gulped the coffee and egg sandwich, then yanked off the drowned kicks to take out the twenty-dollar bill. Half of its printing had been erased by the combination of water, shoe dye, and heel friction. He could barely make out President Jackson's face or the number *20* in two of the corners. The other side of the bill was a web of small paper cracks. Disgustedly, he went to put the bill on the bedroom table, where he found a note. It was scrawled in the margin of half a page hastily ripped from a pad.

Fever 106. At emergency room on 12th and 7th.

Without knowing why, Apollo began to panic. Cursing under his breath, he threw his wet kicks back on and smoothed out the bill. He stuck it into his shirt pocket under his parka.

The rain was even thicker now, as he trudged back to the Korean market where he'd bought breakfast. He picked out a box of chocolate donuts and carried them to the counter. But when he held out the bill, the guy pulled a blank face and shook his head. Apollo surmised it was the hostile expression stamped onto his own face that inspired the refusal, yet he could not unlock his muscles. When the pretty blond girl in back of him placed her two carrots on the scale and held out a twenty-dollar bill that was far from crisp, the clerk's face abruptly changed into an indulgent smile.

He tossed the donuts onto the counter and dove back into the rain. The ailing bill had stood no chance because it was part of the short circuit that made up his world. The cash register at Tina's Afterhours was full of similar currency that was worn, cellophane-taped, or velvety with grime. The same bills passed from johns to hustlers to dealers to bartenders and back to johns over and over. That was how hermetic his world of users was.

It wasn't the fear of facing two whole days with the two dollars he had left or even the inconvenience of trying to change that twenty that got under Apollo's skin. It was the fact that although dead President Jackson's face worked for everybody else, Apollo was obviously not considered a citizen of the realm. Dead or dying people were all that were available to him, and they were coming through less and less often.

Thoughts of this nature shot a rage through him as needlelike as the rain under which he hunched as he headed for the bank up the block. Though he had never had an account, the bank had not escaped his notice whenever he passed that corner. Inside it were people who had always elicited the same dumb contempt in him as he did in them. At certain predictable hours, he could see them crunched into a sullen line at the cash machine in their strangely drab outfits, dangling briefcases or pull-out car radios, making money appear from the machines. Or else they were squirreling it away in some system Apollo had never understood. Yet their different sense of time and its rewards was almost palpable to him, who no longer had any pleasures since he had quit dope. He was convinced these camouflaged clones had some long-term way of enjoying themselves that they were hiding from him, who was still trapped in his world of quick tricks and shoddy results.

There was, he knew, a necessary protocol for banks. Those times he'd gone to the bank with his sick friend or skulked near a teller's line while a john withdrew money to pay him had alerted him to the things that caused suspicion. So he rehearsed his plan carefully. It was to wait in line until a number flashed and stroll casually to that number, acting like he knew what he was doing.

Apollo wasn't sure he had chosen the right line, behind two black girls who were sulkily dissing somebody named Tahara who had cheated on her time sheet. But when an officious-looking woman wearing a tweedy skirt yelled out "payroll," his hair stood on end. The woman had bellowed the word just the way commands were barked out in jail. His eyes narrowed in rebellion and his muscles stiffened as he shifted to another line.

So close to his eyes that he could see the pores on it was the freshly barbered neck of the white man in front of him. The short-cropped hair gleaming with gel, over shoulders enlarged by calculated exercise in a gym, held a disquieting fascination. He couldn't pull his eyes away from that neck, its white shirt collar and suit. It was as if it held some power to sentence him to slow destruction. He'd never been so close to the feeling. It kept tensing the muscles in his mouth and chin into a grimace, against which he kept fighting. It was also what tuned him in to the man's conversation in a spooky experience of eavesdropping.

He was talking to a similarly suited partner about girls at the office. One of the men had lost a "bundle" taking a girl out to dinner who'd never "given her pussy up." The other ribbed him about "not keeping your cards close to your chest."

Apollo had no control over the astonished feeling the conversation caused. The portrayal of a white office female as "pussy" and the use of the word "bundle"—which in his world meant ten bags of dope—seemed borrowed and false. So this was how they talked—by stealing phrases, expressions, and sensations from his world to portray their own boring lives! What a laugh that they needed to talk like him to talk about pussy! They should know that he hadn't even jerked off or thought once about wanting sex since he stopped getting high. And what was he getting out of their rip-offs? He made up his mind that this time the tables would be turned.

The continuation of their conversation added perplexity as well as a sense of inferiority to his strategy. As if there were some connection between lack of pussy and making a living, the two were suddenly talking about the economy. Something about the middle class having to pay an unfair share of taxes. The hard, flexed tone of their righteous indignation sent Apollo into manic laughter. But when they glanced behind them, he shut up fast. What were taxes, exactly, and how did they affect anybody's life? Did what they were talking about have some bearing on his fate that he was too stupid to understand? No wonder he was stuck where he was if his future had been consigned to their manicured hands.

Suddenly they left the line and shifted into a now-empty line marked "Privileged." Apollo intuitively sensed he was to remain where he was. Finally a number flashed, and he followed a blinking arrow to a teller. But he was unable to escape from the irrational feeling that every eye in the place was on him.

In his world, at times like this, you stiffened your pelvis and strutted, careful to let your arms hang low to swing in an apelike way and brush against your crotch. Automatically he felt himself shifting into his dominant display mode. But the sudden realization that the two men near him wouldn't be caught dead walking that way curtailed it, and he bounced awkwardly to the teller window.

The pale blond man with a crisp collar and stiffened

hair seemed obviously gay. One or two types like this wandered into Tina's from time to time. A half-flirtatious, half-intimidating scenario flashed immediately into Apollo's mind. The fag, he felt, wouldn't be able to resist his body if only he could see it without the clothes. He wanted to inform him of this, since it wouldn't be obvious under his shapeless parka. Through the Plexiglas window he wanted to communicate some of the ingrained machismo he was sure the guy wished he himself had. Flex a little even, then ask him to change the ugly twenty.

But the absurdity of this approach in a bank curtailed that thought as well. Without warning he was forced into the unexpected strategy of trying to act polite and unobtrusive. Why hadn't he thought of such an obvious thing before?

Apollo's thoughts went frantically through his meager mental file of polite public behavior. Hotly he realized that it was something that was part acting like a pussy and part speaking like you were entitled to what you wanted. But the two opposing strains twisted into a nervous jumble of intentions. The street was not a place where humility and pushiness combined in that way. He found himself fumbling in his breast pocket for the twenty and holding it up by thumb and forefinger in front of the glass.

"Listen, lemme change this?" he heard himself blurt out. "I put it in my shoe and the face of the president got washed some away."

The teller was unimpressed—in fact, he was embarrassed. If any male animal power was apparent in Apollo at that moment, he did not appear to notice. "Do you have an account here?" he asked with eyebrows arched in doubt and strained patience.

Apollo knew what an account was but not whether he should lie about having one. So he said, "Kind of." And through the corner of one eye he thought he caught the businessmen at the Privileged window eyeing him with amusement.

"Account number?" sighed the teller.

"Listen. My heel rubbed it is all. Gimme another one, would you." Aggressively, he shoved the worn bill through the slot.

The teller withdrew from it as if it stank. Gingerly he pushed it back toward Apollo with the end of a ballpoint. "Go speak to an officer."

The word "officer" was panic through Apollo's stomach, so he fell back into street pride and took the bill from the slot with angry contempt. He hunched up his shoulders and shoved the bill back in his pocket. His eyes spit flames. "You think I need this fucking business? I don't need your fucking bank!" he said, and now everybody really was staring. Fixing his best glare on his face, he stomped toward the door.

He didn't want to go home to find out if his friend was back or if he'd lost him to the hospital. And now he noticed the bum lying in the corner of the lobby where the cash machines were. Perhaps he hadn't been there when Apollo had entered. But now that they were the only two in this space, the image of the ill man could not be avoided. He smelled the acrid odor of urine coming from the man's clothes and noticed the dirt-caked ankles above the sockless shoes.

It wasn't until Apollo had charged halfway up the block with a destination for the twenty-dollar bill that he realized of whom he was thinking. Through grime and puffiness, the black and stubbled face delivered its overwhelming memory of a father he had not seen for years.

Back in the cell after the methadone that I got this vision. It was a methadone dream, 'cause though they be lowering my dose, a few minutes after gulping the stuff you get a little bit fucked up. I'm lying in the cell with heat boiling in my armpit about to make me going to come. There's a cat lying in my armpit having her kittens.

I got to lie so still, 'cause the babies coming out of that pussy one after the other make a nest of my armpit that they mix up with her belly. Then out come the afterbirth and the cat gulps it down. Abuela walks into the cell and says, You are the father. All of a sudden one of them cats turns into a tiny Baby Pop saying his mother's no good so he wanting for me to come out of the cell.

That dream is a sign that I got to start planning my release. To save money they been hurrying up my detox schedule—fourteen days instead of twenty-one, the bastards. I'd like to tell 'em I shit on the cunt of their mothers. They fill me up with such hate that most of the time I'm thinking about the dope waiting for me soon's I get out. I ain't gonna become a junkie again, but now and then on the weekends I'm gonna find the Big Man and get me some of that brand called D.O.A. Dead on Arrival. I'm gonna do it up but I ain't gonna go overboard this time, being that I got my boy Baby Pop waiting for me and I don't want to look too bad. Fuck Monica and Angelita and all them other lying pussies, they ain't gonna hear from me till hell freezes over.

Now let's see here, what that I got to figure how I'm gonna get through the urine checks which the Parole talking. Oh shit, don't you remember what Sugar Bear did and it worked fine every time? You get yourself an empty nose spray bottle and you go to the subway station to start looking over the people that be waiting for the train. You find somebody you know he needs money but you know he ain't into dope or no drugs. You got to look him over good. Check out the eyes, the arms for marks, the color he got in his skin. The hands. The nails got to be clean.

Excuse me, you says, but you want to make ten bucks by urinating for me in this little bottle here?

Then you got to take the bottle and tie it to your fly with a piece of thread. Wrap the thread right around the neck of the bottle. You put the bottle into your underwears right up under your dick. Now when you fill the cup for the urine test, you take out the bottle under your dick and squeeze that instead. Somebody want to watch you, you say, what's a matter, you gay or something?

I keep thinking about that cat eating up all the afterbirth. You are the father, she kept saying to me.

XVI

THE GUY LOOKED FAMILIAR, LIKE THE GHOST OF somebody. Whoever it was, he had lost weight and aged. He stood out against the night like a white burn on a negative, but he flickered, as if you could put your hand through him. An old candle in a tired night.

He was part of the landscape ruled by the Big Man, whom Apollo knew would not turn down his fucked-up twenty-dollar bill. The Big Man turned down no one. You didn't have to have a barbered neck and a suit, talk pussy, or wait in the Privileged line to get his attention.

Apollo vacantly wondered whether the dope the Big Man had would be as good as it had been the last time. Though he had been unable to remember what it felt like to be high before, now that he had made the decision to buy a bag, he suddenly remembered the feeling of that last shot bought on 112th Street. The Big Man would charge ten for a bag and works and give a good ten-dollar bill as change. Apollo would do it only this once and be fixed up until he went to work the day after tomorrow.

If everything was figured out, then why was this half-memory flickering on the Big Man's space? Not that Apollo was complaining. The sight of this ghost from some past was an improvement over the disjointed fragments of memory about his father and mother that had been torturing him as he walked up here earlier this afternoon from the bank. But he wondered how he knew this white guy in battered sneakers and too-large jeans who kept haunting the two-block rectangle of Ninth Avenue from one corner to the next and back.

Thinking about who the guy could be lured Apollo into a tunnel that traveled through the thick tar of a night. The night seeped into his nostrils, ears, and eyes, and slowed his bloodstream. Deep within this sluggish blackness he remembered who the person was. It was the crazy trick who had wanted to do dog training. The one who'd watched him shoot up and then gobbled his toes like a dog. *Remember?* Apollo saw the memory from the depths of the tar. *And now look at him.* He'd been swallowed up by the night as well.

The guy flickered on the blackness of Ninth Avenue among the other users like a moth caught in tar. His bones showed through his clarified face, and his expression seemed to eat itself. Apollo wondered what he had done to end up here. The question was answered almost immediately, as Big Man's black limousine pulled to the curb. The ghost of the foot gobbler got first in line. Big Man was wearing an enormous tent of pleated black silk as a shirt and numerous bracelets and rings adorning each hand. In one of his arms he clutched his red-haired Pekingese, who burrowed into the flab of his chest as if it were too sensitive to face the users on this black nocturnal block.

The Big Man sang out his hellos almost jovially as the throng of hungry users encircled him. The moth from the past was first, flickering in and out next to the Big Man's big face and swollen, overfed cheeks. "You got rockets?" he asked anxiously.

So that was it: the researcher/dog or whatever the hell he claimed to be was now just a white crackhead. This was proof that even white guys with dirty sneakers and cash-machine cards could end up stuck in the night, if their timing and patience went all haywire. Apollo imagined the two shaved-neck businessmen at the bank stumbling into the tar. They kicked and flailed in it for a few moments with their attaché cases, complaining shrilly about big taxes or how much gym membership had gone up. Then they too were still, like flies caught in new amber. They were getting all the pussy they could want now, stuck in the big gooey night. *I'm gonna tax you*, Apollo sang grinningly to himself. *Now* I'm *gonna tax* you.

The Big Man gave him dope and works, and even a little bottle of water, for the ten. But the feel of the glassine bag in his hand had nothing of the magic he'd imagined when he'd finally given in to the urge earlier that afternoon. Maybe because now he'd been awake for almost twenty-four hours and was too exhausted to get excited. The bag felt so concrete and unevocative that he began to doubt that a small, plastic-covered lump could have any power at all. It was like a charm you bought at some magic place or sacred shrine. At some point later in the trip you unclasped your hand and found a piece of stone or a cheap little bell. But maybe if you continued to hold it, it could transform itself.

He told himself this as he passed the entrance to the tunnel, where Mercedes and six other transvestites frantically hooked in garters, stockings, and heels. Stalking in some stylized dance punctuated by yelps and hisses, they flashed jackets open to bare tits in the crisp post-Halloween air. Cars perked along like a ghoul's parade, spitting catcalls or insults on cue from their windows before disappearing into the tunnel.

Apollo imagined the tunnel as a passage into blackness

where a vehicle got stuck and congealed in something it would never get out of. Then the queens would fart into the mouth of the tunnel, and cackles would pass from their big, lipsticked mouths. Suddenly he didn't want to do up the bag. A science-fiction hole in his skin might yawn open and swallow needle and all. It might even chew his hand up to his wrist just because he wanted to do dope this one time.

He was passing a peep show he remembered, which had once let him bring in tricks. He could see Angelo in slurred argument with the Indian manager, who kept waving him out the door. Angelo was stoned enough to see perfect logic to his own point of view, and speeded words spilled from his partly toothless mouth. He boldly insisted on his right to use the booths to hustle tricks in order to make a living. The booths were, Angelo maintained, just like parking meters. So long as a john that was servicing him kept slipping quarters into the slot and the manager kept collecting them, he had no right to fucking complain.

On impulse Apollo slipped by them into a booth and decided he would do the bag. He took two quarters out and dumped them into the slot. He imagined Angelo as a human quarter sinking into a big slot. Suddenly all of Earth was sinking. Apollo went down with it so swiftly that his stomach rose in his throat. The whole fucking world, including his sick friend, his job, and the bank, were being flushed down the toilet. He stood in the light of the sex movie to use its pale colors to tie up and shoot the bag. He realized that he had missed the burial of the needle in flesh as much as he had missed the dope. *It's not the dope that makes the big difference*, he thought as it seeped into his flesh. *It's doing it.* The realization shifted his focus. He was high on heroin for the first time in months and, despite his lack of sleep, could finally see clearly. *Something like getting them to lower taxes or getting office pussy.* Something like a need that sank into the night but re-emerged again and again.

With the withdrawal of the needle, he imagined everything floating backward in slow-motion, not really time reversing, but reversing space: the quarters floating back out of the slot, the cars floating backward out of the tunnel, the moth-man floating clean out of the tar and beating its wings again, dope and blood squirting back out of a vein, crack smoke funneling back out into the black air.

When he got to Tina's Lounge, a couple of blocks from what he thought of as Mrs. Huxton's sex theater, he was shocked to see that the building across the street had been completely leveled. In its place stood murky grayness. Everything on the block had been coated with the demolition's dust. Between the police barriers at each end of the block, every inch of street and sidewalk was inch-thick with the stuff.

On the protrusions and edges and in the cracks of all the building facades, including Tina's Lounge, trails of the powdery stuff clung like snow. It coated the panes of Tina's windows and the accordion folds of her open steel gate. Though Tina hadn't mentioned it, the place was no longer a transvestite-and-hustler bar. Through the filmy windows he caught a glimpse of a sweater or a down coat. Inside, college types were playing pool.

The street looked like a spray-painted set for a play about nuclear fallout, so mysterious, poisonous, and uniform had everything been made by the coat of dust. This part of the neighborhood was changing. It had all happened while he'd been away from it, working at Tina's Afterhours. Where were the queens and crooks now? he wondered. Dully, he took up position in the artificial scene, imagining his rumpled parka and hands that felt spidery against the gray-on-gray. Perhaps because people were afraid of asbestos from the demolition, the street was empty except for him. He enjoyed posing in it in an affirmation of the toxic, as if he were its mascot or logo.

Like an image brightening on a black-and-white television screen, a face burned into focus. To his doped astonishment, it bore a strange resemblance to the teller at the bank. The blond, washed-out teller was made luminous against the gray, like a white hospital sheet on the blurred burn of a fever . . . But what was strange was that there were two images, not one.

Neither was the teller, of course. Revenge was never that perfect. But they were teller types. Two thin, blond gay guys with starched shirts, and overly neat hair. In their pale bleached blue jeans, they stopped and told him they were from Missouri and could not find Tina's Lounge. They'd read about it being a gay bar in the gay guide, but it wasn't there anymore.

This time Apollo did not restrain the calculated movements of male preening that he used for challenge and display. He clasped his hands behind his back and pulled his shoulders down so that the parka was stretched against his chest and upper arms. He revealed their sculpted meatiness and flashed a surly smile.

The tourists responded to the proprietary gleam in Apollo's stoned eyes. Terrified and excited, they stepped aside for a hasty conference, then invited him back to their decent midtown hotel. With edgy delight they snuck him by the desk clerk to the elevator.

It was with cynical amusement that he observed their nervous, provincial hospitality. They offered him a chair, while they perched on the neatly made bed. They folded their hands in their laundered laps. With patient courtesy they asked him if he was a native New Yorker and what he did for a living, trying not to glue their eyes to his crotch, which, slumping, he casually stroked through his pants.

They talked about their families, and Apollo told about his "great" relationship with his father. "I'm his sweetheart," he said. The term must have taken the pair by surprise, because suddenly they became awkwardly silent. So Apollo suggested one of them go to the TV and punch in a straight porno film that would be charged to their hotel bill. With the same Midwestern cordiality, one blond walked uncertainly to the TV. Lapsing into plain-folk candidness, the other flatly asked whether that meant Apollo was straight. Apollo boldly answered that he was, but considered both of them girls.

The offense colored both faces. Apollo understood. Upstanding and reasonable, they'd worked hard to forge a gay identity clean of ludicrousness, ambiguity, or doubt. For that very reason he enjoyed gauging the proportion of insult-to-arousal he had caused, blowing just enough against their house of cards.

Insolently, he stood up from the chair and dropped onto the bed. Start the movie rolling, he commanded, and slipped off his pants. And with the start of the movie, the movie of the past finally replayed. For although Apollo had already gotten high, he had not really found the old feeling until he found this link. It was a sexual mastery that radiated from contempt. It scoped right into others and played with who they were. It took care of him and took care of others without his having to bother to like them. Within it, he gave everything he had, but lost nothing. It was an affirmation that he had never had anything in the first place. That was the pleasure of being high and selling sex to get higher.

So ecstatic and just was this expenditure that the two blonds seemed mesmerized. Below them on the bed lay all of the physical health he had been squirreling away by not getting high, just as those drab ones squirreled away money in the bank. Now he understood what it meant to save and spend, and he hoped that some unknown power in the future would allow him an unexpected accumulation once again. Because his cock was rising in a great arc to fuck the squirming porno actors on television, it fucked the world of banks and fucked the mouths of both men skidding against his tingly, numb skin. It fucked sick friends whom he wished he could save and fathers dying on the floor at cash machines.

They had stripped naked, and their larval bodies showed red marks wherever he had grasped or slapped too hard. It occurred to him that his touch was like a branding iron. It cauterized them into becoming lustier men. Gleefully, he realized how increasing pleasure enlarged them into accepting the role of girls he'd assigned them.

To their reincarnation he offered the blood boiling in his high veins. He gave them what even the best courses in consciousness-raising had denied existed. He showed them the suicidal ecstasy of setting on fire everything that you had saved. He helped them trample their careful masculine gardens and squander their harvests. How wild the blond boys became. How eager they were to relish this real man watching porno and letting them skim off pleasure's overflow. Their admiration for his cock, which had gone stiff all the way to its root near his anus, was not ruined by the thought that they were working on a dope stick. A dope stick was a cock that stayed hard interminably on a high junkie's body. Orgasm was leagues away, and when and if it came, it too would be protracted. But these two were strangers to the junkie world. With eager trust they licked and sucked the magical dick and balls, whose voltage never diminished. All three men hovered and trembled at the same level.

He wanted, most of all, to see the look on the primmer one's face as he pushed his dope stick up his ass. For the night of tar was melting into a rushing ocean. Every tight withdrawal that had marked the last weeks of sobriety loosened and swirled away with it. The white bodies clasping him on either side with suckers fastened to his nipples and cock were like huge sails tugging on his floating body. He gave in to the rushing current that made swollen the huge bladders of silk. He was shooting into this ocean a hot expulsion he couldn't distinguish from peeing or coming. With the help of two white butch queens, Apollo and heroin had finally reached white waters.

In his underpants, the primmer and taller of the two blonds looked piqued. He was standing near the television, which he'd angrily shut off, counting out the sixty dollars Apollo had demanded. Behind him lay the shorter, rosier one, still naked, his forearm shielding his eyes to conceal his embarrassment at having ended up with a hustler.

As Apollo pulled on his wrinkled clothes and worn-out kicks, he studied their leather-trimmed luggage and extra pairs of polished shoes by the bed. He made note of the fancy digital travel clock on the night table. Then he saw the one who was standing shoot a meaningful glance to the one on the bed, who grimaced.

So then. They'd finally figured out who they were.

Who was he? Somebody who chipped,* he told himself. It flushed out the system and cut loose hang-ups. Going back to the old desperate ways was out of the question, but right now he had three new twenties from the butch queens in his parka pocket. Whatever he decided to do with the rest of the night would be no problem, even if he hadn't slept in twenty-four hours.

So he hailed a cab. Encased in pleasure, nearly crowing in freedom, he rocked in his seat, as it took him back up to 112th Street, one of the best copping spots in Manhattan, just to see it again.

The new night setting was full immersion into the old world. Memory, which had been nonexistent for the last months, brought back the image of his last trip there, feeling sick, next to his sick friend, to get a bag. His friend had been in much better shape then.

Apollo felt a touch of nostalgia for the old days, when getting high was a freewheeling affair and before his friend was hit so badly by AIDS. The thought put an idiotic half-grin on his face.

The driver caught it through his rear-view mirror.

"You okay?" he asked.

Apollo nodded, mutating the grin into a beatific smile. Soon the corner floated into view, like a slide of itself

* shot dope now and then

taken at night. It was a memory from the past that he could not imagine becoming real again—that school you used to go to whose corridors have shrunk, that town with different neighbors. Two cold whites of eyes floated in the darkness of the block where he had always bought the stuff. He figured they were the eyes of the dealer. They drew him onward like a fish drawn at night by a phosphorescent lure. But as he got nearer, he noticed that the dealer wore a hat with a glowing *X*. He turned back toward the cab, but it had already crept to the next corner and was continuing through a green light.

The person wearing a matted stocking cap with a big white *X* on it was hurrying toward him as he backed into the street. Now the *X*-cap was raining blows on his head while trying to trip him at the same time.

"You fucking junkie bouncer," it hissed, "where's your queen bodyguard now?"

With great lucidity he recorded the blows hitting him. But his nerve endings resisted them with strange numbness. *What is it like to be high and then beat up?* he remembered. *This is happening to another body, not mine nor his.*

"You killed Angelo's cousin," he said as part of the script.

"So what if I did?"

He felt bizarrely monolithic, his body rhythms so slowed down that he would not fall. He took the beating half as punishment deserved and half in resentment, with an eerie sense of irony. It was like when the effect of a Novocain shot at the dentist is tested successfully with a probe for lack of feeling.

When it was over, he copped the best brand, D.O.A., and dragged himself west to a shooting gallery in black Harlem, a repair garage during the day, where he figured he'd be less likely to run into the *X*-cap again. The place was full of old-time junkies, in their forties and fifties, with some old-time ideas. But nobody was fazed by his ripped parka, swollen eye, and bloody lip. Blood was an abundant commodity here—junkies squirted it from their spikes into soiled water glasses or wiped a dribble off a punctured neck. However, few shared needles these days.

He took his place among them and politely shot up a man who was having trouble finding his one remaining good vein, in his armpit. But as he withdrew the needle, the man jerked into convulsions and fell off his chair. Someone came running with salt, and Apollo pried open his mouth and tossed some in. Then he clamped the lips together, hoping that saline in the mouth would hit the bloodstream and prevent the guy from O.D.ing, while another guy mixed a shot of saltwater. Here in the shooting gallery the problems and their solutions were all familiar. Everything fit together fine.

When the guy revived, Apollo took his shot and fell out on a mattress on the floor. The old junkies let their eyes rest on him and began philosophizing between nods.

"Lookit that young punk crashed out on the mattress. Remember just a few months ago, when he was looking so wasted?"

"Come back fine, like he was in Hollywood or something."

"Or jail."

"Yeah, they feed 'em good nowadays."

"They got a warrant for me. Maybe I should turn myself in and get me away from the stuff for two months."

"Might be just as good as going to one of them detoxes."

"Yeah, they take you off in seven 'stead of twenty-one nowadays."

"That way they can put somebody else in your bed."

"It's legal to be greedy."

"Know what cracks me up? Can't smoke in the hospital no more. I went into one of them detoxes and got through the sickness."

"Don't tell me. But you walked a few days later just to get a cigarette?"

"You got it."

"And those methadone motherfuckers *lower* you instead of increase you if they find opiates in your blood."

"Now that's perverted."

"Downright vengeful if you ask me."

"Lord, take a look at that baby boy's veins. They're so good I can see the valves in 'em."

"What I wouldn't give for pipes like that again. Wouldn't have to hit in the neck no more."

"I bet you gonna be doing that till you're eighty."

"If I live that long."

"When that happens you become a saint or something."

" 'Member that seventy-eight-year-old junkie living up here in Harlem we used to call 'Mother'?"

"A real purified glow to her face."

"How'd she go finally?"

"The bone-crusher got her. She was in such a hurry she didn't draw her shit through no cotton or a cigarette filter."

"Oh yeah, them particles can sneak right into the heart!"

"Reminds me of the time the tip of my spike break off in my vein. But I dug the sucker out with a tweezers 'fore it could travel through me."

"Lookit the jeans on that kid falling off his rear! You know, they wear them big clothes like that so they can hide a weapon in 'em."

"You'd think it would be a obvious tip-off to the law."

"Come on, Rupert, how they gonna come down on just a *style?*"

"It's the mentality of the new generation I don't like. When they got a slight advantage, they sport a lot of gold jewelry."

"Just challenging the other no-gots in the neighborhood to make themselves feel big."

"You think anybody falls for that image shit?"

"What they don't know is we all been lyin' to each other from day one, and we'll be lyin' till West Bubba."

"Each and every one, some of us lie better than others, that's all. This one probably lied eight times today."

Apollo's inner alarm system jerked him out of the deepest nod as he felt the force field of shadiness. He hopped to his feet, disoriented.

"Don't bust a nut, junior, we was just statin' an opinion."

"I want to do up half more a bag," he said.

He propped himself on a broken-backed chair and tied up, then cooked some more. He could feel the dried-up bodies of the old junkies getting off on how easily it slid into his young veins.

The shot gave him a strange speed rush, as happened sometimes, so he started to rap about his big plans for the future. The old-time junkies sat back and laughed and slapped their knees.

He felt jerky, like a marionette.

XVII

What an old maid I am getting to be, losing the nerve to be in love with death!

—ARTHUR RIMBAUD, *A Season in Hell*

THEY SAVED ME, BUT FOR WHAT? NO APOLLO, AND no word from him. The apartment's abandoned, the undumped-garbage smell overpowering, a fungus worse than the thrush that had coated my throat in the hospital on the dirty dishes in the sink. The note still there, right where I'd left it a month and a half ago. Fever 106 . . . Light bulbs are burned out like they'd been left on for weeks.

He never came once to see me in the hospital. And when I called home, nobody ever answered. Finally, they said the phone was disconnected. He's been sucked back into the depths, just as I feared.

I myself have become a human syringe, with a Hickman's catheter sunk into my chest for shooting drugs directly to the heart. A way of slowing the spread of the cytomegalovirus that caused the fevers and has spread to my retinas, they told me. The junkie's dream, I suppose. If I ever run into him again, maybe I'll suggest he get one of these implanted.

You could dump anything into it, making suicide easy. But for the moment I hook up an intravenous contraption to it twice a day. Drip some Gancyclovir through my veins to stave off the threat of blindness.

Conversely perhaps for Apollo, there was the feeling of something leaking out of his body, so that a part of his self was leaking away. A feeling of shame. He spent some nights in a flophouse in the West Thirties that rented out chicken coops. At least, they looked like them. Each dormitory floor was divided into crude little wooden-partitioned cubicles with padlocks, containing a wooden bunk with a mattress. The roofs were chicken-coop wire, the bathroom communal.

Getting in and out of your padlocked coop wasn't that easy. There were drunks and paranoids in the hall. Across from him was a young girl on welfare. He spent one night padlocked in her room with her, but when she told him she could think herself into becoming Michael Jackson, he got scared and moved back into his coop.

He'd never gone back to the apartment or to Tina's Afterhours since that first night of getting high. And when the place got shut down by the cops right after elections, word about the manhunt for Apollo leaked out.

Tina's Lounge remained changed, welcoming no hustlers or drags. Even the sex theater had become a straight porno movie house. Everyone in the crowd was now crammed into another after-hours, over a Portuguese restaurant. They had a video monitor with a wide view of the street so that they could check you out long before you rang the buzzer. The evening began at 3:00 A.M. and was often a desperate waiting game. With Apollo's return to hustling, this was the new place of operations. That or Port Authority in the afternoon. Rumor had it, however, that another club would soon be opening. In Apollo's mind the power behind it had to be Huxton.

He stayed away from the apartment of his sick friend and tried not to think about him. Near the beginning there were tricks on that mother trip he knew so well who fell in love with his skin and lost look and pressed their attentions on him. While it lasted, he took what he could. They bought him little address books so he could come back to see them and "get organized." But just like everybody else out here, he always lost his address book. He remembered telephone numbers and faces, but not names. He could tattoo a telephone number on his mind if the trick allowed him to hear it only once. Then he played the game of calling and saying, "What's up," without announcing who it was. Even if there was perplexed silence on the other end of the line, he bided his time. It saved the embarrassment of the guy not remembering his name and his not remembering the guy's. If the guy recognized his voice immediately, Apollo knew he'd made inroads. Or he got bolder and called collect. If the guy accepted the call, he'd saved a quarter and it probably meant the evening was in the bag. Then there was always the intimidation technique, standing outside the building at two in the morning and howling up at the window like a newborn in the middle of the night.

The routine of addiction and hustling mass-produces looks and personalities. Slowly but surely over the next few months he felt himself falling into one of the several stereotypes. There are those who get skinny and mangy and lose their luster as the street takes hold. With diminishing sexual appeal they get bitter and violently impatient. Or they go the other way: discovering a sexual part of themselves that is clinging, whiny, and willing to accommodate. But there are others who thicken in a stolid-looking male way with a hint of blowsiness. They wring their appeal out of an increasingly unreasonable pride. Apollo was lucky enough to belong to this last group.

Was it an enlarging liver or the grease and starch he

gobbled whenever he had the chance that had begun to develop the slight gut? A filled-out face and extra body weight gave him a more mature look, a broader swagger. Now he attracted johns who were looking for real rough trade instead of son figures. He had to adjust his sexual techniques to incorporate a new surliness, a little casual sadism. Then when he lapsed into dope passivity the tricks got hot at seeing the giant take his tumble.

Flippiness, he knew, was the great sexual tender. To see a burly lard-ass who reminded you of a construction worker moan and grow passive under your mouth or touch turned worlds upside down and set hearts beating. So what if it necessitated a shot of dope? When he got out of bed, he was still just as surly and as uncompromising, just as unattainable. That's what made them keep dropping coins into the slot.

When he caught a case of head lice at the "Chicken Coop Hotel," he shaved his skull. He made jokes about his new hairstyle being called "twenty-five to life." He found himself housing olive fatigues and an army jacket from a willing trick. Then he traded his sneakers in for construction boots. They turned his walk into a new stomp. He developed a seedy bravado, bawdy humor, a new corniness. Such exhibitionism added to the sham "take-control" image and lured more of the same type of trick.

One freezing afternoon in early winter he found himself at a chain pharmacy with a balding-businessman trick. The guy had said they had to stop to get condoms because he'd run out at home. For some reason all the brands were in a glass case. The trick was adamant about the brand he wanted, Trojan Plus, which were tapered and golden in color. But among the native languages and alphabets of the Syrian manager and the Korean and Haitian clerks accumulating at the condoms case, no one could locate the package the customer kept pointing to. When the correct package was produced after several wrong ones, Apollo satirized the laborious process by loudly assuming they now

wanted him to try them on for size. There were various tit-
ters and embarrassed eyes. So he kept insisting. The trick
was humiliated and thrilled by the public display. There he
stood in a suit with a briefcase with a skinheaded tough in
fatigues drawing raucous attention to them both. Little by
little, performance was becoming a larger share of Apollo's
hustling skills.

He was also taking on the poignant narcissism of the
aging outlaw—the type who spouts testimonials to his own
self-worth. One time a drunken trick sent him from the
after-hours club to find a slice and two packs of cigarettes,
one pack as a tip for Apollo. When he finally found the
cigarettes and the pizza at that ungodly hour, he brought
them back to the club. But he was so stoned that he never
counted the change. The trick accused him of housing
some of it and threatened to tell the manager. "Nothing
against you," he slurred drunkenly. "I just wouldn't want
to put other johns in danger from somebody stole from me,
you understand?"

Apollo stood tall and stuck out his chest: "You tell him,
and this what he gonna say. 'This individual Perk been coming to my establishment for years and I have confidence in
him. Why don't you go to that nowhere bar up the street
to see if you can find any dick to suck. Then maybe you
come back here and won't complain so much.' " It didn't
matter to Apollo that he didn't even know who the manager
was.

The man really did complain to the manager, and
Apollo was thrown out for the night. His charades of honor
were thin protection against winter weather and the fact
that without the trick he'd be sleeping in the cardboard
village tonight. After the bust of Tina's Afterhours, the
whole block had been cleaned up. The village had moved
to the docks, where the inhabitants surrounded it with a
half-circle of trash-can fires for warmth.

In order to get there with the shot he was saving, he
had to pass Tina's and the old sex theater. Across from

Tina's the big hole of demolition had been filled by an improbable skyscraper with a big banner advertising condos. Midtown had become a patchwork of crumbling deco and new, half-empty towers. A fragmented rhetoric jumped out at you as dying after-theater restaurants tried to speak of old sophistication and showmanship against the new faceless and monstrous facades. None of it fit together, and it was a little like Apollo's mind. As if to contribute to this schizoid display, his thoughts kept up a frantic soliloquy as he moved toward his cardboard home. He added false plans and tired legends to the decrepit buildings collapsing under the weight of the faceless new.

Underpinning it he saw Mrs. Huxton as entrepreneur of a new midtown empire that had savvily adapted to the new rules. She would combine the old tricks of selling fast kicks with fresh mass marketing. In his mind he saw the megaclub she was planning in deco that recalled the old days of Times Square but was bolstered by new neon. Her waiters all wore jackets, and the hustlers and the johns were all top-drawer. With rich tricks coming to the neighborhood, he was sure his fate would change.

When he got to the cardboard village he saw that one of the plastic garbage-bag tents was empty. Quickly he dived into it and pulled the flap down. Inside it was a small kerosene stove with a little fuel left. He lit it for warmth and used it to cook up his shot. The new shot was good and smoothed out the running monologue in his mind. With a feeling of luxury, he began a new round of legend making.

My life: a hand of cards played illegally in the trashiest of places, thrown down between shots of the best dope there is. That's why I'm used to the wild cards falling. Being on the edge is the only thing that ever gave me the feeling of being alive. Let's face the truth: if my only friend tried to stop me from doing half the things I done, I would a killed him like that, if only it didn't involve too much trouble or me going out of the way.

What gives me my legendary strength is knowing that when I suffer, it ain't no big deal. Come to think of it, I saw my mother suffer at the hands of my father, which was something you are supposed to get used to. When shit happens every day, the eye of the storm is something an old soldier like myself might even seek out. I'm a big bad elephant stomping toward the pit, just like my dad.

"Dad" was like a pebble dropped accidentally into the hollow well of the soliloquy. It brought everything to an abrupt, echoing standstill. Instead, he imagined the prematurely old father figures at the shooting gallery, slapping their thighs and laughing, shouting, "Right on, baby, right on!"

My bourgeois friends formed a reliable support group, now that I was out of the hospital and having trouble being on my own. How happy they were to see me back in the fold after my perplexing detour into the underworld. Now they were willing to run out and fill prescriptions or help me figure my dwindling accounts. A couple of times a week they brought hot meals or came over and cooked.

I'd gone to the hospital in a terrific panic that had knocked all the tongue-in-cheek philosophizing out of me. After they'd brought the fever down and gotten rid of the thick coating of thrush on my mouth and throat, I became a cooperative patient. I suppose there's no greater brainwasher than the lifesavers who take your fate into their hands no matter how brief the respite they offer becomes. As a matter of fact, it occurs to me that the legendary French Bluebeard Gilles de Rais supposedly heightened his pleasure in torturing children by setting himself up as a fake savior who ran into the room and stopped his henchmen. Then, as the saved child sighed with relief in his arms, he switched and became the torturers' leader. Accordingly, as time passed in the hospital, the medical attitudes that had seemed so plausible gradually led to conclusions that seemed more and more deranged. It was, apparently, their business to keep the cells of my body functioning. But what they in euphemism called "quality of life" was considered an entirely private affair. This lack of concern for the libido once again alienated me, and I began thinking of Apollo and wondering where he was living and how he was getting by. It was obvious to me that he'd gone back to dope, and partly because lengthening his life span was not his top priority.

Thoughts of this nature would torture me as I hooked up to my intravenous gadgets twice a day for my Gancyclovir infusion. Despite, or perhaps partly as a result of, my friends' good intentions, I was getting more and more sullen and withdrawn. Sometimes I even lapsed into an infantile state in which I berated Apollo for abandoning me. It didn't matter that he had never learned to show more than inklings of supportiveness, like getting me some orange juice once. What I unreasonably expected was for him to realize that he represented a world. Without it, I'd come crawling back to who I was supposed to be, despising myself all the way. But, of course, his world was notoriously unhelpful when the chips were down.

I was preparing for the evening infusion when a key began to turn in the lock. He walked in as if he hadn't been gone more than a few hours, though the change in his appearance made it seem like years. He was still handsome, almost strikingly so, but his physique showed a new loutishness, and his millimeter-long haircut made his usual saucer eyes look a little slitty. Or perhaps it was the puffiness of his face that had whittled them down.

I didn't challenge the sudden visit or question the fairness of his still using his key. Instead, what little heart there was left in me beat with anticipation . . . as if, despite my knowing better, he'd come bringing some new antidote to pain or secret of oblivion.

In a strange charade of casualness we sat on the couch "catching up." Both of us were painfully aware of his new manner, the booming voice, the heavy-handed boasts. He claimed to be proud of his independence and vowing to "make it on my own." Maybe he'd go to school, he said, after he landed a construction job. He said he was living with a buddy who asked for no rent because "he believes in me." But when I kept repeatedly asking him for details, he turned sullen and said, "What you all up in my business for?"

"That's something you'd never say if you weren't getting high," I said in the ridiculous pose of the reformer.

"So what the fuck!" he answered and picked up a glass as if he were about to fling it against the wall.

He was, it turns out, basically homeless. And when he saw the pain in my eyes caused by the avowal, he took advantage of it by asking if he could take a shower. In my pitiful need to fantasize for a few moments that our domestic arrangement still remained, I agreed, though I knew I was no longer in any position, physically or financially, to have somebody in my home who was in constant need of dope.

But for the moment he played house by weaving out of his soldier-of-fortune hand-me-downs into an image of the adolescent I'd known. It was astounding. Aside from being somewhat heavier, the naked image brought back the budding, sensual Apollo of a few months ago. But then, how much could he have really changed in such a short time?

He ran to the scale and weighed himself and seemed happy that he'd put on weight. Weight is, I know, a valuable commodity among street people, as it is among us HIV-positives. In an attempt to make the scene even more domestic, I decided to do the infusion usual for that time of day. In his underpants, he helped me set up the paraphernalia. But instead of taking his shower, as I infused he began to cook some dope in a spoon over his lighter. When I threw him a reproachful glance from my tubed-and-needled installation, he winked and gestured toward the stove. "Remember how I always said I wanted to cook? Well, I ended up doing a lot of it."

So he had his medication, and I had mine. I knew that even if what he took were prescribed by a doctor, it would have been unlikely to be portrayed as an escape from mental anguish in the direction of pleasure—even if that doctor knew Apollo was using it to numb the discomfort of having to sleep in the freezing outdoors. The doctor would have to use the alibi of observable symptoms, such as an improvement in sleep patterns or more manageable behavior or a decrease in negative verbal expression. That was their only lexicon.

Our separate infusions became a perverse duet in which he was getting happier only for the moment and I was killing off germs that were bound in the future to return. In the face of the human condition, is there really such a thing as "medicine"? I was tempted to ask for half a teaspoon of his concoction mixed with mine. But the big-brother memory of the hospital's rescue from my last trauma squelched the impulse with ideological guilt.

When he finished his shot, he sat and watched me continuing mine, which takes about forty-five minutes. He was fascinated by the catheter implanted in my chest and asked a lot of questions about how it worked and how it was maintained. He was much less interested in the substance and its purpose than in the way it was administered. Junkies can go on forever about needles and penetration, how to locate veins. I now had a passage that was permanently available, so I explained how the Hickman's catheter on my chest allowed fluids to travel directly into my circulatory system by way of the heart and how an internal valve in the device prevented flowback.

His growing familiarity with my predicament lowered more defenses and increased the fantasy feeling that he had come home. Sensing this, he lolled in his high on the couch, and our warm and gentle chatter continued. It was the least anguished of my twice-a-day infusions that I had ever experienced. But when his remarks made it clear that he thought he had moved back in, I had to speak up.

There was no way, I explained, that I could deal with his problems in my condition. He took the remark as a blunt, blanket rejection and coldly informed me that he didn't need anybody's help, including mine. When I said he'd misinterpreted me and that I'd always care about what happened to him, he cut me off angrily, then burst into tears and renewed his pleas to start living here again.

I've got to admit that as thrilled as I was by the short session of playing house, and as radical as I liked to think I was in terms of security and health, the idea of dealing with him brought out the new reactionary in me. Infusion schedules, uninterrupted rest, and pinching pennies had edged out some of the old appetites and squelched my perverse bravado. I wanted to hold on to my shrinking island, so I stuck firm.

His breaking down had humiliated him. He dressed quickly

and sullenly without bothering with the shower. He put on the fatigues like a man reinstalling his pitiless shell. Using the boots for emphasis, he stomped about the apartment. Brazenly he threw open the refrigerator and stuffed his mouth with food. Then he tremblingly marched to the VCR and started to unplug it. The action was accompanied by a stern and nasty monologue about the "need to survive out there," but his voice was shaking.

I was still hooked up to my contraption and couldn't get up in the middle of my infusion. So I challenged him to name how much money he thought I owed him. I'd learned some lessons in life, I said somewhat sarcastically, with him as teacher. But I didn't want to pay a higher rate than I did when he sold me sex. As far as I was concerned, the total education wasn't worth more than about fifty dollars, one sexual experience, and the VCR was worth a hundred and eighty.

Crazily wounded, he tossed the VCR on the couch. Why don't you take that vase, I said. It's worth about fifty dollars. I couldn't sell it for shit on the street, he snapped. So in black burlesque I suggested more objects in the apartment, purposely choosing those few remaining selections that would fetch little price outside the realm of yuppiedom. Becoming part of the strange comedy routine, he picked up each classical CD, Italian bath brush, StairMaster, Noguchi lamp, or abstract silkscreen I indicated and dropped it in laconic rejection on the floor at my feet. Then, in an explosion of rage, he started tearing all the drawers from the dresser. He threw the contents on the floor and pawed through them for money. He ripped the couple of dollars from my wallet and tossed the wallet in the sink. Then he smashed a wooden chair against the table, splitting both. He shook the VCR in my face, screaming, You think I need your shit? and smashed it on the floor as well. The neighbors below started pounding on their ceiling. Frantically he stripped some silk shirts from the closet and stuffed them into a shopping bag. He threw my CDs on top, then stalked out the door.

Since that time, my mind has circled the robbery again and again, as if it were some monolith, an incomprehensible edifice of secret motives, secret fear. I've queried each sealed entrance of this horrible

*structure, which can produce cold violence and betrayal. But I'm
locked out of it and half hoping not to get in, to find that self inside
I've been avoiding.*

*Now that I know he is gone for good, I feel that old protective
veil of excitement receding like an illusion, like someone being de-
prived of a drug. This must be how death comes, a peeling away.*

*Was I just a naive bourgeois who broke the rules in a depraved
context? Was the cure of the leper—through enough daring and
sacrifice—just an illusion? I lie in bed with eyes closed, arms
spread, and palms turned up, still trying to expel this pain into
the atmosphere, where all are forced to breathe its fumes.*

At one moment he wanted to hurt Apollo so much that it
would even penetrate the heroin and both of them could
feel the pain. At other times he reasoned that doing time
would get the boy off heroin and it was his responsibility to
turn him in. Being a full-time medical patient had, he realized, instilled a sense of "civic duty." If Apollo had done
this to him, a sick friend, what would he do to others? Finally, he saw his snitching to the cops as a simple cry for
contact, the only way left to reach out toward him.

When he called the cops and described the cardboard
village and where Apollo had said it was located, they did
not react with surprise. If they'd wanted to, they could have
taken the time to comb Apollo out of the neighborhood
haunts. But going to the trouble of recognizing Apollo's
face, which resembled that of thousands of mug shots of
people his age in the precinct files, required more motivation. Now they had two charges, the assault of Casio and
the robbing of a sick man whose apartment he'd trashed.

Their unmarked car cruised toward the village in the early
morning, as the fires were growing paler against the putrid
light. Two chubby near-rookies had been sent out to do the
dirty work. They were to pick up a youth who'd been wanted
for more than seven months, just because somebody had
put it on the day's agenda.

Both cops were white. Both would have said that they'd "paid their dues." One had nursed an alcoholic father and had turned the tide of family do-nothings by becoming a cop. The other was the son of an abusive mother with a bitter vengeance for "those who preyed on innocent people."

Like some outlandish antigen attacking an already sick body, their blue-and-white police car pulled up to the squalid cardboard village. With a melancholy disgust, they watched a man crawl out of one of the two plastic tents and take his morning shit into the gray river. He didn't fit the description. Their suspect was much younger and not as dark-skinned. Finally they saw him, climbing from the tent in his stained fatigues. His head was still nearly hairless, and his sallow face was pinched into withdrawal. He was vomiting thin liquid in the dawn light as shaking passed through his thick torso.

When he was done, he wiped his mouth on his sleeve and walked jerkily to the sidewalk. As he began moving north, the car pulled away from the curb and began tracking him at a crawl. Then they pulled over and called out his name.

"Apollo Nelson?"

"Name's Perk."

"What kind of name's that?"

"Spanish. Perdido. Perdido T. Colón."

"Get over here, we want to see your I.D."

He reluctantly approached the cop car, and the two men leapt out. They laid him out over the hood and made him stretch his arms over his head. As soon as they began to frisk him, they pulled out his works and a knife. They sat him in the front seat of the car. One climbed back behind the wheel and the other got in back. As his nose ran and his face twitched from withdrawal they began firing questions.

"Why no I.D., Perdido?"

"I lost it."

"What's your address?"

"I ain't got one."

"Why aren't you working?"

"I can't find a job."

"You know this needle's illegal?"

"I'm waiting to get in a program."

"What's your social security number?"

"Three-five-six, oh-nine, seven-eight-nine-one."

The cops phoned in the name and number and came up with nothing. The stink from the suspect was beginning to fill up the car. They were fairly certain they had the right man but didn't want to make an error. The waste of time and space for bringing in somebody and booking him just because he had works on him didn't win you friends at the precinct. It was primarily because of this that they lapsed into a desperate note of levity. Perhaps the grimness of the sick junkie stinking up the car fueled the need for entertainment. Or maybe they hoped their brand of humor would spur him into an infraction that would make it worth bringing him in.

"Bet there's plenty of free pussy over there in that village."

"Don't know."

"Why not, you a dick junkie or something?"

"Yeah, are you one of those sperm slurpers?"

"You should try a little muff now and then. I bet you'd forget all about being a faggot."

"Sneezing in the suitcase is much more fun than chewing on the stick."

"I guess you two cops would know."

"You calling us faggots, you dumb punk?"

Apollo put his hand on the door, but the cop sped up and pulled so tight to a parked car that he could not open it.

"Don't try to jump on us, punk."

"We're telling you now that you're cased."

"We got a reason to believe that you're Apollo Nelson."

"You better own up now if you are."

"Next time we see you we won't be so friendly."

"Don't lie to us, faggot!"

"What the fuck do you want?"

When they saw the wave move through his stomach and his cheeks balloon out like a squirrel's, they knew he was about to upchuck all over his lap and the car. The cop in back dove forward to roll down the window. He shoved Apollo's head outside but banged it against the window of the other car. The cop at the wheel pulled the vehicle forward so that the suspect could vomit onto the street. He grabbed him by the collar and yanked forward so that the stream of vomit would clear the side of the cop car.

When the heaving subsided, Apollo slumped against the window with his head hanging out. With force out of nowhere, he dove through the opening until he had emerged to his waist. Then, kicking the hands and face of the cops who grabbed for him, he squirmed and crashed onto the pavement. He reared to his feet and shot up the street.

XVIII

Tina's last performance took place early that following spring. The notice for it read:

Tina Shaughnessy
Appleton Funeral Parlor
Tuesday, 5:00–8:00 P.M.
One Night Only

To the Irish barkeeps of the neighborhood, "One Night Only" meant there would not be an extended wake. But a large majority of the queens saw the notice in theatrical terms. Tina's private war against illness, like Jacqueline Susann's, had been fought silently and alone. Although Baby Pop was still living with her, he had not known that she had AIDS until her first—and only—stay in the hospital with pneumonia and TB.

Now that she had gone so swiftly, the fact that she had taken him in had another level of meaning, which gave his fears and hopes new depth. Well-fed and sensibly medicated at fifteen, he was the only male image at the funeral. Not one of Tina's protégés or any of the queens' boyfriends had bothered to show up.

Baby Pop could also have been considered her widower, since her death had canceled his domestic situation. In a few days he'd have to vacate her house. Bereft and touched, he stood staring down at the heavily made-up face in the coffin, girding himself for his male role in tonight's serious event. A few queens approached and offered their condolences in the need to ritualize him as husband.

Inside him, a rage burned at what he considered Tina's maltreatment at the dreaded hospital—the same one that had housed his father only as a prelude to arrest, that had diagnosed Baby Pop with HIV, and that employed the *cafre* of a rich doctor who tried to trade drugs for ass. Bleeding into his mind was one incident in particular, when a nurse had yanked an intravenous needle out of Tina's arm and hadn't noticed that the puncture in her flesh was spouting. Half the bed sheet had been drenched as the nurse strolled casually out of the room. Baby Pop ran down the hall to get her with the distinct impression that queens and homeboys didn't speak her language. He also remembered the doctor's contemptuous dumping into a wastebasket of the fish dinner Baby Pop had brought, even though Tina had begged for it. As far as the doctor was concerned, his fasting regime in response to her backed-up liver was more important than the fact that she'd said she was famished. At that moment Baby Pop had made a mental note to go to law school and sue that doctor. As far as he was concerned, Tina had died of starvation.

———

The queens were thick in attendance and on this occasion displayed a rare sense of modesty. Baby Pop had never seen them so subdued or dressed down. He'd also never seen them with so little makeup and this early in the evening, before it was even dark. Their heels were low and their hemlines long. To mourn they had abandoned the exaggeration and parody of dress and gesture with which many tackled situations. Quite a few of them knew they were HIV-positive, or they were dealing with full-blown AIDS. In addition, the death of Tina raised the question of who could ever again open a queen's bar.

In the harsh fluorescent lights of this funeral parlor, which was one of the few that accepted the corpses of queens or people who had died of AIDS, the effect was one of a sorority of pallid sisters squelched by drugs or disease, yet darkly determined to push ahead in sullen dignity. The five-o'clock shadows peeking through the foundation of some were no cause for irony, as no one at this moment was using fantasy to face the grim horizon of the future.

With their innate sense of ritual, they revered Tina's last appearance in a group Ave Maria and farewell kisses to the corpse. Then the hushed room with its tired faces seemed to wilt the air itself. The unfriendly wattage of the fluorescent lights pressed on everybody's spirits. One by one they wandered into the reception room to have a smoke.

They gravitated toward Angelita, who'd flown in from her new affluent life in California after her very recent sex change. Here was a positive image around which they could rally and from whom they could seek advice.

They asked her how the operation could have changed her legs, which now looked so much more feminine and shapely. Angelita kindly told them that they too could improve the texture and silhouette of their legs by wearing several pairs of nylons—as many layers as they could stand. The pressure was kind of isometric and toned them up.

They admired her pineapple-shaped bouffant, and she

generously explained how you do it: you freeze the hair around liter-size Coca-Cola bottles with a ton of hair spray, then you pull the bottles out and tie the giant curls together.

Finally, they touched on the operation and asked how long it took to heal. Angelita said she'd been told she had to stop hustling for two months, and that she had another month to go. One queen asked if it was true that the depth of your pussy was based on the size of your dick, which she'd heard kind of got turned inside out during the operation. Did that mean that people with little dicks would end up with shallow pussies? Angelita calmly responded that that was a question the asker should discuss with her doctor. Then another queen piped up and asked whether doctor-made pussies were higher up on the groin instead of right between the legs, since a guy's cock and balls were higher up on the body than a born-woman's pussy. Angelita said that was true but that there were variations in the way that guys were hung. The base of some dicks began quite low, and those would make better pussies.

Then she loosened up completely and told a funny story about her two visits to Leavenworth prison. Her wealthy sponsor had spent six months there for running an escort service. When she'd gone to visit him the first time, the female guards in the women's section had searched her thoroughly, because of the epidemic of drug smuggling. They'd found what she had between her legs but let her go through the women's line anyway. When she came back a month later, they'd searched her again. You can imagine their astonishment when the searchers discovered that the dick had disappeared.

The story of the stymied prison guards livened things up and got the queens chattering. It soon became apparent that life had started up again and would go on. Even the sobbing Mercedes blew her nose and began to gossip. She confided in another queen that Angelita had always said,

"Let's see who'll be the first to get my pussy once I've got it made." The two conjectured about how rich or how powerful the lucky man would be.

From his position across the room, Baby Pop gravely watched them reanimate. As the only official man at the proceedings, he had appropriately avoided the girlish rap. Instead, he began wondering if he should bother mentioning to Angelita that his dad was getting out of jail this weekend. But as he watched her, he couldn't match her successful image to the present condition of his dad. Instead, he considered the possibility of living with Casio on his social security. Since his father still had trouble walking, he might need Baby Pop's help. And he himself knew that physical deprivation could cause another early slip back into the complications of AIDS. He was determined to continue his healthy life style, and maybe the release of Casio would give it a chance.

As dwindling as life within his sphere may have seemed, unbeknownst to him another chapter was just taking place. Baby Pop would probably have had trouble remembering the homeless girl he'd met and had sex with during his period of starvation and camping out at Grand Central. The encounter had flowed almost unconsciously from the fatigue and desperation of both. On this very day, the labor from their fleeting union began. The birth was in line with Baby Pop's family, where generations had usually occurred in the slim increments of fifteen or sixteen years. If seventy-eight-year-old Abuela had lived only another eight months, she would have become—probably also unknowingly—the great-great-great-grandmother of the child.

XIX

IT WAS JUNE, AND THE CONSTRUCTION WORKERS were used to the mangy, outspoken street person who'd made the sidewalk in front of the site his home. He would ask for handouts and relentlessly heckle when anybody shook his head or said no. Sometimes his desperation and black wit were entertaining, but a couple of times the bum got out of hand and a wrench or hammer had to be raised to the insolent face or thrown at his head as he ducked.

By July, he'd become a kind of mascot at the site. The guys began tossing him their lunch leftovers, which he stuffed down before you could blink an eye. Then one of them passed him a cast-off pair of construction boots, which he sported by rolling up the cuffs of his dirty fatigues to show the tops. He stomped around the site all day like some fantasy construction worker or *Playgirl* stallion.

His wisecracks and preposterous charades made the day pass faster. Some of the guys took a liking to him despite his cracked lips, stinking clothing, and sallow-colored skin. He walked and talked like a mature animal who had been down for a thousand years. But little kindnesses brought out the kid in him and brought a grateful gleam to his eyes. Probably because he thought he was God's gift to manhood, he'd dubbed himself with the unbelievable name "Apollo." When he appeared in his rags and with his matted hair, the guys enjoyed asking him to strike bodybuilding poses to prove he was a Greek god.

By August he started turning up with merchandise suitable for the guys or their girlfriends. He'd fence gold and silver chains, an occasional pocketbook, or a shirt still bearing a price tag. The guys spent part of lunch or their coffee break bargaining for the hot goods, ribbing and baiting the mange-ass, or tossing him loose change. They gave him errands or shit work, which he performed eagerly. Most surprising was his unsquelchable interest in the project, a sleek new dance club to be built on the site of this old Irish bar. Improbably, he claimed to be a personal friend of the one ultimately responsible for the contract, whom he named as a certain Mrs. Huxton.

Orders, however, came from the ex-owner of the joint, a cranky eighty-year-old man named O'Hara, who always chased away the mange-ass when he saw him and always complained about how much better the place and the neighborhood had been when the space was a simple Blarney Stone and types like that never came this far downtown.

Each feature that was added to the new interior as it neared completion—the svelte booths, strobe lights, and aluminum bar—seemed to thrill the mange-ass more. He stepped up running errands for the crew and doing odd jobs at the site, talked more and more often about the important role he would play in this business and about opening night. He was sure he'd become a waiter, doubling as bartender some evenings; and he had even designed in his head the sharp vest, white shirt, and crisp bow tie he said was waiting in his size.

Then, near the end of the afternoon, he'd disappear for a while and return in a changed mood. He'd be out of it and vague and lost in his own world. He'd be half-smiling and still and could stare at his boot tip for an hour. Some of the guys said he had to be high, but he became so manageable that nobody pushed the issue. His cranky face would be relaxed into a moonlike glow, and his mouth would look drugged and sensual.

It was at such moments that he'd ask the boss in a sweet and childlike voice if he could crash out at the site for the night. If the boss said no he'd pout and beg like a practiced whore.

It was unusual to lock a street person up with expensive installations in progress. But sometimes the boss would give in and let the baby-doll mange-ass have his way. They'd pack up for the night and bolt up the tools and other valuables while he climbed onto a shelf or bench. As they locked him in, he'd fall out in a happy delirium, mumbling about his Huxton lady and the details of their joint glorious venture.

Maybe it is no dream that the veiled woman lunches with slow elegance in the midtown Brazilian restaurant. She wears white gloves. Under the veil her looks have been plucked by tweezers and made up a shade lighter than her own skin. From the way the waiters dog up to her every need or hang at the table to light the cigarette in her old, trembling hand, it's obvious she still has clout. More, anyway, than that wide-eyed but aged blonde in a suburban getup who seems to hang on her every word.

At the moment, the blonde is gabbing on about her fabulous middle-aged son, who has grown up to be an investigator but still lives under her nose. She boasts one minute about his glorious ca-

reer, then sinks into her fears for his safety, trying to pry information out of the older, higher-class woman about a babe she thought he was dating.

The old one lets her gab on, because she knows the more innocent one has always thought of herself as her sweetheart, her protégé, and can't resist spilling the beans those few times they now come together. She keeps some things she knows of this son close to her chest for fear of upsetting her simple friend, 'cause as a businesswoman she understands facets of him that his mother perhaps could not deal with. Both dames cluck and nod and shake their heads like old harpies, so that anybody peeking from afar would take them for your typical senior citizens lunching.

In the back of the mind of the veiled one, new plans are being hatched. Of these she drops only carefully phrased hints to the dumb blonde. This venture will outrank every sex palace and club the neighborhood has ever known. Ancient as she is, she prides herself on her savvy business sense, which she feels keeps her going. A slew of old haunts have closed in Times Square, but she won't be left behind by the big change. The city may be planning a new convention center, but she's devising ways of entertaining the tired male with the new modern methods. There is no way, she realizes with her sixty-odd years of experience, that mens' needs and tastes will be chased by the new tight-ass goody-goodies from Manhattan forever. And there'll always be those needing work, who'll get stuck in her net.

Those together countries like Holland and Denmark that made a smooth industry of adult entertainment provide the inspiration for this new club. One entire room won't ever have a liquor licence. Those between the ages of eighteen and twenty-one would be stuck there, waiting all night for the johns who drink, dance, or dine in pleasanter accommodations above.

Then they'll come down and make their selection. So strict will be the surveillance and so hand-picked the clients and personnel that the old betrayals and fucked-up behavior won't have a chance. In fact, even intimate encounters will occur in a special wing, so there'll never be a complaint from customers that a trick ended up getting mugged or beat up in a hotel room.

Now the luncheon takes a turn, as the two begin their griev-
ance session; bitter stories of betrayal are the old girls' bread and
butter. In that self-pitying but turned-on tone of old ladies who
lunch, the blonde tells the story of her husband's fuck-up, which the
veiled one has heard hundreds of times before. Her story is the one
of disappointment and loss that some grow to treasure. But when
the veiled one launches into her tales of things gone wrong for her,
they leave the domestic shit far behind. Though fellatio for money,
drugs injected into festering holes, and deadly diseases hovering
everywhere are mostly left out by the veiled one, the stories make the
blonde's eyes big as saucers.

Distant-acting as the veiled one is, she keeps close track of all
the individuals who make up her world. She has her favorites and
pets who she thinks she nurtures as projects in rehabilitation. One
by one they betray her and throw away their own chances for a
secure future. Such disappointments have hardened her heart but
also make her a wronged mother rather than a purely get-over busi-
nesswoman. She can claim that each time she reaches out, it's re-
turned by shit and betrayal. But this time, high technology and
brilliant marketing will eliminate all of that. The new business, like
clockwork, will be programmed for fabulous success.

He waited on the corner with the razor blade in his mouth,
on the flat of his tongue and pressed gently up against the
roof. Maybe the wheelchair would fool them into thinking
he was an easy mark. But he could jump up from it using
his arms on the rests and get to them with that blade before
they knew it.

Ever since Casio had come up here to 112th to cop and
been taken off by a laughing teenage junkie, he never
showed up without that razor blade. The kid had tipped
over the chair and gone through his pockets. But now with
the blade Casio was ready for anybody. Then he'd cop and
roll up to a cab, which took him to the SRO hotel room
seven blocks away.

This time, however, he had an escort. Right across the street Baby Pop was buying a dozen eggs and two cans of Chunky Chicken soup. He was going to cook up a feast for Casio on their illegal SRO hot plate.

Casio copped just as Baby Pop was heading back. The guy who'd passed him the stuff he recognized as Carlos the hustler. He wondered if the guy remembered he'd been a manager at that theater where Carlos used to turn tricks. Casio hadn't been to the old haunts once since he got out of jail. And Baby Pop had informed him that most of them did not exist anymore.

With his stuff in his pocket, Casio gave Baby Pop a sign. The boy started to wheel him back toward their SRO room.

Baby Pop had told him that the *cabrón* who'd wasted him was doing really bad. He looked like shit, never turned tricks, and God knows where he got the money for drugs these days. But Casio kept planning anyway to get over to the old 'hood with the blade in his mouth and see what kind of trouble he could cause for the *cabrón*. The only problem was, he needed a cab to get around. By the time he'd spent his social security money on the dope, there was only enough left for food.

When he was wheeled into the elevator, he opened his mouth and carefully picked out the razor blade. In his pocket was the new bag, and upstairs a comfortable chair and a TV with cable stations were waiting. Baby Pop was standing in back of him with dinner in the bag. He'd cook it up and also help Casio do his shot if he was having trouble finding a vein. Casio made up his mind that as soon as he himself went back into rehab and got off the dope, he was going to give some serious thought to organizing finances. He really wanted that boy to go to college.

They hit their floor and Baby Pop pulled open the elevator. He wheeled Casio down the hall toward the room, where everything was kept as neat and balanced as Abuela had used to keep it. There was a framed picture of her on the dresser, and Casio had pressed the lock of gray hair inside.

All in all, things were going better than they had in a long time. What more could a man ask for when he had a roof and some food, no trouble from bitches, enough dope, and a son by his side? Whenever Casio laid eyes on his son, he'd think of Monica, whom he resembled, and wonder if Florida was keeping her away from drugs. Then he'd think of Angelita and wonder what she felt like as a real woman now. Spitefully he'd fantasize that her pussy was too shallow for his tool. He'd seen her dick once, and it really hadn't amounted to much.

Apollo hated the whole bunch of them. They belonged together: Huxton, Pargero, Pargero's mother, and maybe even his own white mom. Here he was, standing in front of the new club he'd built with his own hands, and they wouldn't let him in. It was just down the street from a restaurant owned by a fancy nigger who used to be a model. Between the two establishments they kept the block clean, sending out white bouncers with attitude to do hourly sweepings.

He couldn't believe who he saw entering that lounge. No one belonged to the old crowd. Those that were left, like Mercedes and Cubby, were all on Eighth or Ninth avenue, without any bar to go to. The ones going to this new club were white and collegiate-looking, with haircuts that probably cost a lot. It was all part of a plan, he realized in his most lucid moments, to clean up Times Square. But who had devised this plan, and how had he enlisted so many supporters? Part of the plan had obviously been what turned Forty-Second Street, the main drag, into a ghost town. But the joke was on them. Instead of getting rid of the dealers, hookers, and users of the Deuce, they'd scattered them. Now they infiltrated every block of Eighth and Ninth avenues.

As Apollo watched the couples or groups filing into the club, he noticed that some of them clasped theater programs and not one seemed to be looking for a hustler. Well, maybe they just had that white shyness but were different once they got inside. But when Apollo tried to tell the doorman he was a friend of Mrs. Huxton's, he said they had no idea whom he was talking about. This was a private club and Apollo had better move on.

Cruising outside was worse. The whitebreads traveled in packs. When you waylaid them on Eighth Avenue or threw them some of your strut, they got scared. They started to walk faster and said they'd call the police. These guys didn't like muscles unless they'd been made in a high-tech gym and were packed in the right clothes. Let the sissies suck each other's pussies then. In his day they'd been looking for real men.

He took to coming back to the block with the restaurant and club with shopping bags of boosted merchandise in his grimy hands. If he had the right merchandise even the yuppie fags stopped for it. A shirt with a Ralph Lauren label or the right watch style caught a greedy eye. He made some sales, but they were cheap bastards and never gave in until they'd got over.

Weeks went by like this, and nothing was easy. He had to sneak onto the block while the bouncers weren't doing their sweep. If they saw him, they'd chase him with their bats and trash his merchandise. Then one day he was nodding a couple doors from the club when what he considered the inevitable happened. A black limousine pulled up. But instead of a bevy of fags on a rented joy ride, a gorgeous woman climbed out who looked a lot like Angelita. With her was a fierce-looking middle-aged dude. He was so craggy-faced that he looked like he'd been carved from granite. He had a pharaoh's jaw with a Kirk Douglas hole in the center of his chin. His head swiveled like a gun turret and his eyes pierced Apollo like lasers. Then he took a black notebook from his tuxedo pocket and his hand moved staccato to jot something down. Giving Apollo a deathlike smile, he took the jeweled arm of the beauty and marched her into the club.

Who would believe the account of a man whose mind was riddled by drugs and months of deprivation? How likely is it that a down-and-out junkie with a year-old crime could even make any cop's list? But in Apollo's mind the man was Pargero. And the fact that he'd seen him going into the club he thought belonged to Mrs. Huxton only clinched the conspiracy theories in his mind.

There was, he thought, some justice in being busted by a cop in a swank tuxedo, especially one with a fierce and foxy transsexual on his arm. And there was, he admitted, no longer any reason to resist him. Jail almost seemed inviting, 'cause the world was mixed up and everything happened upside down.

If junkie queens somehow became real girls and rode in on the arms of the law itself, while cops went after drag queens and rented limousines, why shouldn't he have to pay for a crime he barely remembered the feeling of committing? Apparently you could never predict how your actions would bear fruit. Maggots grew on yesterday's live meat. Then the creatures sprouted see-through wings that looked classy in some light. Soon they too would be part of the dung heap. So if Pargero wanted him, he could take his body.

Like a faithful whore waiting for the beating from her pimp, Apollo waited near the club for the evening to end and the cop to resurface. And in the wee hours he did, the babe looking flushed and pressing closer to his arm. But though Apollo stared brazenly and sensually into his eyes as if to say, Come on and get me sucker and make my day, old Rushmore breezed right past him and into their waiting limo. The door slammed shut, locking Apollo out and leaving him where he'd always be.

If Pargero didn't want to take him in this megaworld of cold blank stone, he'd go back to the hotbed of the first mix-up.

He'd go home.

He went to the phone and called 911.

911? This is Apollo T. Nelson himself, and today's your lucky day. 'Cause my ass is the most wanted one in town. Check your books, and I'll be waiting for you on my mom's roof. I ain't gonna give you no address, and I ain't gonna turn myself in. Send the faggot detective Pargero to get me. He'll tell you I'm wanted for attempted murder, if you don't believe what I'm saying.

Don't ask where I am—I told you I'll be at my mom's. I can't even get in the club I helped build, so where the fuck else do I have to go? Only cops and sex-changes who hated their own dicks can get in now. Remember to send the faggot Pargero. I'll be waiting for his sweet face to come and take it raw.

There was no bread on the roof for anybody this time. It had been almost a year since he'd been up here. But even so, he nourished the mad hope that the pigeon would swoop downward out of nowhere. He imagined the touch of its claws on his face as he heard his mother two floors below rising to begin her morning rituals.

Her chanting floated softly in the air. He thought of her standing over him with the sun peeking through her blond hair. *The bird is eating out of your mouth again . . .* Although the chanting was saying something different, he imagined it was repeating those words again and again. He lay back and waited for the arrival of the bad detective. In his mind he saw his mother in her Indian cotton blouse and sweatpants go to the door to let him in. He waited and waited for her betraying finger to point up to the roof. The

226

hours were passing but he couldn't keep up with them. They flew right by him like something too high to grasp. Slowly but surely they lightened the sky, leaving him stuck in the same dark moment like the moth in tar.

He called and called for the bird.

Pathways to Vibrant Health & Well-Being

Profound Stories of
Physical, Emotional, and Spiritual Healing
To Encourage and Uplift You
On Your Personal Journey

Powerful You!
PUBLISHING
Sharing Wisdom ~ Shining Light

PATHWAYS TO VIBRANT HEALTH & WELL-BEING
Profound Stories of Physical, Emotional and Spiritual Healing
To Encourage and Uplift You on Your Personal Journey

Copyright © 2014

Cover Design by Jodie S. Penn
Editor: Sheri Horn Hasan

Published by: Powerful You! Inc. USA
www.powerfulyoupublishing.com

Library of Congress Control Number: 2014901142

Sue Urda and Kathy Fyler – First Edition

ISBN: 978-1-4951-0047-5
First Edition March 2014

Self Help / Women's Studies

Printed in the United States of America

Dedication

*This book is dedicated
to each woman who follows
her own pathway with courage and faith.*

*"We ourselves feel that what we are doing
is just a drop in the ocean.
But the ocean would be less because of that missing drop."
~ Mother Teresa*

Table of Contents

PART TWO: EMOTIONAL HEALTH & WELL-BEING

PART THREE: PHYSICAL HEALTH & WELL-BEING

Well-Being is for Everyone

Especially, YOU!

FOREWORD

The thought of a pathway may conjure up an image of one that stretches out clearly, perhaps with a few winding turns. However, the healing pathways taken by the women who share their powerful stories in this book are anything but straight and clear. There were detours, loops back, dead ends, descents into valleys, and hills to climb. These brave souls were willing to confront the profound questions about their lives: What has meaning for me? What do I really feel? What do I need to be my authentic self? Ultimately, through courage and perseverance each woman found her unique path for a life of authenticity, joy, and well-being.

Forging a new life pathway isn't easy. There are new choices to be made, even ones that may not be acceptable to others, yet these are the ones that are ultimately empowering and offer the reinvented life. It takes courage to follow your heart, do the inner healing work, and then take the outer steps. As I often like to say, "personal growth is not for wimps."

We often connect "health" with just our physical selves. In fact, vibrant health and wellbeing include four aspects: mind, body, emotions, and spirit. As you work with one of these aspects, the others will inevitably shift as well because we are whole beings and these aspects are interconnected. Meditation, affirmations, visualization, yoga, Pilates, emotional release work, joining support groups. All of these and more were utilized by women in this book as they found a new sense of life purpose and direction.

Where do you start? With whatever you are guided to do. Spirit is always whispering to us, giving us directions for an authentic life. Unfortunately, we are generally so busy with the To Do list that we don't listen until something challenging happens.

From the time we are born, others have expectations of the pathways through life they envision we will follow. The child's eyes, ears, and emotions absorb these expectations as they learn about life from parents, other adults, and their daily experiences. The positive events and the negative ones are all woven together in a complex inner tapestry of memories and emotions. The unconscious mind holds all of them and begins to run the show.

Have you ever done something and then wondered *Why did I do that?* The unconscious mind has pulled up a pattern. Here is an example of how our unconscious minds work: When I was working as a therapist, a woman who had inherited quite a lot of money the year before came to see me. She wanted to understand WHY she lost it all in less than a year through unwise decisions. We uncovered her powerful beliefs from childhood—*you don't deserve money, rich people are not nice, and you'll never be successful.* The inner pattern was unconsciously triggered and she lost the money. Once she understood the dynamics of the situation, her tasks became forgiving herself for the loss and creating new empowering messages about her ability to handle money wisely.

Patterns are set from early childhood—of perfectionism, not loving oneself, putting others' needs before one's own, feeling unworthy of success, expecting relationships to be difficult and fail, and a myriad of others. These patterns then setup pathways for our lives as we unconsciously struggle against them or continue to fulfill the unconscious mind's directives. It is a rare person who is taught authentic living and shown how to develop their unique skills and talents.

When I lead training workshops in Louise Hay's philosophy, we work on discovering parental messages and how the unconscious acceptance of negative ones has limited us in adulthood. This isn't to blame our parents because they were doing the best they could due to their own patterns.

In the discovery process we also find that many others in our young lives, including other children, also affected our feelings of self-worth. Were you ever on a play ground where another child taunted you or called you names? Whoosh! Right into the unconscious mind goes another experience that confirms "I'm not good enough". And because children can't process situations intellectually and emotionally the way an adult can, they often carry blame and guilt into adulthood for difficult events, such as a parent's divorce—something they couldn't possibly have caused.

As we grow into adulthood, everything may seem fine on the surface level, and even enviable to others. Others see a woman with a wonderful career or what seems to be a loving relationship, but have no idea that this outer life hides underlying emotional pain and distress. Sadly, this seems to be a normal state for many women. As the cultural norms have changed, women are attempting to "do and be all." They are doing their best to be successful, meet others expectations and look good, while inside they are distraught. We are taught to wear a mask - the mask of *"I'm OK, I don't need any help"* or the mask of *"Everything is perfect in my life."* We are taught to look good at all costs. And then the mask falls off....

Sometimes it's a slow process of building awareness that your life isn't working. More often, a sudden, unexpected event shakes you to the core. It could be an accident, illness, a partner wanting a divorce, or a physical violation. There is initial shock, disbelief, and disorientation. *This was not in my plan! This isn't a part of my pathway!* And because few of us were taught healthy ways to cope with these unexpected events, the woman is suddenly afloat in a sea of emotion, a place of uncertainly, and feelings of betrayal by life and even God.

As the women in this book courageously share their intensely personal journeys through these events, it will help you understand your own challenges with more clarity and less fear.

Difficult events happen to each of us at some point. Even though the emotional skills may not be developed to cope with them, there is a choice in how to respond. It's normal to feel like a victim at first—*why me?* However, refusal to let go of the anger leads to depression, helplessness, and resentment.

In her amazing little book, *Heal Your Body*, author Louise Hay lists diseases and symptoms, connects each one with possible emotional/spiritual causes, and then offers affirmations that help heal the disease or symptom. Anger, resentment, guilt, fear, and criticism are often listed as possible causes. Many readers find the connections in this book to be about 85% accurate for them. Recently, even scientific studies are verifying many of the connections in Louise's book.

When a challenging event occurs in your life, it is normal to feel fear and anger. But as the fog clears, there is an opportunity to stop feeling like a victim and let go of the fear and anger. Once that space is cleared, there is room to accept emotional responsibility. The women in this book decided not to be victimized by the challenging events they experienced. They began seeking pathways for healing in body, mind, emotions, and spirit.

These authors discovered a variety of techniques for their new pathways. Some began meditation to quiet the mind and consciously create a profound connection with their spiritual self, learning to feel the expansion and Oneness with a Source greater than themselves. This connection opens the mind and heart to a depth of

Inner Wisdom we don't usually access from the conscious, problem solving mind. Meditation offers a profound way of listening to the whispers of Spirit we might ignore otherwise.

Other women discovered the power of bodywork to release trauma. Many sought emotional support from other women, either individually or in groups. Unhealthy relationships were let go, and nourishing ones developed. Some did healing work with their inner child. They discovered that forgiveness of self and others creates a sense of freedom. And they began practicing gratitude, a daily conscious appreciation for all aspects of their lives.

My own shift in awareness began during a difficult time in my life as a stressed out social worker in a rough part of Los Angeles. To deal with the stress, I began meditating, and this daily practice proved to be my first step to wellness.

As I continued on this path, I discovered books that told me "we create our own reality." Although I'd never heard that growing up, the concept immediately resonated with me. I learned about affirmations and visualization and eagerly applied them to my life with wonderful results. Using these techniques I transformed my career and finances rather quickly. Manifesting a wonderful relationship and physical healing of chronic fatigue syndrome took longer! My awareness of the power of the unconscious mind grew, and I attended workshops to explore the connection between my experiences and emotions.

Another process I learned—intensive breathwork—helped me access and release old emotions. One dramatic incident demonstrated how the cells in our bodies store emotions. As I was studying a practice test for a psychology exam, I read a question about Phenobarbital. Immediately I began to hyperventilate and fear flooded my body. Suddenly I was a child of about six years old being told "be brave" as I lay on a hospital gurney being prepared for yet another surgery on a congenital cataract. Although in a fearful child state, fortunately a part of me remembered my breathwork training and how to relax into the experience to let it flow. I began to nonverbally comfort the child and tell her it was OK and natural to be scared before the surgery. For about 20 minutes I continued the intensive breathing, and then the fear simply dissipated. All those years I had suppressed the fear I felt, trying to be brave because adults told me to!

Situations in your adult life, like mine, will bring up the experiences that need to be healed. Learn to explore the roots of the feelings that surface. If you are angry about something that seems unjustified given the situation, look for a childhood experience that might be related. One woman I worked with found herself very upset at a park because she felt one of the mothers wasn't paying sufficient attention to her child. Exploring the roots of this feeling, my client realized she was still angry at her mother for not paying attention to her.

As you read the women's stories in this book, you will be moved by their courage and willingness to go deeply into themselves to heal the past and find their pathways to vibrant health and well-being. They took risks, learned to love themselves, and found new ways to embrace the journey of life.

You will be inspired for the possibilities of living your life in a more expanded and authentic way. There is great power in telling your story of transformation and there is power in reading someone else's. You will find yourself and your life challenges in the pages of this book. It will give you tools for your own well-being.

Begin to listen and pay attention to your life. Listen to the whispers of Spirit and be guided to techniques for your vibrant health and well-being. Be willing to love and accept yourself more fully each day. Start and end your day with gratitude and affirmations. Ask yourself meaningful questions: How is my body speaking to me? What am I feeling? What is going on around me that needs a response? Take a deep breath and quiet your mind and ask: What can I do today to bring me more joy and well-being? Start asking these on a daily basis and welcome the transformation in your own life.

Finally, as you read these stories, remember to have a profound appreciation for the mystery of life and allowing the times of "not knowing." We can only be willing to find our own soul journey, and support others in finding theirs.

Love and blessings,

Patricia J. Crane, Ph.D.
www.heartinspired.com
www.drpatriciacrane.com

INTRODUCTION

"A hero ventures forth from the world of common day into
a region of supernatural wonder:
fabulous forces are there encountered
and a decisive victory is won:
the hero comes back from this mysterious adventure
with the power to bestow boons on his fellow man."
~ *Joseph Campbell, The Hero With a Thousand Faces*

The word *pathway* conjures up an image in the mind that's usually a pleasing one. Perhaps winding this way, perhaps that, sometimes lined with flowers or tress—it opens us to feelings of peace and calm, bounty and growth. A pathway is a beckoning from Mother Nature.

The pathway in our minds is often unobstructed and leads us to a specific place—most times, a place of peace or a garden of Eden or a magnificent castle. A pathway in our minds is idyllic, joyful, and abundantly perfect.

The pathway that our authors follow is not always the one we conjure in our minds. The pathways they follow and write about in these pages are often so overgrown with weeds that they must forge a new path. Others' paths—abruptly obstructed by the likes of a fallen tree—are never to be walked again. Still others' pathways are so windy and filled with sharp turns that their journey is akin to navigating a maze.

And then there are those who travel a path so very narrow, it's as if there's no clear way, no sign posts, and the whole forest becomes a prison in which they are trapped.

Though each of them walks her own path and speaks with her unique voice, they all share a common bond—the Hero's Journey.

And what you'll learn as you read their stories is that each author is an incredible woman.

The Hero's Journey, as defined by Joseph Campbell, is one from the known to the unknown and back again, a transformational process from which one returns with greater knowledge or wisdom. When this knowledge is shared, it benefits all who hear about it.

Each of these women—our authors—has followed the Hero's Journey; each is a hero in her own right. They have traversed a pathway that's often brought them to, and then *through,* unimaginable circumstances, and here they share their journeys with you.

As you open these pages, I invite you to give yourself over. Yes, it may be painful at times as you immerse yourself in their narratives. You may find your own journey woven into their words, and you may wonder how it's possible that you share their emotions with them.

You may feel a twinge of guilt for living such a blessed life when others have been through so much...but mostly you'll feel a kinship with these women as you discover that their strength and gumption is not unlike your own.

You see, the truth always rings through, and there's no doubt that you'll see yourself and your own truth in these pages.

Each of these women is connected by an invisible thread and a bond so strong that we feel ourselves all to be one and the same— even in our own individuation. And now we unite.

I honor these women, so bravely baring their souls—sharing their losses and grief, breakups and failures, fears and shortcomings, mistakes and mishaps.

I honor them, too, for baring their souls and sharing what they've discovered—the openings they've walked through, the wounding they've endured, the pathway they've blazed, and the healing they've received.

You'll find much hope, encouragement, and optimism in these pages. You'll find joy, willingness, and love. You'll also find yourself.

As you venture through life on the pathway of your choosing, know this: there is always a way and it will be shown to you as long as you believe in, and persevere on, your own pathway to vibrant health & well-being.

With much love and deep gratitude,

Sue Urda
www.sueurda.com

PART ONE

Spiritual
Health & Well-Being

"We delight in the beauty of the butterfly,
but rarely admit the changes it has gone through
to achieve that beauty."
~ Maya Angelou

Healed To Be Whole

Yataye "Yah-Tay" Keaton

"Get out of the car!" I scream at my teenage sister Abrielle as I approach the passenger door of her friend's car.

"Who are you?" asks the young man sitting behind the wheel. Also in the car is her friend Raquel.

"How do you know this guy?" I yell at Abrielle as I tug on the door to try to open it.

"Just leave, don't say anything—just go!" Abrielle says to her friends and sighs heavily as she leans on the door and steps out from the passenger side. I don't give her time to say another word before I lunge at her and slap her across the face.

My God, this girl should know better! I rage in my mind. *Where's her darn common sense?*

Abrielle, clearly humiliated by my behavior, says nothing and walks away. I'm angry because she's not where she said she'd be. In addition, I'd received a call from Raquel's father telling me he'd found some inappropriate pictures at his house where the two girls were supposed to be studying.

"Get in your car and go home!" I shout, still enraged by her disobedience and disgusted by her connection to these inappropriate pictures. It isn't until I get into my car and drive away that I become aware of my extreme reaction. *What the heck just happened?* I wonder. *What's wrong with this scenario?*

It doesn't take long before I recognize that I've just duplicated the dysfunctional "communication" pattern of someone I used to know; someone who used to treat me in the very same manner.

From One Generation To The Next

I look up and there she is, standing five-feet eleven-inches tall with her right hand on her hip, in the doorway to my bedroom. My heart skips a beat as I swallow and think *what did I do now?* She has to be standing there for some reason—or so the expression on her face tells me.

I never know if my mother is happy, sad, or mad, because she wears the same look on her face more times than you can shake a stick at. But this time is different. As she approaches, she tells me she has something important to say and summons me to sit at the foot of my bed.

I make my way across the bright orange bedspread that looks like flames of fire and, with each move that brings me closer to the edge of the bed, my eyes grow bigger and my throat drier. I tremble with horror, so greatly do I fear this woman.

Not sure what she wants to discuss, I know this: I'd better be ready to explain! Even though it won't make any difference, considering my mom always talks and never listens. I always feel invisible, like what I have to say doesn't matter. I've never known her to ask my thoughts or feelings about any given situation—she comes from old school thinking that "a child should be seen and not heard."

My anxiety about being in trouble for something slowly begins to disappear as a different aura emanates from my mother. This isn't going to be our usual *Mom yells at me and tells me how I didn't do something right,* or *I get blamed for something my younger sisters have done*—you know, the oldest child syndrome...get the mess beat out of you because you know better, or *should* have known better!

She mentions *her* mother and how prior to her mother's death in December 1970 they didn't have a great relationship as she was afraid of her mother, too. Then she tells me she doesn't want us to have the same type of mother/daughter relationship.

Here's the thing, though—*we do,* and she created that environment and set the tone years earlier...

A young girl growing up in the projects, I'm already exposed to certain hardships based simply on the rough environment in which I live. However, my home atmosphere is a battlefield of the mind and emotions. My mother's very militant in her child rearing, and punishes me using whoopings and *curse you out* tactics.

She always finds something to fuss about, and I feel like I can't do anything right. And don't let my younger sisters do something wrong—she'll decide I should have prevented whatever it was from happening and yell: "You're the oldest, you should know better!" Her famous line is "use your common sense Yataye—use your *damn* common sense!"

I go to sleep one night, forgetting to sweep the floor or wipe down the kitchen sink. I wake up to her beating me and hollering "why didn't you clean my kitchen like I asked you to?"

"Mom, I forgot this one time!" I cry.

"I don't want to hear that shit!" she replies, "get your ass up and go finish cleaning my kitchen like I asked you to!"

In disarray from being beaten awake, I jump to my feet and run into the kitchen as fast as I can thinking *gosh, I can't get a break, she's always on me–dang!*

My mother knows I'm afraid of her. Frankly I think she wants it that way. I can't talk to her or tell her what I think about our relationship and how I believe she treats me. She's the judge, jury, *and* executioner; her decisions are made before she even hears the case.

"I don't want to hear it, *period!"* is her cross-examination. "Now get out my face, and go sit down somewhere before you make me hurt you, Yataye!"

As you can see, our communication skills were not affirming, and we didn't have the chance to enhance them because she died thirty-nine days after my sixteenth birthday.

Love You Like A Mother With The Heart Of A Sister

Eight years later, now twenty-four, I'm still dealing with my inability to adequately communicate and let my voice be heard. Not taught how to effectively do so—as it wasn't modeled for me during my youth—I struggle to express my thoughts and feelings, and often listen during conversations only enough to reply back. I have an answer ready and waiting in the wings because that's how I was conditioned by my mother.

Now in the Navy and stationed in Jacksonville, I decide together with my middle sister Mercedes to have our baby sister Abrielle come live with me. I'm excited and nervous—happy to have the support of the military to provide her shelter and a stable environment, but nervous because we've been apart for some time now.

I'm unsure how well I'll do as a parent, considering my own upbringing, but in my heart of hearts I *know* no one can do it better. I ventured into the world on my own—no mentor or leader to guide me through this game called life, and I intend to ensure that Abrielle gets a better start than I did!

About to embark on the road to parenthood, I'm physically prepared to handle my new obligations, but not necessarily mentally or emotionally ready for such a huge commitment. I have new responsibilities as a single parent—I can no longer come and go as I please, and for the next four to five years I have to see that Abrielle has what she needs. Also, I must attend school meetings and functions, and provide structure and routine, including chores to help her develop self-discipline and time management skills.

I experience the many challenges that come with raising a teenager and worry about her hanging out with the wrong crowd, getting into trouble in school, and not passing her courses. Also, I concern myself with whether or not she'll follow the guidelines set forth at home.

One day, after being told not to bring anyone home, I find out she allowed a male classmate into our apartment and I explode. Clearly she disobeyed the rule—no one in the house without an adult present! Without listening to her or giving her the chance to explain, I punish her immediately. Later I find out the boy came in simply to use the phone to arrange a ride home.

"Broken Little Girls Become Wounded Women"
~ Iyanla Vanzant

Shortly after slapping Abrielle it suddenly hits me—here I am perpetuating the same dysfunctional habits that governed my own mother/daughter relationship! This blows me away!

"God, please help me!" I break down and cry. On my knees, arms outstretched across my bed, face down, I moan as tears cascade over my cheeks. My heart aches desperately because not only did I embarrass my sister, but in the act I caused her physical and emotional pain. I'd injured her with *no* consideration of the potential depth or long-term impact of my conduct.

Without fail, I've repeated the dysfunctional "communication" pattern again, this time in the rearing of my younger sister. I begin to realize that I *am* compassionate, but I don't exhibit charity at home. I see also my unusual ability to understand situations from various angles, but that I lack the necessary patience and am extremely controlling.

The emotionally wounded young woman I model is in the parental image of my mother. For me, this woundedness goes way back—two, three, maybe even four, generations: My mother and me; my mother and her mother; my grandmother and her mother; and my great-grandmother and her mother, too, based on the stories I've heard.

It's so true—broken little girls do become wounded women if their brokenness isn't addressed, cared for, and mended. I see how the women in my family tend to carry that baggage into other areas of their lives and ultimately hurt the ones they love most. I believe this is what happened to my mother and, without fail, her conditioning trickled down to me.

A spiritual teacher arrives in my life shortly after this incident and my mending process begins. After much prayer, soul searching, and seeking to understand the brokenness and fruitless patterns of miscommunication, I gain a new perspective of the historical hurts that haunt the women in my family.

Through divine intervention, God reveals to me the challenges and hardships of my mother's life and her inner struggles. My ability to better understand my mother allows me to have empathy for her and to understand that she did the best she could with what she knew and had available to her at the time in terms of information, resources, and support. In turn, this knowledge aids in the healing of my relationship with Abrielle.

Over the years, I gain active listening skills and problem-solving solutions that promote healing within me spiritually, mentally, and emotionally. I immerse myself continuously in self-help material and seek counsel and wisdom from my elders and seasoned mothers when warranted. And through this ongoing process, I am healed to be whole...

ABOUT THE AUTHOR: Yataye "Yah-Tay" Keaton, Designer, Certified Coach/Certified Youth Worker is the Founder and CEO of From The Heart Designs, LLC. Her vision of bringing harmony to one's dwelling space and personal life created this "unique labor of love." Passionate about young people, "Yah-Tay" assists with clarifying direction, developing visions and creating plans that will guide them safely toward their said goals, dreams and aspirations. "Yah-Tay" is also a Natural Hair Advocate and the visionary behind Real Rootz Apparel, a clothing line and organization that champions African-American women, teens, and girls who have chosen to return back to their natural hair texture.

Yataye "Yah-Tay" Keaton, MPA, BSS, BFA, CC
From The Heart Designs, LLC
www.FTHDesigns.com
ydesign@FTHDesigns.com
855-4-Y-DESIGN (855-493-3744)

The Garden of My Heart
Robin V. Schwoyer

"Feed the trees, Robin."

With these words from my mother, I run around, scoop up leaves, laugh, and drop them at the base of our trees. One tree in particular receives my special attention. Extra leaves for the growing apple tree, which sits front and center on our lawn.

I'm three years-old and love the walks my mother and I take each day. It doesn't matter the season—winter, spring, summer, or fall—we're out walking. There's something in the fresh air we both need.

It's on these walks she teaches me to listen to nature; to be silent so I can hear the voices of the sky, trees, birds, water, and garden. Of course, at three, silence isn't my specialty! I want to laugh, dance, twirl, poke things, and imitate all the sounds I hear.

When feeding the trees though, noise is okay, especially the sound of fallen leaves crunching under my feet. Up and down I jump as my mother laughs. Right here, in these moments, are the beginnings of my life as a caretaker...and caregiver.

It's the early 1960's and my mother is a stay at home mom who had me later in life, compared to her friends who married and had children right out of high school. Often, I sense a loss or longing around her. It seems our ability to connect occurs around activity, especially outdoors activities. The apple tree is a focal point for many of our years together.

"A seed hidden in the heart of an apple is an orchard invisible," my mother says, remembering a Welsh proverb. When the tree bears fruit a few years later, I recall cutting open one of its apples and finding the standard five seeds. They bring her joy and make me curious.

My mother's oscillating moods require constant navigation by the family. My father is happy when she's happy, and evasive when she's moody. My sister learns to come to me for attention, guidance, and protection. I go to the apple tree. There I sit, ponder, and study the bees buzzing from flower to flower.

There seems a cycle to her moods, much like seasons for the tree. Fruitless times of coldness and emptiness; other times of promise and new beginnings as flowers and leaves bud in spring. Then the splendor of a tree in full bloom with its intoxicating scent of apple blossoms wafting through the air. Summer has its vibrancy as the fruit ripens and the tree fills with life, and birds and insects come and go, tending their nests.

The light dances across the leaves as its branches sway in the breeze of early summer evenings. As fall comes, so does the harvest, sometimes good and sometimes not so good. The leaves change colors and drift to the ground, bringing back the fun of raking, stomping, and mulching. Yet, there's a starkness and fear that set in.

Beyond BeLeaf

One year when I'm about twenty, we notice the tree doesn't seem to have the same vitality. My mother and I sip our coffee, sit nearby, and wonder if it's age or disease. She remarks how majestic trees are to her. They develop strong roots, withstand the elements, reach for the skies, and provide for us in so many ways that she feels they hold an inherent wisdom. I agree.

"How are you like the tree?" I ask. At first, she seems intrigued, and points to her many creative projects which have yielded successful outcomes, and likens this to fruit, harvest, and seeds. But then she switches as some part of her processes more deeply, and anger arises.

Suddenly, the sweetness of the apple conversation turns bitter. Rage overcomes her, and I watch as the leaves drop from her tree in a storm of regrets, hurts, and beliefs rooted deeply in a soil of fear and self-doubt. She goes into the house. I stay with the tree, tending seedlings which have sprouted beneath it.

As a child, I used to think the tree was dying when its leaves fell. An empty tree with a bunch of bare branches looks sort of dead. Then someone explains that the tree is just resting. Leaves come and go, but the tree remains. I wonder why with humans it's harder to shed our leaves...our beliefs...our hurts...our transgressions...our doubts...and simply know when to let go...

"Beyond BeLeaf" living is what I come to call this way of learning to move through the cycles of our lives with forgiveness and faith for new possibilities. Sometimes with trees you have to spade the roots to stimulate new growth. So it seems to be with humans. Sometimes, we need to cut our roots and use what life has given us as the compost, and accept change, allow growth, and soak up love like leaves soak up the sun.

My mother and her mother are ill when I'm in high school. I do what I can to help. My grandmother passes away and my mother recovers. I find myself in a care giving role to help maintain balance and keep the peace. Even in college I work part time and commute to be home to care for family. When my mother is diagnosed with a stage 3b breast cancer, care giving takes on a whole new intensity during the following years.

I study death and dying in a couple of courses in college and become familiar with caregiver roles and cycles. I begin to see my life through this lens, which is very helpful, especially in identifying tendencies towards co-dependency. Now in my mid-twenties, I feel compelled to be healthy as I go through this time with my mother and family. I know somehow that I will need to have the strength of a tree to persevere and support the others.

My mother struggles with her diagnosis and prognosis. She feels betrayed by her body and her God. I'm the filter and buffer for my father and sister, so they can carry on with their daily lives. My father has an important position in a chemical company, and my sister is still in high school. Meanwhile, my mother's sister also struggles with health issues and requires care.

Both are in their early fifties and face the prospect of an early death. How strange it all is! Again and again I go to the garden—to our vegetables, flowers, trees, and my saplings (I raise apple trees and Japanese maples to sell), and our beloved apple tree for solace, strength, and inspiration.

Days turn into weeks, months, and years with surgeries, treatments, and medications. There's the pain of it all, and the stigma of hair loss which really bothers her. Her hair loss is not like the loss of leaves; this tree is indeed dying in her mind.

The third week of her chemotherapy cycles are always the hardest for me. Her moods swing to darkness and the vileness of her words course through my veins like venom. These are trying times as I try to survive the poison while understanding the person.

Truth is, my mother's a beautiful person with incredible creativity and an old soul spirituality whom I love dearly. Yet, I learn later that abuse earlier in her life afflicted her to her core. Depression fuels her inward spiral and isn't helped by her fierce independence, defiance, and denial that she needs help.

Trees can face incredible storms, but not just because they're tall and strong. It's because they're flexible. All trees have a certain bendability built into them, so they can weather the elements. Woodworkers will tell you that they seek certain types of wood from trees that face the winds. It makes the wood stronger. Flexibility is not one of her natural traits.

One Of The Strong Ones

Mom passes away in September 1991, right after her fifty-sixth birthday. I continue to care for my father and sister, and provide balance for them as we move through our grief. My aunt passes two years later. I find this to be very bitter. There seems to be something relentless about my need to care for others while caring for myself.

Then the apple tree needs to be taken down. She's diseased and well past her prime. My beloved tree, who's been my refuge and my muse! I thank her for our years together, grateful for all the lessons she's taught me, and appreciative of the many quality moments experienced with my mother and family because of her: Delicious fresh apples; warm pies; shade from the sun; and simple moments of fun and admiration.

As it turns out, care giving is very much in my sap, so to speak. My interest in healthy life cycles and lifestyles lead me to become an ordained minister and holistic practitioner of various healing modalities. I create and lead a spiritual direction and healing circle for caregivers since 1992, called The Caring Circle ®.

According to a November 2012 report from the American Association of Retired People (AARP), 65.7 million caregivers provide care to someone who is ill, disabled, or aged, and make up 29% of the U.S. population. More than 66% are women, and 34% provide care for two or more persons. These people spend at least twenty hours per week care giving, and their stress levels are reportedly quite high.

In my life, care giving attains new levels, as I have a son with autism when my father—diagnosed with Alzheimer's—moves in. Primary caregiver to them, I have also the rest of the family to tend to and work obligations, which take their toll. I credit my early years with the trees, the garden, my family, and my mother's teaching me to enjoy the silence and the wisdom of nature, as my saving grace.

Before my mother dies, she reminds me how upset I'd get when we'd plant seeds and have to select which plants we'd keep to cultivate. I wanted to keep them all. She'd tell me to take the weak ones out to make room for the strong. I understood the concept but felt bad for the ones we plucked out.

"You are one of the strong ones," she'd point to me and say, "it's my time to yield and go. This will free you up, so you can grow in new ways. Take what you've learned and let it be fertile ground for you and all the invisible orchards contained within."

So, now I offer a gift sown from years of striving to remain vital and vibrant as I care for others. Regardless of external weather and circumstances, deep within is a beautiful tree sustaining us with sacred counsel and seeds of hope, yielding amazing orchards to be savored. We must choose to thrive and breathe deeply every day, celebrate joys little and large, forgive, let go, express gratitude, take walks, dance, doodle, sing, create, ask for and accept help, set boundaries, develop strong friendships, admire the trees, and tend the gardens of our lives with love—especially the gardens of our hearts.

ABOUT THE AUTHOR: Robin is a renaissance style woman being an artist, author, gardener, Reiki Master-Teacher, entrepreneur, inspirational speaker and retreat facilitator. As a coach and consciousness guide, she uses intuitive art, sound healing, success coaching and stress reduction to activate and empower a person's transformative process. Robin has expertise in caregiver issues, being a special needs mother, Alzheimer's daughter, and founder of the Caring Circle®, a holistic support group for caregivers. She is the founder/director of HeARTs for Autism®, a nonprofit offering creative lifestyle support for Autism families. Robin's great passion is for helping people to live vitally, creatively and abundantly.

Robin V Schwoyer
HeARTs Wellness, Inc.
www.PinkHeartsWellness.com
www.HeartsforAutism.org
rvschwoyer@gmail.com

Soul Food

Ericka Crawford

Why can't I stop eating? Why am I so attached to food? Why do I eat what I know isn't healthy for me? Why do I choose pastries over fruit? Why do I choose soda over water? Why do I eat the bread on the table? Why do I choose French fries or chips over the side salad? Why do I reach for food when I'm stressed?

God, why do I expend so much mental energy thinking about food? Why is it that some people eat whatever they want and don't gain a pound, while others who watch everything they eat struggle with their weight? Why does food take up so much of my life? Why can't I break the cycle? Why? Why? Why?

Always big—as in muscular—they called me "Big E" as a kid. Active in sports—basketball, softball, track, discus and shot put throwing—I loved working out in the gym and enjoyed seeing what my body could do. "Quit" wasn't a word in my vocabulary! Luckily I never had to actively manage my weight as a kid, and remember thinking that I never wanted to be fat. I saw how extra pounds limit peoples' mobility and negatively affect their desire to live full lives.

The Yo-Yo Effect Begins

As I mature into my late twenties, I gain thirty pounds during my M.B.A. program and another fifty over a two year period while working a stressful job that requires twelve to fifteen hours per day. After an eighty-pound weight gain—*how did this happen?*—I decide to change my unhealthy and obviously unsustainable lifestyle.

A new job at Bayer Healthcare in Berkeley, California, sends me west where, shortly after arriving, a friend introduces me to cycling. Within three months I drop thirty pounds and purchase my first real bike—a beautiful white and blue Cannondale complete with clip-in pedals and a mileage/rpm tracker—for my thirty-first birthday.

The new bike, in addition to my discovery of the Perricone

Prescription weight loss program, results in a ninety-pound loss in eighteen months. Stronger than ever, I love my body again—my cute clothes, the muscles in my legs, my extra energy! I vow to *always* exercise and *never* again become overweight.

Two years later I meet my wonderful partner and we decide to relocate to Portland, Oregon. Six months pass and I begin to experience knee pain that requires surgery. Nervous about gaining weight due to exercise restrictions, I see a general physician for a physical and to discuss my concerns.

The doctor enters the room, introduces himself, and tells me my chart looks great and I'm in good physical health. I express my concern about gaining weight while recovering from my upcoming knee surgery and ask for guidance.

He looks down at my medical chart and inquires about my family history.

"Is your mom overweight?" he asks.

"Yes."

"Is your dad overweight?"

"Yes."

"Are your grandparents overweight?"

"Some of them."

"How about the rest of your family—brother or sisters, aunts and uncles?"

I look down and say "yes, many of them."

"There's nothing you can do—you will be overweight too," the doctor replies.

"That's why I'm here," I protest, "I don't want to be overweight! How do I break the cycle?"

He looks at me and says "it's in your genetics—the likelihood of you being overweight is pretty high no matter what you do."

I exit the doctor's office deflated and angry—I'd hoped for a better answer than that there is no hope!

During the next four years, many life changes—including a long knee surgery recovery, a move to San Diego for a job with eighty-percent travel, and two abdominal surgeries for endometriosis and fibroids—result in a whopping ninety-five pound weight gain! Once again I've lost touch with myself and need to make some major changes...

I start Dahn Yoga where I learn to reconnect my mind, body, and spirit, which results in a forty-pound loss in six months. To speed up the loss of the remaining fifty pounds, I join Medifast Weight Loss Center, which turns out to be the doorway through which I meet my real weight issues once and for all. But not before I lose fifty pounds within five months, put back fifteen, and keep yo-yo-ing back and forth.

I realize that, while Medifast helped me lose weight on a set food regimen, I have not started my deep internal work yet. Determined, I recognize the only way to gain more power over food than it has over me is to face it head on...literally...I can't take it anymore; I have to do something to break the cycle!

Please God, there's so much I want to contribute in this lifetime, I pray. Thinking, worrying, and feeling guilty about food sucks out the energy I need for greater endeavors in this world...

The War

I plan a feast for my final battle. A little crazy, I know, but I've tried *everything*—exercise, gadgets, diets, etc. Now I sit at my dining room table, alone, just me and *all* my favorite foods from *all* my favorite restaurants.

The candles flicker as I gaze around the table at each beautifully presented plate: Filet mignon, potatoes au gratin, asparagus, and sourdough roll; lasagna, salad, and garlic bread; chicken Jalfrazi, rice, and naan; carne asada taco, and chips and salsa; cheeseburger and fries; Washington Roll (spicy tuna inside, salmon on the outside); BBQ ribs, macaroni & cheese, beans, and slaw. And, to wash everything down, red wine for the steak, Indian and Italian, margarita for the Mexican, diet soda for the hamburger and fries, and a glass of water just in case. For dessert, a cupcake with a candle on it.

I look around the table again in gratitude for being able to put food on it, but also with remorse for all that I waste while so many in this world go hungry. I pray for guidance to break this food addiction cycle, for myself, my family, and all those who struggle with their weight.

The Final Battle: Breaking The Cycle

And so my battle begins...my prayer ended, I become a conscious neutral observer, and the questions about food and drink start scrolling through my mind:

What beliefs about food have I accepted? What agreements have I made? What information has been programmed into my brain? Why do I have so many emotions around eating—sadness, guilt, shame, joy, pleasure? Why don't I respect food as fuel and nourishment? Why don't I respect my body? Why does food have more power over me than my will, spirit, and brain?

I watch in fascination as my mind settles down to focus on this internal battle, and open my journal to record my observations. The judge sits on my left, while on my right is perched the victim.

You shouldn't eat that! You'll feel awful afterward! Why do you keep doing this to yourself? You will always be fat—it's in your DNA! Why try—who cares if you're fat? Why does your weight really matter? You're fine the way you are! Why can't you simply stop eating? Why can't you be stronger? Why do you keep self-sabotaging? Why? Why? Why?

Tears stream down my face, and a bright light appears between the judge and victim. My message comes forth: *The judge and victim play out this war and you watch, instead of taking control over your life! Take back control of your brain—you're the master of your life! Food and drink have no control over you! Live in a space of joy, love your body, and be strong, healthy, and create the life you want! Food is neutral, not good or bad; food is fuel from the earth to nourish your physical body. Give up everyone else's beliefs about food; give up your inner critic and your emotions around food. Trust yourself and your body to know what's good and what it needs...*

Tears of gratitude splatter onto my journal pages and smear the ink. I notice, as I ask my questions, that answers come to me effortlessly.

Q: Why do people lose weight and gain it back again?

A: They're following someone else's regimen, diet, and beliefs about what's good or bad for them. People trust others more than they trust themselves, they lose the weight following a specific regimen but when it stops they gain the weight back because they never change their beliefs about food or themselves. The answers are not outside you, they're inside! Listen to your body—it will tell you the truth!

Q: Why do I eat what I know is not good for me?

A: Habit! Habit forms neural pathways stronger than your will. Creating new neural pathways via new habits breaks the cycle! Envision a mental image of a healthy vibrant you, hold the image forever in your mind's eye, and take action every day to create it. You get to create you! You're the only one who can!

Taking Back My Power

Today I agree to:
- Take back my power and no longer judge food or myself!
- Define my own truth and stop believing what everyone else has told me regarding what's healthy for my body and brain, and what's not!
- Listen to my body, and meditate to create new beliefs and neural pathways in my brain that support me, my health, and well-being!

- Choose foods that contain nutritional value and fuel my body to live well!

I close my journal and say a final silent prayer before I begin to eat: *Heaven, I wish to truly taste and enjoy this food and to let go of all judgment. I send love and gratitude to Mother Earth, who grew this food with her fertile soil, sun, and water; the farmers who worked to grow and harvest the food; the animals that gave their lives; and all the people who supported getting this food to my dinner table.*

I eat—for the first time ever—with pure love for myself, the earth, and all of humanity; for those in the world who are hungry and those who struggle with their weight. I take a few bites from each plate in complete silence, free from the usual war raging in my head. I blow out the candle on the cupcake, and know the war is over...

Reflections

Ending the war makes space for the light to enter. I'm grateful that weight management has been my issue to overcome in this lifetime, as it's been a great teacher and helped me awaken to live a conscious life. Sometimes I still overeat—gain fifteen pounds and lose it again—but view this as my reminder that I have all the answers I need inside that guide me and others to the light within...as we continue to nourish body and mind with soul food...

ABOUT THE AUTHOR: Transformational leadership and life coach Ericka Crawford teaches individuals how to tap into their infinite potential, and to realize and actualize the life they desire in order to return to their natural state of health, happiness, peace, love, joy, and abundance. Founder of "Light Leadership - Leading from within," Ericka draws from twelve years experience as a coach, mentor, speaker, inspirer, and author, and eighteen years in diagnostics, medical device, pharmaceutical, and biotech companies. She has served three years on the board of directors for the Southern California Healthcare Business Women's Association and is a Dahn Master (Energy Principle Yoga and Meditation Instructor).

Ericka Crawford
Light Leadership
www.light-leadership.com
ericka@light-leadership.com
760-212-4099

The Great Dragon Empress
Miriam Belov

The City of Light does sparkle, just like the champagne Kate loves. Born in Romania in 1922 as her parents fled Russia, she was just a baby when in Paris and had always wanted to return. Almost eighty-eight years later, in the spring of 2010, she is now in its midst. What joy! Statues everywhere, glittering in the sun. Boulevards of stately trees add a touch of green elegance.

We were all thrilled when Kate, now widowed, shared her desire to travel to Paris for a "girls week out"! Despite my sense of foreboding—worried about the long airplane flight and that a great deal of sightseeing in just one week might prove too much for her— my mother insisted...so off we went.

Our first few days in one of the most beautiful cities in the world prove to be wonderful—the Eiffel Tower, Cathedral of Notre Dame, Versailles, the music of French spoken everywhere, and the chic ambience enthrall us all. Paris by evening is just as beautiful as we sip champagne on a cruise down the Seine. In the Louvre, Kate and her entourage—her other daughter, granddaughter Maddye, and I— are able to get close to the great Leonardo da Vinci painting and smile at the Mona Lisa.

On the first warm day, Maddye and I travel to Giverny where Claude Monet lived, gardened, and painted. The entire day seems like we've stepped into an idyllic Impressionist painting. However, upon our return Kate is in bed. She'd fallen during the day, as well as the night before in her room. The sparkles are beginning to fade. She can't get up and it's painful for her to move.

Our flight home is fraught with concern. She's immediately taken to the hospital, where we discover she's fractured her hip! We're all shocked, as we had no idea her situation was that serious. She seemed so strong and stalwart!

An immediate operation and rehabilitation follow and I focus my attention on my mother's recovery. People tell me to expect the worst since she is old. But I refuse that notion, as does Kate.

You *Can* Go Home Again...

Three years pass—years filled with happiness and love. Kate lives with my family—my husband, Maddye, and I. Although she cannot move around the house as much or watch TV with her granddaughter after school in her usual seat on the sofa, she is content.

When she develops Bell's palsy in June 2012, it turns out the cure is worse than the disease. She's given steroids which negatively affect her system. The summer consists of rushing to the hospital when she can't breathe and a number of infections. Finally, after several weeks, it's rehab time again.

However, just prior to her scheduled release, Kate experiences two strokes. Now ninety, she returns home, though diminished in physical strength and mental concentration.

Years earlier, I promised my mother she'd never be in a nursing home away from us. I keep that promise. Comfortably ensconced in her cherished room, she is taken care of tenderly.

Asked what she enjoys most in life, Kate answers "everything!" with such gusto and intensity that I shall never forget it! Throughout the following fall, winter, and spring, Kate retains her sense of humor and enjoys her Coca Cola, a drink she's loved her whole life.

Kate deserves it—that and her beloved Chinese food! Our entire family loves Chinese food. It's a ritual we've shared together every week since I was just a child living with my father, mother, and maternal grandmother, and it continues even now. How Kate loves it–and all of us!

A devoted wife, daughter, and mother, Kate made family the center of her world—and she is the center of the family, an empress who rules with love. She taught us by her vibrant example the importance of family, honesty, commitment, respect, and that each and every moment of life is precious and to be savored. Yes, mother Kate!

"The Dragon Spirit Searches The Sea" ~ Tai Chi Sword

Through my involvement with the United Nations, I become friends with Madame Lu Hailin, the wife of the Chinese Ambassador and a most remarkable woman. Everyone from every country appreciates her charming warmth. She graciously invites a delegation of women to China to tour her country.

I haven't been away for more than two days over the past three years due to my mother's condition. My world consists of brief forays into New York City for business and mainly of moving to and from my mother's room. How can I take a ten-day trip to the other side of the world? On the other hand, how can I resist—especially since I was brought up on Chinese food and played tai chi for decades?

Off I go, and that spring my appreciation of Chinese food and culture expands! Transported to a land I'd seen only on painted scrolls and fans, I am enthralled.

Madame Lu wants us to explore as much as possible, including the many contrasting elements of her fascinating country. From trees planted in cities to combat pollution and flowers blooming throughout the countryside, we move on to experience modern China. We travel the high speed train from Beijing to Tianjin, fly around the country, and end in Hong Kong—China's post-modern international hub on the South China Sea.

Along the way we visit the Forbidden City, the Temple of Heaven, a green tea farm, an operatic performance under the moonlight on West Lake, and behold beautiful silks and carved jade dragons everywhere. I do tai chi on the Great Wall, which looks like a magnificent dragon undulating over the mountains into the distance—like a female sovereign motivated to help the world. Dragons in China are associated with wisdom and auspicious powers. The great dragon empress in China can represent the feminine divine, the center of the universe, the source of life...

All this, complete with two banquets each day comprised of the most delicious Chinese cuisine ever! The culinary excellence and aesthetic delicacy of the culture are amazing! Overwhelmed by the generosity extended to us and the wide range of experiences offered, everyone in the group agrees it's been the trip of a lifetime.

Only The Best

Upon my return, I see that Kate has weakened further. At her ninety-first birthday party several days later in June, she doesn't eat the Chinese food, drink champagne, or interact with any of us. She becomes more withdrawn which saddens me terribly.

Finally, though hesitant, I call hospice. The night before the nurses and social worker arrive, I have a clear "dream-vision." In it, my deceased father and maternal grandmother appear before me and say "make sure Kate is comfortable!"

"Of course!" I reply.

"We're here to make the patient comfortable," are the first words spoken to me by the social worker. I become quiet upon hearing these words and surrender to the process. Clearly all is in perfect timing and correct action.

After the appropriate medicine, Kate becomes engaged again. When I ask for a prognosis, the nurses tell me nine more days. Obviously, they don't know my mother. For the next two months Kate's constitution stays strong!

Bringing her the fragrant pink roses she loves from her garden, I play her favorite music. We laugh. I pray. Lavender relaxes her. We reminisce. I don't want to leave her side; every moment becomes precious.

Late one afternoon Maddye receives a makeover at a Chanel counter and looks amazing. We rush home to awaken Mom and show her. Hearing the story, she looks at Maddye and, without missing a beat, says "only the best for us!" Then Kate drifts back to sleep. I laugh heartily, for she's said that very phrase many times.

During this period I meditate with her often. Her consciousness intrigues me. In previous decades I'd shared my international studies, discoveries, and work with her, including various modalities of healing and meditation. Mother is already familiar with deep breathing and other exercises I'd encouraged her to use for her wellbeing after her fall in Paris.

Like a sentinel on the edge as Mother hovers between this life and the next, I use my knowledge now to help her transition. The atmosphere in Kate's room becomes so refined it's palpable. It is filled with such spirit that I feel my psychic abilities deepen.

The nurses are amazed she has clung to life for so long. They sense something special around her. I share my work with them. They feel the great love we all have for one another.

A majestic dignity surrounds her as the tunnel of light beckons her forward. The here and the "other side" compress into moments of now. It is time for Kate to move on. In early August she starts to change. Her complexion no longer pink, her body starts to shut down. But her soul shines on. I meditate on how to help her.

Shortly afterward, I receive a directive which then culminates in a beautiful vision.

The following day is Saturday, a Shabbat, and Maddye tells her grandmother it's ok to go. We have each said this to Kate to let her know we will be fine and take care of one another even when she is not here in the physical.

Twenty-four hours after my vision and a few hours after Maddye has spoken with her, Kate exhales her last breath just as I enter her room. I am honored to be present at my mother's very moment of departure.

Her passing has been a pathway for me to reach a state of vibrant intuitive wisdom and compassion. Kate's transition was the ultimate healing for her in a grace of release.

Kate's soul, after ninety-one years on earth, is free now as she drops her body. I think of her as the "Great Dragon Empress" whose glory shines on brilliantly, whose memory is a blessing always of the feminine divine, the center of the universe, and the source of life...

I compose and read the following poem at Kate's funeral:

The Great Dragon Empress

In between breaths Kate rose up into the Light,
As gently as a rose opens itself and offers its petals to the Divine.
Purity arising from a perfect consecration while clinging to Truth,
She was surrounded by Love as she surrendered her life into the great eternal embrace.
I saw her soul rise up through her body as a plume of light,
Shimmering, iridescent pastels: all sweetness.
It began at her feet and grew larger as her soul being traveled through and finally
Reached her crown: all glory.
I was humbled to witness. I was honored to help her on her journey.
She is now all Love and Light.

ABOUT THE AUTHOR: Compelled by her passion, Miriam Belov, MAT, RMT made several global excursions and then founded The Wellness Agenda. For over 35 years she has been involved in mind body spirit work, creating programs for countless individuals and institutions—including The Metropolitan Museum of Art and The United Nations. With a Master of Arts from Brown University, Miriam teaches via all media, corporately and civically. She is a certified Reiki Master Teacher, a public speaker who often leads meditations and a #1 Best Selling author. Miriam has appeared on various TV shows, hosted her own radio talk show and created *the download "Relax...Feel Great! Stay Young"* to help and inspire others.

Miriam Belov, MAT, RMT
The Wellness Agenda LLC
www.wellnessagenda.com
Miriam@wellnessagenda.com

My Resurrection
Stacey Hall

"We can't tell the extent of the damage yet, but she's sustained a considerable amount to her face and head due to blunt force trauma..."

I struggle to make out the voices around me, but they fade in and out.

"As soon as she regains consciousness, we'll run a series of tests to better assess what we're dealing with—but you can..."

You can—what? Confused and disoriented, I try desperately to open my eyes at least to see the faces of family members I sense around me. My eyes move frantically back and forth beneath my lids. My right eye feels like it's glued shut. I manage to squint through the sliver of an opening in my left eye, and vaguely make out the silhouettes of my aunt and goddaughter Alanna standing over me.

"Grandma, this can't be happening!" Alanna sobs uncontrollably. "Look at her! I can't take it!"

"Don't worry, honey, God is going to fix this," I try to call out to her, but can barely speak. The pain is excruciating. I reach out to take her hand as she turns toward me, but the expression on her face scares the hell out of me.

Oh my God, what must I look like? I wonder. In that moment I vow not to look in a mirror under any circumstances! With that, I embark on a twelve-day journey that changes my life forever.

My stomach starts to churn. Bile rises into my throat and I shoot straight up on the gurney, lean over, and vomit blood and what appears to be teeth. (I learn later that it's swallowed fragments of bone from my shattered face and skull.)

"We need you to leave the area now," I hear the doctor tell my family. "We're going to take her for a CT scan immediately."

Exhausted, my body collapses onto the gurney. The nurse begins to cut the clothes from my body, my head throbs, and I lose consciousness.

I awaken to find myself lying in bed in a small room with an I.V. dripping slowly into a swollen vein in my left arm. Alarmed, I try to call out for a nurse but my mouth won't open! I'm barely able to fit much more than the tip of my tongue through the tiny opening in my mouth.

Filled with fear, I tap the corners of my mouth gently. I realize I have to be careful or I'll cut myself on the crude stitches and wires now holding my jaw in place. I burst into tears, unable to hold back my emotions. Confused, alone, frustrated, and growing angry, I'm desperate for answers! How did I end up here—like this? As the tears stream down my face soaking the pillow, I lean back, take a deep centering breath, and try to focus...

Dream Interrupted

"Wow, Mom, you look amazing—like a real executive!" my twenty-one year-old son T.J. tells me enthusiastically. "Anyone would want to do business with you! Be confident and you got the deal sealed!"

"Ooh, thanks baby!" I reply. Giving myself a quick last minute glance in the mirror, I have to agree with T.J. I've spent hours finding the perfect power suit for this meeting, the last of a series to secure funding for my proposed holistic health center.

"Give your mom a hug and wish me luck!" I say with a smile as I grab my briefcase and head for the door.

"You don't need luck when you've got beauty and talent, Mom! You need a ride to their office?" T.J. leans over to hug me.

"No hon, I'll be fine. Besides, it's a beautiful day out—I'll walk to the stand and catch a cab."

As I make my way toward the main boulevard I take in the beauty of this perfect summer day and savor the place I've reached in my life, grateful for what I've accomplished despite many hardships along the way. Securing this funding is a pivotal next step in fulfilling a lifelong dream.

Feeling like a kid in a candy store, giddy from the notion that everything I want in life is mine for the taking, I notice a young man in the distance walking toward me. I check the time, realize I'm late for my meeting, and decide to call my associates.

I rest my briefcase at my feet and reach into my handbag for my cellphone. Suddenly I sense a presence, look up, and *bam!* pain rips through my entire head as my knees buckle from the force of the blow. I fall to the sidewalk and another blow bashes my left temple.

I hit the ground headfirst, catch a glimpse of the pipe in his hand, and see my own blood on his striped oxford button down shirt. He reaches down, grabs my handbag from under me, and looks directly at me for a moment. I catch his cold, dead, icy stare and see the hate in his eyes. Next the cold steel of the pipe greets my face with a third and final blow, and he's gone.

My head spins as I make a desperate attempt to drag my paralyzed, almost lifeless body back to my house one block away. I raise myself onto my elbows trying to get into a crawling position and notice the sidewalk beneath me is stained completely crimson with my blood. As I raise my head to call for help, I swear I see two enormous angels hovering above me...then everything goes black...

More Than Just A Pretty Face

I awaken to the sound of muffled sobbing outside my hospital room. I hear my son's shaky voice cry:

"That's not my mother—that is *not* my mother!" as if trying to convince himself that what he's seen is not reality.

My heart breaks knowing I can't comfort him, especially on such a massive dose of morphine, and I begin to cry. Suddenly I hear a familiar voice telling him that no matter how dim my prognosis, everything will be ok.

My body relaxes instantly when I hear "Mama Lauren," one of my church co-pastors and a woman I've grown to love as a mother, coming to check on and pray with me.

"Remember that you are much more than a pretty face," she tells me. "Know that God will restore you, but you must find it within you to forgive—not just the man that did this to you, but everyone who has ever hurt you, including yourself. Trust the healing process, and remember your church family is always here to support you."

True to her word, she alerts members of my congregation who visit daily, along with countless friends and family, to show their love and support. Having miraculously survived the attack, I'm determined not to let my spirit be broken.

During the next few days I undergo the first of five surgeries overseen by five specialists in oral and eye surgery, neurology, and plastic surgery. I fade in and out of morphine-induced sleep, and am told later that during this time the two surgeons who operated on me—both people of faith—visited me daily to pray over me, hoping for inspiration on how to put me back together.

I experience also a visitation: I hear the unfamiliar voice of a man call out to me, and when I open my eyes I find myself in the presence of not one, but two, larger than life heavenly beings.

"I am Michael," says one. Both are winged, with muscular Greek Adonis physiques, and tower more than seven feet tall...

"And I am Gabriel," says the other. "We've been with you ever since your grandmother Laura passed, sent to help you and keep you safe..."

They proceed to detail specific events from my life and explain how they lifted me up from the sidewalk "when you couldn't lift yourself" and carried me to safety.

"We'll be with you always...call us whenever you need..." And with that, they're gone...

Anatomy Of A Healing

Twelve days after my nightmare begins, it seemingly ends as I'm discharged from the hospital to begin my road to recovery. I return to my childhood home, mostly for financial reasons. I can't help but wonder how I'm supposed to heal here since it's a place of dysfunction and unresolved issues from past abuse. Afraid it will turn out to be a living hell rather than a place to heal, I have no other choice...

I promised myself in the hospital not to look in a mirror, but anxious to see my face I peek the instant I'm home. Anxiety quickly transforms to regret, then to sheer horror. My face swollen and my features distorted, I'm unrecognizable!

It isn't long before depression sets in. I can't sleep, and when I do I awaken screaming from flashbacks. It's as if the attack raises every demon from my past, and they rise up like corpses of unresolved issues I'm forced to reckon with now. Too much for me to handle, I decide it's impossible for me to adjust to life here...

I need an immediate change of scenery. Ready to return to work as a massage therapist, even if only part time, I start job hunting. Days later, I come across an ad for an opening at an ocean front resort in Montauk, N.Y.

"What do I have to lose?" I figure, even though it's three hours away from New York City.

I know I'm going to take the position the moment I arrive. The ocean views are breathtaking!

"If I get to see this every day, then this is exactly where I want to be!"

I'd lived by the ocean several times before and found it always a place where I most connect to God; where I shut out the rest of the world and hear God's voice with crystal clarity. Now I want to get away from it all, silence the incoming traffic, and let my healing process take its natural course.

Every day after work I walk the beach and rail at God.

"Where have you been?" I cry out. "Why did you leave me when I needed you most?"

Bit by bit, time spent on these walks allows me to find lost fragments of myself and to discover parts I'd never known existed. As I begin to converse with and reconnect to God, finally I hear the one voice I've longed to hear for years.

Here it's as if God—after a prolonged period of silent abandonment—answers my prayers. My walks bring about a rebirth and restoration...a reintegration of my mind, body, and spirit...and, in answer to my pastor's prayer, I find forgiveness walking on Montauk's shore.

Now, on any given day, you can find me on the beach here, dancing, and thanking God, Archangels' Michael and Gabriel, and my pastors for the fortitude to face my demons, the faith to forgive, and the courage to survive my resurrection...

ABOUT THE AUTHOR: In 1998, after graduating NY College with a degree in Massage Therapy, Stacey began her career as a Licensed Therapist. In 2000, she founded Essence of Life, a private practice offering a unique fusion of holistic services, combining traditional healing arts with modern medicine. In 2010, combining her skills as a certified coach with firsthand experience with violence, Stacey rededicated her career to helping women heal. Utilizing her unique talents, she helps women breakthrough barriers, transform old patterns of behavior to live vibrant, joyful lives! Stacey maintains thriving practices in NYC and Montauk, NY, providing Massage Therapy, One-on-One/ Group Coaching, Health, Empowerment, & Transformational Workshops.

Stacey M. Hall, L.M.T., C.H.C.
Essence of Life Holistic Health Services
www.Essenceoflifeholistichealth.com
Stacey.hall.eol@gmail.com
917-396-2758 / 631-276-1628

Walking Through My Personal Hell

Wendy Martens

"No, no, no, Jamie's *not dead!* I scream at my husband John. "It's someone else—*not my Jamie!*"

My eldest son is dead? This can't be true! We saw him only twenty days ago on our daughter's birthday when Jenny turned eighteen!

Numb, I stare into space as my heart pounds in my chest, my mouth hangs open, nausea overtakes me, and my legs begin to shake until they finally give way completely and I crumple to the floor. Like falling shards of glass, my world shatters into a million pieces.

It's my forty-ninth birthday—February 23, 1998—and this news simply can't be true! *Jamie's roommate Bill is wrong, it's someone else, and I need to go to New York to prove it!*

I call my father, repeat what Bill has told John and me over the phone, and plead with him to get us a car and driver to take us to New York City immediately. We collect Jenny from her "100 Nights to Graduation Party," climb into the limo, and begin our journey to hell...

The Early Path

The night before my twenty-two year-old son Jamie's death, I would have described myself as a subdued wallflower—a woman without backbone. Molded that way by my narcissistic mother and absentee father—who loved me only when I was the "good girl" who got good grades, stayed out of trouble, and never spoke back—I spent my childhood alone and depressed.

It didn't help that my father traveled all the time, and my mother and brother Steve bonded—*against me!* They would sit and paint and I'd try to join them, but would leave shortly after they'd begin to ridicule my painting efforts. They watched horror movies late into the night, and would come into my bedroom where I lay sleeping and scare me by acting like monsters.

One Fourth of July holiday, when I closed the sliding glass door because the smoke from the backyard barbeque drifted into the house, my mother—on the phone and distracted at the time—saw the smoke, ran toward it, and smashed into the door.

"You tried to kill my mother!" Steve screams at me as—only eleven years old—I cower in the bathtub behind a locked bathroom door. She'd cut her knee on the broken glass, and blamed me afterward for making her knee so ugly.

Two Steps Forward, One Step Back

I fall madly in love with John in high school. At least I think it's love. I hurry through college in three-and-a-half years in order to get married, and believe I've found eternal bliss. We wait a few years to have children and are blessed with two sons, Jamie and Jared, and a daughter, Jenny.

I shower the unconditional love that I hadn't received from my parents onto my children, who are my joy, my life, and my happiness. During those early years, we look and act like the "perfect" family—I'm the happy little homemaker while John goes to his corporate job each day.

But lonely and with very few friends, I fear everything and everyone—I can't talk about politics, books, or my internal hopes and dreams—my life is solely about loving and taking care of my wonderful children. I think if I keep them close and constantly worry about them, they'll be safe from all bad things.

Oh, how wrong I turn out to be....

"A Friend Is One Who Walks In When Others Walk Out."
~ Walter Winchell

After an autopsy is inconclusive about Jamie's death, we surmise the cause was Long QT Syndrome (LQTS) because we discover our daughter, Jenny, has it and it tends to run in families. LQTS is a heart rhythm disorder that causes heartbeats to continue to move farther and farther apart, which can trigger a sudden fainting spell or seizure, or—in a case like Jamie's—sudden death.

Losing a child is the worst thing that can happen to a mother. At first it feels like a giant claw grabbed part of my heart, ripped it out, and scurried away with it, never to be seen again. Unrelenting fear becomes my largest obstacle. I trust no one, and can no longer relate to John, my husband of thirty years. We start therapy together, but he's referred to another therapist and eventually quits.

I, however, am determined to change, and have to learn to trust my therapist Sue, a stretch of unbelievable proportions for me. If you want to change yourself at the age of forty-nine, you have to be determined! I bare my soul, listen to words I don't want to hear, dig so deeply that at times I think I'll *never* discover who I want to be.

And the tears, oh the tears—I cry everyday as the pain of my childhood, my marriage, and my loss come gushing out like the stomach flu. I can't sleep, I want a divorce, and I'm so scared and lonely that I can't concentrate. If I remind John to take out the trash, he retreats into his depressed world and won't talk for three weeks. Later, he is unable to comprehend the rest of the family's hurt and resentment.

When I tell Sue I want a divorce she lays down the law—no divorce or separation for one year from the date of Jamie's death. However, we'll work on my personal strength, which grows daily, and prepare gradually for my transition from married to single.

So, as I push myself to put the pieces back together in therapy, a close friend and I begin to walk five to twelve miles every day—sun, rain, snow, ice, or dark. We talk incessantly as I spill my guts about how I want to divorce John—I can't stand him and have no clue who he really is. His life-long depression has caused a huge rift in our marriage and family.

Meanwhile, I'm able to revel in nature and the changing seasons, which help play a huge role in my transformation.

Baby Steps

I can't wait the required year to ask for a divorce. Christmas of 1998 is a total disaster both physically and emotionally. John wants me to decorate the house, but I can't—everything is just too sad. When he buys everyone a bust of Jamie for Christmas, a feeling of nausea overcomes the three of us as we open this present. This gift— so bizarre in our minds—causes us all to seek refuge in our respective bedrooms.

I ask John for a divorce and to move out as soon as the kids return to school. This catapults him to a new low, which requires hospitalization.

"We no longer have a family!" my children cry, and tell me I'm the one who's destroying it. They stay away at school as much as possible and I suffer their absence severely. Friends stop calling me—a combination of not wanting to choose sides in the divorce and fear of becoming a member of my "Child Loss " club.

Working on my grief is complicated since it doesn't involve only the loss of my son. In my shattered world I'm engulfed in a cauldron of pain in so many areas: Grief over Jamie; my decision to divorce John after thirty years; the loss of friends; the sadness and separation of my two remaining children. I recognize my life is divided into two parts—before and after Jamie's death.

Again, my largest obstacle is unrelenting fear: of living my life on my own, of what will happen to my children, of moving into my own place and—even more—of standing up for myself and accepting responsibility. My feet seem cemented in fear, and I don't know which way to turn. Yet I proceed onward in search of my own power and strength.

At times the pain is intolerable. Often I find myself possessed by horrible bouts of loneliness and sadness, and scream: "Someone please help me—how do I run a household by myself, how can I go on living? I need help!" The only one I can turn is to Sue, who remains steadfast and loyal.

Standing up to fear turns out to be easier than I think. I make a pact with myself to do one thing I fear each day, no matter how big or how small. When my stomach turns to mush and the anxiety creeps up my spine, I say to myself *this is it for today, do it no matter what.* And, then I do it...

The strengthening of my fear muscle begins, and grows stronger each day until my workout always includes something I know I have to tackle. I reach a point—finally!—where I fear little. Oh, I'm not saying that fearful things don't continue to crop up, but now I meet them head on and discover most of the time that the thought of fear is far worse than the actual event. I am transforming from a wallflower into a woman—finally...

"My Father Considered A Walk Among The Mountains As The Equivalent Of Churchgoing." ~ Aldous Huxley

As the months and years pass and my conversations with Sue delve deeper, I discover a spirituality I've never experienced before. I fall in love with nature—it becomes my church and a place of prayer and solitude. I walk daily and begin to breathe in life. I switch jobs to one that's not only more lucrative but also fun, and I reach out to new and different people.

I fall in love with life and myself, learn how we're all connected, and begin to forgive my parents, friends, ex-husband, and others by whom I'd felt betrayed. I wake every morning with a smile and many positive reasons with which to start each unique day. I've learned to give love to everyone and, amazingly, to receive it right back.

I've finally reached a point in my life where I experience happiness and incredible strength. To be truthful, the journey is never really over, and I'm not saying my life is perfect—there are always new challenges and rough spots, but I've learned huge lessons from my son Jamie's death.

I walked through it all, and know now that Jamie is always with me and that one-day I'll walk with him again. Now I understand that learning and growing as a result of hardship has consequently left me more knowing and wise. It's these lessons that make my life colorful and enriching, and walking through my personal hell ultimately brought me new life—a life I'd never have known had that horrible day not occurred.

ABOUT THE AUTHOR: Wendy Martens M.A. is a Certified Psychology of Eating Coach and Teacher. Her desire to help people came after the sudden death of her son in 1998. Determined to change her life, she worked with a therapist to heal. Inspired by therapy, she got her Masters in Counseling at George Washington University. She started New Pathway To Health LLC in 2010, which combines Mind Body Nutrition and the Psychology of Eating. She works with individuals, groups and Corporations to address not only food, but also thoughts, feelings and beliefs clients have about their lives, bodies, and the effect of stress.

Wendy Martens, MA, Psychology of Eating Coach and Teacher
New Pathway to Health LLC
www.newpathwaytohealth.com
wendy.martens@newpathwaytohealth.com
301-602-9286

My Soul's Whispers
Linda Albright

Fear and lying—*my friends? How can that be*? I mean, I'm a spiritual leader, a dedicated spiritual student, and a licensed teacher of spirituality and self-actualization! My entire persona and purpose is to bring light and love into dark places—to show the way to hungry women of the world who need an avatar to guide them.

Fear and lying?

Oh yes. They're not just my *friends*...they're my confidantes, my guides, my go-to girls—my constant companions!

I don't realize I've been lying to myself for years because—from the outside—I have it all. Successful my entire life—that's what we *do* in my family—and raised in an upper middle class environment with doctors and lawyers and *really smart people,* I'm groomed for success early on and I live it.

Throughout the decades, from an Ivy League education to the successful launching of several exciting companies, a long-term marriage and the raising of three "productive" children...I have it *all.* Or so it seems...

Miraculously, I mastermind what most people would deem to be impossible—but as an entrepreneur that word doesn't exist in my vocabulary. I convince my husband Bill of fourteen years to uproot our settled Los Angeles life *completely* and move three thousand miles away to a lovely little town in the middle of Connecticut because I've had enough of big-city life.

Connecticut? Yes, a state so tiny few people can point it out on a map...and not only that, I think it's a great idea to uproot my newly widowed father from the home he shared with my mother in Louisiana for more than thirty years and move him with us.

So here I am, settling into a gorgeous 5,000 square-foot Tudor home next to a stream I hear gently flowing outside my bedroom window every night. One big happy family: A husband, three kids, two cats, an eighty-one year-old grandpa, and a growing business—all coexisting peacefully under the same roof. I have it all. Or so it seems...

The Genie Of True Happiness

Except I'm not so happy. The problem is I feel hollow and like *something is missing.* However, by the time my successful life is in high gear, I feel I have no choice but to stuff the genie of true happiness—in this case my soul's whispers—back into the bottle.

When I say I'm not so happy, I don't mean simply that Bill doesn't really want to move, or that our different political preferences make for fireworks at the dinner table on a regular basis—Obama lover vs. Tea Party conservative. Nor do I mean the challenges inherent in moving my Asperger's father in with me twenty-seven years after leaving home.

That's not what I mean at all. That's called *life*—which is filled with change and necessary adjustments, often accompanied by temporary sadness or disappointment whenever we choose to live big and take on new challenges. I'm not talking about these, I'm talking about the insidious bits...the undertow...the deeper soul longings that *never go away* no matter where you live, how much you weigh, what you're wearing, or the color of your walls.

Afraid to realize—let alone admit—my deep unhappiness, I simply ignore it. *How can I not be happy?* I implore myself whenever I have the guts to actually *ask* myself that question. In fact, I'm not sure it's even *the real me* asking the question...

Happy? Of course I'm happy—I have it all! The five thousand square-foot home on a stream—with a Starbucks only a mile away!—a gorgeous classic New England town, healthy successful children, and a business on the rise. What more do I need?

But am I really happy? As people and situations enter my life, this becomes a question I can no longer dodge. Some are sacred friends and guides who delicately give me the safe space I need to stare the facts straight in the face. Others are fleeting acquaintances planted on my path to show and teach me the truth about my soul and spirit.

Eventually I realize that because I don't have the guts to be honest, everything is *wrong.* Miserable in my marriage (and so is Bill), I can't fathom failing! I'm not a failer! I'm not a quitter! That "truth" was instilled in me *long ago*. Failure is something *other people do, not me...*

The only time I remember failing was back in high school when I didn't make the cheerleading squad. While at first it felt like the end of the world, eventually I turned it into a *good* thing by refocusing on student government, journalism, and community leadership. In the end, I was *grateful* I hadn't made the team, and learned that I'm good at turning even failure into success.

So here I am, forty-four years old, newly uprooted with a gorgeous home and a gorgeous family in a gorgeous town. Yet I feel trapped because—in my family of origin—we only *do* success. I tell myself:

Divorce is not an option because that's failure, so you'd better learn to suck it up, sister, like you've been told literally by a few loving family members. Simply copy the older, wiser women in your family who apparently know how to do this and you'll be fine. They survived—why can't you?

However, I have a problem. Someone like me doesn't know how to *suck it up* or ignore her authentic yearnings of spirit. Someone like me feels it's a *spiritual sin* to bury one's soul whispers. I have no choice but to begin to listen.

Soon the persistent, deep-level, habitual lying to myself—the lying that runs my life and prevents me from reaching true happiness—comes clear. So the lying stops because I choose to no longer live an inauthentic life and understand that thriving means I need to release both Bill and myself from the stranglehold of a dead-end marriage. And this is a good thing...until...

Fear—lying's closest companion—arrives with a vengeance.

"You're gonna turn your life on its head?! Don't you know you'll ruin your kids, and sink your business? And this unseemly news might very well lead your elderly father to his death!

Releasing The Genie

Somehow I plow ahead and do what I have to do. Spirit takes fear by the hand and says: *Shush now, come along—it's not so bad...you know you can do this, what they say doesn't matter. You know the truth and what's right for you. Of course it will work out in the end, you are guided. Step forward—yes, it's hard...yes, it's scary...yes, there is stigma and pain and judgment and unfathomable reactions from family members! But you know what's right—trust it...*

Finally, I hear my soul say: *I am here and you will not fall, you will not fail...have the courage to do the impossible...I...am...here.*

And so I do what previously seemed impossible.

Today I'm a divorced mother, daughter, entrepreneur, and friend who somehow managed to stay in my beautiful 5,000 square-foot Tudor home on a gentle stream in the middle of Connecticut. The three kids, two pets, and a now eighty-five year-old Asperger's grandpa are still under my roof. I have a perfectly imperfect life, one that hasn't brought financial ruin, broken children, or the death of any loved ones as I feared might happen. Utterly messy and wildly unruly, my life is aligned with my true soul's purpose and *I love it.*

For the first time—for as long as I can remember—I am happy. Truly deep down in my bones *happy...*

A quickening takes residence in my soul whenever I find the courage to honor Spirit's calling. I had no idea. It's as though Spirit says: *"Well done. Now we can accomplish some real work...now we can deliver your gifts, serve the world, and help raise the vibration of the planet. Thank you for showing up for work today. Joy is your reward!"*

As a light-worker, I feel it's my spiritual duty to align my life with my own highest truth. And no matter how scary, blasphemous, or unpopular it is to follow my truth, I know I must, as I have many precious gifts to offer and much work to do on this planet.

By the way, my longtime friends fear and lying? I believe they got bored and wandered off to take up residence elsewhere. How do I know? Because the month I filed for divorce, my income tripled my previous best month ever, and today I run a multiple six-figure business that helps women entrepreneurs make great money doing what they love. (The most I earned when married was $11,000 per year—I easily earn that now per month.)

My father flourishes—it seems he survived after all. In fact, despite his bent-over body, he recently built and installed a two-hundred pound tree house in the front yard for his grandkids.

And my kids?

Time will tell, but my worst fears about their ruin, depression, and insurmountable trauma have not materialized, nor do I suspect they will, as Bill and I have committed to a loving and compassionate divorce. Any maternal angst that creeps in is offset with the knowledge that I've taught my tween girls they have a voice—one they can use to right any inherited patterns that no longer serve. They need not blindly follow; they each have a beautiful song and the world wants to hear their precious melodies.

I know now that facing the *impossible* straight on and removing the self-lies and fears inherited from family and culture actually places me on the fast track to true freedom and healing. I know also that trusting my soul's whispers allows me to dance through the scary dark corners of my life to the other side where—intoxicated by the resulting light of true freedom—I flourish...

ABOUT THE AUTHOR: As founder of the Wealthy Woman Movement, Linda is passionate about helping heart-centered visionaries make good money with their natural gifts and talents, because she knows when women like you are financially and spiritually empowered, the world becomes a better place. Linda has decades of experience building successful companies, ranging from a chimney sweep business to an investor-funded dotcom. In addition to running her own lucrative company, Linda serves on the Advisory Board of the national networking group Over 40 Females, and is a Founding Board Member of the Copper Beech Institute, an exciting new center for mindfulness in Connecticut.

Linda Albright
Unleash Your Business
www.unleashurbiz.com
linda@unleashurbiz.com
860-550-2741

Shaktipat*:
The (Best) Shock of My Life
Regina St Clare

Shakipat: Spiritual energy transmitted person to person by mantra, sound, touch, voice or gaze—like a spiritual shock treatment!

Valentine's Day, Shantivanam, India, a Catholic/Hindu Ashram

I sit on a bench in a grove of banyan trees and glance up for a moment from Father Bede's book, *The Marriage of East and West*, as a middle-aged Indian man dressed in a traditional white kurta pajama catches my eye and approaches. I remember him from a few days earlier—I'd noticed his Indian style rudeness.

"Hello, I'm Jeff, may I join you?" he asks.

I nod yes reluctantly and give him space on the bench.

"You look like an American," he remarks.

"Yes, I'm from New Jersey," I reply.

"And how do you like Father Bede's book?"

"I love how he merges east and west ritual and liturgy in this Catholic/Hindu temple."

"Yes, my father was Catholic and my mom was Hindu, so it suited them just fine," he tells me, then shares that he's at the ashram seeking Father Bede's counsel as his beloved father has recently passed away. He confides sorrowfully that now, with both parents deceased, he's lonely and lost.

"I'm sorry to hear that," I say sympathetically.

"Never mind, what about you?"

"Well, right now, I have a sore throat."

"I have an Ayurvedic remedy for that," he says. "May I get it for you?"

I'd taken Ayurvedic remedies successfully in the past, so I nod my consent.

When he returns I stand, and he hands me a small white pill and a cup of water. I pop the pill into my mouth and, as I do, our eyes meet and a strange energy passes between us. Only later do I realize that a tiny Buddha has landed in my third eye and, simultaneously, that I want it out!

On my last day at Shantivanam, Jeff and I walk along the path toward the river and he continues his story of grief and grit. Forced back to India from his duties as a humble Catholic priest in a small depressed parish in New York City, and an only child—like me—he's faced with honoring his Indian father's will. His father's wishes—which turn out to be much bigger than he realized originally—include his having to marry and take on the management of his family's multi-national business. I feel sorry for him.

That night, my last in India before I'm to return to New Jersey, in my private hut I reflect on my most recent dream at Kodaicanal.

"I fell into the Black Hole of Calcutta," I tell my roommate Mary, though I realize I'm being absurd. However, my dream was so vivid and unexpected, and Calcutta such a scary and depressing place. That night—in my reverie—I revisited the dream to find a vast, deep black hole. At the bottom I see a tiny, vivid point of crystal clear light and fall asleep invoking the Hindu prayer: *Lead me from darkness to light, from the unreal to the real, from death to immortality.*

One Month Later, Mumbai (Bombay)

My head buried in the *Bhagavad Gita,* I'm having tea at Mahalaxmi Race Course in Mumbai, waiting for Jeff to return from a business meeting. Ongoing complications between the New York and Indian lawyers have delayed our departure for the States. Meanwhile, we travel the country on overcrowded Indian trains, buses, planes, and local rickshaws, and depressing Calcutta reminds me of my nightmarish dream.

Even though Jeff tries to accommodate me comfortably during our prolonged wait to return to the States, I don't enjoy this taste of myself as the wife of a wealthy business man in India. I have no interest in the races, rarely ever have my nails done, and don't want to wear the popular sari pants. I live on coconut water, creamy cool lassis, and biryani to avoid spicy hot food—perfect for my impending return stateside twenty pounds lighter with my Indian husband.

No doubt Jeff's inept childlike charm is growing on me. Our first and only sexual encounter is more humorous than amorous, and we agree it's a hilarious scene to save for our movie. Since Jeff has so many contacts, including Shirley MacLaine and a myriad of Indian

stars and directors—making our movie should be a snap....
hmmm...*Zellweger and Vivek.*

While I endure Jeff's business obligations impatiently, he encourages me to do something constructive. I choose a ten day Vipassana meditation retreat in Igatpuri. After trying Indian classical Kathak dancing, I decide to put that on hold for my next life. I have a sitting with a famous Indian guru and ask him what I should do with my life. He tells me to go back to New Jersey. *Sigh.*

Even though I'm beginning to realize that Jeff's shakti power probably landed that Buddha in my third eye, I finally get the Buddha out.

"In the future, please ask me before messing with my mind, thank you," I tell Jeff.

I reflect on the whirlwind of the past two months since we eloped from the ashram— the mysterious wedding ceremony with no relatives or friends in attendance. Since we needed to marry quickly in order to get back to the States for business, Jeff finds a priest and witness who speeds up the process and avoids Indian red tape. Still, we don't leave quickly and seem to be in a stop-and-start-to-go phase.

Reluctantly, I'm getting used to being married to an overwhelmed, quirky, former Catholic priest. With great personal concern, Jeff assures me the estate settlement is moving forward. So I concentrate on our plans to honor his father's wishes. We will adopt children, set up an educational foundation, and make movies.

I ponder how I'll break all this to my family and friends after forgetting to tell my former boyfriend not to pick me up at the airport.

Three Months Later, New Jersey

Home at last, friends arrive eagerly to meet my husband, the "guru." Armed with gifts, Jeff dispenses Indian jewelry to men and women alike. A few friends and family gather for a second wedding ceremony, stateside and simple. Jeff is the center of attention with his funny stories, charming antics, and his ability to make connections.

His greatest fan is my personal physician, for whom he arranges an appearance at a holistic conference in India. A close spiritual friend confides mysteriously that she's sure Jeff is "just what I need," though I'm not sure why. There are always a gaggle of spiritual friends present to listen to his crazy wisdom stories.

My accountant is another story.

"Where's the money?" he asks.

"In litigation, of course," I reply.

"Yeah, sure," he says skeptically.

A friend's husband, who happens to be a former mercenary, tries to convince me Jeff is not who I think he is. And my cousin is suspicious when Jeff lavishes his best pieces of jewelry on my family.

Sudden legal business complications force Jeff back to India in a rush and he leaves me behind to sell my little house. When he doesn't call I worry and begin to miss him. I revisit the tiny point of light and, even though I'm not Catholic, pray the rosary. Within hours Jeff calls and asks me to join him. Knowing he needs me, and armed with spiritual books, I trudge east.

Valentine's Day, One Year Later, Highlands, New Jersey

It's the anniversary of our first meeting. A fax arrives for Jeff, who's in California on business.

"Your father is doing fine," it says.

Stunned, my head is spinning as I recall Jeff's first words to me about grieving his father's death. I sink into a chair, close my eyes, and find the light.

I realize now that—caught up in Jeff's fantastical stories—I overlooked so much: How many times I used my credit card for our activities; my cousin's jeweler who declared the diamonds fake; and the missing CDs and family jewelry from Jeff's and my joint safety deposit box. I begin to understand that my dreamlike nightmare forewarned me about this event, and provided me the tiny point of light to get through it. I recall also the spiritual friend who met Jeff and told me this experience would be good for me.

"I will always love you...this had to be," are Jeff's last words in a beautiful card from California. Somehow, I know, deep down, that all this had to happen.

Sometimes We Have To Con Ourselves To Get To The Truth

I face my substantial material loss with pure trust. Once again, I enter the light. I'm at the bottom of a deep well and there's no way out. I focus on the light, and the sides of the well open like a cone, providing me a way to crawl out of this hole. When I arrive at the top, Jeff is there in his giggly mood. We shovel dark, rich earth into the hole and plant flower seeds.

I realize the pull of karma is strong; if there are karmic seeds that need to mature they will. I can either learn from my experiences of deception, or remain confused and angry. We frolic around the planting and I thank Jeff for all his efforts. Must not have been easy to play the con to save a poor wretch like me! I never see Jeff again, and choose to get the lesson and move on spiritually...I remember him as my cosmic clown.

Over time, I realize the deeper message in this karmic event was really about my own greed. I wanted to have it all! Someone to take care of me so that I could rule and not be ruled, and absolution from all responsibility so I could be the free spirit...but ultimately, in the deepest sense, that earned me only isolation.

How dangerous to be unconscious! Our karma can drive us to hell and we are not even aware of it. Difficult at first for me to see, now I know that not to face my lack of wisdom, or learn the lesson from it, causes more harm than good.

Now, my life is a kind of heaven on earth, and that little point of light has matured into my personal guidance system. A huge price to pay for finding my true self? Not at all. It's the same journey everyone must take to sort out what's true, real, genuine, and, most of all, to do it with true love and gratitude.

The little Buddha in my third eye reappears as the happy Buddha, with his big accommodating belly.

"You did good, kid," happy Buddha winks at me. I'll be darned— that Buddha looks just like Jeff!

ABOUT THE AUTHOR: Regina St Clare, Ph.D, Certifier of Virtuosity Leadership Training and Coaching; speaker, author, Seven Power Words of 3V Success; psychologist, specializing in group process work with families, on the job, and cultural groups to develop the dynamic harmonic for clarity, coherence and resolution. CEO of New Life Options, an accredited performing artist; Quaker, Buddhist, "recovering intellectual" and creator/champion of the innovative Love Ping Pong—the finesse of making your partner a better player. Regina and her life partner Frank (approaching the combined ages 160) are mastering the two ball drill—yes two balls at one time.

Regina St Clare
21 John Adams Ct, Monroe Township, NJ
www.reginastclare.com
rstclare1@gmail.com
732-668-6757

Renaissance
Kathy Sipple

The coffee's brewing already at four-thirty a.m. on this Saturday in July as my husband John and I load the car for our weekend trip to Madison, Wisconsin, four hours away. A forty-something husband/wife realtor team, we get by, but a declining market and being on call for clients 24/7 has left us with a general malaise and yearning for a different way of living.

More alive and hopeful than I've been in a long time, we have tickets to hear His Holiness the Dalai Lama speak and today holds new promise. I tingle with anticipation, imagining the spiritual enlightenment that will surely be forthcoming.

The shrill ring of the phone startles me out of my reverie. Glancing at the clock, I confirm it's 4:48 a.m. *Weird*, I think, *no one calls us this early.* John picks up the receiver, murmurs something, furrows his brow, then says "let me put Kathy on."

Uh oh, this can't be good.

It's my middle sister Karen calling from Detroit. She gives me the news:

"Julie lost consciousness last night. We're not sure what happened yet. If you can get here—you should. She may not make it..."

The next four hours are a blur as John and I race to join my family by the bedside of my youngest sister. We drive, mostly in silence punctuated only by my periodic outpouring of memories, musings, and outright panic.

One of my favorite people in the world, Julie is beautiful, intelligent, graceful, sophisticated, witty, compassionate, and philosophical. In short, she makes an impression. Highly educated, she's a creative at heart who works on documentary filmmaking in her spare time and teaches ballroom dancing to pay the bills.

I love Julie as both a sister and a friend, and respect her in a way others might deem unusual for the eldest child to feel about the youngest. There's much I don't know about her—not for lack of interest on my part, but because she's always been cool and mysterious, even to those of us who think we know her well.

"I won a log rolling contest at the lumberjack event in Alaska—no big deal," she told the family, allowing us a mere glimpse into her wild, adventurous, colorful world. At seventeen she won a Caribbean cruise limbo contest, and was rewarded a bottle of rum for making first place. Once she traveled to Amsterdam, arrived at three a.m., and realized her "hotel" room was actually a houseboat. Her life is a mosaic of similar stories. I always assume she has so much to tell, there's simply no way for her to share it all.

Julie's flirted with danger before, but always ended up okay. I pray this is one of those lucky times. Now thirty-seven, she's slowed down a little, but I wonder if she overdid it with partying...that explanation soothes me—it seems manageable. Maybe Karen was being overly dramatic? I doubt it, yet hope so.

Raindrops pummel the windshield as hot tears stream down my face, and I imagine the unimaginable. But if anybody has the spunk to get through this, she does—I can't imagine our family without her.

Symbol Of Hope

Driving into the city, I see the Renaissance Center—Detroit 's iconic landmark building, the tallest in Michigan—originally conceived by Henry Ford II and financed primarily by Ford Motor Company. Built in 1970, it remains a symbol of hope for better times ahead for Detroit and its citizens.

Our arrival at Henry Ford Hospital feels surreal. It's an oasis of quiet, urgent competence emerging from a streetscape of burned out, abandoned buildings. People in the street look like they've seen better days.

John and I join my parents, my sister Karen, and Julie's boyfriend Norm, already gathered in the neurological intensive care unit waiting room. Doctors are busy with Julie and, after a round of heartfelt hugs, we process what's known so far:

Julie complained of nausea and a severe headache to Norm last night. She told him to call an ambulance before falling unconscious. At the hospital a team of neurosurgeons discovered in her brain an arteriovenous malformation (AVM)—a congenital condition she's likely had since birth. An abnormal collection of blood vessels, the AVM ruptured suddenly, causing a condition similar to a stroke.

The situation required immediate surgery to remove a large menacing blood clot, and though Julie still needs further surgery to repair the blood vessels in her brain, her condition is not yet stable enough. Doctors predict she'll need weeks—even months—to regain enough strength to withstand this surgery. Even then, there's a thirty percent chance she won't survive, and no telling yet how much brain damage has occurred.

Scanning the worried faces, I feel the love we all have for Julie and one another. She *has* to make it—failure is not an option! "Team Julie" begins with the six of us. We don't know how long this effort will last or exactly how we'll each contribute, but we intuit our strong bond and know we'll do whatever we can and stay as long as it takes.

I step into the role of communicator and craft an email message to let others know what's happening. As I write, I realize I'm woefully unprepared to explain what an AVM is, and how it happened. But I do it. The email isn't great, but I can't imagine having the same phone conversation over and over, so email it is for now...

I have about forty email addresses for family members and some friends I know will want to be kept in the loop. But I don't know all of my sister's co-workers, friends, etc. Why would I? I hit the send button and pray.

Sending Out An S.O.S.

It's not long before well-meaning friends and family call our cell phones, wanting more details, and asking how they can help. Email access is limited and we have to restrict cell phone usage to when we're not in Julie's room, so communication is challenging. We need a better way to handle this. I take a walk to get some air.

In the hospital lobby I notice a poster for CarePages.com, a blog site where a patient's family can create one online central place to share updates about a patient's condition. I sign up immediately.

In the movies, when a patient comes out of a coma, it's often dramatic and sudden. In Julie's case it happens gradually and takes several weeks. She regains movement first in her eyes, then limbs, then her mouth, and finally forms words—all as she gradually awakens. It will be several months before she speaks, begins physical therapy, and relearns to walk. It will be six months before she returns home.

During those six months I report Julie's successes, ask for and receive help, prayers, coordination of housing and food for "Team Julie," advice on surgery, insurance, rehab centers, and more on CarePages. Visitors from Motown to across the U.S. and abroad check Julie's progress. We consider each visit to the site and every comment a prayer for Julie. Followers, including classmates, neighbors, coworkers, friends, and family—even members of her medical team and family members of patients we meet in ICU—grow to more than 500 people. I help several other families start their own CarePages as well.

Throughout the fall reports of the nation's financial crisis continue to air on the nightly news. Bank bailouts and a 22% unemployment rate in Detroit—the worst in the nation—paint a bleak picture, for sure, but despite this, we feel blessed to have Julie with us. Every day is precious and nothing impossible.

The word "renaissance" means rebirth in French and is an apt name for what we experience during Julie's awakening. Julie amazes us with her spirit of determination. She works hard, never complains, and focuses on making the most of each day. She watches the summer Olympics from Beijing when alone in her room, and I wonder if she draws strength from seeing athletes compete for the gold—goodness knows she works every bit as hard as they do.

In September she asks me to procure an absentee ballot so she can vote for Barack Obama in the upcoming election. My heart smiles to see her re-engage in civics as she struggles still with basics like talking and walking. I start to let myself believe she'll be alright.

A New Day...

From the first posting on CarePages a few days after Julie's brain hemorrhage in July 2008 to now—more than five years later—Julie's following grew to 516 individuals, 27,117 virtual visits, and more than 2,261 messages of support, love, and affection.

The day Julie's released from her physical rehabilitation facility in January 2009 her room is abuzz with family members, a dozen friends and hospital staff, and a Detroit Free Press daily newspaper reporter and photographer. Many present didn't know Julie prior to her brain bleed but came to know her through the blog, about which the Detroit Free Press wrote an article that included a picture of Julie and focused on how her CarePages blog helped us through a difficult time. Julie waves goodbye to the "paparazzi," as she jokingly calls the press.

Back home again, I feel out of place. Fall 2008 all but killed the real estate market and selling homes is not an option. I realize both Julie and Detroit have taught me a few lessons about reinvention. Just as Detroit can no longer afford to rely on the auto industry for its sustenance, Julie can no longer work as a ballroom dancer. Detroit—gritty, talented, and risky—is a breeding ground for innovation, as was Julie's triumphant struggle against the odds. Her indomitable spirit encourages me to reach within and strive to reinvent myself.

Before long, word gets out about my own story, and a public radio station in Chicago invites me for a live interview. A month later I'm asked to present seminars for business owners. By the end of 2009, I'm voted "Indiana's Most Influential Woman in Social Media." Wow, I'm doing what I love, helping people, and earning a living at it! How wonderful!

Five years later, my social media business continues to thrive and I concentrate now on my passions—natural health, the environment, and the arts. Happy, healthy, and more fulfilled than ever, I don't think my change in career would have been possible if Julie's situation hadn't required my full attention. Turns out the renaissance I needed didn't include the Dalai Lama at all...

ABOUT THE AUTHOR: Kathy Sipple is a fusion of business coach, story teller, public speaker, tree hugger and marketing professional. Excited by the opportunity of social media for business, Sipple formed "My Social Media Coach" in 2009 with the mission of making social media marketing understandable and manageable for entrepreneurs and other small business owners. Kathy resides in Valparaiso, Indiana (just outside Chicago) with her husband John. She holds a B.A. in Economics from the University of Michigan in Ann Arbor and is a member of Mensa. She is a reiki master/teacher, an avid hiker, nature photographer and community gardener.

Kathy Sipple
My Social Media Coach
www.mysocialmediacoach.com
kathy@mysocialmediacoach.com
219-440-4620

God Only Takes
The Very Best

Tracey Cox

My husband Shawn and I awaken with a start to the sound of a car backing into our driveway.

"There's a car or truck in our driveway," Shawn says, alarmed.

"It's ok," I whisper sleepily to him. "Just a car turning around in our driveway—happens all the time..."

We both fall back asleep until 1:30 a.m. when I wake suddenly, this time to a gurgling, choking noise. I nudge Shawn to get him to stop, but he doesn't respond.

"Shawn, you're too loud," I say, as I nudge him gently once again. When I don't hear his normal response—"can you please stop"—I get up and turn on my bedside light. I call his name again to wake him, but I can't. Alarmed, I pad down the hall to get our middle son Jabari, and ask him to wake Jelani, our eldest son, because Daddy's unresponsive.

Why isn't he responding? I wonder. I take his pulse and, though it's shallow, he's still breathing and in my mind I figure that means he'll be alright. Jelani comes in and begins CPR on his dad, and I ask Jabari to call 911.

The police officers arrive and one questions us about whether or not Shawn smokes or drinks. I recognize one officer who used to live around the corner from us, and tell them Shawn was neither a smoker nor a drinker. He ushers our sons off the bed and, as the medics perform CPR I keep an eye on my children, the youngest two of whom are still asleep in the house.

Finally, it's clear they're going to take him to the hospital and I go downstairs to gather my things. The officer who knows us tells my sons and me to be prepared because Shawn doesn't look good.

"Thank you, and I hear everything you are saying officer, but we operate on faith in this house!" I respond. "Now if you'll excuse me, I have to get to the hospital."

"Yes, ma'am," he replies. "Please be careful driving."

The ambulance has already departed, so I get into my car and drive to hospital praying all the while *Lord let him be alright!* There's no one else on the road, and I call my cousin Nicole—a nurse at the hospital to which they're taking Shawn—to tell her what happened. She stays on the phone with me until I arrive.

It's funny, I remember getting out of my car to walk into emergency room and how it seemed to take forever to get to the door. Inside, I'm directed to Shawn's room and, as I approach the door a doctor comes out.

Lord let him be wide wake and sitting up waiting for me! I pray.

But to my dismay when I pull the curtain open around his bed, Shawn is covered up under a white sheet. I notice eight nurses in the room and sit down on a chair to wait for a doctor to arrive and tell me what happened. Finally, one of the nurses speaks.

"You know he's gone..."

I look up at her. "Yes, I know."

"Is there someone I can call for you?"

I ask her to call Nicole, my cousin who works at the hospital. Meanwhile, I walk over to my beloved husband and uncover him. As I look at him, talk to him, and touch him, I think *what's wrong—why aren't you saying anything?* I bend down to hug and kiss him, and behind me I hear the soft crying of a nurse who's watching me cradle him. I wish he'd open his eyes, tell me he loves me, and that all will be well.

Finally, they ask if I'll sit outside while they prepare to move him. I comply, and as I move outside I take a long deep breath and pray to God for comfort and strength to be able to get through this. Then I begin to make phone calls.

Always Friends

Shawn and I meet at the South Second Street Youth Center pre-school in Plainfield, New Jersey, where his mother Veronica Cox is the director and my nana Margaret Smith works with her. He used to tell everyone I'd be his wife one day since he was going to marry me.

"No I'm not, little boy!" I'd respond.

My family and I visit cousins who live around the corner from

Shawn. My family jokes that he can smell me from far away—he always seems to know when I'm there! My cousin laughs and takes bets to see how long before Shawn comes walking around the corner.

"He's *not* coming here!" I protest, when suddenly the door bell rings and it's him.

"Tracey, you have company!" my cousin yells. Shawn comes in for a while and sometimes we go to the movies together. My sister and usually I go along on school trips, and one day we're on the same bus as Shawn for a class trip to the Bronx Zoo.

He stares at me the whole time. I remember looking at him, giggling, and turning away with a smile. He smiles too—he always has such a beautiful smile and I love his happy cheerful personality.

Always friends, though we live in different towns—I'm in Piscataway until my sophomore year in high school when my family moves to his hometown of Plainfield—I remember his shock upon seeing me on my first day at Plainfield High School.

"What are you doing here? he asks me.

We graduate from high school together in 1985, marry in 1992, and are together for twenty-seven amazing years.

God Needed Another Angel

The medical examiner comes to me the morning after and says an autopsy has to be done because Shawn was young and it definitely wasn't a heart attack. They tested for food poisoning and a host of other things, but he says Shawn's cause of death was a natural one.

Later, the medical examiner sits with me for two and a half hours and explains that although Shawn's cause of death was not a heart attack, the electrical impulse in his heart was interrupted. He says he's dumbfounded because Shawn was forty-three, didn't drink, didn't smoke, and was athletic. He tells me he feels badly because he doesn't have a better explanation.

But, you know, God always knows best, and the man who's been my husband, my friend, my everything, has now been called home by God, and I have to plan a funeral for a forty-three year-old healthy man.

Had I not had the faith I have—my faith in God, trust in the power of prayer, and a strong will—I might not have survived Shawn's passing. Not a day goes by that I don't think *I wish he was here*...I have my moments when I scream "this is unbelievable!" It *still* seems so surreal to me! There are days I cry, and wish I could stay in bed and not come out—days when I say to myself *I can't do this!*

The only way I can deal with it is to assume that God needed another angel...does that make me feel better? Not necessarily...I stay strong also because—forty-three when it happens—our children are nineteen, sixteen, and turning eleven. I'm a full time stay-at-home mom and soon I have to go to work full time. It's difficult to continue to give my boys the life to which they are accustomed, and I fight not to have the pressure of being their sole provider now.

I also have attitude—my temperament is raised—when I hear women say "oh, I suffered a death," when they mean a divorce. I don't have the option of reconciliation, I have to go to a gravesite and talk to a stone—that's what I have to deal with. If someone had told me a month or two before that this would happen, I would have said "not to my husband!" It was a normal time in our household and this came out of the blue.

Three Years Later

Our household still grieves, especially in November when I always had Shawn home for the entire month. He worked the Monday and Tuesday of Thanksgiving week, but didn't have to return to work until the following year. Having him home—the cuddling, the hugs, the kisses—I miss all of that...

I have every stitch of my husband's clothing still in the house—if I had to get rid of it, I'd feel like I'm getting rid of him. Subconsciously, I'm not ready to let go—he's been my life. I don't know anything else, he's always been my best friend, a wonderful husband, and awesome dad. Women would kill for a husband like mine. I was a lucky woman to have a man like that, and I couldn't have asked for a better husband.

I can't teach my sons how to be men, and I worry often—how do I get them to be the young men that I want to raise them to be? I can't show them how to be those things. I struggle with the loss of him, not a day goes by that I don't say if he was here things would be a little easier. I'm left to take care of a whole entire house, to make decisions I would have made with him. I wasn't the kind of stay at home mother who let him do everything.

Often people say to me "I couldn't do what you do, you're very strong." I don't believe that God has shown me the reason why he's taken Shawn, and I prayed to write a book, and God has answered my prayers. It's tough being a single parent. I grew up in a single parent home, and I certainly didn't want that for my boys. We were going to grow old together.

Here I am three years later, I still go about my day though some are better than others. When I don't want to, I don't do, when I need to be quiet, I pray an awful lot because that's what gets me through the day. My eldest son Jelani is the spitting image of his father. Even though his Shawn is physically not in sight, we see him still through our son, and in spirit—and we know he'll be with us forever.

Am I bitter? No, because I believe God only takes the very best...

ABOUT THE AUTHOR: Tracey Cox is currently employed by Rutgers University, and is a Mother of three sons. She was lucky enough to be married to the love of her life Shawn, and all their years together will forever live on in her memory. Tracey considers herself to be an inspirational person who is dedicated to any and everything she put her heart and soul into. Tracey, currently lives in Plainfield, NJ, and enjoys all the time she gets to spend with her family and friends.

Tracey Cox
Coxbabygyrl34@gmail.com
www.Serenityhealing411.blogspot.com
908-969-1779

Spiritual Surfer

Cheryl DeVaul

"You smell like death—what are you going to do about it?" asks Pat. As cruel as that may sound, it's actually her way of showing concern for me. The chief operating officer and my boss since 2005, Pat is a force of nature. The best negotiator I've ever met, she's direct and her humor often smacks me in the face with truth. Twenty years ago she battled breast cancer and survived.

It's been a rough year at work and the contracts I oversee require air travel. And, for some reason I attribute to having moved furniture, I experience constant lower back pain. Doesn't stop me from working, though it keeps me awake most of the night.

During performance appraisal time in 2009, Pat says it's time I think about running a company. I never say no to Pat because it does no good. In fact, I learn early on never to complain about my workload because I always end up walking out of her office shaking my head at a new assignment, wondering how I'll get all the work done. But I always end up learning a great deal, as Pat is a phenomenal business woman from whom I've learned much over the past five years.

A few weeks later, Pat calls me into her office to inform me we'll start meeting with the owners of a small business to purchase a company she wants me to run. As if I don't have enough to do as head of human resources and overseeing staffing contracts! But I spend much of my life trying not to disappoint my parents, my teachers, and my bosses.

From an early age my hardworking parents pass on to me messages that become mantras which—I find out later in life—come with a price. Among these are "hard work is the only way to get ahead," and "be thrifty and save." I'm taught also that I'm born of original sin, and that I'll be judged for all of my sins when I die.

Shame is one moral compass that keeps me in line, guilt is the other. I'm very afraid not only of God and dying, but of everyone and everything.

I can't understand how God allows good people to suffer and die, or how people can wage war in his name when he's supposed to be a loving father. In college, Edgar Cayce is a reading assignment and represents the beginning of my search for new thought and happiness. Unfortunately, Cayce is over my head at the time but is the universe's way of letting me know there are other ways to believe beside the traditional monastic dogma and philosophies.

My spiritual surfing takes me from Cayce in my twenties to Louise Hay in my thirties to Unity in my forties to Science of Mind in my fifties. This awakening to a new way of thinking is not an instant remedy—it's application of knowledge that brings about change, but unfortunately I still have both feet in the material world and only my big toe dipped in my new reality. I espouse to anyone who will listen my "New Thought" philosophy—how we create our own reality through our thoughts.

Fortunate to live on the east side of Cleveland, Ohio, in my forties, I attend classes by Sarah Weiss—a wonderful medical intuitive who teaches me to meditate. The spiritual director of Spirit Heal Institute, Sarah plants numerous seeds in me that—at the time—I neither feed nor nourish.

The Phone Call

The negotiations in the fall and winter of 2009 take up a lot of time and every month it becomes more difficult for me to function. I go to bed by seven p.m. every night and spend most weekends in bed, exhausted. However, sleep eludes me for hours because I can't get comfortable enough for my back to stop aching. I hate taking pills so I put off taking ibuprofen until I can't stand it, then fall asleep in an absolutely rigid position to keep my backache from returning.

Once the new company is purchased, I finally go to the doctor and schedule a colonoscopy for May 2010. Far too busy at work since 2005 to see a doctor, I miss no more than two days a year due to illness. Ah, how I embody the archetype of the martyr and don't even realize how I may be suffering at my own hand...

The colonoscopy is a horrible ordeal starting with the prep. I don't leave work when I'm supposed to and get a late start on the laxatives and fluids to clean me out. By the time I get home I'm in horrendous pain and spend the next fourteen hours emptying my bowel. It feels like I had six months of poop stored in my body.

"Normally we don't deliver the results of a colonoscopy over the phone," the doctor informs me, "but I can tell that you're a strong woman and also one who's hard to get a hold of—you have colon cancer."

I thank her, hang up the phone, and immediately apply what I've been practicing for ten years—the methods learned on my spiritual journey. First and foremost is the lesson from Unity and Science of Mind—a spiritual, philosophical, and metaphysical religious philosophy within the New Thought movement—that states "do not accept outward appearances as truth. Know that in the **creator's** mind you are perfect."

I return my focus to work and refuse to react negatively to this news. I remain neutral about it and don't discuss it with anyone. Other than keeping Pat informed, I don't talk to people about my feelings or fears. Refusing to talk about it is my way of rejecting the out-picturing of my thoughts. It also keeps people from telling me their cancer horror stories. Cancer doesn't run in my family so I have no idea what I'm in for, but I know instinctively it's going to require a great deal of courage. I worry I won't be courageous enough.

I have surgery in June 2010 to remove a seven pound tumor and undergo a full hysterectomy. I find out later that when toxins can't be released through normal elimination they exit through other avenues like perspiration, which is why I smelled like "death."

Of course, being the good girl I am, the nurses call me the perfect patient and my surgeon says my recovery is miraculous. I leave the hospital weighing ninety pounds but grateful to be alive. I try not to think about the huge leach of a colostomy bag two inches to the left of my navel.

I refuse to cry when I look at my misshapen body and pink stoma that spews feces and gas directly from my intestines. *How on earth can anyone love me now?* I think, until guilt sets in that I'm being vain and should be grateful to be alive.

Fortunate that my son is in between colleges, I'm grateful he comes to stay with me and help with my recovery by preparing and cooking food. Weak after the surgery and chemo, I wouldn't have eaten regularly—or at all—if he hadn't been there to fix whatever food I'm able to tolerate.

Pat finally opens up to me and tells me she's battled cancer twice before in the past twenty years and that it's returned for a third time. I can't believe it—she's so strong! She becomes my rock through the whole ordeal and both of us determine to beat *"it."*

We make fun of the fact that we're wearing wigs. Pat decides to go with red, curly hair and I choose a shoulder length blond bob. We both own more than one wig and frequently switch from day to day, laughing at our vanity. So many of the young people wear their bald, beautiful heads like a badge of honor, but not us! Without my wig, I look like the twin sister of *The Lord of the Rings* ' character Gollum/Smeagol.

Serious Spirituality

In August 2011 the cancer is back. I experience my first dark night of the soul in the hospital after my second surgery. Labeled Stage IV from the very beginning, I refuse to accept it, so it never dawns on me that I'm not supposed to live. I do everything right—according to all my books—so I *should* be healed...

Finally, I begin to take my spiritual practice seriously and do the deep work I should have done thirty years earlier. It's taken a colon cancer diagnosis, two surgeries, three years of chemotherapy, and several dark nights of the soul to bring me to the point of acceptance of help from wonderful people the universe brings into my life: *Heal Your Life* trainers Dr. Patricia Crane and Rick Nichols of *Heart Inspired,* two people who become not only close friends but angels guiding me toward total healing.

Through their help I face a lot of old wounds and release them through forgiveness. Contrary to my early teachings, I learn through this process that after this life there is no judgment, and this takes away all my fear, all my worry!

Meanwhile, Pat's fight with cancer escalates. Her doctors insist she take medical leave, and says she'll either be back in six weeks or dead.

"Pat, we're the only two people I know who'll get to the Pearly Gates and think about how much more we could have gotten done if only we had one more day at work!" I laugh. She transitions before the six weeks are over. Like everything else she did, she gave 150% and died on her own terms.

I end up having an honest conversation with my oncologist and we agree there's nothing more that can be done for me. Does that mean I want to die? *No!* I want to see my son get married and have kids. But it's so beautiful on the other side—and the universe is so huge, so humungous, that you can't even imagine what's beyond this plane and this realm—that I'm ok. I have so many of my questions answered that I now know it's an option...death is no longer a worry.

I accept that I may be one of those people who lives with cancer for the rest of my life. Whether I live six months or ten years doesn't matter, it's what I do with the rest of my life that matters. I *do* deserve to live and I *can* heal myself, but if/when I transition it's okay because it means I have even more work to do on the other side...and a new adventure!

That's what these three years have brought me: The ability to accept death not as an *end* but as a beginning—a transformation. Now I am a spiritual surfer no more...

ABOUT THE AUTHOR: A Heal Your Life™ coach and workshop facilitator, Cheryl DeVaul offers coaching/training to individuals who want to improve their current life situation through her Training with Spirit company. Cheryl's 30 years of experience in human resources for both large and small corporations includes coaching managers on a wide variety of topics—from basic supervisory skills to leadership training—on a daily basis. She holds a B.A. in Education and an M.B.A. Cheryl's own journey of living with cancer allows her to share with clients her unique perspective and invaluable insights about healing and how to live an empowered life.

Cheryl DeVaul
Cheryl's Training with Spirit
www.trainingwithspirit.com
cheryl.h2empowerliveheal@gmail.com
505-268-0816

Rage And Love
Catherine Allen

I give every last ounce of energy to being the best Christian, wife, mother, friend, servant, and teacher I can and should be. The nurturer of spirits, advocator of the helpless, saver of lives, I always try to do the right thing but no matter what I do, it's not enough.

Married to a minister, we have three children, one of whom has a life-threatening medical condition. One night I announce that I've done all I can do for that day and must go to bed. I achieved a lot, all of it good, all of it work of which I am proud. However, working in the midst of critics—even when doing great good—takes its toll in the form of drained energy and heavy burdens.

My hands shake all the time these days, and tonight I'm empty and more hopeless than usual. The medication I take does its job of turning everything, both real and imagined, into vague wavy unknowingness...tonight, I'm all used up.

Suddenly the door flies open, the switch is flipped on—I squeeze my eyes against the brightness.

"Where's the checkbook?" he demands.

"In my purse, in the office."

The light flips off. The door closes with a bang.

Sinking again, I welcome the nothingness as a respite, if only for a few hours, from too many responsibilities, too many sorrows, too many battles, too little support, too little understanding, too little acceptance.

The door swings open again. Again I'm blinded by brightness and attacked with urgency.

"What did you write check number two fifty-seven for?"

"I don't know," I mumble, "if it's not there, I'll have to figure it out tomorrow."

He sighs disgustedly, flips off the light, and closes the door. I try to sink again in order to hold onto the rest I desperately need and hope to find. But he needs me to answer his questions. Again, the door and the light. Again, another question.

So I get up, drag myself into the office, sit in the interrogation chair, and resign myself to answering *all* of his questions. He has a list.

Part of me is numb and empty, but I submit to what he requires even though I already told him how defeated I feel, and that I'm all used up. Still, he asks, and I answer. Finally, he asks how I'm feeling and what I think about things. I pour my heart out to him, hoping desperately for even a hint of understanding and support.

Instead, he leans back in his chair, rests his hands on his belly, and begins to laugh at my grief and heartache, and at everything he thinks insignificant. Then he calls me a lunatic.

I snap. I admit it. The fiery beast in me rises, burns away my emptiness, and replaces it with a fire so hot—an anger I've never let myself feel or express. I throw the fax machine at him, for starters, then everything I can get my hands on. I scream at him, chase him from room to room and, when he tries to stop me by grabbing hold of me, I slap and hit him with all my might. When he's able to restrain me, I fall onto the floor sobbing so hard I can barely breathe.

As I sit there, the fire rekindles itself with the reality of how, in a fit of laughter, he threw me headlong over the emotional cliff on which I'd been teetering. And all I know is that our life together is over. Sure, we may keep on living, but the life I worked so hard for—our marriage, our family, the lives of our children, all of our identities, everything—is now destroyed, since he destroyed me.

The Line In The Sand

I'd never have left him. *Never.* I couldn't have. Anytime I got angry I'd repent and beg God for forgiveness because I knew anger was bad, wrong, a sin. I see now, a decade after our divorce, that he didn't make me into this person so willing to keep going and going, and giving and giving until I was depleted, only to get up and go and give some more. I never drew a line in the sand that said "do not cross, or else."

Ultimately I did leave home—as a failure—to get the help I thought I needed and to protect my children, so convinced was I of the terrible person I'd become. But he isn't the one who taught me those lessons, though certainly he reinforced them.

No, I knew the beast from another teacher, one from before I was even born. My mother's womb was not safe from this teacher. Her anxiety and fear fed my own and followed me into this world, and our fears were real. Some of my nightmares are just memories. Like the picture in my mind of the little girl standing with her nose in the corner, in trouble of some sort. She's probably three or four. She leans slowly to the left, just long enough to sneak a peek into the kitchen, where her parents are fighting.

The sounds seem far away—yelling, slapping, crying—but what I see in that peek is burned into my memory like a photograph...my dad in a rage, hand raised to strike my mother with the next blow. My mother, though she's been knocked to the floor, yells in defiance through her tears.

I never thought about what that little girl felt. This memory is like many others, something I seem to watch from a distance. But, these are *my* memories, my living nightmares, I'm the little girl. As I write this memory, I weep for the first time for what she must have been feeling. I step inside her body, inside *my body*, for just a moment and am consumed with silent terror. Helpless, I feel myself squeeze into that corner, trying to disappear. Forgotten for now, I must stay still to finish my punishment in blessed invisibility. I am so quiet I almost cease to exist...at least I try.

Invisibility becomes my best defense against the anger that unpredictably turns to rage and violence. My childhood play centers around preventing myself from being noticed in any way. Better to have *no* needs at all—no voice, make no sound—than to possibly incur a wrath I don't believe I'd be able to endure. Always good...I live for being good. I go to great lengths to make sure every detail is just right so that there will be no unpredictable disappointments, punishments, or emotions of any kind...only praise for my goodness.

The unpredictable violence continues around me as I watch in silence. I see bad things happen that I can't stop. Even when bad things happen to me, I simply disappear and watch the girl from a distance. It's easier that way. It's how I survive. When the beast shows up, I become invisible. I hide and pretend he's not there.

I get so good at pretending he isn't there that I become confused about what's good and what's bad over the years. I'm able to see and feel, but pretend I'm not hurt at all. If I become angry for any reason, I chastise myself, and believe anger in any form is bad and something to be avoided at all costs. When events happen in my life, I make them okay and deal with everything that comes my way—

good or bad, it's all the same.

I grow up, marry, have children, and life becomes more and more unpredictable. When my daughter is born with multiple medical challenges, it becomes increasingly difficult to maintain appearances, and harder for me to do everything that needs to be done to keep our lives going as I think they should. I do my best. But every now and then I lose my temper and yell at my kids, only to apologize and weep with remorse at how terrible I am. I try with all my heart and soul to be good, to be perfect, to solve every problem, to prevent every possible mistake, to make everyone happy, to be holy. But I'm a terrible failure at everything.

A Beast With A Message

I know, I know. I look back now and see how totally awesome I was in so many ways. But, I hated myself for my inadequacies then, judged and condemned myself for every mistake. It's no wonder I allowed others to do the same, and that there was never an end to what I had to do to prove my worth.

Ten years ago, I thought my anger destroyed me and everything I loved. I've come to understand now that the beast I feared was simply a distortion I'd witnessed of someone else's nightmare. The beast who came to me that night arrived to wake me up and save my life. He came to say "you are worthy of love and support, not because of what you do, but because of who you *are*. Stop *doing* and start *being* the person God made you to be...you are valuable."

Now, when I seethe in anger, I know it's my opportunity to recognize that it comes with a message. The more volatile my anger, the more important the message—and I know I can't allow my anger to burn freely lest it become the beast of my nightmares that rages against others. But neither can I ignore, deny, or push it down, as then it transforms into a silent beast that rages against my own body, mind, and spirit.

Anger lets me know I need to take a closer look to see what action is required, and holds up the mirror that shows me the one I'm angry with is *me*—the one to whom I've forgotten to listen, value, and love. And anger not only awakens in me self-preservation, it also introduces me to a stronger ally...it shows me it's in partnership with *love*.

In love, anger sends me inward to tell me I've neglected my values, tried to become invisible again, and allowed others to walk right through me. Anger reminds me of causes I believe in and provides me the passion and courage necessary to face my fears and stand tall. The more I observe my anger as a guide, the more I discover that love is the one sending the message.

Throw me in the path, love tells me, *between your heart and any situation, and you will know what to do...*

I've learned to trust the love that dwells in my heart and to ask for its guidance, too. When I *choose* to be worthy of love and support, I reinforce that I am valuable—because God made me so— and that my two best allies are rage *and* love...

ABOUT THE AUTHOR: Catherine Allen is a mentor and guide for women, mothers and caregivers, especially those who walk the overwhelming and inspiring path through the medical and special needs world. She has a degree in Sports Science, is a Licensed Massage Therapist and a Trained Life Coach, but she most loves writing and speaking to live audiences about the sometimes brutal, but always amazing, journey of living life with her special needs daughter, who she considers one of her greatest teachers. Catherine's life work is to inspire and empower those who choose to live on the Positive Side of their Circumstances.

Catherine Allen
www.catherine-allen.com
www.facebook.com/LivingOnThePositiveSide
www.twitter.com/catallen143
catherineallen143@gmail.com

The Battle with Bereavement:
A Love Story
Anita Pernell-Arnold

A three year old black girl in a yellow playsuit stood before a full length mirror watching herself cry. All alone, the sorrow, pain, and hopelessness followed me throughout my life.

I believed I was not loved, a belief I carried so deeply inside of myself I was unaware of its presence. It became encrusted in a defensive, impermeable core that influenced all but one person's attempt to love me..

Vince (a.k.a. "Bicky") swept away all doubts about my lovability through his immediate and consistent love. We marry six months after the day we met. This man vowed to the congregation at the wedding that his role in life was to insure that he supported my success in whatever I wanted to achieve.

He gave me three daughters I could not have naturally—two adopted and one stepchild. We spent thirty-four years and ten months together before he fell ill. I watched each of his systems and organs fail painfully—respiratory arrest, dialysis, and a stroke until he passed away at home peacefully one morning.

I held myself together until the daughters came. They said their good-byes, and the undertaker came and took my beloved out on a stretcher, his head covered with a black blanket. Immediately I was thrust—although I did not know it then—back in time to the little girl crying in front of the mirror.

This was the one time I had nothing left to give. I withdrew and grew cold.

My cousins and my best girlfriend Mary came to protect me. I cried uncontrollably and had many meltdowns—often I screamed that I couldn't do this alone, that this pain would kill me. The pain felt as if someone was performing surgery on my abdomen without anesthetic.

I realized much later that I had been writing about the loss of love more than forty years earlier

This verse even though, written forty years ago describes my emotions:

Despair (an excerpt, 1973)

> Hate somber, sullen, surges and restrains.
> Love brilliant, bliss billows and yearns.
> Tossed tomb tumbling into ravine,
> Deep death in stillness wanders,
> Awaits the love of redemption.

My Path: Arduous, Painful, Scary, Exciting, Despairing, & Spiritual

Immediately after my husband Vince's celebration of life services I joined a hospice bereavement group for spouses which met for seven weeks and included individual and spiritual counseling. This group has been a major stabilizing force for the past three years.

We have vowed to remain together to celebrate important events and holidays, and welcome opportunities to support each other through relapses and breakthroughs. We have searched for and found spiritual messages and educational materials about life to share.

I increased my spiritual studies, and wrote and expanded my prayers each time I had a revelation.

Turning point: A parishioner told me she admired my progress through my grief and started steering others toward me. Eventually, she said I should start bereavement work at the church. My first reaction: Nothing could be more distant from my natural inclinations.

During a retreat, a priest suggested I seek counseling about the problems I was having regarding the non-responsiveness of my husband's children to my calls and birthday presents. My priest suggested loving my children from a distance. This eased some of my pain.

I began to focus on my prayers. I had been reciting a mantra every day. I realized my prayers needed to include requests to God for support for the problems with which I was struggling.

About the same time, a friend gave me a *Daily Devotional: Strength and Guidance for Daily Living. Episcopal Church of the Holy Spirit.* Surprisingly often, the scriptures for the day were exactly what I needed to meet that day's challenges. The current sources of my strength come from a daily devotion period which includes a selection from the above mentioned book, a psalm praising God, a selection from *Joy For A Women's Soul,* and my personal prayers.

Reminiscing led to reading poetry I had written in the early 1970's. It revealed a central theme of my writing—despair and loneliness. The death of my husband Bicky broke open my "encrusted, defensive, impermeable core." I suffered and mourned. I believe my worst suffering was caused by not knowing why I hated to be alone.

I had to find a way out of this fog to the present.

I asked my friend Virginia to come and live with me. She stayed with me for five months. When I would tell her about a struggle I was having, she would find a very fitting scriptural reading that she would share and discuss.

She located the scripture in the Bible that said that marriage is dissolved at death. This led me on a path of acceptance and at midnight on New Year's Eve—only about five months after Bicky's death—in a timeshare in Disneyland with two girlfriends, I removed my wedding rings.

"Love The Questions." ~ Rainer Maria Rilke

My best friend, Mary, to whom I tell everything and who spent so much time with me at the time of Bicky's death, listens faithfully. At the end of the first year she says:

"The way you talk about loneliness is excessive and you should try to understand what this means."

Well, I am a psychiatric rehabilitation practitioner, who learned introspection skills during my training. I decide to turn them on full force.

Sitting on the steps in my house I discover:

I am afraid of being alone!

My thoughts race. *The people who loved me are gone, therefore I am incomplete. No one knows what is happening to me...people like me die alone...I am afraid to become emotionally dependent on my nephew...In my mind aloneness is an unnatural state—not enough money, isolated...in pain. I cannot make other people love me....I cannot do anything about it.*

Several weeks later I'm thrust back to the memory of that scared baby girl crying in the mirror, lost and alone. Only now I hear my mother's voice from another room:

"Why are you crying? You don't have anything to cry about, stop crying!" No asking what's the matter? No hugging.

My thoughts begin to race in many directions.

I remember pictures of me as a baby. I search and find pictures of me at seven months old sitting in my grandparents' and parents' laps. They look very pleased. There's also a picture of me in a studio at two years old, all dressed up with a toy.

This was during the 1930's Depression. According to the stories I had heard, my parents were poor.

These images did not fit with my recollections of being unloved! I realize. *What poor people would take an unloved child to a studio to have her picture taken?"*

Where were we when I was crying? In a small one bedroom apartment. I had the bedroom, while my parents slept on twin beds in the living room. Is this a lack of love for me?

Previously, we lived in a large brownstone house with my mother, father, grandmother and two aunts. (One of those aunts became my surrogate mother—I told her everything I can't tell my mother.) Can you imagine all the attention I received? Suddenly, all that attention was gone! No wonder I was crying, no wonder my mother did not understand. My parents finally had a place of their own.

I was a very sickly child. I had allergies and asthma. They consulted doctors until they found an allergy clinic at New York University Hospital. When I was having an asthma attack and gasping for breath, I remember the times fondly when they would heat bath towels and lay them on my chest until I relaxed and went to sleep. No lack of love here!

My mind shifts to my parents' upbringing. My maternal grandmother was a college educated woman and aloof. My great grandmother raised my mother and her siblings. My father's mother died when he was nine, he was raised by an older sister. His father was in another state.

The psychologist in me poses this question: *How could they give what they had not received?*

I feel the Holy Spirit directing my thoughts which leads me to this question: *Well, what did my parents do?*

My mother made pretty clothes for me (we even wore mother and daughter dresses) and costumes for plays. Maybe not the lace, bows, and ruffles I wanted, but very nice clothes. *Alice Blue Gown* is one of my favorite songs!

My mother taught me to play the piano. My parents gave me ballet lessons. They went to all my performances, even through college. They sent me to the best public school they could get me into, to college and graduate school. My father discussed politics, values, race relations, and how to interpret issues in the newspapers.

My parents gave celebrations for each of my achievements. They were overprotective, but they only had one child. They told me many times they were afraid I would die. Even so, they raised a giving, affectionate, cuddly person.

Suddenly it hits me: *No wonder I am afraid to be alone!* I had to reach seventy-five years of age to discover how many ways my parents loved me, contributed to the person I have become, and the many things I have been able to accomplish. I feel my parents and Bicky's spirits surrounding and protecting me.

"Healing Is Letting Go, Getting Better, Becoming Who You Are." ~ Rachel Haomi Remen

My goal is to bring the death of a spouse or a partner to the general conversation of the American public to increase the knowledge of its severity and the positive supports available.

In my family, all of the women lived many years after their husbands died. None of them ever talked about the pain. People live much longer now, the senior population is swelling. Seniors are the center of social networks that depend on them. Mental health issues and suicide have increased, and many people stumble or become stuck on their path through mourning.

My thoughts about an integrated psychological/spiritual curriculum to help spouses and partners in bereavement compel me to search for books on the subject, which I cannot find. I experience a message from the Holy Spirit to write one. The curriculum has morphed into a book that guides facilitators and the bereaved through a psychologically and spiritually integrated process toward healing and recovery.

I am a romantic. My battle with bereavement is a love story. Bereavement can open the door to new loves. Mine did not work out. Oh, but the joy of loving and being in love!

I am not afraid to love again. I do not worry about rejection or pain without which I would not know joy. The joy of being loved, and having been loved, contributes to my power, hope, and resilience.

ABOUT THE AUTHOR: Anita Pernell-Arnold, MSSW, CPRP Retired, Founding Fellow of PRA is the co-founder of the PRIME Institute, at Drexel University, Department of Psychiatry. Mrs. Pernell-Arnold has been the director of mental health centers and mental health systems. She developed and researched services for African Americans and multicultural training. Mrs. Pernell-Arnold has been an investigator and trainer for federally funded projects - most notably, the study on Inoculation Against Discrimination for African Americans with Psychiatric Disabilities. She is a facilitator of Mourner's Path groups in the Episcopal Church. Mrs. Pernell-Arnold is the author of *Paths Through Despair to Faith and Gratitude*.

Anita Pernell-Arnold
Transformation International
arvapba8@aol.com

I Know Things

Sue Urda

I know things. Now, I *know* that sounds simplistic, or "so what," or even like a "non-statement," because, well, everyone knows things. But that's not exactly what I mean.

I know things that knowledgeable people would say are not knowable. But I don't give much credence to what people say—I know what I know. I just know it.

I Know It In An Instant

It's 1970 and hot. We moved recently to Arizona from Michigan, and I'm in the fifth grade. Having moved three times since the first grade because of my dad's job, I enjoy making new friends. It feels like an adventure to me!

Gene is the tallest boy in our class. Cute, even though he seems to have only one big long eyebrow, I distinctly remember feeling weirdly about him the first time I see him. It's like there's something not quite safe about him. Maybe it's the glint in his eyes, his nasally voice, or his "too clean cut" matching shorts, shirt, and white tube socks coordinated with his brand new navy blue Keds—I still don't know what tipped me off.

Still, he's cute, and I develop a crush on him. A few weeks later I'm with some girlfriends on the monkey bars during recess.

"Hey Sue!" Gene calls out to me. "C'mon down here..."

I climb down and walk over to him.

"Hey look," he says to all his friends, "its gorilla legs! I told you so!"

The boys all laugh and point at my legs. Admittedly, I have more long dark hair on my legs than most girls my age. My face turns even redder than it already is from the hot Phoenix sun and I run back to the monkey bars—crushed by my crush.

Why hadn't I simply stayed away? I knew there was something not quite safe about this boy...

That isn't the last time I choose the wrong person to have a crush on, though I decide to stay away from boys for a while—well, at least until the sixth grade.

I Know Things In My Gut

"Hey, there's an 'Open House' sign—turn left here," Kathy directs me. It's a Sunday afternoon and we're out doing our usual Sunday house hunting ritual. We've been searching for a new home for nearly six months, and are at the point where we think we'll never find one. We must have looked at more than fifty houses, townhouses, and condos already and nothing seems like a good fit.

We drive in and the neighborhood is lovely. A small community in a beautiful park-like setting only fifteen minutes from our business, this seems like what we've been looking for. Why haven't any of the realtors shown us this neighborhood yet? I feel a twinge in my belly...it feels good!

The "Open House" sign is on the lawn of a three-unit building. *Oh man! Of course it's gotta be the middle one!* We specifically want an end unit so we have neighbors only on one side of us. We value peace and quiet, space and privacy.

"I knew it was too good to be true," sighs Kathy. "Let's go."

"No wait," I say. "Let's go inside anyway. We might as well see what it looks like in case an end unit opens up—and for some reason, I have a good feeling about this place."

We make an offer on Wednesday and move in six weeks later. Ends up we have almost no neighbors anyway—there's a single mature woman on one side, an elderly couple on the other, and tall bushes separating our decks in the beautiful backyard. The interior, spacious and open with tall ceilings, wide doorways, and wall to wall windows across the entire back of the family room and living room, looks out onto our yard and the woods behind us. Yep, we found our peaceful haven, our very own slice of heaven...

Our next few moves are much the same. We find the perfect bayside house in Cape May, N.J., with all the features we want. I remember still the excitement we shared when we drove up to what would become our new home. I felt deep in my gut that we'd be very happy there—and so we were.

When the warm weather and the beach start calling even louder, we pick up and move to a condo in Marco Island, Florida—sight unseen. It's like living in a vacation paradise and, truthfully, it's tough to be serious about working at first with the blue-green water and white sandy beaches just across the street. Our family thinks we're at least a little bit crazy for moving so far away where we don't know anyone, and wonders how the heck we can plan to live somewhere we haven't even visited...

I know in my gut it's a good move for us. When we sign the lease, I have butterflies in my belly–the good kind. Now, nearly two years later, we live happily only a few miles north in another magical place...and we're lovin' it.

I Know Things In My Body

Here it is again–that sudden tingling and weakness in both arms, especially near my elbows, and in both legs right around my knees. I steady myself by bending my knees slightly so they don't buckle, and focus attention on my breath. *Breathe in, breathe out. Repeat. Okay, that's better.*

It's the same sensation I had as I walked into the meeting room of our biggest client right before they essentially fired me. Some might say the writing was on the wall, but before I saw the writing, I felt it in my body. I knew something "bad" was about to happen. And here it is again.

I know I shouldn't say yes, but how do I say no when it will hurt her feelings? I rationalize.

How can I tell her I don't think she's a good fit for us even though she says all the right things–the same things that, when I hear them from someone else, make me say yes. How do I tell her–when she's got perfect credentials–that she can't start a chapter for our network? How can I say that her energy just doesn't feel right, that something's off and just doesn't ring true?

Who am I kidding? I'm such a wuss.

I say yes anyway, and within two months we cut ties. It's the first time we've ever done this, and although I try, it's definitely not amicable. She's simply not complying with our guidelines and may even mar our reputation–and besides that, she's obstinate, mean, and even a little bit crazy.

When will I learn to honor this tingling sensation? When will I stand in my truth?

I Know Things In My Soul

Well, we did it again! I tell myself. *And that was a great talk, Sue, but where did it come from—this time?*

Packing up after one of our national tour events, Kathy and I discuss today's happenings, the women present, and the high vibes we're floating on still. As always, we discuss my presentation to the group and—the same as every other time before this one—how my talk came out differently than I'd planned.

It's not lack of preparation. I'm completely prepared and professional. I know the drill: know your audience, pick a topic, make an outline, write the speech, prepare some notes, and practice, practice, practice.

It happens that this time, just like my previous talks, my presentation really isn't like the others at all. No one is ever quite the same.

Sure, for the most part, basically the information is the same and definitely on topic. I hit my talking points and occasionally even use the same examples. However, there's a part of it for which I can't account and for which I surely can't take credit—the part where the words that pour from my mouth aren't the ones I've prepared...they're not even ones I remember!

Where do these words come from? I wonder. I have my theories...

It's as if something or someone takes over. I used to resist this. For years, I thought I had to stick strictly to a script, not veer from my notes, and pretty much memorize word-for-word the exact talk I want the audience to hear. I'd agonize over what I planned to say, and the occasional perfectionist in me loved this.

It works for me for a long time—until it doesn't. I find it increasingly hard over the years to be so rigid and not let the *other voice speak through me*. Sure, I fight it, I want to be certain of what I'm delivering, I want to control the experience for myself and everyone in the room, but frankly it becomes too difficult.

These days, I allow and even welcome the words as they pour through me. Sure, I still plan, prepare, and practice, practice, practice—but now I know better than to try to subdue my *knowing*. Instead, I open myself to it. Before I take the stage, my ritual is to ask for guidance. My intention is: *Allow the words to flow to me, through me, and out to audience so that I deliver, and they receive, all that is in their highest and best good.*

This really works for me. I feel good about messages that flow...whatever they are.

Knowing Is Power

I consider myself an amateur at this *knowing* thing, but believe I'm getting the hang of it little by little. At times I play with this by testing myself. I try to tap in and feel my way through instead of using my thinking logical mind, and all its "rules" learned over the years...I must say, though, that I love my mind and it's served me well; but there's a time and place for everything, and right now is the right time for to me to simply be with my knowing.

To tap in even further and develop this amazing gift—a gift I believe we each possess—I practice mindfulness and gratitude every day. I meditate and plan down-time, so I can "chill", relax, and commune with nature. We move near the beach so I can go there every day if I like, and have a pond in my backyard for those times when I don't make it. I surround myself with people I love and like, and who support me in my growth.

I've found that the more calm, clear, and open I am, the more easily my knowing comes through. And I *know* this works be me, because, well...*I know things.*

ABOUT THE AUTHOR: Sue Urda, aka the Connections Catalyst, is an Author, Speaker, Inspirer, and Co-Founder of Powerful You! Women's Network & Powerful You! Publishing. Sue is a two-time honoree on INC Magazine's list of the 500 Fastest-Growing Private Companies. Having started 3 companies since 1989, Sue knows the challenges and joys young businesses face, and she is committed to helping entrepreneurs and all women thrive through connections. Her award-winning book, Amazon #1 Bestselling Books, and 100-day transformational video series are designed to inspire women to embrace and feel their personal power. Sue's personal mission is to connect women to each other, their visions & themselves.

Sue Urda
Author, Speaker, Inspirer, Connections Catalyst
Co-Founder of Powerful You! Inc.
www.sueurda.com
www.powerfulyou.com

Surfacing Into Consciousness

Sheri Horn Hasan

I awaken the morning of my birthday and, as I emerge into consciousness from my hazy dream-like sleep state, think I hear my teenage son's voice outside my bedroom door say clearly the word "schism!"

Trouble is, I know he's at his dad's house and nowhere near my vicinity! His voice seemed so real, however, that I open my bedroom door to confirm that he is, in fact, not here...

What to make of this? I wonder. *I'd heard it clear as day!* There's no doubt *at all* in my mind it's a message of some sort to which I should most definitely pay attention! *But why? And how?*

Immediately I text a friend to tell her about this strange occurrence.

"I'll have to look up schism," she texts me back.

"Split, as in the psyche!" the editor in me shoots back to her. "That was my immediate thought...I've been pondering how and why I attract people with mental health issues, and if they're merely projections of my own inner instability, and then comparing my ex-husband to John.

Sheharyar–extreme irrationality due to high anxiety, John—highly strung nervousness. So I thought, are they really different in the end, or merely manifestations of a variation on a theme—all of which really stem from me internally?"

"Yeah, I was thinking chasm, as in rock," she replies. "The chasm allows you to go down deep. Crack things open. Feeling that discomfort is an invitation to find a way to get comfortable with yourself."

I look up the word "schism" which, as defined by Merriam Webster Dictionary, means: division, separation, discord, disharmony. I learn that schism is the basis for the word "schizophrenia." I laugh.

The Fluidity of Choice

Recently, I'd ended a nearly five-year relationship with my boyfriend John when he began to exhibit major symptoms of commitment phobia. I figured now that his kids were both in college, and mine would be leaving soon to start his college "career," it was ok to start making future plans—together.

I turned out to be wrong—dead wrong...

As an intuitive editor, professional astrologer, and past life regression facilitator, it's my belief that the universe is benign. While it may not always give us what we want, I believe it always gives us what we *need*. The trouble is identifying the difference between the two...

How do I maintain this philosophy of life and reconcile it with what's happening around me? I wonder. *Why am I being asked to get rid of something I need—a loving relationship?* I lack the clear insight necessary to appreciate exactly how the universe is acting in my own best interest here!

Initially overwhelmed with negative thoughts and emotions, I felt forced to end this relationship based on my own sense of dignity and pride, but deep down inside I *know* that he ended it, not me. He simply didn't have the guts to confront me and express himself, and so began to shy away from spending time together and making any future plans.

As feelings of insecurity and worthlessness begin to surface from below, I become irrationally fearful. *Am I doomed to be alone forever?* I cry. *What did I do to deserve this? What's wrong with me?*

Determined to get to the bottom of this, I begin to see how these negative emotions obscure my vision and cloud my perspective. I've long pondered the nature of perspective, and several years ago became aware that *my* perspective is always a matter of choice.

So I tell myself now it's time to walk my talk. I can choose to believe that all events in my life happen for my greater good, that even tragedies have their silver linings, and that I'm here on earth to increase my level of consciousness in order to achieve true happiness for my soul.

When I choose otherwise—to believe that I've been dealt a "bad" hand and that others owe me for that, or that I'm weak and in need of sympathy and empathy—I do myself a disservice in my quest for greater consciousness. Likewise, when I choose to bury my head in the sand, mire myself in my own misery, or blame others for my misfortune, I'm missing one very big truth: that my perceptions are my choice!

I remind myself that another may see things only from his or her perspective, while I view the same issue from the opposite perspective—even though we're both looking at the same thing!

Why not turn things around? I ponder. Just as one would rotate an object in one's hand to see it from the other side or from a different angle? That way I can view it from a different perspective! And inherent in that concept is neither good nor evil. Inherent in that is simply a "difference in perspective."

I begin to grasp this intellectually and apply it to my current situation. Suddenly I see how another's perspective—even if it's opposite to mine—is also a matter of choice. The fluidity of "choice" then becomes apparent, and I understand how choosing to look at a situation one way is as easy as choosing to look at it another way!

And, my choices can change! What I choose to believe today does not have to be what I choose to believe tomorrow. Such "fluidity" of choice makes changing what I believe less of a crime in my own mind. As one who prides herself on being a woman of her word, of meaning what I say, and of staying true to that, this is quite a revelation!

I realize that initially my perspective is that John left me. However, when I choose consciously to realign my thinking—to change my perspective—I understand that I'm the one who ended the relationship because he simply couldn't give me what I need...

Bridging The Gap

Two weeks later I surface once again into consciousness from sleep one morning as a voice in my head I can only describe as coming from the great beyond says: "Conversations About Consciousness!"

Though it sounds ludicrous to say out loud, this voice reminds me of the one in the movie *The Ten Commandments*—stern and definite, like the voice of God speaking to Moses on top of Mount Sinai.

Again, what to make of this?

In addition to being an author, editor, and writing coach, I'm a professional psychological and archetypal astrologer familiar with Jungian psychology as it applies to the interpretation of an individual's natal, or birth, chart. I know enough from my studies that, according to Carl Jung (himself an astrologer), we all have a conscious mind and an unconscious, or subconscious, one.

Merriam Webster Dictionary to the rescue once again! Unconscious means *not aware of something*, while subconscious is defined as *existing in the part of the mind that a person is not aware of; existing in the mind but not consciously known or felt.*

Hmm, I muse once again...*but isn't part of the point of life soul growth and greater consciousness? And isn't bridging that gap between the conscious and unconscious important for those interested in greater soul growth and increased consciousness?*

While I do not recognize what's in my subconscious brain, I know often that what bleeds through to consciousness comes in the form of dreams and/or dream states. This information, this *knowing,* which flows across the boundary between my subconscious and conscious minds, takes the form of thoughts, insights, and revelations—in short, the *elixir* or *gold* of the Hero's Journey—as they rise into consciousness.

Ah, I get it now! Therein lies the importance of the word *schism* spoken to me from out of the blue that day! This voice came to me from deep within my soul, and its purpose was to alert me to the two different sides of my own psyche—my conscious and unconscious minds—and the "split" between the two...

"As Above, So Below; As Within, So Without..." ~ Hermes Trismegistus

Several months later I decide to join a small group of like-minded souls to practice Deep Memory Process past life regression work. During the course of my own regression—facilitated by another practitioner—I'm surprised to arrive at an answer about how I manifest people in my life with mental health issues and why...

As I enter the regression state (a cooperative venture between client and facilitator whereby I allow myself to relax and simply go with the flow and describe the images that arise from my psyche), I see a woman in her bed with long, dark, disheveled hair protruding from the bedcovers.

Then I see myself walking around the bed to rouse this woman, as I begin to recognize it's afternoon. I realize this person is my mother, and that she's sleeping late because she'd fallen into a drunken stupor the night before. I don't know how, but I know my father has left long ago—he either abandoned us or passed away.

As my regression proceeds, I'm guided forward to see that I love attending school and when I graduate from high school I obtain a job as a secretary in a business. The time period seems to be around the turn of the century and, because I have no husband, I find a way to support my mother and myself through this job.

In those days, private and personal lives are completely separate, and it isn't long before I realize I can never marry because I cannot disclose to any male suitor that my mother is an alcoholic.

Eventually, I don't try to stop her from drinking. Instead, I fall into the routine of going to work each day, returning home every evening to make dinner and to put my mother—by now in a drunken stupor—to bed. Essentially, I live a lonely, solitary life, except for work where I am well-liked and respected.

Suddenly one night, after leaving my mother in her usual stupor on the couch in the living room, I see myself at my kitchen table—talking to someone who isn't there! *Oh my God!* I realize immediately that once the true horror of the sameness of everyday life—with no prospect of a future family—set in, my mind created a relationship that *didn't really exist—and I fabricated a husband out of loneliness and sheer desperation!*

Holy s*#t! Was I crazy? Maybe so, but now I can certainly understand why! Talk about gaining a new perspective! Instantly, I'm able to sympathize and feel compassion—*for myself*—and suddenly it dawns on me that it's *not* about whether my internal "craziness" causes me to manifest relationships with people onto whom I project my fantasies, it's about avoiding entering into such *emotionally desperate situations...*

Wow! Making the unconscious conscious isn't easy! However, more determined now than ever to gain greater insight into myself, surfacing into consciousness is a journey I'm definitely willing to take...

ABOUT THE AUTHOR: An Amazon #1 Bestselling author and editor, Sheri combines her 30+ years experience as a writer, writing coach, editor, and professional astrologer with her knowledge of literature, archetypes, mythology, psychology, and writing to skillfully guide authors toward publishing their work successfully. Having worked with 100+ published authors, Sheri relies upon her finely-tuned intuition and insight to help authors achieve their goals. Sheri's business, Karmic Evolution, rests upon the foundational philosophy that writing is healing and that good writing is revealing. Additionally, Sheri's astrological readings and life coaching help clients move from chaos to clarity to achieve higher consciousness and soul growth.

Sheri Horn Hasan
Karmic Evolution
www.KarmicEvolution.com
Sheri@KarmicEvolution.com
732-547-0852

I See Me

Lisa Milich

"We need to be apart because this isn't working," I tell my husband Gerard as we sit in marriage counseling. These words take everything in me to say and weigh heavily on me, as I know the extreme pain he suffered in the breakup of his first marriage.

He's a good man, but I realize for the first time in my life that I have to take care of myself. I've been dying slowly on the inside from over giving and responsibility. I'm numb, burnt out, disconnected, and exhausted from all that life demands of me. In my determination to be the strong, perfect, responsible mom and stepmom, wife, friend, family member, and career executive, I've lost something so incredibly valuable—*me*.

Outwardly life seems good. I own a beautiful home, am raising three healthy children, have a dedicated husband, and a rewarding but challenging career. In reality, however, my marriage is falling apart—and so am I—from the complexities of a blended family, years of trying to break through the glass ceiling, and the added financial stress of supporting two families.

What happened to the free-spirited, vibrant, fun, and creative woman I once was? I wonder. She no longer exists! A mere shell of who I used to be, I'm empty. My depth of despair is overwhelming, and all I want to do is run as fast as I can away from my own life—the life I thought I wanted.

Good Girls Finish Last

Growing up in a working class family in Bristol, Rhode Island—two brothers and me—my youngest brother gets all the attention as he's the one always in trouble. My middle brother is the quiet, responsible one. And then there's me, the eldest—always striving to do the right thing so someone will see me.

My mom's friend dies of cancer when I'm twelve and my parents take in her two boys. Our family expands from three to five children—two biological, two adopted—and me. I'm surrounded by men except for my mom, the matriarch.

From the early age of eleven, I start working—with a paper route and babysitting—and never stop. A dreamer, I aspire to improve my life always—to do better than my parents' did. Dad's a bus driver, mom a secretary, and we live paycheck to paycheck. Sometimes it isn't enough, but we're incredibly loved and thankful for all that we have.

I inherit strong values from my parents and the notion that if I live with integrity and work hard, I'll be recognized and rewarded for what I do. Driven by my desire to succeed, I put myself through college while holding down two jobs. I'm the first in my family lineage to graduate from college.

One of my first jobs after receiving my business degree is with a large, multi-national corporation. It's very much a male-dominated company and I work around the clock in my attempt to be recognized and promoted. Sadly, this never seems to happen. Instead, I stagnate in middle management for years and watch others—mostly men—come in with less experience and get promoted. Frustrated, I work ten times harder to try to move up the corporate ladder. I learn quickly that working hard doesn't translate into fairness or recognition.

At the age of twenty-nine I marry Gerard, a divorced father with Joshua, age four, and Paige, age two, and become a stepmom overnight. At thirty-one, our daughter Lexi is born. Since I'm the primary breadwinner, as Gerard had not fared well financially with his divorce, I have no choice but to work through my entire pregnancy and thereafter...

Superwoman No More

As I drive from marriage counseling, questions swirl through my mind: *How did I get here? Why is this happening? Where did I go? Who am I anymore?*

Turns out I define myself as "superwoman"—you know, the overachieving career mom who single-handedly and perfectly accomplishes everything possible. I care for family and friends, meet unrelenting employer demands and deadlines, and manage a busy household—one with the added complexities and injustices of raising and supporting a blended family both emotionally and financially, I might add.

Yes, that's who I am...

For a long time, I accomplish this with relative ease and grace, or at least I think I do, until the burdens became too heavy to bear. I set impossible goals that can't be achieved and measure my own worth in terms of productivity and tangible accomplishments. In retrospect, by living up to modern society's definition of the "superwoman," I live in a constant state of overwhelm and stress. I've been trying to be something I'm not in an effort to please everyone else and have the perfect life.

In my mind, I never measure up. I'm the good girl off to the side, waiting for someone to do the right thing and really see me. I'm the strong, principle-centered career woman who works harder than most to try to break through the glass ceiling to no avail; the early entrepreneur who strives for success but never seems to reach it.

I'm the compassionate mom and step-mom who puts a lot of effort into children who others criticize because of their own shortcomings. No matter how hard I strive to be successful and perfect, I never quite make it in an honored and truly visible way. I receive no big recognition for my gifts and talents, no awards or accolades on a plaque, just criticism and judgment from my own self and others who don't know me for who I truly am: A deeply compassionate and courageous leader.

Determined To Heal

The days that follow my separation are painful ones. Despite my best efforts to bring balance and healing to our marriage, Gerard isn't ready to accept my statement because of the pain, hurt, and disappointment from his first marriage. He can't come to terms with what seems like another failed marriage.

I know I can't sacrifice myself another minute. It's in these days that my pain and suffering is darkest—leaving behind the life I've known for nearly ten years proves to be extremely difficult for me.

The stress manifests in my body with weight loss, a scare with breast cancer, and some internal bleeding. My mind, body, and spirit are giving me clear signals that I must act to take care of myself for the first time in years. Painful as it is, I pack a suitcase for myself and Lexi and go to live with my brother. A few weeks later, I move into my parent's motor home.

The irony of my choice to live in a motor home when I have a large, beautiful home of my own baffles friends and family, but I don't care what others think. I know staying means losing myself completely, and I'm no longer willing to sacrifice myself—mentally, physically, emotionally, or spiritually. Anyone who knows me knows determination is my strongest quality.

In the four months that follow, I begin to reconnect with myself despite being unsure of where my marriage—or my life—will take me. Eventually, I move back to my hometown and into a small apartment owned by my aunt and uncle that overlooks the bay. The months that follow are most blissful and healing.

Each day I experience amazing sunrises and sunsets, and begin to nourish my soul by doing the things I love most—communing with nature, diving into arts and music, reading, decorating, having fun with family and friends, and balancing my business and work. Slowly I began to feel more aligned to who I truly am despite the pain and uncertainty of where my marriage or life will end up.

Most of all, I begin to live life without so much responsibility. I set boundaries and learn to say no to that which does not align with what I value most. I take steps to actively heal and, with the removal of a benign lump in my breast, all my other symptoms start to disappear and my health improves.

Miracles From The Heart

Unbeknownst to me, Gerard has been healing, too. A year into our separation, he surprises me with a conversation that opens us up to healing our relationship. This miraculous moment changes my plan to file divorce papers that very next day, and slowly we reunite...

My entire yearlong journey has allowed me to finally reconnect with who I truly am, and to begin to appreciate my own unique gifts. These gifts are not associated with some fancy title, big house, monetary reward, or a list of accolades or achievements on a wall. My gifts are authentically mine, uniquely expressed. And for the first time in my life, I find meaning in work that's better aligned to who I truly am as I become a certified life and business coach, and obtain a Master's in Holistic Leadership—all so I can help others live their lives from the inside out.

The more I align to this, the more abundance flows into my life in the form of the right people who show up to support me and the work I do, from fulfilling relationships to—yes!—even financial prosperity. In my insatiable quest for learning, I dive also into the expressive arts, lead the reinvention of a multi-million dollar company, run a small business, and raise a family.

"How are you able to do this?" friends and acquaintances ask me all the time.

"With clarity about who I am, what gifts I bring, and the relentless determination to a higher purpose that serves others, I can truly move mountains, take care of myself, and nourish my soul at the same time," I answer.

The way to fulfillment is through the heart—not the ego. No longer will I live by societal roles and expectations. As I weave through my own life and help others who seek the same support, I am reminded that we are all here for a purpose: To bring our own unique gifts in love and support to one another.

These days, boundary setting and letting go is a constant in my life. Letting go allows me to be myself and discover my life's purpose. That life purpose is not necessarily what I *do*, although the work can manifest outwardly in that way. It's more about who I *am*, how I show up, and what unique gifts I bring into the world to help others.

For far too many years, I'd sought something outside of myself to make myself happy—the next career opportunity, promotion, or planned purchase, etc.—when in fact, now I see it was—and is— always in *me*.

ABOUT THE AUTHOR: Lisa Milich is a reinvention strategist on a mission to help women break the rules, rediscover their value, reclaim their voice and live their dreams fearlessly so they can have a more prosperous life. As founder of Inspired Living, a leadership and wellness collaborative and Living Your Way, a women's life and business coaching brand, Lisa is dedicated to helping success-driven women trade in the life they have for the life they want. A certified holistic coach and leadership practitioner, she is equipping women with the tools to lead a more lucrative, purpose-driven life that has lasting impact.

Lisa Milich
Inspired Living
www.startlivinginspired.org
lisa@startlivinginspired.org
401-787-3937

PART TWO

Emotional
Health & Well-Being

*"Those who do not know how
to weep with their whole heart,
don't know how to laugh either"*
~ Golda Meir

Stopped Dead In My Tracks
Sabrina Umstead Smith

The memory of the smell of smoke overpowers me as the elevator door opens and I step out and walk down the hall toward my old apartment. It feels like the longest journey of my life.

I stand in front of the door and see the indentations near the lock from the axe used to force the door open. Drawn to touch the remnants of burnt peeling paint on the door, they resemble ocean waves. I remember how the overpowering stench of fired smoke filled my nostrils every time I took a breath.

I touch the door knob, still trying desperately to make sense of all that happened. I stand at the door, frozen, shake my head and try to hold back the river of tears that start to flow down my cheeks. If I hadn't relinquished the keys I would have entered the apartment one more time to gaze around the rooms where my life as I'd known it went up in smoke, destruction, and death.

I head back to the elevator, my emotions a tangled ball of yarn. The pain is excruciating—*I have to get out of here!* I panic. *Why did I come back to this place, anyway?* Standing in front of the elevator door I press the down button. *Really, I can take the stairs, it's only three flights,* I think. Instead, I wait.

The elevator chimes, its door opens slowly, and there *she* stands— the woman who changed the trajectory of my life.

I recognize her instantly as I step in and, though I do my best to look through her, anger and rage race through my entire body. *Surely she must see it on my face,* I think. She glances at me quickly, and I secretly silently dare her to utter a single word, so I can respond with words that cut her deeply—words sharp as a double-edged sword that leave her bleeding. I want her to feel the depth of my pain.

Finally, she recognizes me and gasps: "How's your husband?"

Instantly, my volcanic emotions erupt and I reply "my husband is dead!"

At that moment the elevator door opens and I storm out, leaving her speechless. I walk quickly down the hall to the stairs, out the front door, and break into a run toward my car. I fumble for my key, plop myself into the car, and begin to sob and scream uncontrollably, all the while banging on the steering wheel.

God, please wake me up from this horrible nightmare! I pray, hoping for answers and some kind of relief.

The Air That I Breathe

October 14, 1988, my husband Eric and I—newly married and expecting our first child—are found unconscious and presumed to be dead, victims of a fire in our third floor Brooklyn, N.Y., apartment building. However, a firefighter on the scene insists on administering mouth to mouth resuscitation, whereupon we're both taken to a hospital that has a hyperbaric oxygen tank.

My mother explains to me two days later what happened and that I was placed one time in the tank and regained consciousness, while Eric went in twice but remains unconscious at a different hospital. She explains also that doctors told her she needed to make a decision about terminating my pregnancy because they feared my child may be born with a variety of health challenges because I'd lost oxygen.

They said they didn't know—today's technology certainly wasn't available then—and that it was a roll of the dice. Five months pregnant at the time, I'm fine when my mother tells me she decided not to terminate my pregnancy because I haven't seen my husband yet, can't travel since I'm still in the hospital, and because none of us knows what's going to happen.

Devastated, so many emotions zoom through my mind. I try to keep my emotions stable and do what I have to do to keep myself sane, because whatever I do is certainly going to impact the child I'm carrying. Eric and I had been looking for a house, climbing the corporate ladder—we had dreams and plans for our unborn child, and were building a business to help others with their career plans. Now he's on life support in a hospital several miles away.

A few weeks later Eric dies without ever regaining consciousness. I'm told to take it easy and do not return to work. I move in with my aunt, dumbstruck and numb, while my family surrounds me with as much love and support as they can. How did this happen? No time to dwell. I have to keep my emotions in check for the life of my child—our child—yet to be born. Every now and then I feel the baby kick and move. I remain prayerful but wonder why this happened to me and what I did to deserve this...

Fast forward a few months and my son Erick is born. I learn he has a host of health challenges as a result of injuries sustained from the fire, including cerebral palsy and mental retardation, and at three days old he has his first surgery—a tracheotomy. A tube in his stomach, he's never able to take food by mouth.

Test after test is done and I learn that his condition requires extraordinary care that can only be found at Children's Hospital of Philadelphia (CHOP) or Boston's Children's Hospital. I decide to go to Philadelphia to live with my mother. My mental state is not important—I focus on Erick and making sure he has *everything* he needs to thrive.

The Grieving Process

And I do just that. Erick thrives for three and a half years, and after he passes on July 9, 1992, I still think I have it all together. There's nothing I can't handle; after all, I survived the death of a husband and a child, and I'm fine.

My mother passes away in June 2003, and almost a year later I realize my life is just a mess—she was my rock and my source of strength. I'd remarried and my husband Rosy is amazingly supportive, but I'm still wounded and in pain. Counseling, support groups—I try them. The counselors and shrinks all tell me I'm fine. Support groups prove too painful, so I keep moving and mask doing what I have to do to live my life—or at least what's left of it.

All the while anger and disappointment simmer inside. Finally one morning the eruption occurs.

"I'm not going to work today, and you can't make me!" I tell Rosy defiantly. "I'm staying in bed and doing what I damn well please!

Not knowing what to do, Rosy reaches out to a friend who calls me and says "Sabrina, it's time to surrender—you need help and I'm going to help you find it." She calls me back with name of a shrink. Just before I meet with the shrink at my place of work I lose it and blurt out all my feelings of anger and hopelessness.

"You've been through a lot, you're depressed, and we're gonna peel this onion back one layer at a time," the psychiatrist tells me. I'd been to three shrinks over the years between the death of my husband and my son, and they all told me I was fine, but I realize now I never had the chance to go through the grieving process.

I start therapy and my healing takes time. For me it's first about acknowledging that I've been deeply scarred and that it's all right for me to feel that pain. I need to heal my anger, pain, suffering, and inability to forgive for all I'd been through. Secondly, I have to realize I really need professional help to work through the process. Not very good at asking for help, at times I still struggle. Third, I have to learn that sharing my healing journey is *so* helpful to others.

The emotional stuff I've experienced may be exactly what helps my neighbor, co-worker, girlfriend, or stranger get through a major life crisis. I learn that, despite what I went through, I experienced it for two reasons: For me to grow as an individual and to help somebody else get through it as well. We really are stronger than we think, and together we can remove any barriers that try to hold us back from being amazingly powerful human beings.

Each session with my shrink ends with a homework assignment. One assignment in particular is to find my son's legacy. At first I have no idea what that's going to be, but when I discuss it with Rosy we decide to start an organization that will provide college scholarships to young men. That's the beginning of my healing. My therapy lasts three years, and I begin to feel good about who I am and who I've become. I feel like I mean something to this world...

Going Back

A few years after therapy ends I decide to again visit the place where my life changed forever. At the time of the fire, newspaper articles said it started as a result of children playing with matches, but residents said it was crack cocaine related.

Originally, I spent a lot of money trying to find out who was responsible—someone had to pay! But nothing came of it. I needed my resources and energy for my son, and after he passed thought: *Ok, I'm done, let's just keep moving and live life the best we can.*

Rosy and I travel to Brooklyn where we're able to gain access to the building thanks to its superintendent. I knock on the door of a neighboring apartment, and learn that the former resident no longer lives here. Another neighbor overhears my conversation and leads us to her uncle who lives down the hall and who she says knows how to contact my old neighbor.

She takes us to her uncle's apartment where we introduce ourselves, shake his hand and the hand of his son, and I begin to share my experience.

"I remember that fire—it started in my apartment," the older man says. My heart skips a beat. *I just shook the hands of the men responsible for the death of my husband and child!* I realize.

We drive home, some 150-plus miles, speechless. Once home I collapse on my bed, and it's hours before I realize what just took place. My journey, which had simmered for so many years filled with pain, suffering, and self-destructive behavior, has passed...I can actually breathe freely, knowing that I've healed and forgiven.

"I wish you could have seen the look on your face when you shook that man's hand," Rosy says later. "I'll never forget that look."

Now, as I share bits and pieces of myself, I learn that others are encouraged to take on challenges that may otherwise have stopped them dead in their tracks...

ABOUT THE AUTHOR: Sabrina Umstead Smith is an experienced manager who has worked for top corporations. She's a self-starter who runs her own nonprofit. She's a gifted speaker who connects with both audiences and individuals. Sabrina gave her son a meaningful legacy through Erick's Place, a charity she founded to help chronically ill children and their caregivers. In running the nonprofit, she applied the organizational and leadership experience she honed over 25 years at Verizon and affiliated corporations. Sabrina is the creator of Forgive 4 U, a program that defines the six essential steps to overcome emotional roadblocks.

Sabrina Umstead Smith
Forgive4U
www.forgive4u.com
powerfulyou@forgive4u.com
856-371-2360

Wide Awake
Kay Larrabee

I jolt upright in my bed gasping for breath. My heart pounds, and beads of sweat form on my neck and chest as the words *I want a divorce!* echo over and over again through my psyche. I moan in anguish as these words—my spouse's—fill me with terror and suffocate me. I take a deep breath and look at the clock. It's three-thirty a.m.

For more than twenty-two months—648 days to be exact—I cannot sleep through the night. Not once. Sometimes I collapse on the sofa during the day to try to make up for the sleep deficit I've experienced the night before. Most often, though, I simply lay in the fetal position wide awake and unable to function.

Do you know what lack of sleep does to a person? Without REM sleep, we lose our minds slowly, along with our ability to think clearly, make decisions, handle stress, and function in general. I spiral downward into depression and despair and question the necessity of my existence. After all, who really cares if I disappear?

Breaking Point

I hit rock bottom when I resign from a job that's my primary source of income because I can no longer deal with its demands—in fact, I can barely function.

Journal entry, early December 2009: *Finally I decided to give my notice—I'm grateful to have a job, but I cannot handle it emotionally. I have to take care of my health and start to live my life without being in a continual state of depression.*

I know I have to step away from making a living to work on *me*. Depression is only part of my problem—I need sleep and I need it now! Terrified—this terror bubbles up inside and bursts out of me every night at three-thirty a.m.—I wonder where it comes from and why I'm so afraid. Does it come from the message I learned from my family that I need a man to support me? Or is it a result of being so emotionally beaten down during my twenty year marriage that any self-confidence I once had is gone?

Undoubtedly connected to my physical challenges—weakened arms from a childhood disability that cause me to struggle to open jars and locked doors, or to light a match—I wonder now how I'll handle the day to day physical rigors that come with running a household on my own.

Journal entry, late December 2009: *I am scared of everything. A lot of things in my life don't work, and I can't move forward! I'm depressed, and can't sleep because of all of the anxiety inside of me about what's going on in my life...I believe it stems from my husband leaving me. My marriage was the one thing I was sure of—that I could count on. If that can end, then there's nothing on which I can rely....nothing is for sure—employment, relationships, health. I must accept this and still carry on with my life, unafraid. But how?*

It doesn't help that I find it difficult to ask for assistance—I don't want anyone to pity me because I have a physical disability—and I know I've always worn a mask of strength and confidence. Always the one who helps others, I'm confused because I don't realize that my family doesn't know how to respond to me as a person whose strength has been crushed by personal catastrophe, so they stay away when I need them most.

Into The Loving Arms Of Morpheus

I never even consider taking sleeping pills. In my condition, I might have been tempted to take the whole bottle! I don't want to tempt fate, yet still I can't sleep soundly.

The first doctor I find prescribes antidepressants that make me so nauseous I have to stop taking them after only a few days. Several support groups to which I reach out are not accepting new members, others are on hiatus. I *know* resources are available—a good doctor, therapist, support group, and friends—but I have to find them!

Only when I move back to New Jersey to be near family am I able to muster the courage to try antidepressants again. Unfortunately, this prescription makes me sick as well, and now I find myself waking up each night around three-thirty a.m. not only panicked and terrified, but with added nausea and a burning sensation running down both arms!

I don't give up. I research antidepressants and visit a new doctor for a different prescription. He recommends an over-the-counter sleep aid also. I take them both and—hallelujah!—sleep through the night! The third time's the charm, as they say, and I'm happy to report that *this* prescription works without any ill side-effects!

It's Christmas Eve 2009, and I don't realize until I'm able to sleep through the night again that I haven't done that for almost two years!" Amazing that something we take for granted becomes so crucial when it's gone!

Until now, the only vision I had when I closed my eyes was of me careening down a black hole with nothing to hold on to for support. Once able to sleep through the night again, my vision changed. Now when I close my eyes I see myself in front of a large audience making a speech to empower others. Quite a change in perspective! What a wonderful holiday gift—and one for which I am eternally grateful!

I don't want to become dependent on pills, so I take them for a couple of days and try a day off. In total, I needed to take them for only three weeks to get back on track. Finally I'm able deal with the crisis through which I've been living and start the true healing process. I begin therapy as well...

In therapy I realize my insomnia is a manifestation of Post Traumatic Stress Disorder (PTSD.) I begin to understand that the challenges I faced with my spouse and adopted children were *huge* and that I shouldn't feel badly about having trouble dealing with it all, especially when you factor in the additional stress of a divorce. Anyone would break!

No sooner do I find the necessary tools to help me sleep through the night than *boom*!—another major health crisis emerges: *I'm diagnosed with breast cancer!*

After surgery and seven weeks of radiation treatments, I say: "that's it—*enough!* No more bad stuff!" It's tough, but this time I don't freak out, I simply deal with it. During my divorce, help was everywhere around me but I was too broken to see it, so most of the time it was hit or miss. During radiation treatment I was told "you're gonna be tired, take a nap," so now I tell everybody "I can't do this by myself and I'd appreciate your help..."

My Recipe For Wellness

My body has to heal now from *both* the cancer and my internal emotional devastation before I can create my new "normal." I realize

I've been resisting the reality of *what is,* and until I accept *what is –* that I *am* divorced, *am* living alone, *am* a cancer survivor, *am* a person with a physical challenge, *am* totally responsible for my life— I can't choose to embrace my life with empowerment and grace.

I start to mend and begin to honor myself—to treat myself with love and respect. Since sleep is the lynchpin of my well-being—I know without a doubt that without proper rest and renewal I might not have survived the additional challenge of surgery and radiation treatment—I make my bedroom into a sanctuary. I want my surroundings to totally reflect *me*! The great thing about being on my own is that I don't have to compromise my taste or style for anyone else.

Finally I allow myself to buy new linens, curtains, pictures, and pillows, which I delight in showing my sister. She doesn't grasp the symbolic nature of my purchase, but I know this is a big step for me, and that I'm on the road to recovery by allowing myself these items! It's so empowering to look around my apartment and know that everything is here because I *choose* to have it here.

I splurge on a matching robe, pajamas, and slippers also. I want to feel safe again as I snuggle in my bed each night. I begin a night time ritual that includes cleansing my body through meditation/relaxation and gratitude, and I even mist fragrance over my sheets right before I slide under the covers. It's amazing how soothingly a fragrance can relieve the stresses of one's day! Since my bedroom adjoins my bathroom, I redecorate that as well, coordinating it with the color scheme in my bedroom.

In addition to making my personal physical surroundings more pleasing, I decide to add enjoyable activities to my life, such as ballroom dancing. That's right, even without a partner I decide to plow through the fear and head to the ballroom solo. It's great exercise and so much fun! Now I'm planning to ride in a hot air balloon (pretty daring for a woman who hates to fly!)

I take responsibility for my own health now by exercising (including ballroom dancing!), keeping up with annual screenings and check-ups, and eating properly as well because *I am worth it!* I treat myself to monthly full-body massages. This ritual flushes toxins and stress from my body, and leaves me completely refreshed.

All of this progress would be pretty empty without a supportive community of friends and family surrounding me. After feeling so alone during my divorce, I realize how important relationships are in my life. I rid myself of toxic friends—you know, the ones who suck you dry and feel so badly about themselves that they find it necessary to hurt others—and find much more positive and supportive friends. Many of these relationships grow out of building my own business, and are with other women business owners.

In a relationship now with a man who shows me the affection I deserve, and who accepts me completely, my life reflects the inner peace I'm now finally capable of achieving. Though there are no guarantees in life, I can carry on because I can always count on *me*. Oh, by the way, I also make it a priority to get my sleep, so that I can face each day refreshed, renewed, relaxed, and wide awake!

ABOUT THE AUTHOR: Kay Larrabee is an author, speaker and coach who takes her clients *from fear to fearless*, as they travel through unexpected life transitions. Due to Kay's own challenges, which include a long difficult divorce, unrelenting depression, and a career crisis or two, she speaks straight from the heart. Kay has been sharing her expertise and message with audiences for 15 years. Her current program *"From Messy to Manageable: How to Carry on When Your World is Turned Upside Down"*, inspires audiences to make a crucial shift in their mindset so that they can move into their new lives with grace and empowerment.

Kay Larrabee
Women on the Mend
www.TheDivorceConciergeOfSouthJersey.com
womenonthemend@hotmail.com
856-628-5272

Fresh Air

Sheila Murray

The special gown closes in the front and accentuates my cleavage, yet chills run down my back. How can I be *so cold in the middle of July? Why is this taking so long? I'd be home by now if Debbie hadn't asked to come along so she can prove the lumps I've been monitoring for two years are nothing to worry about...*

Everything progresses as usual with the exception that my sister Debbie—a mammographer—is behind the scene. The technician takes multiple views...wait...more views...wait...*more views...wait...*I'm the only person left and am out of magazines. My dread increases as two o'clock turns into six o'clock...

Finally, Debbie and the doctor enter the room with the same look on their faces—a look that says *gee you're not gonna believe this, but...*

Forty-two years old and I have breast cancer. Can't say I'm surprised as I've had lumps for two years now. I started having mammograms at thirty-nine at Debbie's urging. Eight years older than me, she's always been the diligent guardian of me by my mother's design. However, despite being given a clean bill of health after biannual mammograms followed by ultrasounds, I continued to schedule appointments six months apart.

"Really, there's no need—you're fine," they'd always tell me. But I feel it, the knowing that's nagged me all my life. The only way to truly believe your own knowing is to be empowered, and I was far from that. A master at compartmentalizing, I'd shut it down because, after all, who am I to have any special way to know what is unknown.

But it's something else that stops me in my tracks: Why is Debbie—who pressed for a closer look at my films, insisted they take more views and that they keep looking—the one to deliver the news...*again?*

An eerie familiarity washes over me, and even though the doctor and Debbie are with me, I feel alone, panicked, unworthy, paranoid, and inferior. I've based my life on these feelings and beliefs for forty odd years...

Then I hear the doctor say "very early stage," as Debbie repeats "it's all very manageable" several times.

The Dream

The water like glass, the air hot and still, my three year-old self sees my mother and sister up on the bow on my family's boat. Told to "be a good girl and stay put on the back seat," I feel alone but enjoy watching my dad's strong back as he steers the boat from the captain's chair.

I see my dad coughing. He leaves the steering wheel and, as he comes right in front of where I'm sitting, he leans over the side of the boat coughing uncontrollably, unable to breathe, unable to stop.

"Dad?" I cry out. "Daddy? *Dad!*" I yell for my mom, but she doesn't respond—Debbie doesn't hear me either. Just then a rogue wave appears from out of nowhere, crests, and washes him overboard!

The boat rocks only once and then is still. I see Dad's white t-shirt and khaki pants as he floats downward. No one hears me screaming, I'm insignificant—told to be quiet, stay still, be a good girl. I learn that no one listens to me even when I do what I'm told. I feel so alone with a sense of dread, fear, anxiety, alienation, loneliness, panic, and unworthiness.

Every time I awaken from this recurring dream—which continues for nine years during childhood—I have the overwhelming feeling that I'm going to be in trouble for letting this event happen. I have already developed at three years old the belief that I'm responsible for everything, no matter what. *How can anyone be responsible for everything?* I wonder.

It feels so real and I taste the fear for days afterward. When I tell my sister about it she says "it's only a dream, don't worry." I stop telling my mom because she scolds me, saying they'd never ignore me and how could I possibly think like that would happen.

Another belief solidified: I *am always wrong and don't know any better.* These emotions, feelings, and beliefs become deeply seeded in the bedrock of who I am.

But during the years of this dream I feel I have a sixth sense—that I know more than the others. This scary, unsteady feeling, makes me paranoid that perhaps I'm a witch! Vulnerable and exposed, I have no way to erect boundaries or create a safe space in which to speak of it and test the waters while attending Catholic school daily and church every Sunday.

The year this dream starts, I remember the phone ringing. My father, a carpenter lies broken and crushed by a crane meeting a building. The only thing that saves him is a large spool with cable wrapped around it.

This terrible accident leaves him curled up in a ball in the emergency room when my mom finds him, every bone in his back broken. He heals and is able to resume his career as a union carpenter, but for the rest of my memory everything is about how much Dad cannot do.

The Summer Of '72

Then it happens—in the summer of '72...Dad's life now revolves around how much mobility he doesn't have any more, but he's a trooper. He's going into the hospital for a myelogram—an x-ray assessment of the condition of his spinal cord—and a procedure to block the pain from the accident. He and I are talking in the kitchen, waiting for my mom to finish getting dressed.

Suddenly, right in front of me, I hear the unthinkable—my father coughing out of control. Bone chilling fear grips me as I watch, helplessly repeating "Dad? Daddy? *Dad!*" just as in my dream! He's retching and coughing up blood. My mother hushes me, tells me it's no big deal, but I'm unnerved and trembling as I wonder *is this a coincidence? Did I do this?*

Debbie, an x-ray technologist, is proud to be attending my father's doctor. She's all about the science of the situation. Little does Debbie know I'm all about what no one else can see, the feeling no one else can feel, the dread from the nightmare I've watched nightly for nine years that's manifesting right in front of my eyes now! That *knowing* I've had, contained within the feelings and beliefs bound up within my dream.

They put up the films on the screen to see my dad's spine to begin the procedure.

"What's that?" Debbie asks the doctor suddenly. She's zeroed in on what looks like a mass where his lung should be. "Should we do a chest x-ray?"

Dad's been given strict orders not to move or sit up, but Debbie runs into the room where he's being prepped.

"Sit up, Dad, we need to do another x-ray to clear up some confusion," she tells him.

Despite my father's protest they take the picture. I cry all day at home, waiting to hear something or for someone to come back and tell me that my worst fear—the one I've dreamed about for years—is a figment of my imagination.

The procedure never happens. My father undergoes surgery instead, and is given a prognosis of six months to a year.

Breathing Deeply

Diagnosed with cancer, I'm frightened out of my wits. Once again, I'm broken and inferior, especially around Debbie. Major emotions from the past surface around her, and I begin to rage. Without the tools necessary to comprehend from where this rage originates, I'm left without leverage to settle any disputes between us.

The lumpectomy shows no clear margins. I opt to have a full mastectomy, and forgo reconstruction because I'm in fear of infection and simply want my life to get back to normal. Uncertain how far my cancer has progressed, I don't know if chemotherapy is going to be part of the process.

Despite being overwhelmed and consumed with fear, I soon learn my cancer is hormone receptive—suppressing my hormones starves out the cancer—and that my lymph nodes are clear. This is the best of all scenarios!

Ecstatic, I return to life as I know it, but soon discover that life as I know it is unsatisfactory—the beliefs I've held since childhood leave no room in my life for joy and peace. My diagnosis and surgery point this out to me like an orchestral crescendo—with my sister as the conductor!

What am I to do? I fret. *I'm tool-less!* I begin to search for a better way, knowing I need to find the right tools to help me identify joy in my life. My old beliefs—that I'm unworthy, undesirable, and inferior—need to be removed!

Though I'd had therapy previously in my life, it seemed only to smooth over some rough spots without really getting to the heart of changing my negative beliefs about myself.

Eventually, I find someone better than a counselor—I find a life coach! A coach is one who trains or directs. *Yes! I need to be trained how to be happy!* My life coach, Doreen Shea-Marchetti, guides me patiently for the first few months to understand that everything happens *for* me—not *to* me. Originally, I have no idea that every point of my unhappiness and dissatisfaction were chosen by me at a very young age.

She shows me that any anger, agitation, frustration, fear—or any other feelings I didn't know I was experiencing—stem from beliefs I adopted years earlier as a small and traumatized child. I begin to heal all of these beliefs and learn that everything happens in divine time and for my highest and best.

From there I'm able to release (not easily, of course, as my ego mind holds on with a steel grip!) my baggage from all of the panic, anger, dread, and feelings of inferiority from childhood on. I begin to understand that if a certain situation triggers me, it's presenting itself to show me something about *me*—a belief I hold, a feeling I have. It's *always* about me until there are no triggers left, and then I can simply enjoy my life!

Along the way, I allow so much healing around my former beliefs and emotions that I let the heat of them burn out. As a result, I can honestly say that my reactions now turn into calm responses instead of emotional outbursts. Now I see also that these previous outbursts were never fueled by immediate triggers, but rather by events from much earlier in my life.

Over the years I tell Doreen about many amazing life stories I want to write. But my work all sounds too much to me like the "blame game." Her response is simple: "As you uncover and heal your wounded emotions and feelings from your past, your writing will emerge with a fresh air..." And so it has—I breathe deeply and am grateful!

ABOUT THE AUTHOR: Sheila lives on Cape Cod with her husband. They have two sons, one married with a beautiful little girl and the other entering college in 2014. Sheila is a Massage Therapist, Reflexologist, CranioSacral Therapist & Reiki Master. She has her own practice, Release ...Therapeutic Massage & Bodywork in Sandwich Massachusetts. Sheila believes that the rich experiences in her life have moved her into a space in which she can help others live their lives to their fullest potential.

Sheila Farkas-Murray
Release Therapeutic Massage & Bodywork
www.releaseoncapecod.com
Sheila@releaseoncapecod.com
774-313-9167

Dangerous Obsession

AmondaRose Igoe

Oh my God, I'm so fat and ugly—physically undesirable and imperfect in every possible way!

I belittle myself with this kind of negative dialogue every single day, every time I look in the mirror. I find numerous reasons to dislike my body, and my constant inner critic barrages me with self-critical and self-defeating statements.

I really believe that if I can control how I look on the outside, I'll feel better about myself on the inside—that everything in my life will suddenly become perfect. *When it comes to eating and my relationship to my body, how the heck did my life spiral so out of control?*

Before I can get a handle on these self-defeating behaviors, I find myself literally at a place where I don't care if I live or die...

"Before You Find Out Who You Are, You Have To Figure Out Who You Aren't..." ~ Iyana Vanzant

A chubby kid, my mother repeatedly makes negative comments about my eating and my weight, and I'm picked on by my peers. My issues begin here, but the reality is that I spiral out of control initially at age fourteen when I start my first diet. Finally, I experience life as a thin person!

It feels so good to control the amount of food I eat. For the first time in my life I actually love the way I look! It doesn't take long for me to become emotionally hooked on what it feels like to be thin—so much so that I can't stop losing weight. Eventually I have to quit my weight loss program because they tell me I'm getting too thin. In my mind, the thinner the better...

Soon, what was supposed to be a simple, balanced diet turns into a vicious cycle of yo-yo dieting. I gain and lose weight over and over again during my high school years. Whenever I embark on another diet, I become even more obsessed with my weight and my eating. Before long a totally destructive eating disorder starts to grab hold of me.

By the time I'm in college, my behavior is extreme. Going on and off numerous diets over the years leads me to full blown bulimia, anorexic tendencies, laxative abuse, and extreme compulsive exercising. My food and body issues start to take a serious turn for the worse.

Every time I overeat or gain weight, I beat myself up emotionally for being weak-willed and out of control. This only leads to purging— a very dangerous and crazy behavior. Like an addict who craves a drug, my drug of choice is food, and always I end up trying to cleanse my body of the "drug" I just abused.

Eventually, I begin to purge most of my meals. I take up to sixty laxatives at a time in an attempt to get rid of the food I just ate. My behavior is certainly life threatening, and intellectually I know I can die from it. However, I don't care! My self-esteem is so low that I believe my life has no value, so what difference does it make?

I want to believe that my crazy out of control behavior around food and my weight is a result of mental weakness and lack of willpower, but I begin to realize it's much deeper than that. No longer impacting just me, my situation begins to affect other people in my life as well.

"Out Of Difficulties Grow Miracles." ~ Jean de La BruyĂre

Newly married to the man of my dreams at the age of thirty, I begin to see clearly how my behavior impacts our relationship in a big way. Tony and I are supposed to be enjoying our honeymoon in the beautiful Caribbean, and I'm obsessed with my weight and every bite of food I put into my mouth.

While other newlyweds are taking pleasure in the breathtaking views and romantic locations, I find it impossible to enjoy this special time with my husband. I spend our honeymoon petrified of gaining weight and log several hours each day in the gym trying to burn calories instead of enjoying this time with my new husband. Forced to admit to myself that I can't spend the rest of my life with Tony obsessed about food and my weight, I realize doing so will surely be the death of our relationship!

A few weeks after our honeymoon it becomes even clearer that I can't go on this way and that I must decide which is more important—my new marriage or my long and out of control relationship with food and my weight...

One night after binging—as I'm getting ready to purge all of the food I've just eaten—I hear Tony pull up in our driveway. Most brides would be excited to hear their new husband coming home from work, but not me!

Oh my God! I panic, now I'll be stuck with hundreds of calories in my body turning to fat! How am I going to get rid of it all while he's home? To me, Tony was intruding on my binge time!

Soon after this incident, which emphasizes my high level of frustration and fear, something inside clicks, and I realize I can't go on this way. I need help—now!

"You Are Either Working At Your Freedom Or You Are Accepting Your Bondage." ~ Robert Adams

I start to seek out support groups for compulsive eaters and food addicts, and meet many other individuals who struggle with food and their weight, though most of them don't go to the same extremes as me. The best part of attending support groups is that I finally have a place to share my experiences and feelings so that I can get my eating and crazy behavior under control and begin to heal. I learn that I'm not alone—they've got me and I've got them!

Eventually I realize with crystal clarity that food and my weight were never the source of my problem, and that my bulimia, compulsive exercising, and laxative abuse represent a form of slow suicide. I begin to understand that killing myself with compulsive eating behaviors is more socially acceptable than taking my own life.

For many years, I've carried a hole deep inside my heart that I try fill with food—my sadness and pain run deep. My issues with eating and my weight are literally symptoms of my self-loathing and low self-esteem—I hate myself so much that I try everything in my power *not* to deal with these emotions...

Raised to believe that God is punishing and judgmental, I never heard anything good about God as a child growing up. When I begin to attend support groups I hear others say things like "God loves me exactly as I am," and "God loves and accepts you every day."

It's here that I first start to grow spiritually and emotionally—to develop a relationship with a loving, caring, and supportive God. Prior to this I never felt God's love but now I begin to open up to loving myself...I realize I can create a God that works for me and who totally loves me, no matter my religious upbringing! So that's exactly what I do—create a God that adores me, loves me, accepts me, cares for me, and supports me in every way possible.

My new relationship with God is the most important part of my healing process because I know if God loves me unconditionally then I'm worthy of love. Over time, I let go of eating addictive-type foods that seem to trigger me to eat more.

After close to a decade of attending support groups, following a specific food plan and releasing my crazy behavior with food, I feel truly and completely healed emotionally, physically, and spiritually in my relationship with food and my weight. However, I'm afraid to let go of the support groups and food plan that I've followed for so many years because I don't want to slip back into my unstable life-threatening behavior.

Every ounce of my being tells me I'm finally free and that I can actually eat normally and release the support programs on which I relied in my deepest darkest hours. But I'm scared to change what's worked for so many years. My only option is to ask God for guidance and to trust the answer I receive.

God, if you love me so much, why did you allow me to become addicted to food and to suffer from this addiction for the rest of my life? I ask.

The response: *My dear child I would never give you something to suffer with for the rest of your life. It is no longer part of you. You are free to eat normally...*

I ask again just to make sure I heard correctly, and the answer comes back exactly the same.

Today, I can say with absolute joy that I am totally *free*! My positive relationship with food and weight is something I cherish every day. And the best part is that I know now that I love myself exactly as I am. Yes, all of me!

The self-hate and condemnation are gone, replaced with love, respect, and joy for the life that I've been given. As a result, I appreciate my body more because I put it through hell and it didn't quit on me—it hung in there through some very rough times! I'd like to believe that my body—along with my spirit—must have known that healing is part of my path and that someday I'd inspire others with my personal story.

It's now been more than twenty years since I've binged, purged, yo-yo dieted, abused laxatives, or compulsively exercised, but this transformation didn't happen overnight. I had to be willing to grow and to let go of self-defeating behaviors that no longer served me. I had to commit on an ongoing basis, keep an open mind spiritually, and possess the strong desire and willingness to change.

Today, free of my food issues because I love who I am and how I show up in this world, I make healthy choices because that is what my body desires and deserves. I eat food that makes my body feel alive, exercise like a normal person, and maintain a size six to eight. Best of all, I feel an incredible sense of gratitude knowing I am free to live my life fully without this dangerous obsession...

ABOUT THE AUTHOR: AmondaRose Igoe, the 6-Figure Speaking Goddess, is an Award Winning Speaking Expert and Best Selling Author who specializes in helping business owners attract more clients and income with speaking by showing them how to design, deliver and book speaking engagements. The power of what AmondaRose teaches has helped her clients from around the globe including North America, Germany, Switzerland, Romania, England and Australia. AmondaRose is the author of Pain-Free Public Speaking, a contributing author in the number #1 Best Selling book series "Chicken Soup for the Soul" and was a featured expert on the FOX 4 Television Station.

AmondaRose Igoe
6-Figure Speaking Goddess
800-610-9056 (Toll Free)
www.6FigureSpeaking.com
www.AmondaRose.com

Neglected Child
Lillian Kui

"What are you doing, Dad?"

"Just need to fix this pipe."

"How do you do that?"

No answer.

"At school we use tape and glue."

"Can't use those here."

"I fixed my friend's lunch box the other day. I just opened the box and...so what do you suggest next time?"

No answer.

"Dad, what do you think I should do next time?

Silence.

"Dad?"

My eight year-old self realizes the stark reality of my situation: My father simply...doesn't...care...

I begin to sob uncontrollably. My mother, with us in the kitchen cooking, comes over to investigate. I tell her what's happened and immediately she starts to yell at my father for being so inattentive.

My father yells back in self-defense, saying he was focused on the task at hand and didn't hear me, then leaves the kitchen. I sit there drying my tears and feeling badly now because I've caused a fight. I feel kind of stupid—he *really didn't* hear me—but sad at the same time, and proceed to try to explain all of this to my mother until she turns to me and yells:

"Of all the things to cry about, you choose *this?"*

The Raging Teen

My family's system is a hierarchy: My mother's at the top; then my father; my twin sisters; Margaret; and me. My mother is a master manipulator and has arranged the family in such a way that if we need to tell my father something, we have go through her. If my sisters or I get into an argument, my mother talks to us separately instead of getting us together. Indirectly she sends the message that we aren't allowed to talk to each other. And so we don't. We *never* talk about our feelings—they're like a foreign language that's forbidden.

My teen years are spent in my parents' room watching TV by myself while the rest of my family is off doing their thing. I don't have many friends since I distrust people in general, and don't really know much about relationships.

My mother uses her love as bait, and it's this emotional abuse that's the worst part. If we do what she wants, she shows affection— if not, we get the silent treatment. We're left out of family conversations or activities, and either she gives us the cold shoulder or shreds us to pieces with her criticism and judgments.

I grow to hate her. She bullies us and acts like it's ok. I hate living at home and think about running away several times, but just can't do it—partly because I know it would devastate her, and also because I know she loves us in her own way. Why else would she work a full day, come home, and immediately put a full meal on the table? I see how hard she works for us, too. Both my parents do.

As I get older I retreat into myself and my own little world because there's no one to talk to at home. A family of six, we share rooms and that's about all. My sister Margaret and I connect in a twisted love/hate relationship. She stands up for me if someone at school picks on me, but at home she'll pick on me if the opportunity arises.

The worst part is that my father always blames me because I'm seen as the trouble maker since I'm usually raging about some injustice that happened. Resentful and bitter, I often break into a rage when someone pushes one of my buttons. Usually it's Margaret or my mother. I'm like a pressure cooker when I feel they've done something on purpose that they know will hurt me. I blow my lid, and when in that state of rage, I swear I could flip over a truck.

Young Adult Lost

My first year of college I meet a group of church people who invite me to study the bible with them. Eventually, I join the group. These people seem honest and real, and I enjoy their company. They're fun and unpretentious, and I feel safe enough to be myself around them. I enjoy a sense of belonging and this group becomes my adopted family.

I attend gatherings consistently, and soon my mom becomes worried and jealous, but I don't care because for once I'm getting what I didn't from my biological family.

I leave the group after graduating from college as it's strictly for students only. I get transferred to another part of the church for adults, but don't feel the same closeness. Meanwhile, I start dating someone and we marry within eighteen months.

I marry for two main reasons: I really think he's someone I can rely on; and I want to get the hell out of my house! Not the best reasons to marry, but I'm not in my right mind at the time. During the marriage I learn that he's suffered from anxiety pretty much his whole life, though I never knew it when dating because he hid it so well.

Eventually his illness becomes so bad that he loses his job, becomes paranoid, and stops going out altogether. I become his caregiver, as basically he turns into an invalid. I look at my situation and think *this is not how I want to live the rest of my life!*

We divorce and I begin a two year relationship with a man just out of an eleven year prison sentence for manslaughter. Needless to say, there are issues in that relationship as well...

Slow Awakening

By this time I've worked at five different jobs in a span of two years because I'm trying to find my purpose in life. Eventually I own a small jewelry shop and think being my own boss works best because I always find myself working for evil female bosses.

A year or so goes by and I'm bored out of my mind. Often I have a sense that I'm supposed to help people in some way, but don't know how. A natural counselor, friends come to me for advice. I even have a social work job but that doesn't cut it because I see how broken the system is and want to find a better way to help people.

One day my friend introduces me to Louise Hay's book *You Can Heal Your Life.* I skim through it quickly, get an idea what it's about, and immediately know it's going to change my life. I become so scared that I don't pick it up again for a whole year.

A year goes by and I'm still bored, so I decide it's time to read it again more thoroughly. This time I do all the exercises in the book, and its truths jump out at me like a tiger. At first, when I read that everyone does the best they can with what they know at any given moment—including my mother—I think *no f*ing way! She did her best* *to abuse us!*

Slowly I learn that I have to be honest and begin to accept these ideas, and soon everything starts to make sense! I know my major challenge is to learn to forgive my mother and to understand that she did the best she could with what she knew at the time. Eager to learn more, I embark on an investigation to learn about spiritual healing and what that all means. I know right away this is what I want to teach as well!

I sign up for the licensing and certification course to be a *Heal Your Life* teacher and life coach. The training itself is greatly transformational and therapeutic. I have moments of intense crying as I start to allow myself to feel and acknowledge my emotions again. I continue to do my own research and study after the training as well. I begin to pay close attention to my inner dialogue—how I speak to myself and how I really feel about myself.

I didn't grow up in a picture perfect family, and I think it's safe to say I'm not the exception—many people don't. The thing about my environment growing up is that nothing majorly crazy happened, like getting locked up in a basement or anything like that. Rather, the abuse was subtle and quiet, a slow deterioration of my emotional sanity. And it ate me alive.

We all need love to grow and develop into emotionally whole and sane people. But when love and emotional support was withheld, I became empty inside. That's how I felt for most of my life, like my heart contained only an empty space, like something was missing and all was not right. And it hurt; I was filled with an aching emptiness.

The worst part is that I didn't know I felt that way—I had no idea! It was like walking around with a broken leg, like limping, but not knowing why my leg didn't work—all I knew is that it wasn't working. I felt like a broken person—damaged, not whole.

Now I realize that I've internalized the emotional isolation, neglect, and abuse from my family into a deep sense of unworthiness. Subconsciously I hold myself back from succeeding and excelling because of fear and guilt. Whenever I succeed at a job, I sabotage myself by quitting.

I start to understand what real, unconditional love is, and slowly learn to stop criticizing and judging myself. We are usually our own worst critic and that could not be any truer for me! Self-judgment literally paralyzes me from doing and being what I love and enjoy. I learn to forgive everyone I can think of—including myself. I release more hurt and pain from the past, and gradually feel lighter and happier.

I decide that I'm going to really love myself and be good to myself by being healthier. I start to eat mostly fruit and vegetables after learning about the health benefits of foods that are living or raw, and cut out all junk food. As I change my eating habits and mentality, my body responds and I lose twenty pounds in a month and a half without even realizing it!

Now that I know I can give myself all the love and acceptance I need, I no longer seek validation through unhealthy relationships. Also, I've made great new friends, and that emptiness I used to feel has long since faded away. I feel so much more connected now because I know we are all *one*. I'm doing what I love and I know that I'll never again be the neglected child...

ABOUT THE AUTHOR: Lillian is a spiritual life coach who through understanding her own emotional abuse and neglect that she is not just another victim but a spirit who chose these particular circumstances so as to learn and overcome the challenges of the pain suffered, the rage that resulted and the return to the love that was always there. Lillian discovered that she can also help others find their way back to the love that they are a part of as well and to heal through this remembering.

Lillian Kui
Living Your Truth - Life Coach
www.LivingYourTruth.info
Lillian@livingyourtruth.info
917-667-8288

Running With The Bulls

Andrea Hummel

Actually, I've never been to Pamplona. I haven't run ahead of those manic bulls through the Spanish city's narrow streets in that annual rite of masochistic daring.

But many of the risks I *have* taken in my life felt as intense, insane, and animalistic. And yet they were also a source of profound fulfillment, golden mana for a soul passionate to push beyond the restrictions of a predictable persona.

My early life was the antithesis of that kind of excitement. I grew up in a small southern town—safe, protected, insular, predictable. The streets ran up one direction and down the other, no unexpected curves. A Main Street and a University Avenue. The kind of place where, I used to joke, they roll up the carpet on Friday nights.

My two sisters and I walked to school, hung out on the street with the neighborhood kids, had pet rabbits and guinea pigs. In first grade the highlight was being in the school play—as a mushroom. In second grade it was participating in an after-school program—quilling (the art of curling thin paper strips around a pencil, as greeting card decorations.) It was either quilling or football—and a mild-mannered German-American girl like me obviously didn't play football.

Weekends were more exciting. My mother, an economist and artist, painted or gardened with us; my father, a professor, took us to grand openings around town. There was always a radio station, hospital, or furniture store sponsoring a celebration. Our greatest challenge back then was to find the prettiest and best-tasting little cookies to take back to my mother.

I'm not being trite—it really was a charmingly simple childhood. I know many people grow up in challenging circumstances with risks they never chose or wanted. So I'm extremely fortunate to have had an easy upbringing and am forever grateful to my parents for this security and simplicity.

Perhaps that's exactly what made me hungry for more—hungry to taste life fully, experience risks, danger, adventure. I always felt something was missing and I wasn't truly *alive*.

The trips back to Europe were only teasers. They opened my eyes to the *real* world, real problems, and histories. I know my parents shielded my sisters and I from harshness and cruelty probably because of the horrors of their own childhoods in World War II Germany. They suffered far too much loss and sadness to want to repeat that...

There was no one single clarifying moment when I broke out of my shy wall-flower shell and pursued the proverbial bulls. Instead, it was a gradual disquietude, antsy-ness, or maybe boredom with life. Once, in frustration with my predictable world, I tried to fail a high school French exam, deliberately writing all the answers backwards. Even that back-fired—Madame Pierre simply fumed "ce n'est pas amusant!" and gave me an A anyway...

I tried pursuing activities outside my comfort zone: The debate team, cheerleading, acting, a pageant. Most of these "risks" were opportunities that just presented themselves so I pounced on them. But these didn't satisfy me either. I wanted something *big* —messy, dirty, unpredictable—like heading to the North Pole with just a toothbrush and a change of clothes. Nothing in this small town seemed to come remotely close to that...

Feeling Alive

My breakthrough finally came when I finished high school at sixteen. Instead of giving me a car or whatever the standard graduation present is, my parents gave me a plane ticket to Peru!!

Wow! Really? I was stunned! *Nirvana!* Finally, a trip to the unknown! They must have read my mind. And I didn't even speak Spanish, nor had I traveled solo before. Again: *Wow!* I was out of my mind with anticipation and excitement.

So, two weeks later, after hurriedly packing mountain gear and a passport, I was off for a twelve-day hike to Machu Picchu. In Lima I met up with a family friend for a few days, acclimating and trying to avoid getting Montezuma's Revenge (a nasty form of diarrhea caused by unfamiliar bacteria in water) by not eating anything raw.

There I was, standing at the head of the trail high in the Andes, dizzy with altitude sickness. I watched the group's muscular porters hoist bag after bag of supplies onto their backs.

Oh, crap, I thought, *what did I sign up for?! Maybe this is too much of a risk!* But it was too late to change my mind. So I closed my eyes and started walking.

Most days our trail lunches consisted of "American sandwiches" wrapped tightly in soggy toilet paper, with a sticky mint for dessert. But the true mind-boggling experience was learning to push past the achiness and cold at 7,900 feet. Some days I was so exhausted I didn't know whether I could walk another step across the mist-covered awe-inspiring crags. The nights were bone-chillingly cold and the ground hard and damp.

But then I realized the trail back was just as far as the one forward...so I kept walking, one foot in front of the other, knowing one way or another I'd make it to the end. This became a valuable metaphor for my life thereafter.

Another *oh crap!* moment was inching across a narrow rope bridge a day out from the ruins. The guide cheerfully pointed out it had ripped the week before, killing one hiker. But it was the only way across...we had no choice but to keep going forward. So I closed my eyes, turned off my brain, and felt my way across the bridge, hand over hand.

Trust it'll be okay, I kept saying to myself. *This is your time to live, not die.* And I made it!

Finally, stumbling around a bend in the path, suddenly I saw the ruins of Machu Picchu glowing peacefully in the rising sun. *Indescribable! Powerful!* In that moment it all came together. All my effort was worthwhile. I felt like this speechless wonder was mine alone. I'd earned it by pushing through and risking my life.

What I learned from this experience is not to resist challenges. Go with the flow, and don't question the wisdom of what you're doing. I learned to trust that what needs to happen *will* happen. It's like the "trust fall" so popular in personal growth workshops: Fall backward into the arms of a group of strangers and *trust* they'll catch you. Fall forward into a personal risk, and *trust* it's meant to be.

Alive Inside

Over the years, the challenges I set for myself morphed from external/worldly to internal/personal. I grew tired of physical danger: a trip to Israel during the 1990 Kuwaiti-Iraqi crisis; Greece during the strikes; hiding with Guatemalan war refugees on the Mexican border.

What am I looking for out there? I wondered. *Why do I keep chasing adventures outside myself?* That's when I shifted direction and started focusing on internal growth instead. It's also when I discovered peace-building, ShadowWork®, and women's empowerment work.

In 2006, after a painful and long-drawn-out divorce, I made such a leap into the unknown inner world. I completely uprooted myself and left behind everything I knew—family, friends, home, and my diversity training firm—to move north and pursue my dream of foreign policy work and peace-building.

I felt I had to get away, and I had it all worked out: a cool government job in Washington, D.C., and a co-conspirator to move with me and take care of our two little girls, *Kate and Allie*-style.

Of course, the "risk-gods" had to throw me another curve-ball! The job fell through only one week after I moved. And my friend changed her mind about coming along. I was devastated, not to mention mad at the universe. But—*dang it* —I really wanted this adventure! I wasn't going to back out because of a few (major) glitches!

So my five-year-old Sophie and I packed only the bare necessities (clothes, frying pan, air mattress, toys) into my battered mini-van and drove north for three days. I felt alone—except for Benny, that is. Benny was Sophie's guinea pig, a furry pillar of strength, always good-natured no matter how many miles we drove. He was by our side every step of the way, including nights when we snuck him, squeaking exuberantly, into the hotel room.

For me, that little guinea pig was a symbol of having made it; having taken a risk that I needed in order to live fully. If *Benny* could make it in a new city—heck, so could we!

I remember being so ecstatic that I cried as I passed Washington, D.C.'s city limits, little Sophie asleep in the back seat. I felt so thankful, relieved, overjoyed, renewed. After twenty years of dreaming and working to move here—I had finally made it.

Several years later, it turned out to have been one of the best risks I ever took. By the time I'd been living here for a while, I was ready to take another stab at relationships and open my heart to love. Getting back on the proverbial horse after a fall is never easy. But my choice was simple: Skip love in order to avoid being hurt, or take the risk of being hurt and gain the incredible highs, pleasures and rewards of being deeply connected to another human being.

I chose the latter.

Of course, I had to take the ultimate risk: falling in love with a Cuban. That may not seem like a leap, even if you visualize a reserved German with a passionate Latino. But here's the kicker: my first husband was Cuban. Considering how that relationship turned out...I wasn't so sure I wanted to try that particular adventure again!

In fact, when I first found out the man I was dating had the same ethnic background, I just about screamed. *No! Absolutely not! I need a garlic necklace and a wooden stake! I'm not doing this again!*

But my mother had challenged me to "date someone other than all those CIA and FBI types you bring home—a nice musician or something." I wasn't about to refuse that gauntlet! So, as Gilbert fit that criteria, I had to at least give the relationship a try.

As it turned out, that time around the risk did pay off, and we're still married.

I'm taking my latest risk right now, as I'm writing this: leaping into something spontaneous, unscripted, unnecessary. I decided this just a few hours ago—forty-eight, to be precise...

I'm sitting at the airport en route to *Iceland*! Yes, I have my toothbrush, though not much else.

Next year: Pamplona! The bulls are waiting...

ABOUT THE AUTHOR: Andrea Hummel, M.A., is an anthropologist and ritualist. Her passion is helping peace-builders and global movers-and-shakers be more effective in creating harmony and understanding internationally. She helps individuals and organizations take risks, break through fears, discover strengths and tap into their incredible potential. Since 1991 she has been teaching at universities and providing seminars to non-profits in cross-cultural settings. Andrea is launching a new coaching program incorporating Jungian archetypes. She has training in action-based methods including ShadowWork® and psychodrama. She earned her Masters in Washington, DC, where she resides with her family when not traveling to keep up her languages.

CultureWorks Consulting
www.cultureworksconsulting.net
www.linkedin.com\in\andreahummel
Andreachc3@gmail.com
813-727-6064

The Power Of Forgiveness

Dr. Barbara Tucciarone

"Let's dump her in the ravine—no one will find her there," says one of the boys who's just raped and humiliated me to the other. Slumped in the back of the car, my body numb, my mind ablaze with terror, I realize I've got to say the right thing or they might actually kill me!

In shock, I know I have to think quickly if I want to survive. From the crazy way they're talking and behaving, I know they're high. Both drug dealers and addicts, one of the boys is older than me. I recognize him from my high school and remember he was expelled two years earlier. I lean forward slightly and begin the fight for my life.

"My uncle's a police officer," I lie, "and if I don't get home soon, every cop in town will be out looking for me..."

After more crazy discussion between them and a lot of convincing on my part that I'll *never* tell anyone what happened, to my surprise my lie works and they agree to take me home. Instead of my parents' address I give them my boyfriend Bill's.

They drop me at the end of his street and speed away. I wander dizzily down the block to the door of Bill's house, ring the bell and—when he opens it—faint dead away into his arms.

Just Don't Talk About It

For years after my rape I experience continuous nightmares, flashbacks, and remember all of the details—many, many of the details—of this horrific event. It preys upon both my conscious and unconscious mind and interrupts my thoughts daily. Whenever I see a man who resembles either one of my perpetrators, I look quickly the other way to avoid getting sick to my stomach, and begin shaking with fear. For a long, long time I experience so many flashbacks, so many nightmares...

Bill would say "just don't talk about it, just don't think about it, and it will go away." Every year I get a little stronger, but it's several years before I can venture out by myself in the dark and, even then, I look over my shoulder. It's a long while before I can go out alone and not be afraid...

Bill and I marry very young and I attend college at night in order to get my bachelor's degree. By the time I'm twenty-six and the mother of three beautiful boys, I'm so turned on by the prospect of teaching that each and every course is precious to me.

One particular psychology class—in which I'm introduced to Gestalt Therapy and the techniques of noted psychotherapist Fritz Perls—changes my life. The core of the Gestalt Therapy process is to explore one's relationship—and aspects of one's personality, concepts, ideas, and feelings—to oneself or to other people in one's life. Enhanced awareness of sensation, perception, bodily feelings, emotion, and behavior in the present moment is emphasized.

I take it all in, and learn about "unfinished business," the need for "closure," and the "empty chair technique." Taught the importance of finishing unfinished business we have with others in order to move on with our lives, it's explained this is a form of role-playing. I'll always remember the professor saying "you can't have something large, if you're holding on to something small."

Letting go of the old and making room for the new is something that makes a lot of sense to me. We're encouraged to imagine a person who's hurt us sitting in an empty chair, and to express our feelings—we can yell, scream, or even curse at the person sitting in that chair so we can "get it all out" in order to be complete and free.

Several students volunteer to come to the front of the room and participate. I do not. We're asked also to write a letter to a person who's hurt us deeply. These letters are intended to allow us to vent and release our old feelings. We're told to close with "thank you for....."

I choose to try the exercise alone in the privacy of my home. I know immediately who I need to write to and put in the empty chair. I imagine I'm facing first one of my rapists and then the other. I look at the empty chair and suddenly I'm filled with rage.

"God damn you!" I scream, "who do you think you are? How dare you do that to me? You should be shot for what you did to me! I hate you!"

I begin to sob uncontrollably and my tears spill down my checks and onto my blouse. Suddenly, "thank you for not taking my life!" flows out of me, and a feeling—not only of relief—but of deep peace overtakes me.

Thanks to this class, I begin to realize how deeply I suppress my emotions. Although I understand the need for closure on an intellectual level, this technique enables me to rediscover many of my old repressed and deeply buried feelings.

When The Student Is Ready, The Teacher Will Appear

Eventually I'm able share the story of my rape with my two closest girlfriends. My best friend Anita gives me a life-changing book entitled *The Dragon Doesn't Live Here Anymore* by Alan Cohen. This book provides me with much spiritual enlightenment and opens my eyes to brand new concepts. Advice about giving up judgmental thoughts and forgiving freely all but jump off the page!

Anita supports this way of thinking, and we discuss these concepts as I soak them in. I immediately buy copies of this book to give to all my friends, so much respect do I have for its author. The book also references *A Course in Miracles.*

What I remember most from this book is that in life we can come either from a place of love *or* fear. Retaliation, blame, and guilt are all rooted in fear. When we behave with compassion, show kindness, understanding, or helpfulness, we come from a place of love. This makes so much sense to me—both then and now.

I read the book twice, and I must be ready because I sign up for my first yoga class, followed by a meditation class with my neighbor. The first night after our yoga class we're about to enter the meditation room, and guess who's the teacher? None other than Alan Cohen! Amazing! To meet him is such a huge surprise...

Later in life I learn there's no such thing as coincidence. Meditating helps me go within and connect with my innermost feelings. This brand new experience is very different for me, as I'm a thinker—used to living my life from the neck up.

Forgiveness Is A Gift You Give Yourself

Now that I can identify my feelings, I become aware of my extreme level of anxiety every morning when I awaken. As the primary breadwinner, I teach seventh and eighth grades, attend school at night to finish my college degree, singlehandedly take care of my home, husband, and three children, and am constantly worried about making ends meet. Often, I lay awake tossing and turning, trying not to allow panic and self-pity to overwhelm me.

A few years later Bill and I decide to divorce and, my friend Anita points out that I need to practice forgiveness in order to get free. She's invaluable to me during this time in my life, offering tons of support and encouragement.

Immediately I think of the empty chair technique I learned in college. I put my soon-to-be-ex in the empty chair and release my emotional baggage. I write several letters and allow myself to vent, releasing years of pent up resentments. When I'm finished with the last one, a feeling of calmness washes over me. I realize that as I forgive Bill I also forgive *me*. On a gut level, I intuit the famous words "forgiveness is a gift you give yourself." Free now, I no longer need to blame him. For far too long, I've over-focused on him and under-focused on myself. A turning point, I'm energized to move forward in my life and to embrace change...

Months later I find myself doing the same thing regarding unfinished business with my father. I had not the slightest awareness that I'd been harboring deep feelings of anger and blame against him; for the longest time I thought all was well...

This actually prompts me to get myself into therapy. I find a wonderful therapist with whom I resonate. This is my first healthy relationship with a male! I trust Dave almost from the start—he's safe and non-judgmental—and I feel free to pour my heart out to him. I know he believes in me, which helps me to believe in myself.

We peel back more and more layers of my personality as the weeks and months fly by. Initially, I deny having any anger issues. For many years I've suffered from migraine headaches, a spastic colon, and TMJ disorder that causes pain in the muscles that control my jaw movements.

As a result of my work with Dave, I'm able to face my deepest fears and to identify areas where I'm blocked. Eventually able to get in touch with the tremendous amount of internal anger and pain , I deal with these emotions.

As I own my bottled up anger and learn to release it in healthy ways, *every one* of my physical ailments dissolves! The twenty-five extra pounds I carry melt off! *Wow!* I'm so impressed with the *new me*....the woman who has *way* more energy than ever before.....the woman who can voice her opinions now....the woman who can say *no!* and mean it. Most of all, I've become a woman who *truly loves herself unconditionally!*

Now at a turning point in my life, I realize that if I can change this much, perhaps I can help others accomplish the same ultimate self-awareness, self-esteem, and self-love.   Hmmm...

Looking back over that painful yet transitional time in my life, I can see how I grew spiritually and became more alive, passionate, and authentic. It's as if I was reborn! Empowered by my years in therapy, I'm grateful and inspired to help guide others to find their true voice.

Coincidentally, during that time, I receive my master's degree and meet George, a kind, wonderful man—also in the field of counseling and on his own spiritual path—whom I later marry.

Free now to give up blame and judgment—especially toward myself—I live truly in the moment. This creates so much joy, passion, creativity, confidence, and unconditional love—I'm happy to be alive! I look for the good in every situation and in every person, and realize, too, that everyone who comes into my life is either a teacher or a lover, sometimes both. I forgive easily and effortlessly because I understand the true power of forgiveness.

ABOUT THE AUTHOR: Dr. Barbara Tucciarone is a Certified Life Empowerment Coach, Certified Emotional Intelligence Practitioner, and a Certified Hypnotherapist. She holds a Doctorate in Counseling Psychology. Barbara is the mother of four grown children and works full time at her coaching practice in Martinsville, N.J.   She is a Motivational Speaker, Writer, Consultant, and Workshop Leader. Barbara is in the final phase of writing her book about rebuilding and moving on after a breakup/divorce. Letting go and moving on is something Dr. T has been researching for years, and is happy to assist people in rewriting their Life Scripts so they can move forward with renewed confidence.

Barbara S. Tucciarone, Psy.D.
StarCoaching
positivebarbara@gmail.com
908-872-0885

Look Into Your Own Heart

Carole Franques

"So, who do you want to go with?" my father asks as he bends down, takes my hands, and looks me in the eye. Confused, I know I have to think fast, but I'm afraid if I give the wrong answer I'll be responsible for hurting someone.

Only ten years old, I've been ushered into my parents' bedroom with my older brother Eric, asked to sit on their bed, and told they are separating. I feel the tension in the room, see the seriousness on their faces, and realize that no matter what I won't be able to avoid taking sides.

"I'll go with Mom," Eric says.

"I'll stay with Dad," I utter softly—I have no choice, I don't want him to be alone. Even though he scares me at times, I'm closer to him than to my mom. She likes my brother more, anyway.

The next thing I remember is standing in the doorway of the room I share with Eric, a heart full of sadness and shock. Half the room is empty—his stuff is gone, they're gone! *Where did they go? I wonder. When will I see them again?*

When I make the decision to stay with my dad I don't know there's another woman involved. We move in with her and her two young children, and I become withdrawn and live in my room to stay out of everybody's way and avoid conflict.

Thankfully, my parents' separation doesn't last long and we return home a few months later. My parents, only sixteen when my brother was born, married at seventeen and don't seem to know much of anything except how to work hard—both come from difficult childhoods as well.

My parents owned a restaurant, discotheque, pizzeria, and catering business, my brother and I grow up in a very chaotic environment. My father's temper is bad and both my parents yell a lot. Sometimes I seek quiet and a sense of normalcy at my best friend's home.

My parents spend little quality time with us and often leave Eric and me alone with our grandmothers or employees who happen to be working that day. Other times, they busy us with chores and teach us to please everybody else because we're in the service industry. But they never praise me and, as a result, I never recognize a compliment when I receive one!

Through the years, they fight constantly and yell so loudly that often I pick up my keys and leave. *I can't take this anymore!* I think, as I retreat to a local park to clear my head and try to make sense of things. Nature becomes my refuge.

Then one day during my last year of college my mother picks up her clothes and leaves. For three days we have no idea where she is. Frantic, my dad and I contact my brother. Eventually she calls to tell him she's sought refuge at a shelter.

I don't understand and can't believe it! Bereft and at a loss to understand how she can leave me—*again*—I go to the mall with my boyfriend Ali the second day she's gone, and walk into a pet store. Raised with a German Shepherd, I see this beautiful puppy in that sad cage. We ask to play with him and, in that moment, I know my mother's never coming back.

"Don't Start Your Day With The Broken Pieces Of Yesterday." ~ Anonymous

When my mom leaves, Ali is my support. Later, when my dad decides to remarry, Ali helps me move into a home where I'm on my own—with his financial support. We walk down the aisle three years later; it seems the right thing for both of us.

When I become a mother, I take this role so seriously that Natalie becomes my whole world. I live my life around her schedule since my parents were never with me. I try to do right by her and create a life different from the one I've known.

It isn't long before the lack of communication between us takes its toll. Always busy, I rise early, rush to get Natalie to school, work in my father's business—a physical job—and often end up doing bookkeeping for the business late into the night. Day in and day out, I'm exhausted.

I try so hard to be the *perfect* daughter, sister, employee, wife, and mother. When I think about it, I'm surprised the pharmaceutical industry hasn't created a people pleaser syndrome pill yet, because the shoe fits right here...I can't give it my all and make mistakes along the way. I never feel good enough. How can I, chasing an illusion?

I fear being alone and abandoned, and feel always under someone's control. Ali is similar to my father in many ways, but we choose to avoid confrontation and heated arguments and remain silent instead.

I begin to realize our relationship is more one of circumstance than choice, and that I don't really know what love is because I've mistaken security and safety for love. Long ago I transferred my sense of obligation from my father to Ali, and now I see that I never really got to be by myself! A child of divorce, I fantasize that I can save my marriage and keep our family intact, but it becomes clear that I have my head in the sand and am stuck in a swamp, yearning to live a happier and more meaningful life.

Life events catapult me to reconnect with who I am. For forty-three out of forty-six years, I've searched for validation outside of myself and put everyone else before me. Isn't that what a woman is supposed to do according to society's rules? I begin to look at my life and ask questions about why I react the way I do, why I always put myself last...

"Who Looks Outside, Dreams; Who Looks Inside, Awakes."
~ Carl Jung

They say a picture is worth a thousand words. I look at our Christmas picture and it hits me: I have to save myself, my soul, and my health! I realize my daughter deserves so much more than the miserable self I've become. I've lost my wit and energy—I used to be fun, energetic, and optimistic—where did my inner light go? My body is breaking down—both my arms have become numb, I suffer from a kidney stone, and experience digestive and weight issues. I hate who I've become and feel so alone...

I decide to separate from my husband of nineteen years. I've endured enough. I have no choice—my health depends upon my ability to stop pretending I can continue to live this way. I contemplated ending my marriage sooner, but my savings was wiped out and I wasn't working. No family close by to take me in, I worried about where I could possibly live.

While it takes courage to change everything, my main focus is now on Natalie as I try to disrupt her life as little as possible. I remember what happened to me at the same tender age of ten when my parents separated.

When the process of divorce starts, one of the hardest moments of my life is having to say goodbye to my daughter that first weekend of shared custody. Upon closing the door, I sit on the couch and sob hysterically for hours. The immense pain and anguish is difficult to describe. My heart physically hurts.

What is this? I wonder. *Anger? Sorrow? Disappointment? Failure? Jealousy? I've spent the past twelve years caring for Natalie and now she's gone!*

I reach deep into my core to stay strong and resilient. I know I have to face up to the situation and heal my wounds. I realize I don't respect and love myself enough to demand better from others, and now I want things to change! My biggest challenge is one of empowerment, of learning how to put myself first.

Looking back, it's ironic the similarities I see between my mother's path and my own. We both decided to stay and try to fix something we couldn't, both ended a relationship of twenty-four years, both experienced health issues and endured a difficult divorce but, because I had the financial support of my father, I came out better than she.

Also, we both found ourselves with no place to call home for a while—on the day of my move, once all my stuff is packed and on the truck, I find out my financing didn't go through! I never imagined being with just the clothes on my back, all my stuff gone and no address to which to deliver my belongings.

I've tried hard not to bother anyone else with my problems, but now I have to reach out to others to ask for help. All I have to do is ask, but I don't know how. Finally, I put pride aside and in that moment I *know* everything will somehow work itself out—I trust that it will. Blessed when a few friends come through for me, I spend a few nights at a hotel, while Natalie and our dog are both safe with her dad.

Eventually, I understand that I need to look within and see my contribution to all the pain I cause myself. I realize I've followed in my mother's footsteps. I have to open many doors to heal and break the patterns for my sake and Natalie's. Some take longer to open than others, but behind each is a revelation. Upon each new discovery, I can heal the wound and move on to the next. I used to compare myself to an onion from which I peeled off layers, but now I prefer the analogy of a flower blooming, each petal opening at its own pace.

I take each day one at a time and accept the past because nothing I do will change those events, but I can *choose* to do better each day, to rise up and become my authentic self. Unsure when I first begin, I focus on the concept of owning my truth. In the process, I find the buried me—*I get it now!*

My journey takes me to the study of holistic health, energy work, and dream building. I'm grateful for every one of my experiences, as often I can relate to a client's situation. My own soul searching allows me to support my clients on their individual paths to healing. Also, I love working with children to give them the opportunity to release heavy burdens and traumatic experiences *now* rather than later in life.

Everything I've done helps Natalie and I lead a better life. Now that the storm has passed and laughter returned, I remind myself often of Carl Jung's quote: "Your vision will become clear only when you can look into your own heart."

ABOUT THE AUTHOR: Carole Franques has an extensive background in the food industry and has received several certifications following her B.S. degree. Through her own personal challenges and experiences, she has evolved into an intuitive and uses a holistic approach to healing. She is able to empower her clients through life changes to optimize their health and well-being by embodying Spirit, Mind & Body through Emotional Release, Self-Esteem Growth and Food Awareness. She does distance and in-person healing and as a French native, she is able to offer her services to individuals in French speaking countries as well.

Carole Franques
A La Carte Wellness, LLC
www.alacartewellness.com
Carole@alacartewellness.com
571-278-3325

The Long and Winding Road
Kathy Fyler

A Kool-Aid stand—boy do I want one! My mom lets me order the stand offered on the back of a Kool-Aid packet, and I love it from the moment it arrives. Immediately, I set up shop on the side of my Aunt Theresa's quiet street.

My cousins – my helpers – and I are ready for business! I'm in charge of the stand and my "staff" takes care of our clients. What a thrill I get when I hold that shiny nickel in my hand from our first paying customer. The entrepreneurial bug has definitely bitten!

In the fourth grade I start a Rock Club. Yeah, I'm a bit of a nerd. One of my aunts is a geologist and she's taught me a few things about local rocks. As part of the Rock Club, members come to my house—which borders many acres of vacant land—and we venture out to the fields after school. Here I direct them to help me find specific types of rocks.

Then I categorize and display them in an outside building in our back yard. Each girl pays me a nominal fee to be part of my club— my first membership organization! We all have fun for a while, especially me. I love teaching them and being their leader—and getting paid to do it. Wow!

Next I land my first "real" job—an afternoon neighborhood newspaper route. Thrilled when the boy next door comes to my house to hand over his route to me, I think *now it's mine* as he places in my hands a coffee can that holds the customer cards and payment stubs. I'm overjoyed!

Each day I load up the white wicker basket of my pink bicycle with folded papers, and then pack the overflow in a burlap bag that I sling over one of my shoulders. It's a heavy load for my tiny frame, but I never complain—to me its light as a feather because I'm living my dream.

The route is an everyday commitment and I'm ready for the challenge. My favorite part is Wednesdays when I go door-to-door collecting payments. Almost every customer tips me—five to ten cents! On Sundays the papers have to be delivered early in the morning, so my dad—coffee cup in hand—drives me on my route to help make it easier. It's fun having this time with him because he works long hard hours during the week...maybe I get my work ethic from him...

I really love having my own businesses as a kid and being able to make money beyond my allowance. It feels natural and right. I have other passions, too, like being really interested in science to the point where I think about becoming a doctor. So I put off my business ideas for some time in the distant future, since I feel a subtle societal nudge to follow the doctor path during high school. I prepare by getting excellent grades, taking college prep courses, and participating in extracurricular activities—all of which looks good on my college applications.

Medicine Or Business?

In the fall of 1979, my first year of college, I enroll in a heavy load of pre-med courses. I find that I enjoy my "college experience" more than my college courses, and my grades begin to fade, as do my aspirations to become a doctor.

It's my second semester and decision time—what do I really want to be and do? If I can't handle my pre-med courses, maybe I should follow the business route. It calls to me and, besides, many of my friends are enrolled in business school and their courses seem much easier. This way I'll be able to use what I learn in my own business one day. My decision made, I switch my major to business.

For some reason, though they don't say it directly, I intuit that my parents don't understand why I choose to be in business. I feel they'll be much happier if I follow the more traditional and safe route to become a nurse.

If I'm not going to be a doctor, then nursing is the next best thing, I figure. Also, it's a more widely accepted female profession these days.

So after one year of business courses, I switch direction again to become a nursing student. But only a few of my pre-med classes are accepted as part of the nursing program, and it's as if I'm starting over again. It feels like I'll never graduate!

However, nursing it is...I graduate in the spring of 1985 and start my first nursing job that summer. I've waited my whole life to start my career, and now I wonder why I'm not more excited. Looking back, I know my heart was never in it.

The Bug Is Back

Even though I'm a nurse now, the entrepreneur in me reveals itself once more when I start a silk-screening business on the side with one of my close friends. I work three twelve-hour shifts each week at the hospital. This leaves me four days to devote to my new business.

We keep all of the equipment in a make-shift room in my basement. It's a great deal of work with little reward, and my partner doesn't share the same work ethic as me or hold any big vision for our business. Devoting my time to both nursing and the business is exhausting, and I contemplate quitting nursing and making this my full time job—but decide against it. Good thing, because this business doesn't survive.

I find a way to combine my nursing and business skills when I take a job at a small technology firm in 1991. The company sells computers for bedside charting in hospitals. It's perfect! I move out of my home state of Connecticut for the first time and into New Jersey.

I find myself again somewhat unhappy with my current choice of profession—or maybe corporate life simply isn't for me. The job is interesting enough—I get to travel to meet with clients and even begin to climb the ladder—but still, something's missing.

Then comes an opportunity to start a business with my partner, and Network Display, Inc.—a lighted sign and display manufacturing company—is born! Our target customers include large corporations such as beer companies.

In addition, we create a new retail product called a "Glo-Lite" and launch it at a premier mall in northern New Jersey in November 1994. I remember sitting in the mall at a kiosk for twelve hours a day, seven days a week, during the Christmas season thinking" *I gave up my paying job for this?* And yet, it's *my business*. I call the shots, I make the decisions, there's something here for me.

We build the business for the next eight years, and experience several lean years in the process. Though tough, it's also rewarding. As we grow, we're granted a design patent by the United States Patent Office, win several design awards, provide jobs for more than fifty locals, and combine business with pleasure as we travel to various trade show locations.

Our revenues climb to nearly $5 million and we're listed on the *Inc. 500 Magazine's* list of the 500 Fastest Growing Private Companies in 2002. It's an honor, I know, but still it feels eerily hollow.

The same year, we experience a catastrophic loss and, within months, our business is gone. Some people might call this a failure, but for me it's a relief because I'm simply not feeling the kind of "soul" I so desire in my business.

The Road Less Traveled

Looking back now, I see the many threads—woven throughout the years—that make up the beautiful tapestry of my life today...

The nursing profession that I didn't want actually helps save my life. When I undergo open heart surgery at the hospital in which I was formerly employed, I have lots of friends looking out for me. Because I'm a trained nurse, when complications arise I'm able to tell my father that something is terribly wrong and he should call the doctor immediately. Because my cousin works at the hospital and is aware of my rare blood disorder, she shares this with the doctors and ultimately saves my life.

There are more neat correlations with the flow of my business life, too...

The Kool-Aid stand taught me that if I give people something of value that they want, they'll pay me for it. My first membership organization, the Rock Club, foreshadowed for me our Powerful You! Women's Network. I learned that people love to be part of something bigger than themselves and connected with like-minded individuals—and that they're happy to pay for the privilege.

My newspaper route taught me the "get paid for your productivity" model of economics and that a good work ethic goes a long way. It's funny, too, that this thread connects to our Powerful You! Publishing business today. People value stories, information, and anything that connects them to others, and since the ability to understand and provide this is inborn in both my partner Sue and me, I don't believe it will ever change.

The main lesson learned from my silk-screening business is that choosing the right partner really matters. Learning this early on led me to choose the perfect partner not only for my business, but also for my life.

The nerd in me, present in both the Rock Club and the

technology company which taught me programming skills, provides me a leg up now since I create and manage the many websites for Powerful You!

Perhaps the biggest lesson I've learned is from our sign company. If not aligned with my true purpose, I may outwardly seem successful but won't inwardly feel fulfilled. Eventually, if it doesn't satisfy my soul's purpose, it doesn't belong in my life.

We spent three years after the loss of Network Display, Inc. exploring new business ventures, including e-commerce, real estate development, network marketing, and a holistic wellness business. However, everything came full circle when we started Powerful You! Inc.—a company designed to assist women in their business, personal, and spiritual growth.

Powerful You! provides me with all those clichés I deem so very important—it nourishes my soul, feeds my spirit, and allows me full use of the varied skills and gifts accumulated from my vast experience. Although some may say I wandered down many "wrong" pathways, I know for sure the long and winding road is the most beautiful to travel.

ABOUT THE AUTHOR: Kathy's earlier diverse career includes positions as a Critical Care Nurse, Project Manager for a technology firm, and owner of a $5 million manufacturing company. In 2005, Kathy followed her calling to make "more of a contribution to what matters most in this world". Using her experience and passion for technology and people, she co-founded Powerful You! Women's Network and Powerful You! Publishing to fulfill her personal mission of assisting women in creating connections via the internet, live meetings and the published word. Kathy loves to travel the country connecting with the inspiring women of Powerful You!

Kathy Fyler
Co-Founder of Powerful You! Inc.
www.powerfulyou.com
www.powerfulyoupublishing.com
info@powerfulyou.com

Liberation From Perfection

Debra Dennis

"I just don't think this is going to work out in the long term," Gary tells me.

"What do you mean?" I ask him, surprised.

"Well, this perfectionism thing you have—I just don't think I can live with that!"

Oh my God! I begin to panic. And in that moment, I become desperate. *Please don't leave me!* I think, as I realize simultaneously that I've already decided this is the man with whom I want to spend the rest of my life.

Yet here he is, telling me it's not going to work! And, suddenly, I see right smack in front of me this sickness that I created for myself and understand that it's now or never. *Do I—can I—begin to shed my walls and armor?*

This is my scariest moment...but I do believe people cross our paths because they have something to teach us. Although it's hurtful, I know on some level that Gary is right...and now I must begin to delve deeply into discovering why I carry with me this twenty-ton shield that I think will protect me when, in fact, it's the very thing that prevents me from being seen and taking flight...

Imperfect Me

At the age of three and a half, I can only imagine what it will be like to have a baby sister—I dream she'll be like a real live doll I can hold and love and cherish! I want so much to see her little fingers, feel her soft skin, and learn how to help change her diaper...

The time finally arrives! My aunt—who's been caring for me for a few days—pulls her car up to the front of the hospital. I'm wearing my party shoes—shiny patent leather Mary Jane's—with white lace anklets. Whenever I wear my party shoes I'm happy, and today's the happiest day of my life!

It's raining a little, but the weather has no effect on my warm sunny glow inside. I see my mom in a wheelchair, my dad close behind. In her arms rest my new baby sister—chills fly up and down my spine and I feel like I could fly! I run gleefully through the puddles, so filled with life, love, and anticipation am I! Nothing's going to stop me!

Except my mother...

"Why are you wearing *those* shoes today?" she says in her most critical tone. "It's raining!"

Suddenly my throat closes, I disconnect from my body, and my voice deserts me. *Stupid me, why did I wear the wrong shoes?* I think. Then I beat myself up mentally for being so imperfect. The thought *I can't believe Mom doesn't see my excitement!* follows and—in that moment— my life changes...

President Kennedy is shot just after I turn six. Mom and I are seated together on our somewhat modern brown and green love seat in the den when the news comes on TV and Mom begins to panic.

"Oh shit!" she yells urgently to my father, "the President's been shot!"

A good girl, I look up to Mom and want to please her. After all, she's my mentor.

"Daddy, daddy, oh shit, the President was shot!" I repeat.

The silence is deafening as time seems to stop. The red bumps in the shape of my fathers hand on my cheek hurt like heck. I keep hearing the crack and feeling the sting. I didn't know that "shit" was a word only mommies could say.

Mom tells me often that if I laugh too much during the day, I'll certainly find myself crying all night. So, I do the math and make sure to keep my happiness to a minimum. Introduced to shame and guilt at an early age, I learn that my decisions are not appropriate and my feelings have nothing to do with anything. I understand that full expression is meaningless unless I'm perfect.

My elementary school years are flat and lifeless, and I'm yelled at, beaten up, and ridiculed for questions like "why can't I go to my friends' house?" or "why can't they come here?" Everyone else socializes and has fun while my home life is gloomy. Still, I'm friendly to everyone, smile a lot, but all the while the radio station in my head plays a never-ending song of not being pretty, smart, or thin enough.

The Perfect Life

Mom is absolutely stunning—always up on the latest fashion—and looks long and lean in everything she wears. Her style very much like Jackie Kennedy's, you had only to look at the cover of Vogue Magazine and there you'd see my mother.

A beautiful ballerina when young, my mother is diagnosed with breast cancer when I'm ten. By the time I'm fourteen, she's had a mastectomy. One winter evening I peek into my parents' bedroom to see what Mom is doing. The chocolate brown walls and round white bed on the dark hardwood floor give the illusion that the white linen bed is floating like a cloud.

Frail, Mom walks her fingertips slowly up and down the wall in an effort to regain her strength after losing her breast to cancer that year, and I catch my breath watching her. Reconstructive surgery is out of the question, as her once ballerina body is way too thin. When she sees me, she lifts her shear nightgown to show me her scars, and her expression turns wicked.

"It's because of you that I'm a freak!" she screams. I scurry as fast as I can to my bedroom. I must have laughed too much that day because that night I cried myself to sleep. I wasn't the perfect child after all—I didn't wear the right shoes, cursed like a sailor, and caused my mother's cancer! What a mess I am! I'd better "shape up or ship out," as my mother told me often.

Summer camp is the only thing to which I look forward. From age nine, as soon as I get home from two glorious months in Monticello, New York, I count the days until the following summer when life will again show glimmers of hope. No one ridicules me at camp, except of course, *me*. I play sports, swim in a lake, and eventually even make out with a boy for the first time. It's surreal...

A straight A high school student, I never smoke cigarettes or take drugs like most of my classmates. I come straight home from school, take piano lessons, and spend hours trying new ways to straighten my very curly hair.

I graduate from high school and happily move away from life as I know it in Forest Hills, New York, to begin a new life on my own in Bridgeport, Connecticut. Like a kid in a candy store, I try almost every drug out there and get hooked on diet pills and speed during my first year of college.

The buzz keeps me focused on my studies and at peace with the scale. I have a terrible body image—being really perfect is important to me and the pressure I put on myself is enormous...finally, at ninety pounds I'm in total control of my life! Getting my nose fixed is the icing on the cake and—finally—I feel my life is perfect!

An overachiever, I earn a lot of money during my early twenties and get married. I proceed to have two perfect children, acquire the perfect home and, eventually, the perfect divorce. Really! My ex-husband and I remain friends for a long time.

I spend the next eighteen years playing the role of the perfect single mom, raising the perfect children (they really are amazing), and keeping a perfect home. The stress nearly kills me, and I even contract the perfect case of streptococcal pneumonia...

Free At Last

My relationship with Gary now threatened, I start to listen to my own perfectionism and hear this truth: I've literally starved myself of nourishment like food, pleasure, sex, adventure, play, relaxation, and joy because being perfect is more important than being *me.* After so many years of living this perfect lifestyle, I begin to see how huge it's gotten—so huge that it overshadows who I am—I don't even know myself anymore...

My need for perfection holds me back from taking risks. I fear making mistakes and looking bad. In fact, my perfectionism is paralyzing my life! It shatters my dreams and creates missed opportunities. Now I see that what I truly crave is liberation from perfection, so I can become more relaxed in life and less in my head about how I should be.

Freeing myself from perfectionism isn't an easy task, but I catch glimpses of humor in my own behavior. Why do I spend so much time doing my makeup just so it looks like I'm not wearing any—when I go to yoga class? What's the benefit of making sure my hair is in a perfect pony-tail when it's tucked under my hat during a hike? Why do I refuse to leave the house until all the pillows on my couch are in perfect fluffed up alignment? And why have I held myself back from public speaking, not sharing my wisdom, until I know I'm perfect at it?

Studying with a mastermind group of very powerful women helps to release me from my negative body image. Through their loving support, I manage to understand the benefits of liberating myself from perfectionism and how to experience the freedom of full expression without limitation. I open up to more pleasure, laugh more, and am finally *in the game of life,* instead of living on the sidelines, worried about looking good.

Eventually, I'm able to speak comfortably in front of an audience of 100 people! Today I teach workshops on eating psychology and mind/body nutrition to help others liberate themselves from self-hate, negative body image issues, and obsession with perfectionism.

Recently Gary—my wonderful husband of four years now—and I tested my resolve to let go of that which stops me from being fully expressed, spontaneous, and free. I spent a three day weekend with no makeup and imperfect hair! I even enrolled Gary in my experiment, and we went so far as to agree not to shower (a biggie for me!)

We hiked, gardened, and ran through rugged trails with our dog. One of the greatest weekends I've had since my twenties, I spent it free from body hate and obsession with perfect grooming. Along with Gary, I even ate sushi with my fingers, and we had amazing sex. And not once did I fluff up any pillows!

I know now how important it is for me to loosen the chains of my perfectionism—had I not done so, I'd have missed out on just how liberating it is to no longer give a shit! Liberation from perfection allows me to get on a deep level that *I am enough!*

ABOUT THE AUTHOR: Debra Dennis, Founder of Indigo Lifestyle Solutions, a highly respected expert in the field of Household Staffing and Training for the past 23 years, has worked with thousands of families in securing carefully screened Nannies resulting in successful, long-term relationships. With her background in Psychology and Holistic Nutrition, she understands that finding quality staff for your home is just the beginning in creating a harmonious, nourished lifestyle. As a Certified Eating Psychology Coach and Teacher, Debra helps her clients tap into their inner wisdom to find what nourishes mind, body, heart and soul. In 2014 Debra gratefully launched her training program HealthyNannies4HealthyKids™.

Debra Dennis
www.indigolifestylesolutions.com
www.healthynannies4healthykids.com
703-307-7909 mobile
703-385-0011

This Journey Called Life: Lessons Of The Heart

Lela Lynch

Genesis

Before I'm even born I know I'm a mover and a shaker, a winner and survivor. I outperform millions to become the *one*. I live in a world that's safe, and that provides everything I need. My only objective is simply to *be*. I do nothing on my own because I have a guardian angel.

Before the beginning of my existence I have a guardian angel who guides me and gives me free will. At the end of the preparation for life in another environment I have to make a journey through the birth canal and enter into the world in which I will live out loud. I like to believe that I entered this world kicking, screaming, and crying, notifying all in attendance that I arrived with my guardian angel in charge.

This is my first life shift.

In The Beginning...

What happened to me during my first four years of life is a total mystery to me. I initially become conscious sitting under a huge tree in my maternal grandmother's yard. A beautiful summer day many years ago, the sun shines so brightly its warmth washes my face like a ray of happiness. I enjoy the feel of nature, as I listen to the amazing sounds of life all around me and bathe in the innocence of the moment as only a four year-old can do.

I sit there enjoying life, looking up at the huge, beautiful green tree with sun beams dancing through its foliage when—to my dismay—a worm seems to dive at warp speed straight into my hair! I realize suddenly and for the first time in my life that I'm very afraid...I scream and cry, and run toward the stairs of a huge porch.

I know instinctively that someone or something will relieve me of the horrible fear that grips me like a vice and launches me into reality. But of what am I afraid? An adult in the house hears my plea for help and rescues me from the beginning of life into which I've just been catapulted. And so a worm falling out of a tree and into my hair leaves me with no idea how I got here or why, and I make my first conscious life shift into knowing *I am*...

As quickly as I'm introduced to life, my world begins to change rapidly. My sister, a young teenager, lives with our grandmother in Florida. My grandmother comes home from work one day, says she's going to lie down and take a nap, and never wakes up...years later I'm told that my mother and I traveled from New Jersey to Florida because my grandmother suffered from a long-term illness and was expected to die.

Shortly after the funeral my grandmother's house catches fire and my mother, sister, and I are left homeless. My mother leaves my grieving teenage sister in Florida and we begin our journey back to New Jersey. Years later I come to understand that my mother hadn't realized she was leaving a teenage daughter to raise herself. More than forty years pass before my sister and I see each other again. Having had no previous connection with my sister or my grandmother, I don't remember feeling the separation.

On the trip back to New Jersey, I recall we have to get off the first bus and sit in the bus station because we don't have another ticket to continue on the next bus. By the grace of God, my mother manages to get me back to Newark, New Jersey, where she delivers me to my dad.

I say by the grace of God, you see, because I was born to a thirty-nine year-old schizophrenic mother and the fifty year-old son of a sharecropper. However, the one thing I know about my dad is that he decided he wasn't going to remain a sharecropper for the rest of his life. He ran away from the plantation in Arkansas when he was a young man to seek a better life in the north.

I never had the opportunity to meet any of his relatives in Arkansas and he never spoke about his parents or siblings. My mother was institutionalized shortly after she brought me to live with my dad, which represented another life shift.

My dad, his girlfriend, and her three children all live together in an apartment on the second floor of a three-story brick apartment building. Dad and I bond quickly and he treats me like a princess because I'm his only child.

My father keeps me connected to my mother. He has a friend drive him to Greystone Park Psychiatric Hospital—a mental health facility near Newark—and park the car under a window. He sits me on the roof of the car facing that window. When he gets inside to my mother, he brings her to the window to look out and see me. My instructions are to keep looking up at the window until I see my mother.

He teaches me compassion for the mentally ill, and explains that my mother did not choose to be sick, and that one day she'll be able to come home. My mother does come home when I'm nine, but she returns to Greystone when I'm eleven. She remains institutionalized until I'm twenty.

Dad teaches me this lesson about compassion for the mentally ill because I need to be prepared to deal with the cruel remarks other children make to me as well those remarks I hear made by unthinking adults. I will need this compassion and empathy later in life...

...There Was The Word

Every day—as Dad returns home from work and makes his way down our block toward our house—I get a running start and leap into his arms for a kiss. Every day I remember I'm not who others say I am, but rather who Dad says I am—a smart, pretty girl. I reason I must be a pretty child because people always tell Dad he has a pretty daughter. However, his girlfriend takes every opportunity to remind me I'm not as pretty as her daughters. Her children—many years older than me—have no need to pay me much attention. I receive my first lessons in dislike and negativity from his girlfriend and her children. They teach me I will have haters in my life, a lesson I will need later on...

I am so excited to finally attend kindergarten, Dad took me shopping for school clothes and a rug needed for nap time. We bought a tweed multi-color nap rug, and when I arrived at my new school I saw the most beautiful teacher with long hair, a smile that captured my heart, and a voice that opened the world of imagination for me.

Like a sponge, eager to listen to the stories which took me to see the king, to the bean stalk, and to learn of Cinderella's victory over her mean step-mother, I love school! A whole new world opens up for me in more than one way.

Because of my multi-colored nap rug and a raised mole on my ear, I become a target for the bullies. The bullying is never physical, but the verbal assaults are vicious. I don't tell anyone when students bully me—I hope an adult will come to my rescue. I endure this bullying at the same time I enjoy the excitement of learning to color, paint, read sight words, count further, and visualize myself in the stories that Mrs. Barrett, my beautiful teacher, reads as I sit mesmerized at her feet.

My teachers like me, and I love school and excel. Dad tells everybody we know how smart I am. He encourages me to do well in school and never to settle for less than my best. My biggest cheerleader, Dad is my first teacher. Every night he and I sit at the kitchen table and he asks me to read and explain my homework to him. I spell and practice using my spelling words in a sentence each day.

Each week, I earn no less than a ninety percent grade! I excel in math also and continue to make the honor roll. When my report card arrives, Dad shows all of our neighbors and his friends proudly, and often they give me a nickel or a dime for doing so well.

"As Each of Us Has Received A Gift, Use It To Serve One Another..." ~ Peter

By the time I turn six, my guardian angel reveals to me my purpose—I know I'm born to teach! I feel it in my soul; my reason for existence is to teach—it's ingrained in my spirit that my journey will take me to the path that leads me to my purpose...

I observe my teachers and learn what I will and will not do as I become a teacher. I see myself teaching, know how I'll dress, move around the room, and encourage my students. I'm on a mission and I know where I'm going. My life shifts...

Later on, I discover that all the while our neighbors and friends were reading out my grades and my teacher's remarks when my father showed them my report card, they weren't reading for me to hear, but to let my dad know how well I was doing in school. Little did I know that, as a boy, my dad had to help his parents on the land they sharecropped and was totally illiterate because he never had the opportunity to attend school!

The early encouragement I got from my dad and the other adults in the community helped support my vision to become a teacher for life. To this day, I'm amazed at how my dad and the community built my confidence and character, and taught me the lessons of the heart I needed to address the issues that would arise on this journey called life...

ABOUT THE AUTHOR: Lela's faith in God and her guardian angel is undisputable. There's no way to explain how she was left alone at fourteen without a support system, got knocked down by life's circumstances and got up strong. Lela is a Master Teacher who is partner of New Jersey Safe Net, a tutoring/ mentoring program that works with at-risk youth. She is an Inspirational Speaker, a John Maxwell certified Leader Coach, a business owner, entrepreneur and a lifelong learner. She inspires women's groups and youth. It's not where you start that matters, it's where you're going. Connect with me!

Lela Lynch
www.acnteacher.acnibo.com
acnteacher1@gmail.com
New Jersey Safenet (facebook)
862-224-0245

Letting Go
Valerie White

"I'd much rather have *you* as an only parent than most other couples as two parents," an old boyfriend used to tell me repeatedly. I figured that was his way of pushing me to have a child by myself to avoid my pressuring him, since he didn't want kids...

I daydreamed from the time I was young about who I'd marry and what his last name would be. Years before I even started dating I'd lie in bed at night and ponder: *How old will I be and how many children I will I have by the year 2000?*

I'd always pictured myself getting married, not only for the relationship aspect, but also because I wanted to become a mother. I saw dating as a means toward that end. Dating was not my problem. Finding a man I wanted to marry and who wanted to marry me, that's what I couldn't seem to get right!

For so long I thought: *I have to meet someone and get married to have a child and a family.* For years I believed it wasn't right to bring a child into this world on my own. Becoming a single parent because the marriage doesn't work or because something happens to the baby's father is one thing, but voluntarily becoming pregnant without a father in the picture isn't fair to the baby, I reasoned.

Now in my late thirties, pretending it's okay not to be married when that's what I want most doesn't work. I can't force nonchalance anymore than I can force good chemistry between me and a man to whom I'm not attracted. I don't know what to do, but know I *have* to do something. Each "go nowhere" relationship seems to move me further away from my dream of a family.

Thoughts like: *I'm running out of time to get pregnant,* and *is he the one or not?* only add to the pressure whenever I meet somebody new. A failed date seems like another wasted evening to me. Not a good way to think, nor a fun process for me *or* my date, no matter how hard I try to keep my aging egg fears to myself...

I realize putting my future happiness on hold in order to find the right man is not working in a *big way*. I know the common denominator in my failed long-term relationships and short-lived dating experiences is *me;* however figuring out what I need to change and how to make these changes is daunting at best.

At thirty-nine it's clear to me now that marriage *and* children, which I so desperately desire, may not be in my future. Acknowledging I might never marry is truly hard for me, as it triggers my worst fears and insecurities. I can be single and adopt, but never thought of having a child on my own.

I begin to understand it's now or never if I want to use my own eggs, and also that I'll *have* to do it by myself. *Ok, but can I let go of this idea in my head that I can't do it alone? After all, there are a lot of women like me who get to this age who haven't met the right person, aren't married, and don't have kids...*

For the first time in my adult life I decide to take my ex-boyfriend's advice to heart that I *don't* need to be married to start a family. This major shift—this letting go—is incredibly empowering, and I honestly for the first time truly believe it'll be okay. *After all, I can support a child, I can support myself, and if I don't marry is it really the end of the world? No!*

New Jersey And Me—Perfect Together?

I'd wanted to move out of Manhattan for several years, but figured if I couldn't meet a prospective husband in New York City there'd be no way I'd meet somebody isolated out in the New Jersey suburbs. But things reach a breaking point shortly after the terrorist attacks of 9/11, and I—like so many others—must take stock and question what's truly important to me.

I decide I'm willing to go to the suburbs of New Jersey, and won't remain dependent on something happening with or because of somebody else. While contemplating moving to New Jersey I see a fertility specialist who clears me to try to become pregnant through artificial insemination. I research sperm banks, decide upon a donor, and order the "donation."

Meanwhile, I rent a professor's house in Princeton, N.J., near family, and move at the end of May 2002 with the notion that I'm going to do something I've never really done before—relax and work on writing the book for which I have a contract. My newly discovered sense of empowerment leaves me free to date for the fun of it, since I no longer need to find "the one." If I don't have a good time, oh well, I'm simply meeting somebody new and enjoying an evening or afternoon out. If I do like somebody, well that's just a bonus! It all seems an adventure with nothing to lose since I'm not looking for anything to gain for once. Years of angst dissolve along with my shifting beliefs about what's possible and acceptable.

In Princeton I join a round robin dating event and come out with six mutually agreed upon dates—the largest number of matches in the group! I continue also with a New York-based online dating service, only now I have a New Jersey address.

This is a lot of fun, I admit, and continue to date throughout the summer. Amazed by the number of nice men I meet in New Jersey—though not physically drawn to most of them—I enjoy seeing them casually. I realize my time here is turning out to be more socially pleasant than I'd anticipated. I meet and date more genuinely good men in three months in New Jersey than in all the years I lived in New York! And, though none turn into serious relationships, I'm happy as I get ready to try to conceive.

Somehow my New York City dating service profile accidentally pops up in front of a New Jersey guy. Not interested in dating someone from New York—he wants a Jersey gal—Marc notes I'm located in Jersey and contacts me. Right away things between us are good...

Meanwhile, I've picked out a sperm donor and am ready. I drop the other three men I'm dating casually. They all tell me they think what I'm planning to do is fantastic, and that they support me fully. One, who is divorced, even tells me he loves his little girl so much that he wants another child and is willing to donate his sperm—we don't even have to sleep together! He tells me if our relationship works out that's great—we can raise our child together—and, if not, the baby will be mine and he won't interfere! Where do these men come from? Certainly, they're not the ones I'd been dating in New York all those years! I thank him, but decline his offer.

My third date with Marc is the evening before I'm scheduled to be inseminated. It's clearly time to let him know my plans!

"Wow!" he keeps responding, "wow, I didn't expect to hear this on our third date!"

I tell him I understand it's a bit surprising, and he adds quickly: "Well, look, Valerie, I know you've thought about this, I know it's important to you, and I totally support you. But things are going so well for us that if you want to consider postponing this, maybe you and I can try at some point in the future to have a baby together."

Now it's my turn to think: *Wow! Here's a person with whom I can make a family and a life! He's said absolutely the right things to me!* I choose not to go through with the procedure, and instead continue to see Marc. Dating since early September, we marry that February.

My Girl

Having our own child together proves impossible, despite all that modern reproductive science has to offer. I'd seen a disturbing documentary about the plight of baby girls in China years earlier—much as creating our own child would be a joy—we decide to adopt a little girl from China.

Adoptions from China will soon no longer be an option for most foreigners, as circumstances there are dramatically different now. But, as with our marriage, our timing seems to be perfect. When we start the adoption process we understand the waiting time from application to actual adoption will be seven months. Ultimately the wait turns out to be seventeen months. Had we submitted our application a month or two later, the wait could have been nearly a year longer!

It's quite a sight—thirteen squirming little bundles tightly packed together on a couch, all dressed in heavy snowsuits on a hot and humid day. One baby not lumped on the sofa with the others is held by a nanny. Quiet, curious, and particularly beautiful, this baby's perfect features and white cheeks—rosy with eczema from spending the winter in the mountains where she was born—are framed by her shiny brown hair.

Several prospective parents, including me, wonder whose baby is this little doll come to life. A few weeks earlier we'd received photos of the baby meant for us. However, they were taken when she was only several months old, and now she's between nine and eleven months of age. As the other parents are called to come and hold their long-awaited babies for the first time, I realize this little darling is indeed ours!

It's nearly two years since we started the process to adopt. Now, for the first time in my forty-three years I'm going to become a mother! Marc is forty-five when they hand Chloe to us.

We believe now, as does Chloe, that we were meant to be a family. The dear people who gave her spirit a physical body let go of her so that she could live a life filled with greater opportunity than if she'd remained in China. And my letting go of the notion that marriage and family was my *only* option made it possible for me to fulfill my dream of marriage and motherhood in the end...

ABOUT THE AUTHOR: Valerie White, PhD, is a personal and Fortune 500 executive coach who works with people around the world. Her passion is helping others achieve more joy and success as quickly and permanently as possible. She is co-author of *First Impressions, What You Don't Know About How Others See You,* and has been a guest on the Today Show, MSNBC, the BBC and NPR. She is a NYS licensed psychologist, Reiki Master, and is working toward ACEP certification in energy psychology. She has a loving family with a husband, daughter and many furry, four legged children.

Valerie White, PhD
ChangePerspectives
www.changeperspectives.org
drvalw@aol.com
973-543-6380

Who's In Charge?

Vicki Lea Leech

"Something's wrong with Mother!" I tell her friend Dorothy frantically. "Maybe she's just tired, but she seems confused and her speech is slurred!"

"Stop overreacting!" Mother says, outraged after hearing me on the phone. However, I wouldn't be calling for help if there was no reason for concern.

Dorothy, a retired nurse and volunteer, is familiar with Mother's medical condition and defensive personality. I choose to call her, rather than 911, to help me decide if it's necessary to go to the emergency room. Dorothy, Mother's friend since they were teenagers, is the only person who understands how helpless and hurt I feel by Mother's disrespectful manner toward me.

Mother, now eighty-three, has a history of strokes—including transient ischemic attacks (TIA's), or mini-strokes. She's usually discharged after several hours of evaluation, and always blames me for overreacting. Nevertheless, I put up with her lack of concern about her own health and do what I feel is right. Her displeasure makes no sense and I'm angry she's annoyed with me, but don't express my feelings.

Besides, I know the *real* reason she doesn't want to go to the hospital: Smoking restrictions! Mother allows nothing to stop her from smoking—it takes precedence over everything in her life, including me, her only child.

When Dorothy arrives Mother is sitting in her recliner, smoking. Dorothy asks her not to smoke so she can get an accurate check of her vital signs.

"Virginia, your vitals are good—"

Mother smiles, as if to say *I told you so!*

"—although I think you've had a stroke and should contact your doctor as soon as possible."

Mother's annoyed, of course, that someone—*anyone,* even her most loyal friend—is telling her what she *should* do! She neither responds nor acknowledges her appreciation for Dorothy's presence.

"Would you like me to call for an appointment?" I ask her.

"Ok," Mother replies calmly as she continues to smoke.

I walk Dorothy to her car and thank her. She suggests I put into place home care for Mother—out of concern and compassion for both Mother for me.

"I've known your mother a very long time," says Dorothy. "She's a beautiful, brilliant woman who's always had an independent and strong-willed personality, and who wants things her way..."

Then she says something I'll never forget: "Maybe someday your Mother will forget she's a smoker."

"In my dreams!" I laugh.

"It's really possible," Dorothy replies. "Some stroke victims do forget..."

We both smile at the idea of that happening, though I believe it to be impossible.

I'll Do It My Way

When mounting research proves that smoking is connected to health issues in the 1970's, Mother becomes extremely defensive about her "right to smoke" and annoyed at any talk of restrictions. Nothing can convince her there's any health risk, even when doctors medically confirm that my health has been compromised since childhood.

"You've lived all your childhood around me and others smoking," Mother says, determined to believe that these health risks are untrue and that I'm simply overreacting. I know she loves me, but she refuses to acknowledge medical evidence that my health issues are related to her choice to smoke.

My symptoms—including chronic bronchitis into my college years and when working as a stewardess in the 1960's and 70's—suggest prolonged exposure to secondhand smoke. I never smoked, and never had any desire to after being around it all my life.

During my stewardess career my symptoms worsen. It isn't until the 1980's that the airlines accept the possibility that in-flight smoke relates to serious medical conditions. This is a reality no one wants to accept, but I know many coworkers who've died from lung disease and never smoked.

Meanwhile, my mother tells me she's proud to be the only one in our family who's never been diagnosed with cancer. She comes to believe that if she stops smoking the extreme effect on her body will *cause* her to get cancer! I know this isn't rational...

Mother was a brilliant business woman—an in-charge kind of person—who I know would never hurt another person. It's impossible that the devoted and protective Mother of my childhood could have *no* compassion for my health issues.

However, her denial and lack of concern gradually limit our shared time together during most of my adult life. We had a close mother/daughter relationship until smoking became her priority. It's heartbreaking that she allows this to separate us, especially after my son Christopher is born. Loving her from a distance is the only way to avoid the hurt and disappointment I feel.

Yet she's determined to do what she wants to do, no matter what anyone says. Her actions say it all—"I'm gonna do it my way!"

"Adult Child" Caregiver

Mother's neurologist confirms she's had another stroke and his diagnosis is vascular dementia and cognitive impairment, combined with her existing heart disease.

"Your mother's medical decline is now irreversible" her neurologist says. I'm unsure and bewildered by the exact meaning of this diagnosis. Mother doesn't look sickly, she's been living an independent life, and still drives.

I soon find out, as Mother struggles with how to hold on to her independence, that I'll struggle, too, with how to respect her independence as I make lifestyle choices for her due to her current rational limitations. I learn that dementia can cause cognitive deficits equivalent to a young child's ability to reason. Mother's cognitive deficits relate to her health, safety, and lack of concern about her smoking habits—which cause burns in her clothing, favorite recliner, and the carpet.

"It's ok, I had the chair and carpet fireproofed," is her response when I express my concern. She says this with such confidence that at first I accept it as rational. She can be very convincing! As the reality that I'm now an "adult child" caregiver begins to sink in, I realize that Mother—who's always been the decision-maker in my life—now needs me to reverse our roles and become the one who's in charge...

I find a small assisted living home for six residents with a visiting nurse practitioner. All the residents smoke (though restricted to the front screened-in patio), and the home is pet friendly with lots of visiting dogs and cats. These are the two joys of Mother's life, and the two reasons she can't live with me, besides my physical limitations to caring for her.

I see her every day since she's only ten minutes from me, and bring her home occasionally or out for lunch. A few months later, she's doing well with the routine until she has a stroke and seizure. Her cardiologist wants to give her a pacemaker, and the surgery goes well but she declines mentally and can't walk. The doctor recommends nursing home rehab with consideration for long-term care.

I move her and she becomes very peaceful, quiet, and gentle—the loving mother I had as a child. Miraculously, she forgets she's a smoker! When she isn't smoking, all her good qualities emerge once again and she's neither argumentative nor in denial. Ironically, her smoking—which is what pulled us apart—is what brings us back together, as it's no longer a priority for her and she's again compassionate, happy, and pleasant!

Sharing this part of her journey provides us a new beginning. Eventually I learn from her neurologist that, due to her above average intellect, she's able to interact verbally and make "clever" comments better than most others with dementia. He explains that Mother's vascular dementia is a result of her history of strokes during the previous twenty years, and that her irrational behavior about smoking relate to early stages of dementia.

This explains why she never believed me about my sensitivity to secondhand smoke in more recent years—the major reason for our personal conflicts throughout my adult life. Words cannot express how this changes our relationship!

We share five wonderful years together making new memories...the nursing home staff considers Mother their favorite resident. We've been blessed with the opportunity to enjoy an unconditional mother/daughter relationship and to share in ways that change both our lives forever. Mother forgets the conflicts between us, and I let go of all the disappointment and hurt from my past.

What a new appreciation and happiness I feel to know her now as I'd known her as a child! In her sweet smile and the twinkle in her eyes she expresses the same love and trust that she gave to me earlier in life. Knowing I'm able to create a sense of security for her—one that makes her feel safe and loved—is the best possible gift I can give her.

The Call

Asleep only a few hours when the phone rings, I turn on my beside lamp and look at the time on my cell phone. It says four a.m. I pick up the phone and before the person calling says anything, suddenly I know.

"No!" I protest. "Not yet!"

"I'm so sorry to tell you that your mother passed a few minutes ago," says the nurse from the home. "I want you to know her late night aide said she had a very peaceful, brief, and calm passing. If you'd like to be with your mother before she leaves, we can wait to make those arrangements."

When I arrive, the entire staff from the late night/morning shift is there to say goodbye. After five years they're like family. Her aides enjoyed helping her with her favorite hair style and outfit that I'd prepare for her each day. One aide asks if she can put Mother's lipstick on for her. To me, that's such a loving thing for her to do...knowing that Mother liked to look pretty and always wanted to wear her lipstick.

I want Mother to leave with pride and dignity. I lay her favorite comforter over her for the trip to Texas, where I join my uncle, Christopher, and a few special friends to say "goodbye and sweet dreams."

I miss Mother now, but don't feel sad, knowing we shared memories that make my heart smile every day. I'm especially grateful that she passed peacefully in her sleep, which was undoubtedly her plan.

Thank you God, for letting her leave on her terms! Now I know, with certainty, exactly who's in charge!

ABOUT THE AUTHOR: Daughter, mother, friend, and retired Flight Attendant...Vicki became an "adult child" caregiver, when her mother was diagnosed with vascular dementia, and they shared a "six year journey" with her decline. She credits her single working mother with inspiring her entrepreneurial spirit to pursue her creative ideas and passions. Vicki now advocates for dementia awareness, family shared care giving and care planning. Her passion is to assist the elderly and family caregivers by researching resources and encouraging caregivers they can help a loved one suffering from dementia maintain quality of life, and it's possible to sustain a loving relationship.

Vicki Lea Leech
Advocate for Dementia Awareness
VickiLeaJournals@gmail.com
www.vickileajournals.wix.com/advocate-for-aging-
772-879-9109

Emancipation
Michelle Gale

It's opening night at a cutting-edge gallery in Atlanta. Energy is high, the place is packed, and the crowd is moving as one. Suddenly, a large rectangular painting stops me cold. The bulk of the canvas is a muddy shade of brown. Almost lost in the lower half is a little girl in a red dress staring, stricken, at the viewer. Hovering above her head in black lettering the size of which diminishes with each successive line is the legend "I am the worst little girl in the whole world." I am glued to the spot. I am forty. But I have been that very child.

When I was thirteen, my parents and I went to Europe. We spent a few days at a sumptuous hotel in Torquay, a lovely seaside town on the English Riviera. Between the thrill of being *in Europe* and the opulence of the place, I was savoring every moment.

On our second night, we had dinner in the hotel restaurant, an establishment the size of a ballroom dripping with elaborate crystal chandeliers. Waiters in tuxes swept suavely about, diners spoke in hushed tones, and classical music played in the background. I was wearing my brand new green jumper and ordered my favorite, veal scallopine. It was altogether a stellar event.

We finish eating and our waiter arrives with seconds. I decline, as do my parents. My father glares at me. "Why didn't you ask *me* if I wanted your veal?" he asks in a voice full of menace.

Then, in the middle of this roomful of elegant strangers, he starts hollering about what a selfish little brat I am. Heads turn. Everyone in the restaurant hears all about what an atrocious thing I've done. When he has beaten it into the ground, he pompously orders me to wait outside the door of our suite until he and my mother are through. Miniscule with shame, I creep away. My mother shows up half an hour later and lets me in. I'm in bed by the time my father, having evidently had to polish off more whiskey at the bar prior to dealing with us, follows. While the satin comforter slides repeatedly off the silk sheets and onto the floor, my father screams at my mother about how he's going to get a divorce and leave us right then and there. I'm terrified. My mother isn't up to this.

Years later I was visiting my parents, whose marriage survived all my father's threats. My mother was asleep, I was reading in bed, and my father came into my room. He took my desk chair, turned it around and sat down on it backwards, and we talked. I ended up describing what happened in Torquay.

"How come I don't remember this?" he asked.

"Because you were drunk."

We cohabited the planet for forty-five years. That was the only time I ever heard him say, "I'm sorry."

I don't remember how often he attacked me. I do know that I spent my childhood waiting for the other shoe to drop, that we lost our oldest and dearest friends because they found his treatment of me intolerable, and that I had, finally, to surrender to him on every occasion on which we disagreed for eighteen years.

But it was the way he treated my mother that hurt me the most. By the time I left for college he'd picked hundreds of fights with her. After another twenty years of this, she succumbed to a psychotic break in the grip of which she lived the last eight years of her life. After she passed I learned that he'd told her years before that she'd never get away from him, and better not try.

Some Kind of Mind Warp

Ours wasn't a house in which weapons were ever brandished, bones broken, or blood shed. Physical violence was relatively rare. But you don't have to beat someone to break her. My mother and I were violated left and right and never knew from whence the next assault would come. By the time I hit adulthood, she had long since stopped laughing and I had decades of psychotherapy ahead of me. The notion that sticks and stones will break your bones but words will never harm you is garbage.

My mother for her part generally treated me as well as a dedicated, hardworking, emotionally shattered woman possibly could. Yet she'd often turn on me in the face of my father's rage. The price she would have paid for directing her wrath at him was unimaginable. So, either in an attempt to let off steam or to keep me from enraging him further, she'd shove me, glare at me, dig her fingers into my arm. Although I loved them both I also hated them, and there were no sibs, cats, or dogs with whom to ride out the storms. It was the three of us up under each other day in and relentless day out. I was stunned when I read Jean-Paul Sartre's *No Exit*. He'd written a play about us before my parents even met.

Meanwhile my parents danced beautifully together at parties and won prizes for best costume on Halloween. We had stimulating discussions and private jokes that made me laugh until I cried. On a good day, my father was warm, funny, playful, ingenious, and interesting. And he'd go to the wall for me. When a riot broke out at my high school, he was the first parent there. When I got into trouble for having written a controversial article for the school paper, he backed me. And when I told him I wanted to be a psychologist, implicitly asking for not just his blessing but extended financial support, he said, "do it."

From the outside, we looked great. Unless you were around when my father cracked, you'd never guess what went on behind closed doors. My high school boyfriend was shocked when, years later, I told him the truth.

"I thought it was a class act," he said.

No one, inside the family or out, had a handle on the situation. It was like living in some kind of mind warp. With the exception of a few scattered moments of clarity, my mother favored the perceptions of a raging alcoholic over mine all her life. I couldn't reconcile the upside with the insanity and didn't know what battering was.

In some respects I was okay. I had close friends, got good grades, and pursued my interests. In terms of material needs, everyone should have it so good. But I was in emotional pain and had developed some profoundly distorted ideas. Having been obligated to attend constantly to my parents' needs, I paid no attention to what I felt, concentrating on what I thought other people wanted instead. I had a voice in my head that berated and belittled me exactly the way my father did me and my mother. When either she or my father got angry at me, I quaked. And I worried about my mother constantly. Like the girl in the painting, I knew something was wrong with me.

An incident from my senior year in high school reflects what I'd become. My friends and I were heading home after seeing a movie, and one of them turned to me and asked what I'd thought. I ducked the question, doing the verbal equivalent of a tap dance in order to avoid expressing an opinion with which the others might disagree.

I had to conform. I had to be good. I was intimidation incarnate.

The Power of Insight

A step at a time, I won my freedom. After college I moved to Manhattan and landed right in the heart of the feminist movement. I came to understand that my family's nasty little secret was just one instance of a worldwide phenomenon with more ramifications than you could count.

All of a sudden things that had never made sense were crystal clear. I saw a notice in the back of *New York Magazine* for a women's therapy group led by psychologist and author Phyllis Chesler and headed straight to the phone. Finally, I began getting the help I needed—and putting my foot down with my father, who lived under an hour away. In time, the fact that I'd managed to escape sunk in. I remember running around my studio apartment shrieking "Aiiieeeeeee! Free! Free! Free!"

When I was twenty-three, I had a job researching a book on women in their thirties. I'd just finished a fascinating interview with a woman into whose life I had considerably more insight than she did. I experienced this as what I'd later learn to call "high play," and was so exhilarated that I ran all the way home from the West Side to the East Side in two-inch heels. It dawned on me that there were people who did this fulltime, and I decided to become a clinical psychologist. For me this was a decision to apply my strengths to the service of women and children and to make personal development the fulcrum of my life. My evolution into a women's empowerment coach is a story for another time.

It took me years to appreciate the magnitude of my father's illness. The picture clicked into sharp focus one day on the psychiatric ward at Grady, Atlanta's public hospital. A visiting psychiatrist from New York was interviewing a patient at grand rounds. The patient, a grandiose, paranoid, volatile black man in his forties, blew my mind. If you stripped away the trappings, he was the spitting image of my father in one of his states. Only instead of running a company that made stainless steel pipe fittings and flanges, he was on the eighth floor of Grady exemplifying psychopathology. When I attempted to stand at the end of the meeting, my legs didn't work.

I had decades of individual and group psychotherapy, participated in workshops, and became acutely conscious about the quality of my relationships and more discriminating. I did bibliotherapy, filled journal after journal, worked with my dreams, created rituals, and learned to take world-class care of myself.

I no longer recognize myself in the woman who was too timid to tell her friends what she thought of a movie. I have a strong sense of my own authority and personal worth. In order for this metamorphosis to have occurred, the change that originated with a moment of insight had to work its way down to my very cells. Heavy lifting. For years I walked around saying, "no one abuses Dr. Gale" to myself and feeling exultant. I still can't get over my freedom.

In the words of Tennessee Williams, "the violets in the mountains have broken the rocks."

ABOUT THE AUTHOR: Michelle Gale helps forward-thinking women articulate their vision for themselves and bring their lives fully into alignment with it. She has been facilitating women in stepping into their power and purpose for decades. Michelle is a women's empowerment coach with certifications in life and career coaching and a doctorate in clinical psychology. Her experience as a coach, psychologist, entrepreneur, teacher, researcher, and writer gives her an abundance of tools with which to help women meet their challenges and transform their lives. Having recently emerged from a twilight zone called multiple chemical sensitivity, she knows more than she ever cared to about overcoming staggering odds.

Michelle Gale
White Lioness Coaching, LLC
michelle@whitelionesscoaching.com
www.whitelionesscoaching.com
470-377-0730

PART THREE

Physical
Health & Well-Being

"Wounds don't heal until they're witnessed.
Witnessing the existence of a wound
allows the healing process to begin.
If I am stuck in denial, my secrets will remain
locked in my cells, unavailable for witnessing and healing."
~ Dr. Christiane Northrup

The Stress Point
Melissa Brown, MD

I walk through the door of my pediatric practice's waiting room and know I have to pull myself together—fast! *Why does this happen every morning as I start my workday?* I wonder. *I don't want to think about the answer to that question...*

I can't for the life of me figure out why, when making the familiar climb up the stairs to my office day after day, suddenly these steps seem to go on forever. My legs are like lead weights and my body doesn't want to move, so I pause on the stairs, feel the familiar sting in my eyes, and choke back my tears.

How the hell did I get myself into this, I wonder, as I plaster a false smile on my face, continue up the stairs, through the door, and past the children I'll be treating in just in a few minutes. I know I can't let the waiting parents and children see me crying as I come through the door—I have to hide my tears and the pain I'm experiencing.

Once in the office, I forget completely about myself and focus solely on my patients. The morning's internal struggle to get up the stairs dissipates into the chaos of my day. There are lab results to check, patients to be seen and treated, and constant telephone calls from parents about issues that demand immediate attention.

Medical and business related decisions—both large and small—must be made, and my pace becomes non-stop. Hospitalized patients with rapidly changing conditions necessitate hospital resident phone consultations in order to manage acute circumstances throughout the day.

Finally finished in my office for the day, I catch my breath and conduct a mental check to ensure all my patients' problems have been addressed: All phone calls returned? *Check!* Hospital patients stable, or do any necessitate a planned second trip to the hospital to check their condition? *Check!* Charts completed? *Check!* Office staff happy and satisfied? *Check!*

My constant vigilance doesn't end once I walk out the office door. I'm on call 24/7, which means that at any moment the phone could ring and a patient might require me to meet them in the emergency room for treatment of a medical situation or for admission to the hospital.

Home again, it's time to care for family members next. Or the dog. Or friends, whose needs are high on my list, too. What I don't seem to ever realize is the one important person I leave off my checklist constantly is...*me!* And this is costing me dearly...

"It's Not Stress That Kills Us, It's Our Reaction To It."
~ Hans Selye

So involved in caring for others, I've forgotten to take care of myself. Forgotten is probably the wrong word, though—I simply don't consider my needs important enough to put on the list! I know I should do certain things to take care of myself, but always they seem to come after everyone else.

My self-care consists of popping antacids for acid reflux symptoms daily. I deny myself all of the spicy and tomato-based foods I love, hoping that will help. I experience near-constant gastrointestinal symptoms to various degrees, and I find that if I skip a meal sometimes it calms my irritable gastrointestinal tract.

I crave sugar also, and give in to this temptation repeatedly. If I skip a proper meal, I'm ravenous. This only creates a vicious cycle of more cravings, more mood swings, and feelings of general malaise...

Unhappy and constantly stressed, it's like I'm always on high alert for some unknown, unseen danger lurking around the corner. What is this danger, and why must I remain so highly vigilant? Seems it's hiding in my office, since this is where my dread and unhappiness bubble up and spill over into my day when I walk up these stairs.

After months of stomach aches, stress, and misery, I finally feel the need to reach out for help from another doctor. It's the stress of having recently taken custody of our granddaughter, I tell the doctor. Or maybe it's because I'm experiencing perimenopausal symptoms.

A physical exam shows nothing of significance. I'm actually pronounced to be quite healthy and given a prescription for an anti-depressant and an invitation to perhaps talk it over with a therapist.

Not once was I offered a blood test to check for a hormonal imbalance!

My misery upon walking into my office each day continues. I begin to think of ways to escape. This brings up terrible feelings of guilt. Isn't being a doctor what I've worked so hard for all my life?

Think of all you sacrificed to get here! I scold myself. *The time missed with my three daughters during their childhoods, the family events and celebrations—all because I'm always on call or working! The years of study and the delayed gratification for money for so long. If I'm not a doctor, then who am I? After caring for so many for so long, what else would I do?*

I'm stuck in limbo with an office lease that forces me to keep working in order to pay for it, but feel so miserable I'd do almost anything not to have to return daily...

Stress Rules...

One day I reach for my antacids and pop my usual dose, and it dawns on me that I've been downing these pills twice daily for a *full* year to quell my acid reflux! Not only that, but they don't even work all the time—often I still have acid reflux symptoms, heartburn, and pain in my stomach. I still can't eat my favorite foods without paying the price of abdominal discomfort.

What am I doing to myself? Not only with the daily use of a medication that doesn't solve the root cause of my problem, but what am I doing continuing to allow stress to rule my life and ruin my health?

Cancer is a six-letter word that everyone knows and fears. Everyone knows the havoc cancer can bring to the human body, as well the devastation and wreckage it brings to families. Yet *stress* is also a six-letter word, and it can be just as lethal.

But we not only tolerate stress in our society, we celebrate it as a necessary evil on our road to success! We use phrases like "get outside your comfort zone!" Or, "no pain, no gain!" It's crazy! Stress kills and it does so slowly and insidiously. And the death certificates for those that it takes don't list the primary cause of death as *stress*. That's because stress causes other chronic and acute conditions that eat away at the human body and mind.

Our bodies become triggered by stress to produce a chemical reaction inside to either fight or flee. Stress hormones are triggered by perceived danger—it's a survival adaptation. But in this day and age, we're not threatened most days by a saber-toothed tiger, although our bodies react in the same fashion.

Stress that's constant and unremitting produces the changes in our body that herald many different chronic dis-eases like diabetes, heart disease, adrenal burn out, gastrointestinal conditions—even cancer cells grow faster under stressful conditions. It's been said that the effect of chronic stress can be as bad or worse than the health effects of smoking cigarettes.

"The Greatest Weapon Against Stress Is Our Ability To Choose One Thought Over Another." ~ William James

Antacid bottle in my hand, I now realize that the entire year I blindly swallowed these antacids, choked back my tears, and stuffed down my unhappiness was really all about *stress*. I know that I have to start putting on *my* oxygen mask before I can continue to assist those I feel it's my mission to help. It's been too long now that everyone else's needs have come before my own! If I continue this way, I know there will be no *me* left to help *anyone*. As they say on the plane: "In the event of loss of cabin pressure, put your own oxygen mask on first before assisting others." Finally, I'm going to put my own oxygen mask on first!

I know I need a plan, and begin to create a vision for myself in order to get myself out of this mess I call my life. Recently I've become fascinated with personal growth and development courses and, as I begin to create a vision for my future, I'm certain it has to entail separating myself completely from my pediatric practice.

I can't just cut back—no, I have to leave entirely! I think about who's perfect to replace me—I want to insure my patients are well cared for by any pediatrician who takes over my practice. I compile a list and begin advertising for my replacement. In a relatively short period of time I manifest this person—a woman pediatrician who reminds me of myself in the early days of my practice!

This is only part of the answer for me, and I intuit I need to take care of myself from a physical *and* emotional point of view. Once free of the pediatric practice, I join a local gym and begin to exercise. I take long walks with my dog. I'm pulled to return to nature, and venture into the woods near my house to explore. I begin to feel calmer and better physically, but still something's missing...

I'd begun to hear the term "coach" used in a way that has nothing to do with sports. The concept fascinates me. I start to look into what a coach does and how to become one. I discover a coaching school called iPEC and schedule a conversation with an admissions person. I decide to begin this program to further my own personal growth and development, never realizing how key this step will become to my own inner healing.

Through my coaching training, I realize I don't have to accept the victim role in any of life's situations. Rather, I can control entirely the energy I choose to bring to any situation. Excited to once again help others while not forgetting about helping myself first, I can now be in control of my life, my time, and my stress responses—instead of simply reacting.

I actively explore alternative healing modalities, including Reiki and essential oils. I begin to view nutrition with new eyes and experiment with a gluten free diet. Much to my amazement, physical symptoms that I have experienced for decades vanish! I switch to a more plant-based diet including a repertoire of vegetables and foods that I never knew existed. I meditate. I journal. I lose weight. I feel more...balanced...

Best of all, as I look back now, I see my healing process as a journey on the road to health and wellbeing; a journey that steered me clear of my stress point.

ABOUT THE AUTHOR: Dr. Melissa Brown combines 25 years of medical experience with her passion for empowering women to live more healthy lives. Retracing the path that she took to regain her own wellness, she created The Simple System™ to help women who feel plump, pooped and strung out from stress to restore their energy, lose weight and calm their mind without prescription drugs. Dr. Brown is co-facilitator for her Powerful You! Chapter, President of her Toastmasters Club and serves on the Board of Directors for BlinkNow Foundation aiding impoverished orphan children in Nepal. She lives in NJ with her husband and granddaughter.

Melissa Brown, MD, CPC, ELI-MP
Green Light Coaching
www.greenlightcoaching.com
Melissa@greenlightcoaching.com
973-379-3970

Losing 800 Pounds
Monika Emad

It's seven p.m. and I'm locked in my half-bath next to the kitchen crunching away on a family size bag of pretzel M&Ms, looking like a possessed, crazy-eyed squirrel monster. My hunched back is to the door in case someone tries to break it down and take them away from me.

I can't let my kids see me like this, after all my lectures on healthy eating and the importance of avoiding sugar and "stupid food," as we call it in our house! And God forbid my husband should catch me with processed milk chocolate breath and rainbow food dye smeared all over my palms. He'll never let me live it down—not after I've bombarded him with junk food nutrition facts, my "processed sugar is the *real* white death" thesis, or the whole "remember—you are what you eat" lecture series.

I try to better myself every day, as so many of us do, to become the best version of *me* that I can be. Each morning, I wake with the intention to be more kind, loving, patient, healthy, fit, and happy—in short, a force for good in all ways big and small!

I figure that's the goal of most conscious people on this planet, at least those who believe the way to true happiness is through gratitude, purpose, and service. I, too, want to make the world better and add positive energy to it, rather than spreading negativity. Yet with all these wonderful intentions and grandiose goals, I fail on this basic, primal level, as I have so many times before. The guilt starts to set in half way through the candy bag.

For the past twenty years, since moving to the U.S. from Europe, I've been on this crazy roller coaster ride of gaining and losing between twenty and forty pounds each year. The moment I stop the latest diet, which I follow to a "T" for months, I gain it all back with gluttonous vengeance.

Though intellectually I know that food should be simply a form of nourishment, a way to give my body the nutrients it needs to function at an optimal level, it somehow becomes an obsession. It's an escape—my best friend and worst enemy, my partner during joyous occasions, and my comfort during moments of despair. Even when all else in life is blissful, my inability to control this one aspect and make sense of it influences and disturbs everything else around me.

Hard to believe that something so simple—in theory—has so much power over a rationally thinking being...

My Rocky Relationship With Food

When I gain weight at lightning speed shortly after ending a diet, I slowly imprison myself in my own fat suit. Once an effervescent, fearless, and strong gal, I transform quickly into a cynical, antisocial, unhappy mope.

Am I that weak? I wonder. *Am I going to allow this small part of who I am to have such a monumental impact on every other part of my life? I can't believe that all it takes for me to lose my mojo is this tiny inability to control what and how much I put in my mouth...really?*

This, in turn, brings to life the one-woman self-loathing show in my head. *You're weak, pathetic, and worthless!* the show begins. *You have no strength or power—I hate you!*

Great! There isn't much good I can do from that headspace. Nor can I try to love myself or others as those destructive thoughts race through my mind.

After many years of banging my head against my bathroom tiles, I decide I need to get to the bottom of my self-destructive behavior and figure out how to get past it and regain some control.

I begin to accumulate facts, look inward and outward, and educate myself on the topic of nutrition. I read every book I can get my hands on, and attend lectures by M.D.s, brain doctors, and spiritual gurus. I frequent TED talks, Overeaters Anonymous meetings, and health seminars. I see dieticians, nutritionists, blood analysis specialists, and try many different types of eating—including vegetarian, vegan, raw, and paleo diets.

Finally, I sign up for a health-coaching program at the Institute for Integrative Nutrition (IIN.) I want answers to what it means to live a healthy and fulfilling life, and to help me sort through all the conflicting information out there.

Is animal protein good or bad? Should I eat whole grains in the morning or in the evening or not at all? Is fruit ok, or does it have too much sugar? Is dairy friend or foe?

Turns out that specialists in the nutrition field often have very strong but conflicting opinions and different answers to each of those questions. How can I cut through the overwhelming waterfalls of lies and diet instruction gibberish spewed by hacks who pretend they've found the right way or—worse yet—are blatantly out to make a buck?

It's enough to make a person go completely mad, fall down on all fours, start grazing in grass, and mooing! Filled with hundreds of opposing theories, food facts, and health suggestions, the pressure in my brain becomes similar to a space shuttle rocket right before take-off! Finally— miraculously—after I throw all this info goo into my own logic sifter, I'm left with a few golden nuggets. Because even though the major brains out there disagree on most counts, they do share a common thread. And these agreements are enough to make all the difference in my rocky relationship with food!

Life-Changing Find #1 - It's Not Nice to Fool Mother Nature

Since we are the manifestation of nature and thrive when we live in harmony with her, I find that anytime we decide to mess with our green mom, she smacks us upside the head, leaving some gruesome scars. What the earth provides for us is perfect nourishment in its most original and unprocessed form.

To test this theory, I pay close attention to my body—not my brain, since that little addict simply wants piles of junk food to experience a nanosecond high. I crowd out the bad by first eating the good. I follow my gut—literally—and monitor what I eat and how it makes me feel for three months. Journaling is essential. Turns out that when I eat organic and closer to original Earth food, the better, stronger and more energetic I feel. When I throw something down the shoot that's processed or doesn't agree with my unique bio-individuality, I need to stay away from crowds, elevators, and open flames!

Bottom line: If it's in a box, has more than a few ingredients—especially ones I can't pronounce!—I don't put it in my mouth (most of the time.)

Life-Changing Find #2 - The Spice of Life

No matter how hard I try to be good, at times my mini-Tasmanian devil within awakens unexpectedly and tornadoes through a box of chocolates like a starved hyena. At IIN I'm taught that being good all the time is simply unrealistic, crazy, and boring—although I might have added the last two. We all live in this increasingly imperfect, beautiful, yet dirty little world—and unless we live on a mountaintop in the garden of Eden, we have to figure out a way to balance the sinfully pleasant with the righteously healthy.

I had to kiss and make up with my kitchen and start cooking clean, healthy meals at home since you never really know what you're eating at a restaurant. I still give myself license to be naughty ten percent of the time. So one meal every three days includes either meat, dairy, chocolate, alcohol, or refined sugar *or* five weeks every year I get to be a lot less than perfect—*guilt free*. It feels good to be bad sometimes, minus the bloating, indigestion, and fatigue of course...

Life-Changing Find #3 - Chew, Chew, And Chew

This little tip from nutrition brainiacs rocks my world! It turns out that chewing each bite thoroughly—a crazy amount of thirty times or more—produces enzymes that break down food and begin the digestion process right in the mouth. Plus when I eat this way, I find I get full much faster and don't overstuff myself! Eureka!

Also, I stop taking beverages with meals, and instead drink lots of liquid thirty minutes before or after I eat. Drinking during a meal dilutes stomach acid and prevents food from breaking down thoroughly.

Life-Changing Find #4 - What Am I Really Hungry For?

That one is a biggie... It takes a lot of soul searching and talking to myself, sometimes even out loud in public, to realize that reaching for a snack often has nothing to do with hunger. It's either boredom, sadness, happiness, or pure mindlessness, and each one of these feelings is rooted in issues with my emotional—not bodily—needs. I try to eat for fuel, rather than entertainment, solace, or simply to fill an empty hole. Before rummaging through my cabinets, I ask myself what I'm feeling before I try to numb it with food.

Life-Changing Find #5 - High On Life!

There it is—the essence of why I'm writing this in the first place. Once I decide to manifest positivity, focus on the good in my life, and actually do something to change the bad instead of simply complaining, doors start to open!

My "snap out of it" moment occurs when I begin to offer hugs, kindness, love, and consideration to people with no expectation of recognition or gratitude in return.

When I give of myself freely my soul becomes extremely grateful for all the blessings in my life, which makes me giddy all the time!

If you're wondering what I'm smoking right about now—I assure you that when my soul is filled with joy about my life, healthy relationships, a spiritual practice, and a fulfilling career, trivial grub falls to the side. I finally get that I eat to live and that the better the quality of my fuel, the more optimistic, clearer, and happier I am.

"Always look on the bright side of life!" I sing to myself...

I'm at my healthiest weight now—fifty pounds lighter than my heaviest weight—which I've maintained for a year and a half with fluctuations of no more than a couple pounds. Back to my old tricks again, I love life, and bounce with so much energy and passion it's hard to contain myself! And, the changes I've made are simple and so much easier to implement than anything else I've put my poor body through in the past. Also, I became a health coach to help others get in touch with themselves.

Having gained and lost more than eight hundred pounds thus far in my life, I took the long-winded and complicated route to learn how to read my body and listen to its needs and inner wisdom... working with a health coach for a few weeks would have been so much simpler. Live and learn!

ABOUT THE AUTHOR: A former news reporter, creative director and filmmaker, Monika always longed to be a part of something bigger. A loss in her family lead to the creation of the H.U.G. Foundation in 2008, which focuses on the needs of underprivileged children. She opened Olive Organic Tan Spa in 2009 and later O'live Organic Spa in NYC to promote healthy beauty and self-love. To expand her knowledge in the field of wellbeing and help people live happier lives, she became a Certified Nutrition Health Coach and a Reiki Practitioner and is planning to open a Wellness Center in the near future.

Monika Emad
www.theHUGfoundation.org
www.oliveorganicspa.com
www.olivetanspa.com
monikaemad@gmail.com

One Step At A Time

Sheila Dunn

I begin to hit my stride—proud to be a sixty-seven year-old cancer survivor *and* walking a nearly five mile race—when suddenly, as I approach the one mile mark—I trip and fall! Momentarily stunned, I lie on the pavement trying to figure out what happened.

Surrounded by fifteen thousand participants—both world class runners and casual walkers—on this beautiful Thanksgiving Day at the 76th Annual Manchester Road Race in Connecticut, I wonder *how did I fall down in the middle of the race?*

I raise my body gingerly from the road and realize my knees have taken a full hit, and then the pain kicks in...something is very wrong! I look around at the participants, many of whom are dressed for the occasion in festive holiday costumes, and flash back to shortly before the race began.

Hand over my heart, I'd sung the Star Spangled Banner and gazed at the huge American flag supported by two fire engines over the street. Grateful and blessed to be healthy and taking part in this event, tears filled my eyes—I was happy to be getting my exercise for the day and that I'd soon enjoy a wonderful turkey dinner.

I return to the reality of my present predicament when my friend Cliff appears from the crowd, takes my arm, and helps me stand and begin to walk. Though he supports me, I know instantly with my first step I can't make it back to my car—I'm in way too much pain.

"I fell and hurt my knees!" I shout to a couple of guys standing in the front yard of a house we'd passed on the race route. "Can you give me a ride to my car?"

"What, Superman can't take you?" one of them quips as he points to Cliff, who's wearing a Superman t-shirt and a red cape. I'd smiled upon seeing him that morning, but the friendly humor of that moment is long gone now. However, one of the men kindly gives

Cliff and me a ride to my car so I don't have to walk in pain all the way.

Cliff maneuvers my car through the race route walkers and we head to the emergency room. Something is seriously wrong with my right knee—it's so swollen I can't stand or move without pain. An x-ray confirms the worst: My right patella (knee cap) is fractured.

Gotta Dance! Gotta Dance!

"Will I be able to dance again?" I ask the doctor anxiously. Fear fills my heart as I wait for his answer.

"You need to have patience and we'll see how your knee heals—but chances are good you'll dance again," the orthopedist answers. He's optimistic my knee will heal without surgery, and reminds me it was simply an accident and that I must wear a brace 24/7 for ten weeks in order to keep my knee stable.

At the moment, however, healing fully seems impossible to imagine, and I feel as if my world comes to a stop. This is not my plan! Back at home I notice I can't concentrate, and fearful thoughts about my future keep me from a peaceful place. My body tightens, and I feel old, scared, and out of control.

Eighteen years ago, at forty-nine years of age, I faced a breast cancer diagnosis that proved to be a major factor in my decision to retire early. Surgery, chemotherapy, and radiation addressed my cancer, but took a toll on my body. My retirement plan began to involve experiencing all I could while in good health.

I always loved to dance and—since becoming a senior and retiring—am part of a senior dance team that performs at some of the Connecticut Sun Women's Basketball home games. My teammates and I learn new dance routines for the season ahead and practice each week.

Making this team at age sixty-five brought such joy to my life, including the excitement of waiting to go on the court to perform our routine, hearing the roar of the crowd as we dance, and receiving all of the wonderful feedback from the fans!

I fear all that may be only a memory now.

Hung-up on what I should or should not be doing, I feel old walking with a cane and taking the senior dial-a-ride vehicle to doctor's appointments. My thinking does not reflect the reality of my life. Instead of being thankful, my mind becomes my worst enemy as I dwell on my age.

"It's The Heart Afraid Of Breaking That Never Learns To Dance" ~ Amanda McBroom, *The Rose*

I'd started meditating during my breast cancer journey, which allowed me to relax my body and mind. I realize now that I can take the opportunity to use this practice to calm my fears and bring balance to my body once again. Much to my delight, it works, and I begin to let the fear leave my body...

Another positive daily routine incorporated into my life at that time was keeping a gratitude journal. I begin again to write down five things for which I'm grateful in my life with my first cup of coffee every morning. I remember how when I express gratitude and acknowledge the wonders around me, I am more open to receiving.

I sit in a straight wingback chair as my braced leg extends out onto an ottoman, and realize this is my opportunity to allow others to help me. I express my thanks to the man who gave me a ride to my car the day of my accident, my cane which helps support me, the senior vehicle that delivers me to my appointments, the fact that I required no surgery, and to my friends.

As I reach out to friends, a steady stream of visitors, cards, food deliveries, and a whole lot of love arrive on my doorstep—I feel so blessed for all the love and support I receive each day! I adjust my holiday traditions to fewer decorations and no outdoor lights, order prepared food for my holiday entertaining, and hire a house cleaning service. I holiday shop on line. Life doesn't look so bad!

Excited to begin physical therapy now, I feel like I'm back to exercising. My plan consists of physical therapy twice weekly and designated exercises twice a day. After weeks of not moving my knee I need to build up muscle and stretch my ligaments. However, uncomfortable and in pain, I'm afraid I won't be able to move my knee.

During breast cancer treatment I found it helpful to collect in a binder information and documentation regarding my health. I want to do the same for my patella fracture healing journey, so I purchase a three-ring binder, and on a blank sheet of paper write *Right Patella Fracture* in bold letters. Below those words I paste a picture of the Connecticut Sun Senior Dance Team, and insert the page into the cover sleeve of the binder.

I collect and save information from the orthopedic doctor, pictures of the patella, and information about my physical therapy. I make a matrix for each week, with a list of my exercises and the number of times I'm supposed to do them. This makes it easy for me to do the exercises and helps me witness my progress. I check off each exercise as I finish it. Every day, I see the dance team picture on the binder cover and this keeps me focused on my goal to dance.

Weeks pass and my range of motion continues to increase. The day finally arrives when I can remove the brace. I begin to drive again. The exercises became easier. I notice I start to move when I hear music. Things are changing...

The 2013 Senior Sun Dance Team audition is scheduled for early April, and team members from the previous year plan to go for dinner after the audition. I want to be part of the celebration, and if I'm going to drive forty-five miles to see everyone, I decide I might as well audition too! I don't expect to make the team, but I certainly don't want to sit on the sideline and *not* feel a part of the group!

We learn a short dance routine and the choreographer calls us to the stage in small groups to be judged. Cliff is also on the team and I ask him to help me up the staircase because it has no rail. I climb the stairs to the stage slowly, bending only my left knee and bringing my right leg to join it, one step at a time. I'm relaxed—after all, it's my plan to have fun!

They ask us to improvise, and as I feel the rhythm of the music I give it my all. We dance to *Everybody Dance Now* and, as I turn, my black rim glasses fly off my head! That's never happened to me before, and I keep dancing. When the music stops, I stay on stage to try to see my glasses against the black stage floor. *Please don't let me step on them,* I think, and *where are they?*

"What did you lose—an earring?" the choreographer yells. I explain my glasses fell off during the dance routine, and from below stage level someone sees their reflection and retrieves them for me.

"I really wanted more stage time!" I joke with the choreographer from mid-stage.

You Know I Can Dance!

"I made the team!" I shout excitedly into the phone to Cliff the next day. Surprised and so happy about this good news, I start to cry.

My knee continues to strengthen during dance practices. Sometimes a dance step feels strange, but after repeating it for a few weeks my leg feels comfortable. Although my knee injury slowed me down, it simultaneously allowed me to reflect on my life. Once able to relax my mind and body, I could then handle each day without fear.

When I allow others to help and support me, and realize what a wonderful life I lead, it becomes clear that I don't need to impose restrictions on my life because of my age. After all, age is merely a number that represents my years on this planet—no matter my age, I can continue to learn and to enjoy my life!

My wish is to have many more years of good health and tons of energy to enjoy life to its fullest, including many years of dancing. I simply need to stay balanced, appreciate all of my blessings, and take it one step at a time...

ABOUT THE AUTHOR: Sheila Dunn, retired from an insurance career since 2008, is a member of the Senior Dance Team, which performs at the Connecticut Sun Women's Basketball games. In addition, she's become a Certified CT Master Gardener, and volunteers at CATCH (Coordinated Approach to Child Health) as a Healthy Habit Coach, for children grades K-5. Sheila's other volunteer interests include the Komen Race for the Cure, Casting for Recovery, and Big Brothers Big Sisters. Her interests include drawing, photography, decorating, gardening, and scrapbooking.

Sheila Dunn
smdunn12@aol.com
860-461-3932

Owning My Metaphysics

Valerie Lemme

"Tom, hon, wake up—you have to take me to the hospital!"

My husband stirs and looks at me through half-closed eyes. Yes, he'll do it, he'll take me...we've been through this before. He knows the drill as I stand white-faced, dismayed, angry, confused, in pain, and in need.

Two years earlier we'd arrived at the emergency room, my back muscle spasms so intense I shook with anguish and fear. In indescribable agony, when asked "where is your pain right now from one to ten?" my reply was "*fifteen!*"

My back issues are nothing new—they started around age fourteen when, after vacuuming, I had to lie down to ease the ache in my lower back. I'd visited chiropractors for both prevention and pain management for several decades and they helped a bit—for a short while. But the pain continued despite all my efforts and persists intermittently through the years.

I try practically everything: Chiropractic; massage therapy; Jin Shin Jitsu; Jin Shin Do; homoeopathy; over-the-counter pain pills; prescription muscle relaxers and pain killers; myofascial release; heating pads; analgesics; emotional healing techniques; *and* hypnosis. Many of the practitioners are wonderful caring people—I have no beef with them. Everything works to some degree...but when the pain returns, its suddenness often shocks and overwhelms me.

Then I'm in a very intense car accident.

"Is that your car?" asks the tow truck driver as he thrusts his chin in the direction of what's left of my vehicle. "How are you still walking around?"

I'm so concerned about the other people involved, I don't think about my own pain. I feel fine—just a little shaken and wobbly, so I go home with my son Jared who comes to pick me up at the scene of the accident.

Months later, things start to go very wrong. As I enter menopause, my weight skyrockets, and my blood pressure spikes to 180 over 110—a few times reaching 210 over 110. I enter the shower, turn on the cold water, and shock my body into lowering my blood pressure.

I change my diet and drink magnesium because I don't want to take medication for the rest of my life. To me that's like defeat on the deepest level. But my situation only gets worse. A healing practitioner part-time, you can imagine the internal shame and despair I feel and with which I have to live.

Healing The Healer

The pain begins and a day later I recognize its telltale signs and realize it may escalate into another emergency room visit. I've lived in fear for the past two years, using heating pads and taking small amounts of the oxycodone prescribed at my last emergency room visit to control the symptoms. Finally, they run out.

The admonition "physician heal thyself" rings in my ears, a knot forms in my stomach, and a crescendo of symptoms happen all at once as we head to the hospital now. How can I face my clients if I can't heal myself? I want to hide from the world. If there's a small cave I can crawl into and die, I'll do it. That sounds about right, that feels like what I need...

But not today when there are twenty-four people coming to my home for a party! We had planned to prepare this morning. Jared, visiting from Florida and staying at a nearby hotel with other family members, doesn't even know where the keys to the house are kept.

I'm so distracted by my pain that I leave my cell phone home. In the emergency room with Tom, I insist several times that they allow me to use a telephone so I can call Jared. We left for the hospital at 5:00 a.m., everyone's due to arrive at 12:30 p.m., and there's still so much to be done! I need to speak to Jared!

Tom and I fight about the party the whole three weeks before. He thinks we've invited too many people, and makes it quite clear that he isn't happy. Therefore I'm not allowed to be happy, either.

To be fair, the party starts out with only seven guests, but keeps growing—which I don't mind. But for Tom it's an ordeal. I don't listen to him, and he doesn't listen to me. I'd soon come to understand this isn't helping my health.

We arrive at the emergency room and my blood pressure shoots sky high to 210 over 110. They recommend several tests: EKG; chest x-ray; CT scan; and a test to see if there's any blockage in my leg veins and arteries. We agree to the tests and they all come back negative. I know it's not my heart, but because it's mid-back and radiating pain—and my blood pressure scares the attending doctor—they have to make sure.

She's kind and compassionate as she lays her hand on my leg and looks into my eyes. I intuit her empathy, comforted finally by someone who can feel my pain. Tom, as willing as he is to go through this with me, is very angry and fights with me at every step. I want to call my son, am concerned about the party, and he thinks I'm crazy...again, I feel he's not on my side. He thinks I'm mixed up about my priorities.

Finally, the doctor arrives and informs me she wants me to stay and take a stress test, which won't be available until tomorrow. Tom wants me to stay and take the test, even though it means I'd have to miss the party at home. I tell the doctor I don't want to stay—I know the test will be negative, just like all the other tests.

She warns me that the only way I can leave is if I sign a medical waiver stating I'm doing so against doctor's advice. I *really* want to go home. I want to call my mentor Ti and use FutureVisioning to heal. I've been studying and applying the principles of FutureVisioning for the past seven months and finally see that I have to face this crisis myself, at least until I can finally speak to Ti. But without my telephone I can't make the call.

Finally, I get through to Jared. He locates the house key and gets ready for the party. I'm so conflicted. There's one thing I know, though, and of this I'm certain: the pain is diminished but still there, and I have a future self that can help heal me. I've met her before and always she is filled with so much love for me.

Freedom Of Choice

I visualize signing the waiver and tune in to my future self to see how she feels about my choice. What I experience next shocks and awes me! A wave of joy stronger than anything I've ever felt comes rolling over me—my future self is beaming and filled with love. I've connected profoundly to my future self before, but this time it's so clear and true it transcends every other experience I've had until this very moment.

My bliss and excitement strong, I'm encouraged to stand up for my convictions. Suddenly it hits me why I'm here! The comfort I'd felt from the doctor—her attention and concern felt so good—but this feels even better, deeper, and more true. It's *freedom*...freedom to choose to heal my back through FutureVisioning and to increase my awareness of the emotional pain I'd stuffed there.

I've known all this, but teeter-tottered on the edge of real healing and allopathic measures which caused me deep agony. My relationship with Tom has gotten better over time, but still we frequently find ourselves in a negative dovetail pattern. This has to be healed, I know...and even though I've begun to let go of my suppressed rage, anger, hatred, and jealousy, I see now there's more—a whole lot more...

I ask the doctor for the waiver and sign it.

"You're worried, aren't you?" I ask Tom as we walk toward our car.

"Yes,'" he answers, "I'm afraid you're going to die."

"Yes, I know, but when you see your bright future and you're walking on the beach, we're together, right?"

"Yes," he replies.

"Well my future self was joyful when I chose to use only FutureVisioning to heal, so you must trust your bright future, too!" I say, elated.

Tom draws me close and I feel our relationship grow deeper in that moment.

"Once The Door Of Your Destiny Is Opened, It Can Never Close." ~ Lazaris

I get that. I grok it. I do heal. My back pain becomes a signal I understand...when I feel it starting with a twinge now—very infrequently—I know to stop and listen, and not ignore it. I know I'm guided to health and healing when I pay attention to how my emotions are stored there. And most of all, I know emotions are the root of every illness, because my back is better, along with my other physical ailments, too.

Healthier now than I was in my teens, I have the tools I need to heal. Haunted and limited by physical illness in the past, the situation has changed now. When I look into my future that's what I see—more breakthroughs, more love, more effective healings, and me making a difference for my clients in ways I've always desired.

The healing I've experienced in my body, my relationships, my emotions, and my spiritual foundation has exceeded my expectations, and I share this with clients who experience similar healings and breakthroughs through my work. I am grateful, awed, and in wonder at the continuing beauty of life...the vitality of having a calling.

This is what I bring to my clients...*my* healing. My choice to heal opens the door for others to heal themselves. I'm learning to get to the nuggets of truth so much faster now and without the pain. Can you imagine a life where you don't grow through struggle, but choose instead to grow through joy and success?

Ultimately that's the choice that was in front of me. I asked myself: *Which do you want, Valerie?* I realize I'm here to understand, not be understood. My focus changed from what I can *get* to what I can *give*...but still I'm oh so willing to receive. I'm not about sacrifice...I'm about embracing the wholeness of life. The pleasure that surrounds us always—that's my path and passion.

I'm sorry it's taken me so long to get here, but elated to have finally arrived in a place where I own my metaphysics...I embrace this seeming juxtaposition, and in my acceptance find an absolute peace that can't be shaken.

ABOUT THE AUTHOR: Remember life seen through your 15 year old eyes? Valerie Lemme began her spiritual journey to heal and understand the deeper meaning of life at that age. After her lifetime journey, in 2010 she found FutureVisioning and finally, after perpetual yearning, healed her chronic back pain, menopausal symptoms, mood swings, acid reflux, and high blood pressure with FutureVisioning™. Also her relationships transformed and the lack of love and kindness turned into acceptance, honesty and intimacy with her husband, son, friends and family. She helps her clients create miraculous health and happiness, by utilizing the Power of the Future.

Valerie Lemme
FutureVisioning Practitioner, Life and Business Coach
www.valerielemme.com
Facebook: Valerie Lemme & FutureVisioning
Text or call 201-681-9240

Doctors Are Human, Too!
Victoria Pilotti

Not your average pill-popping patient, I've made unconventional medical decisions about my health. Doctors may do the work of God, but they possess the same limitations as all human beings. Motivated to advocate for myself by my anti-medication and anti-surgery beliefs, I say *no* to meds and research the alternatives.

Pain is a warning sign my body sends to tell me something is wrong. I need to know *why* I have pain, not simply how to mask it. In the course of my medical journey, I've learned to ask physicians "what are *all* my options?"

Orthopedist Experience

The pain in my knees prevents me from sleeping as it spreads to my thighs and then to my hips at night. *What's going on?*

"You have weak quads," the orthopedist tells me.

"But I exercise every morning!" I reply. "How can this be?"

"This condition is very common in forty year-old active women," he informs me.

Prescription: Physical therapy

Result: Pain gone

Snap! Crackle! Pop! are the sounds my wrist makes after I lift a heavy box onto a high shelf. The pain in my wrist explodes up to my elbow and I return to the same orthopedist.

No breakage. Diagnosis: Tendonitis

Prescription: He suggests a cortisone injection. *Shocking!*

"Can't I try physical therapy first?" I plead. Only then does he write a prescription for physical therapy.

Result: Once again, pain gone.

I become paralyzed at a conference—frozen with lower back pain—and can't get up from my seat. After reading Dr. John E. Sarno's books, I come to realize that my mind causes this very real acute lower back pain that keeps me from asking the panel a question at the microphone in front of an auditorium full of people.

According to Dr. Sarno, yesterday's ulcers are today's back pains, irritable bowel syndrome, and migraines, and what was once referred to as "psychosomatic" is now called "stress-related." Amazing what the subconscious mind can do to control the body! I join a local Toastmasters Club to become comfortable with public speaking and eventually my paralysis subsides when I address large groups.

Chiropractor Experience

At home with my baby six weeks postpartum, I decide to redecorate his nursery and carry a heavy bookcase up two flights of stairs. This foolish idea results in a severe back injury. Not strong enough to support such strenuous lifting, my back pain becomes so acute that when lifting my newborn out of his crib every two hours I almost drop him each time.

Prescription: The internist prescribes anti-inflammatory medication which I do not take. Instead, the chiropractor teaches how me how to bend at the knees and lift my baby out of his crib. He demonstrates lowering the side of the crib, bending over it, and models with a pillow how to bring the baby to my chest and straighten. Also, he provides me with exercises targeted at strengthening the area of the back injury.

Result: Pain free

Pediatrician Experience

My husband and I don't agree on pain relief when raising our children. He gives them acetaminophen every four hours at the first sign of illness to make them comfortable.

"Isn't acetaminophen hard on the liver?" I ask our pediatrician.

"Of course," she responds. She agrees that repeated doses of medication do not allow time to check if the fever has gone down. I tell my husband that our pediatrician agrees that too much pain reliever can be harmful.

Dental Experience

While waiting for my daughter at the orthodontist's office, I read a brochure about clear braces. Always self-conscious about my bottom front teeth overlapping and that my upper canines are beginning to protrude like fangs, the orthodontist suggests removing a bottom front tooth because my teeth are so overcrowded that there's no room for them all. This makes sense, so I agree.

However, what he doesn't tell me is that there's a possibility I'll be left with a space near my gums. Now I look like I have a speck of food on my tooth!

I've come to realize there are two types of orthodontists: Those who are all too happy to pull healthy teeth, and those who are conservative and try to file between teeth to make room.

Regret is the most negative emotion a person can feel and I regret not seeking a second opinion before I had a healthy tooth removed. I also wonder whether my daughter's two upper canine teeth should have been taken out for orthodontic reasons fourteen years ago, and feel guilty that she continues to wear retainers every night.

Why didn't I learn my lesson? In my twenties my (now former) dentist recommends I remove a wisdom tooth so it will not continue to cause me pain on and off. On the spot, I agree. He struggles so much to extract the tooth that he cuts my lip, and it's swollen for days and oozes with puss. I'm left with a tiny scar years later.

Here is what he should have done: The tooth was growing at an angle toward the next tooth. He *should* have partially sawed away the tooth before attempting to yank it out. Here is what *I* should have done: Sought a second opinion from an oral surgeon or another dentist! At the time it made sense to me to remove the tooth, but I didn't know the dentist possessed neither the skill nor the experience.

Years later, our family dentist refers me to an oral surgeon about a painful polyp inside my mouth. The oral surgeon recommends surgery. While seeking a second opinion the polyp bursts from the pressure of my tooth rubbing against it. The pain disappears and the sore heals without surgery.

After a regular cleaning, a periodontist examines my gums for erosion. He strongly recommends surgery for a deep pocket that traps food. A second periodontist does not. So far I am avoiding the gum surgery.

Breast Cancer Experience

In 1990 my mother's mastectomy pathology report for her ancillary lymph node dissection shows sixteen lymph nodes have traces of breast cancer. Her oncologist prescribes tamoxifen and my mother lives cancer-free for more than twenty years without chemotherapy.

I'm diagnosed with breast cancer ten years after my mother's breast cancer surgery. Four breast surgeons and five oncologists do not relate my cancer to hers, as my breast cancer diagnosis is premenopausal at age forty-three, while my mother's breast cancer was diagnosed post-menopausal at age sixty-five. I choose sentinel node dissection to remove two or three nodes (based on the path of a radioactive isotope injection) over ancillary lymph node dissection (removal of numerous lymph nodes.)

There's no indication of breast cancer in the lymph nodes and therefore no evidence of metastasis, yet four out of five oncologists recommend various types of chemotherapy because of my younger age and the higher levels of estrogen present in pre-menopausal women.

The surgeon who performs my breast biopsy recommends ancillary lymph node dissection. I have a lengthy discussion with his partner about the two lymph node dissection options. He describes a protocol he's conducted with sixty women at a New York hospital where they've found that ancillary dissection is ninety-six percent effective, while sentinel node dissection is only three percent ineffective.

I notice how he plays with numbers, and have to do my own math to convert the three percent to ninety-seven percent. Aha! Sentinel node dissection is one percent *more* effective!

Yet another breast surgeon (my fourth opinion) quotes a study conducted in Florida of one thousand women—obviously a much larger sample size—which finds the sentinel node procedure more effective in predicting metastasis and less harmful than lymph node dissection. Lymph node dissection can lead to a condition called lymphedema, a permanent acute swelling of the arm, in fifteen percent of patient cases. I certainly want to avoid the risk of lymphedema and not have so many lymph nodes carved out of my body!

The biopsy surgeon strongly recommends a lumpectomy and my gut instinct tells me I need a mastectomy because my biopsy shows no clear margins. I cannot have this biopsy surgeon perform my breast cancer surgery for two reasons: 1) He insists on a lumpectomy and ancillary node dissection; but 2) three other breast surgeons recommend a mastectomy and sentinel node dissection. I find out later that the biopsy surgeon's hospital does not have facilities for a sentinel node dissection.

As I make these unconventional decisions about my breast cancer surgery and treatment thirteen years ago, I learn to trust myself. I gather facts through conducting my own research, and reject chemotherapy. Instead, I choose to undergo a bilateral mastectomy followed by radiation, and eliminate almost all carbohydrates, caffeine, and yeast from my diet. A side benefit—my cholesterol plummets forty points in one month!

I choose leuprolide injections—not recommended for a mastectomy at that time—to reduce the production of estrogen that feeds estrogen-positive breast cancer, and the conventional tamoxifen citrate treatment to block the effects of estrogen.

When I begin leuprolide injections, I mention to my physician's assistant (before meeting with the oncologist) that I've been feeling pretty grumpy. She starts to write down a psychologist's telephone number for me.

Then I meet with the oncologist who says much the same thing: "You know, with cancer sometimes we need to speak to people about how we're feeling."

Next I have an appointment with my ob-gyn who laughs and says "well, of course you're irritable—you were put into menopause overnight! I would normally prescribe a light dose of estrogen to make that transition a little easier. But of course the whole purpose is to *remove* estrogen." We kind of chuckle about that.

Now I dread visits to my oncologist. Often I feel like I need to put on boxing gloves to get him to listen to and respect my opinion. When I speak to him again and ask why he did not consult an ob-gyn, he says, "well the ob-gyn unit used to be on the same floor but now they're in a different location."

Oh my God, I think, *really? If you're working with this issue, shouldn't you be talking to the specialists who deal with it all the time? Why can't you pick up the phone and call them since they're no longer close by?*

Instead, he reminds me repeatedly: "If you had followed my advice and taken chemotherapy, it might have stopped your menstruation." Only later did he tell me—*finally!*—that a study out of Europe proved I was right—the medical treatment I chose *was* the most beneficial.

Now I go to an oncologist who is up on the latest research, and who questions medical studies and treatment recommendations the same way I do. In my quest for good health I learn to listen to my inner voice, become my own best patient advocate, and that—although doctors are the hands of God—they are human, too.

ABOUT THE AUTHOR: Victoria Pilotti, Ed.D., a New York City public high school English-as-a-second language teacher, has taught graduate courses at St. John's University and Hunter College, and facilitated numerous workshops for teachers at international, national, state, and city conferences. Victoria advises and advocates for women diagnosed with breast cancer, and her husband Eric counsels spouses and sons. A member and officer of the Toast of Queens public speaking club of Toastmasters International since 2007, Victoria has presented over thirty formal speeches (www.toastmasters.org.) and urges friends and family to be proactive and *think out of the box* about health decisions.

Victoria Pilotti
VPilotti.CWNY@gmail.com

No Laughing Matter

Erika Ruiz

Bleep, bleep, bleep! My alarm clock rings every morning, and the only thing I want to do is cry—cry like a baby devastated by lack of sleep. This particular morning, when my husband Rey comes to rouse me, I refuse to get out of bed.

"I simply can't get up!" I cry, tears in my eyes. "I'm so tired, I want to die..."

Alarmed, Rey insists I accompany him to the doctor after he prepares breakfast for the girls, fills their lunch boxes, and drops them at school. Fatigued after long hours of persistent insomnia, my nights have become longer than my days. I've tried all sort of "sleep well" teas, exercise, yoga, Jacuzzi and other bath and relaxation rituals, but still I'm not able to sleep, and am perpetually alert at three-thirty a.m.

With no way to sleep peacefully not only is my health suffering, but also my daily routine. I'm no longer the same active mom of five children, always ready to assist with family needs, work, after school, and church activities.

At the doctor's office I have no words to explain my current situation, so I let Rey do it for me. When he tells the doctor it's been several weeks since I've slept well, I do the math quickly in my head and realize suddenly that an irregular menstrual cycle has accompanied my problems with sleep. All told, I've spent nearly eight months—*two hundred and forty nights*—with insomnia!

"Lack of sleep causes depression, and that must be the reason why you have no appetite and are depressed!" the doctor explains emphatically. "You must eat and sleep so you can feel good!"

At that very moment I realize my feelings of hopelessness and lack of desire to get up, bathe, or dress every morning—is called "depression." I don't know what to say, words elude me, and my eyes well with tears. Rey takes out his handkerchief and dries my face with a protective gesture and assures me everything will be fine.

The doctor suggests I try a drug newly on the market that's recommended for insomnia. Never a prescription-oriented person, I am reluctant. My natural tendency is toward home remedies— grandma's recipes are more my style. But I accept the prescription because I'm desperate for sleep!

We leave the doctor's office armed with this prescription and a lab order for a hormone profile to try to get to the bottom of my heavy and irregular periods, now approximately every two weeks.

I take my first pill that night, and fall asleep, but don't sleep through the night. About thirty minutes after waking the next morning, I begin to feel lightheaded. I have a bit more energy during the day, but at times feel like my head's in a tunnel. Still, I begin to sleep better, and that's the goal!

Part Of Being A Woman?

I return to the doctor's office, where I'm told a premenopausal period may be the cause of my insomnia and irregularity, and the doctor refers me to my gynecologist. I call my gynecologist immediately, hopeful that he might have the answer or the magic potion to end my sleepless nights and menstrual irregularity once and for all.

"My dear, this comes as part of being a woman," says Dr. T., a pleasant gentleman about sixty-six years old who attended the birth of my youngest daughter.

"Yes, doctor, that may be true, but the frequency of my periods is unbearable— and to be honest, I don't want to depend on a sleeping pill!"

"Well, if indeed this is something that causes you so much trouble, I'll prescribe to try to regulate your periods, but you can only take forty-five pills in a period of four months, and no more, because this treatment is associated with breast cancer."

I leave the doctor's office with a little bit of hope, and rush to the pharmacy. I want to start as soon as possible, because I believe that controlling the menstrual cycle will also restore my circadian rhythm, which will allow me to get rid of the sleeping pill.

On the twenty-third day of my treatment for insomnia—with only seven pills left in the bottle—I sleep more soundly now, but wake up heavily and feel sleepy during the day. This isn't ideal, but at least I'm able to rest more than before. In addition, the treatment to regulate my period is working well, so somehow we're winning the battle with Mother Nature.

But then something happens that really scares me. I'm driving down the turnpike on my way home and my eyes close for a moment. *Oh my God–I fell asleep at the wheel!* I panic. *Thank God it was only for a few seconds and nothing happened...so many accidents are caused by sleepy drivers...*

That night I decide not to take any more sleeping pills. *The risk of falling asleep at the wheel is not a price I'm willing to pay!* I reason. It's not long before my insomnia returns...

Laughter *Is* The Best Medicine!

A recreational specialist for seniors at an adult day care center in Miami, Florida, my job entails planning and implementing activities for senior citizens–those with and without memory impairment. Always looking for meaningful activities, especially ones beneficial for Alzheimer's patients, I discover Laughter Yoga–a wonderful tool for those whose aging process has stolen their memory.

I start with only a general idea about the Laughter Yoga concept and later have the opportunity to take a Laughter Yoga leader course. I begin to notice what a blessing it is to apply Laughter Yoga in my patients' sessions, and the joy it brings to their lives– especially those who suffer from Alzheimer's.

The Laughter Yoga method is ideal because it's something that doesn't use jokes and humor to bring out laughter, and it works simultaneously as an excellent cardiovascular aerobic exercise–even for participants in wheelchairs.

In early 2010, I discover that Dr. Madan Kataria–the founder of Laughter Yoga–will visit the U.S. to teach a certification course. Eager to learn new things to increase my knowledge in the field, I leap at the chance to take this course.

Without a doubt I look forward to it, but lack motivation. Still suffering from insomnia and consistently down and depressed throughout the day, I have great difficulty mustering up enough enthusiasm. As the day of the course approaches, I convince myself it's better not to attend the meeting.

It doesn't make sense to travel alone, feeling sad and unmotivated, I reason. *Anyway, I don't feel like I'm truly living up to the course title's standards, given that I'm not happy with myself...*

I talk to Rey about going, and whether or not I should cancel my flight. As always, he gives me the extra push I need to go.

"This is something you've always really wanted to do," he reminds me, "so why not take advantage of it?"

I realize it's already paid for and I really have nothing to lose. So I pack my bags, still uncertain and dismayed that I'm not feeling better, and arrive at the hotel, which—surprisingly—is awful. Dull and unwelcoming, it's not at all what I expected.

I head first to a welcome gathering in the main meeting room that isn't the least bit inviting. Arranged in mahogany and burgundy, it bears no resemblance to anything joyful or related to laughter itself.

I check into the hotel and go to my room, which doesn't make me feel any better. Though I assumed by now this trip would feel more like a vacation, it seems just the opposite.

What a disorganized, unpleasant facility! I think, as I drop my bags in the room and head back to the welcome gathering. There they discuss the materials, instructions, and agenda for the week, and I have the opportunity to introduce myself personally to Dr. Kataria. Although not as fluent in English as the others, I manage to socialize with several other course participants. We all retire early because our first activity is scheduled for seven a.m.

I toss and turn the whole night—the odd smell coming from the carpet only increases my insomnia—and decide to get up and get ready very early. Because of this I'm the first to arrive at the meeting room.

"Against The Assault Of Laughter, Nothing Can Stand."
~ Mark Twain

Our first session with Dr. Kataria includes a breathing and stretching session. After a breakfast break, the rest of the day is spent practicing laughing exercises, including giggles and gibberish. Some laughs are genuine, others fake, but that's what Laugher Yoga is all about—training your body to laugh for no reason.

My first time as a participant rather than an instructor I laugh so much throughout the day my abdominal muscles become sore! At the end of the day I return to my room, shower, put on my pajamas, and eat some yogurt. I don't even turn on the TV—just call Rey, talk to the girls, and before I know it I'm asleep...

Despite my discomfort with the hotel mattress, I sleep with no interruptions for the first time in a *long* time. Though I'm supposed to meet my group at seven a.m., when I awaken and glance at the clock I notice it's nine-thirty a.m.

I've slept almost twelve continuous hours! I can't believe it—what a miracle!

I brush my teeth, fix my hair, throw on comfortable clothes, and rush downstairs to join my group. When I call Rey during my lunch break I practically squeal: *"Guess what?* I slept almost twelve hours without taking any pills! I didn't wake up during the night—not once! It was great—I *so* needed that!"

Not only does laughing the rest of the week help me regain my rest and much of the happiness I'd lost along the way, it also helps me see life from a different perspective. And, as I begin to view life in a simpler way, I become more tolerant.

I can state now with certainty that Laughter Yoga grants me an inner joy despite my circumstances at any given moment. On a professional level, Laughter Yoga is a great tool that allows me to help rescue the smiles and laughter of those for whom age has stolen much of life's joy and most precious memories...

On a personal level, I have made Laughter Yoga my life's mission because I know now that to laugh with the afflicted is as important as giving water to the thirsty. I have discovered, too, that the antidote to suffering from lack of sleep is *indeed* a laughing matter...

ABOUT THE AUTHOR: Erika Ruiz is a Laughter Yoga World Ambassador passionate about joy and wellness. She has 30+ years experience with recreational programs for children, seniors and adults. Erika was inspired to develop "Laughter Dynamics" - a complete workout that combines brain fitness with laughing, singing, dancing, and playing. Erika's sessions are engaging, fun, and a great means of physical activity for anyone with or without cognitive impairments. Erika leads her Laughter workshops around the world, combining her talents with that of the wellness seeker, helping people to unleash their interior laughter. She is a member of the Association for Applied Therapeutic Humor.

Erika G. Ruiz
Laughter Yoga World Ambassador
www.risasaludyvida.com
er@risasaludyvida.com

My Personal Mount Everest

Summer Keen

Imagine, if you will, watching me attend a breakfast networking meeting where there's a wonderful buffet set up in the back of the room, and my table is in the front. I make my way to the buffet, stand in line with the other folks, and finally reach the steaming serving pans, baskets of bread, bowl of fresh fruit, and the juice and coffee at the end of the table.

I pick up a plate and contemplate grabbing a bowl for the fruit, but decide against it. I go through the line, lifting the lids with one hand and holding the plate with the other. I plop scrambled eggs onto the empty plate, move to the next pan and open the lid. Mmm...bacon! I grab a few pieces with the tongs, then choose a muffin and some butter.

Now to the big bowl of fresh fruit. The strawberries, blueberries, raspberries, and pineapple chunks make my mouth water and I scoop the juicy fruit onto my crowded plate. *It will be okay,* I think.

Finally, I grab that much-needed cup of coffee and, as I head back to my seat—coffee cup in my right hand, plate in my left—suddenly the twitching starts and the plate tilts just a bit. *Only two more round tables to pass until I'm back at my seat,* I reassure myself.

The tremors become almost constant now and the plate tilts a bit more. Oops! A blueberry rolls across the floor and a strawberry gets ready to take a high dive onto the carpet, too. Maybe the blueberry and strawberry have a love-pact!

Only a step away from my seat and—dang!—there goes the strawberry! And it looked delicious, too...

I set down my coffee cup (I dripped only a little), and place my plate on the table. *Yes!* I shake out my arm and check to see if I need to pick up the lost strawberry. No, it rolled under a table so it's simply going to have to fend for itself...

Approaching Mount Everest

Diagnosed with Parkinson's Plus Syndrome (a condition that mimics Parkinson's Disease symptoms and responds to Parkinson's Disease treatment) by a local neurologist at age forty-six in 2006, I make the trip a year later with my husband Dave to solicit a second opinion at the Hershey Medical Center in Hershey, Pennsylvania.

The Hershey neurologist proceeds to give me the standard neurological tests, and asks me to hop on one foot then the other, walk as fast as I can down the hallway, and clap my hands. Next he asks me to join together my middle finger and my thumb on both hands as quickly as I can, then to close my eyes and repeatedly touch my index finger to my nose and, finally, walk heel-to-toe across the room. And these are just the tests I remember!

He invites me to sit up on the paper-covered exam table and, as I begin to take notes in my journal, states matter-of-factly "you have Young-Onset Parkinson's."

At first, I write the words down blindly, but as they begin to sink in I start to cry.

"Why are you crying?" the doctor asks.

"I have Parkinson's!" I blubber.

"But that's a good thing," he tells me. "Now that we know what it is, we can treat it."

He assures me I can still do anything I want—that a Parkinson's diagnosis isn't like it was years before; that treatment and medications have come a long way.

"I even treat a patient who climbed Mount Everest!" he tells me.

He encourages me not to feel sorry for myself, and that's exactly what I need.

Climbing Mount Everest

Initially, there are days when I do feel sorry for myself, and days when I actually get scared. Like the day I have to take a state exam at a testing facility and can't keep still in my chair—I can't control my "herky-jerky" movements. I sway one way, jerk back the other, pick up the mouse and smack it back down on the table. It's awful! Driving home afterward, I pull over to the shoulder on the turnpike to calm myself down.

Tweaking my medication to find the correct dose is like following a recipe to bake a cake—too much flour and it's dry, not enough baking powder and it's flat and won't rise.

Sometimes my foot simply won't raise high enough when going up steps, especially the last step—almost always the last step!—and often I trip and fall. Tripping is one of my worst experiences, because everyone knows we adults don't fly through the air and crash down as easily as we did when we were kids. Now, because we have more weight behind us, the ground, concrete, deck, floor, or carpet are not nearly as forgiving.

When kids fall they are often okay until an anxious adult rushes to them and asks where they are hurt, and *then* the kid will start to cry. Well, it's almost backwards for adults. When I fall, it hurts, and I feel like crying immediately...usually, there's no one close by rushing to me to make a fuss, so I get up slowly, check that there aren't too many boo-boos, and then tell others about it. Then, after days of healing the scabs and bruises, I'm okay.

Over the years, Parkinson's has proven to be an insidious disease—one that's slowly stiffened me up, weakened me, and caused me more and more shakiness in my left hand and arm and stiffness or jerkiness in my left leg. Still, I feel blessed that I don't have the disease as badly as some folks.

Yet—before my Parkinson's diagnosis, I was diagnosed with Crohn's Disease in my early twenties. Crohn's disease is an inflammatory bowel disease that causes inflammation of the lining of the digestive tract, which can lead to abdominal pain, severe diarrhea, and potential malnutrition. Though very lucky to have had a long run of being in remission, I experienced two relatively recent flare-ups, including flu-like symptoms of body aches, weakness, fever, soreness, diarrhea, cramping, and nausea that lasted a month!

I've dubbed my condition "ParkinCrohn's Disease."

Dave is great at not letting me get discouraged. Sometimes I have problems putting my arm into a coat sleeve or pulling a sweater off over my head. So I call him in as my back up team to help out.

Folding clothes can be a horrible chore—even without a disease! One hand folds right along, while the other lollygags along, not keeping up, which makes for lopsided folded shirts. Luckily, Dave works construction and doesn't really care! It helps, too, that we both have a good sense of humor and don't take ourselves too seriously. And, well, almost any situation is funny...eventually...

Parkinson's causes me shuffle when I walk. My seventy-five year-old elderly father lives with us and some days I'm not sure who shuffles more. Once in a while, I challenge him to a race. We just laugh instead.

Moving Mount Everest

Dave and my doctor try to get me to exercise for years and I start walking, but that becomes boring after a few days. Then I pull out some exercise CDs and follow them for a week or so. Again really *b-o-r-i-n-g!*

I practice yoga, which I like, but the class I take meets only one evening weekly and then the holidays arrive. So I join a local gym and attend only once every other week. Mostly I walk on the treadmill. Basically, I don't do much of anything. I know I should do some exercise but have no desire to pursue anything at home.

Then an attendee at a Powerful You! lunch who owns a gym with her husband offers a 14-day program to five winners. Lucky enough to win one of the prizes, I look forward to my fourteen days.

I complete a questionnaire, have a phone consultation, then meet with Joe—a coach who shows me how committed he is to the success of his clients. Joe knows how important it is to work within a person's limits and not expect them to "keep up" as they would in a class at the gym.

Joe's wife Susan handles the nutrition portion of the program, and I also receive lessons on how to eat better. I learn to be sure to eat more often during the day, to remember to drink more water consistently throughout the day, and to stay away from the processed foods that poison our systems.

Next, we set my goals, and Coach Joe helps me make them meaningful. The first is to fit into size ten jeans—something that I haven't done for more than two years. Another is to lose ten pounds. And most important, I want to be able to stand up from the couch in one try. (I usually have to rock myself to get my footing in order to stand up from the couch.)

So de-conditioned I can barely get back up off the floor to move on to the next exercise, I flounder like a fish out of water. But Coach Joe doesn't let me get discouraged. He repeatedly tells me not to expect to do a lot in the class right away, like some other people do. He lets me know what I should expect all along the way.

About the third week in, during some cool down exercises—including a lunge where I'm down on my knees and putting one foot forward (normally I have to push it forward with my hand) my left foot moves forward all by itself! So excited, I can't help but share this news with the rest of the team!

Then, I notice I can cross my legs—something I'd stopped doing months before—for more than a minute once again. And I reach my goal to get up off the couch without rocking!

In addition to exercising more and improving my diet, these past few years of self-development have been mind-blowing as I've learned that I can't help others if I don't take care of myself first! Nobody else is responsible for how I feel, and though it's still a struggle some days, I understand it's mind over matter (if I don't mind, it doesn't matter, as Mark Twain once said!)

I have something to share with the world, as do we all, and perhaps I have these diseases to educate the world about them and to help remind those who suffer diseases like mine that keeping a positive attitude does help! In addition, I know now I'm more resilient than I ever thought possible, and that if I surround myself with like-minded, positive people, I *can* move mountains!

ABOUT THE AUTHOR: Summer's varied work history has taken her from boardrooms in New York City to working for a nudist camp resident, and from high rises in Los Angeles to the basement of a start-up company in Pennsylvania. She assists others with online home business opportunities and self development/growth. "I love the saying 'you don't know what you don't know,' because it inspires me to discover more," says natural entrepreneur Summer. "I've had my trials and am blessed with a great attitude and fabulous support—and I know I need to share my story with others to assist them on their personal journeys."

Summer Keen
Summer Keen Shares
www.SummerKeenShares.com
admin@summerkeenshares.com
866-697-7445

Living My Truth
From The Inside Out
Susan Gala

Sound asleep in my bedroom in the back of my New York City loft on a sunny April afternoon, a loud crash jolts me awake and I hear the scuffling of feet coming from my kitchen. Before I can ascertain whether I'm dreaming or awake, I see from my bedroom five hooded men in my kitchen.

Blurry-eyed and without my glasses, something deep within my essence leads me to walk toward the kitchen, where I find myself suddenly staring right into the whites of their eyes. Some higher power or vibration tingles under my skin for a split second—as if my body and spirit are communicating—and I say quietly: "I'll give you all I have, just please don't hurt me."

One of the hooded men shuffles me all over the loft—hugging me close with his stinky, dirty body next to mine, all the while holding a knife to my throat—as I direct the others to the location of my valuables and cash. Then I'm tied up and held at knifepoint for what seems like hours but may only be minutes as they invade my laundry room, gather together my linens, and wrap up my jewelry, cash, and other expensive belongings. They then proceed to cut my telephone wires and flee.

By some miracle they leave me physically unharmed but traumatized. Frozen, confused, and weak, I finally make my way to my neighbor's door and knock. From there I call the police, who arrive, take me to the station in an undercover car, and question me for hours as I pore through mug shot after mug shot trying to identify my attackers.

Later that evening I lie alone, motionless in my loft, and attempt sleep. But with no sense of security, my body leaves me and I'm numb...

"If You Surrender Yourself To Your Essence, The Whole World Surrenders To You" ~ Rumi

I'm fit—I run, bike, swim, travel, and live a happy life as a successful lingerie designer in New York City—when suddenly my life comes to a halt. I become lost—physically, emotionally, and spiritually—and stuck, painfully stuck deep inside my body. Trauma paralyzes me, while fear keeps me up all night and exhausted. There are nights when I wake up and can't move due to excruciating back and pelvic pain.

One evening the pain is so fierce I end up in emergency room. X-rays find nothing and the physician writes a prescription for pain killers. I tear it up...I realize all this pain, stress, and trauma is not just happening in my mind.

I continue to suffer from lower back pain, hip pain, and eventually sexual pain, and begin to turn inward. I seek chiropractors, active release therapy, acupuncture, massage, Pilates, physical therapy, and discover bodywork. Shattered, I don't want to live a victim—in pain, stressed, abandoned, and disconnected.

Then one day I take a walk two blocks from my loft and enroll in the Swedish Institute of Health Sciences to become a licensed massage therapist. I know this is my opportunity to transform the deprivation of my body, and to help me to eliminate this traumatic event.

All I have to do is trust this purpose will be the beginning of my healing journey. I want to listen to my soul and win back my sacred body. I want to journey beneath my skin and discover my inner beauty to heal. I know my rhythm can be found again.

In massage school I meet talented body workers who discover my creativity and purpose. I excel here and am asked by my mentors to help tutor students. I befriend a classmate in whom I develop a deep trust and reveal to her my secret pain. Overcome with joy, she inspires me to read Louise Hay and use her flash cards.

My mind, body, and spirit are healthy, but this pain still grabs my attention so I research it to find a solution. Though I always have the best doctors, body workers, and acupuncturists, it's an underlying pain that no one seems able to address. I know my body isn't failing me, and suspect it's the trauma trapped within that prevents me from living a life of joy.

"Ruin Is A Gift, Ruin Is The Road To Transformation." ~ Elizabeth Gilbert

Years later, at the height of my health profession I own a Pilates studio, am licensed in massage therapy, possess certification in integrated pelvic core therapy, and practice yoga and essential oil therapy. Yet I live with debilitating trauma, fear, and pain. No one knows—I look normal, but don't feel it.

To nourish my soul again I know I need to heal deeper and let go of past hurts, old paradigms; forgive those who wronged me, and learn to forgive myself as I begin to lead more from my heart and core. My mind-body connection wants me to release past emotional pain in the pelvis so I can live more freely.

Bodywork heals...I know my mind has the power to heal and that I can't navigate this journey alone. It will take an integrated community, and I must delve deeper into my limiting beliefs, use the power of affirmation, and seek a healer to open up my heart again and re-connect me to my core. I find an incredible Eye Movement Desensitization Reprocessing (EMDR) therapist, and closing my eyes use deep visualization and conscious breathing with centering.

I learn that power in the female body comes from the pelvis. The first and second chakras in the pelvis encompass huge emotional centers—of passion, sexuality, or of deep trauma. Eventually I learn also that many events in our lives can turn into chaos: natural disasters; rape; physical and emotional abuse; traumatic childbirth; menopause; hysterectomy; endometriosis; pelvic pain; sexual pain; and incontinence...and that all of these events affect our feminine center—the wisdom of the sacred.

I begin to realize that the trauma of the robbery I experienced became trapped in my pelvis, and—unable to release these suppressed emotions—my body became unbalanced over time. As my body denies me freedom, I experience pelvic pain, and when I go to a medical doctor, I'm asked a million different questions, but never if I ever suffered a trauma.

Stress, pain, trauma, and fear can deplete the body and block energetic flow. Many times, the body will react to a difficult situation or event by freezing to protect itself. After the difficult period ends, the body remembers its self-protection mechanism and will continue to freeze and restrict anytime the memory is triggered. This enables the memory, or emotional trauma, to permeate your being.

These restrictions manifest in the pelvis, the center of gravity and the birthplace of all movement. Emotional traumas imbalance the deep core along with the psoas—the group of muscles whose action is primarily to flex and rotate the hip joint—and create restrictions in the root and sacral chakra. The root chakra is related to basic needs such as food, clothing, and shelter; the sacral chakra to creativity, passion, birth, and sensuality.

I know the experience of having emotional trauma trapped in my body. I know how it feels to have my body go deep into self-protection mode to the extent of being almost paralyzed by the restriction. It was from this experience that I began to truly tune in and develop a profound level of awareness of how my body reacts to stress.

Painful traumatic events will live in our bodies for years until we are ready to release the energy that restricts us, I learn. When the energy isn't flowing properly in our bodies at the time of an event, it becomes blocked only to re-occur when another life-threatening event happens.

My Sacred Purpose

As with every moment in life when faced with deep uncertainty and loss, we are most gifted with the opportunity of rebirth and growth; a chance to choose how life will flow and align. I believe that, as women, we must become aware of our body's reactions to stress, pain, trauma, and fear. We must recognize that our bodies have frozen and take necessary action to release the restriction. I am blessed with the awareness of what pleasure brings to my body when I move it energetically. Movement is my medicine.

Only through my intuition do I discover that all this painful emotion and trauma is blocking my emotional identity in my creativity center—the center of power, the inner world of my deep pelvic core that keeps me from the freedom my body craves, from freedom of movement..

When I emerge fully from deep within my core, I'm able to create an aligned life. I need to have courage and commit to transformation from the inside out so I can be fully alive and present. According to author Louise Hay, physical symptoms are merely tangible evidence of what is going on in your unconscious mind and how you are really feeling deep inside.

"Your emotions play a crucial role in ensuring that your needs are met," Hay says. "So if they are ignored, your subconscious mind must find another way to gets its message across and help you see that your deeper needs are not met."

There is now research to prove how chronic pain is deeper than we can imagine.

"Finally, science and spirituality meet and it has been proven that there is a physical and emotional relationship between brain chemistry and the physical/emotional health," states a report from Stanford University.

After many years of successful study and achieving my own personal healing, it becomes clear to me that there's a missing link in women's health and that most women know little about a most crucial and intimate part of their body, the "pelvic core..."

This intimate center deeply influences our quality of life and it's obvious there is a need to educate women on this sensitive subject. Exercise is a vital part of healthy living and so I created "Feminine Fitness Within" for pelvic-core health, through which I educate women about how to re-connect to their physical, emotional, and spiritual anatomy.

I'm a licensed massage therapist, integrative pelvic core therapist, STOTT Pilates® practitioner, and am certified in therapeutic essential oils for healing, with more than twenty years experience.

It's my mission to help women heal their pelvic core, unveil emotion, and turn pain into pleasure, power and presence. Women need not suffer in silence, but rather learn how to empower their pelvic core for a life of renewed vitality. The greatest gift of all my research is that I now live my truth inside out in order to let go of pain and embrace joy.

ABOUT THE AUTHOR: Susan Gala is the founder of Feminine Fitness Within®. She helps women heal their pelvic core, unveil emotion and turn pain into power, passion and presence. Susan is trained as a Licensed Massage Therapist, Stott Pilates Practitioner and Certified in Holistic Pelvic Core therapy. She has advanced training in multiple bodywork techniques and is recognized as an educator, intuitive healer & movement specialist. Susan provides live workshops globally, offers online teleretreats, events/workshops and sees clients privately in NYC and via Skype worldwide. Her decades of practice and research have developed into radical Feminine Fitness for self-care. Connect with Susan Gala.

Susan Gala
www.susangala.com
info@susangala.com
www.twitter.com/susangala
www.facebook.com/FeminineFitnessFromWithin

Minerals Are Mandatory!
Marlene Pritchard

"Marlene!" cries my sister Marilyn, in near hysteria on the phone. "Daddy's having a massive heart attack—they're on their way to the emergency room now!"

My legs go numb as I hang up the phone. *How can this be? These things happen to other people and other families—not mine! My family, both immediate and extended, has always been blessed with good health!*

It seems an eternity before my phone rings again. My hand shakes as I hit the answer light. Dad now has two stents in his heart and, after losing consciousness on the table, is in critical condition. They want to transport him to the Arkansas Heart Hospital via ambulance—there's nothing more the doctors can do for him at his local emergency room.

Dad's heart begins bleeding into his lungs when they move him from the bed to a stretcher. I listen to my sister's voice on the line and experience a feeling of helplessness like never before—I just hope to make it to Little Rock to say goodbye to him in person.

Oh God, this nightmare doesn't seem real—someone tell me it's not really happening! I begin to pray like I've never prayed before, and pack my suitcase quickly to drive to Little Rock. *Oh God,* I think again, *this isn't a bad dream—it's really happening!*

It's a five-hour drive from my home in Jackson, Mississippi, to Little Rock. I drive in silence, staring at the highway, trying to figure out how this could have happened to my precious dad. A seventy-seven year-old grandfather in relatively good health for his age, he takes no prescription medications. His only regular supplements are vitamins and a mineral sachet called Sango Coral Life that I recommended and mail to him every month.

What caused his sudden heart attack? I wonder. *There can't possibly be anything in either of these supplements—the vitamins or mineral sachet—that could trigger a heart attack!* I think, as I continue to race toward the hospital.

I arrive at the hospital to find my dad stable but with only half of his heart still working. They've placed two stents in one part of his heart and a balloon in another chamber, which is attached to a machine that assists Dad's blood flow by mechanically pumping blood through his heart to the rest of his body.

Weak, but fighting hard to survive, his fate is in the hands now of the nurses and doctors who monitor him around the clock and give Dad the medications he needs to maintain life...

Knowledge Is Power

Now Wednesday, four days post heart attack, Dad lies in bed with the balloon in his heart still. I have had four days in his hospital room to research the medications the nurses are administering to him. He's constantly having blood drawn to check his blood gases, and I see his bruises are not nearly as bad as I would have thought.

My nursing background keeps me on top of what is happening in his room, and makes me very curious. I ask questions when I need to, but other times simply observe very closely the care that's being given to Dad. I do feel better knowing the Arkansas Heart Hospital has an outstanding reputation along with excellent nurses and caregivers.

I have much time on my hands—Dad sleeps a lot because he's so weak. I continue to research whatever I can find to help him in his current condition. My iPad is extremely useful in this type of situation!

Thursday morning when my dad's cardiologist Dr. Harrison makes his usual rounds, he orders the balloon removed from Dad's heart. This procedure is completed without complication.

On Friday, I notice a large bruise on the inside of Dad's right ankle where an "x" is marked for the pulse count. Pulses are routinely taken in cardiac patients three times per day with every shift change. The balloon had been "threaded" up this leg to his heart via his femoral artery. I fear immediately he'll experience decreased blood flow in that leg because the balloon-assisting machine is now removed and Dad's heart has to beat on its own. I say a prayer that this won't be the case, and continue my research on my iPad...

The next morning when Dr. Harrison makes his rounds, I pull the blanket back to show the doctor this bruise. To my amazement, the bruise is all but gone! There's a slight greenish tint where the bruise had been, but that's all! I stand there, astonished...

When my mother sees this, she tells Dr. Harrison and me that Dad has not been bruising much since drinking the "water with the mineral sachet." She's referring to Sango Coral Life—the same product that relieves my acid indigestion and increases my energy—that I mail to my dad each month. Sango Coral Life has been adding more than seventy trace minerals and electrolytes to Dad's diet every day since he began drinking it about a year before his heart attack.

Dad is aware that he bruises more easily now that he's older, but the major effect he's noticed since taking the mineral sachet in his water is that his bruises don't last very long. One time, when helping my brother pull up carpet and tile in a house he was redoing, Dad hit his hand on a sharp point in the kitchen. It bruised on impact and normally the whole top of his hand would still have been bruised for quite a while.

The next day he discovered the bruise was all but gone...and now, in the hospital, they put in an intravenous line and he hardly bruises at all! *Incredible!*

"You Can Trace Every Sickness, Every Disease And Every Ailment To A Mineral Deficiency." ~ Dr. Linus Pauling

It's been fifteen months now since Dad's surprise heart attack and Dr. Harrison himself tells us it's a miracle Dad is still with us. I'm happy to tell you he's had an amazing recovery and is doing fine today. Dad takes a couple of medications now, but he always drinks his high pH mineral-rich sachet. There's no doubt in my mind that the Sango Coral Life mineral sachet played a vital role in his healing process.

I asked myself immediately following Dad's heart attack what role this product, if any, might have played in healing his bruises so quickly. However, at this point, I know that my dad's water alkalinity increased with Sango Coral Life, just as I know that my sister's eczema of the past three years disappeared after only four days of taking this mineral sachet.

Aware that alkalinity is important from my nursing background, I started taking Sango Coral Life two and half years earlier and since then feel better, sleep better, and have more energy. In addition, it relieves my heartburn and acid reflux, and I no longer retain fluid in my ankles or fingers.

Fifty-two, I have very few complaints, aches, or pains. A former nurse employed by my family physician—who always preached to me how vitamins are necessary for good health but minerals are mandatory—my check-ups have always been good. Though I can't prove it, I believe Sango Coral Life also helps me with weight loss.

After Dad's heart attack, I'm offered a pre-workup by the hospital—a scan and lab work—to see if I'm a candidate for heart disease. I accept their offer, and afterward a nurse tells me they couldn't believe my lab results—that they're incredible for someone my age! I'm not surprised—during my research at my father's bedside I saw confirmation after confirmation that minerals are crucial to good health.

Striking The Right Balance

When I conducted my own research about how alkalizing my body might create a healthier environment that would prevent disease, I discovered that many doctors agree that viruses, bacteria, and cancer cannot live in an alkalized body.

They've known this since the early 1930's when Dr. Arthur Guyton—one of the recognized authorities on human physiology—found the immensely positive effects of lowered acidity and higher alkalinity on a person's health. Dr. Guyton spent the better part of his life studying the effects of different pH or acid/alkaline balances to the body.

"The cells of a healthy body are alkaline while the cells of a diseased body are acidic," Dr. Guyton pointed out in his research. He writes in his *Textbook of Medical Physiology,* used to train medical students: "The first step in maintaining health is to alkalize the body. The second step is to increase the number of negative hydrogen ions. These are the two most important aspects of homeostasis."

I learn that Dr. Guyton found that when the number of negative hydrogen ions is increased, the number of electrons available for the body to use as antioxidants to repair free radical damage is also increased. This allows the body to heal quickly and to maintain a high level of health, and this information is what originally convinced me to try alkalizing my blood through increasing my mineral intake.

I know that things happen for a reason, and I believe now that my father's heart attack is no different. My family has grown much closer—we appreciate every minute we have with each other more now than in the past! By the same token, I know I found Sango Coral Life to introduce it to my family, friends, and relatives to help them better their health.

This mineral rich sachet, which increases my water's pH level immediately through the addition of seventy trace minerals, is the highest quality I have been able to find. I do not believe all mineral sachets are equal! I find it to be inexpensive but *priceless* in terms of helping me get my daily dosage of required minerals.

As I continue to think about my own life and how my dad's heart attack might impact my future health, there's one thing I know for sure: Everyone's unique but what we all have in common is the fact that minerals are mandatory for our long-term health and survival!

ABOUT THE AUTHOR: Marlene is passionate about preventative healthcare—a must in our current society!—and helping people achieve optimal health through education and awareness. A former nurse, Marlene's commitment and dedication now focus on getting the word out about natural and affordable ways to get and stay healthy, and on sharing her professional knowledge and experience. A contributing author to *Zero To Hero In 90 Days,* and a female visionary author for several online women's communities, Marlene owns and operates two traditional businesses. Married for 26 years, Marlene has three children, resides in Mississippi, and is a true southerner at heart.

Marlene Pritchard
www.SouthernStyleMarketing.com
www.SangoCoralLife.com
MarlenePritchard1@gmail.com
601-291-9981

How Seeing With New Eyes Saved My Life

"Chia Cheri" Avery Black

No matter what I do, the shadowy figure won't go away. It intimidates me all day and through the night.

Why are you here? I ask, struggling for strength to regain control of my mind. A fog clouds my thinking. I know about hallucinations. I was Deputy Director of Mental Health for Philadelphia.

Fear grips me as I can't control this *thing*. I remember horror stories about patients seeing images threatening them. My mind swirls—I've just received a diagnosis of Stage 4 cancer in my uterus, lungs, and liver—my chance of surviving past five years is less than ten percent according to my medical prognosis.

I call a friend.

"Please help me," I plead.

"Let love overcome," he responds, reassuring me that I am a child of God and that I can reclaim my health. He guides me to transform the frightening image into a guardian angel. I'm grateful for this realignment with God, my source.

I call my oncologist. She quickly halves the dosage of the narcotic pain medicine prescribed for my chemotherapy in the hospital yesterday, and the image disappears. Still, I resent this mistake and am angry for giving in to chemo—the indiscriminate killer of cells— even though I was out of my mind with pain when doctors persuaded me.

I resent especially that the hospital waits for days to give me an enema—which instantly eliminates the pain I experienced before chemo. *What? The pain was from constipation—not cancer? I wouldn't have submitted to chemo if I'd known!*

I want to help my body heal itself. I learn that nutrient-packed chia seeds keep constipation away! That's a start—now what about the causes of my cancer? That would be helpful...

Why Me?

Growing up on a Kansas farm, I inherited much from my mother—her cheerful personality, optimism, and strong work ethic. She died at seventy-two from a series of strokes, living ten months after treatment for colon cancer. *Were her bodily functions compromised from the chemo?* I wonder. *Surely it's not my destiny to inherit that!*

I know how to live more healthily from reading *The China Study* years ago. However, I submit to fast food and chocolate bars, and the charts say I'm obese...*ugh*...but I quit smoking twenty years ago, exercise some times, and periodically try to lose weight! Regardless, I'm forced to admit I've been fooling myself.

I'm not angry I protest, but anger explodes at the cancer, the carcinogens in our environment, and my careless self.

The side effects of my first chemo treatment are devastating. I can't eat, drift in and out of sleep, and lose twenty pounds in three weeks. So weak I can't carry a glass of water, I begin my second round of chemo regretting that I'd started but afraid the cancer is too advanced to heal the natural way.

"Cheri, you're as red as your shirt!" a nurse shrieks during my chemo treatment. My face and blood pressure blow up like a balloon! Nurses race to pull the plugs. Within minutes, I return to normal. A doctor explains that protocol requires reintroducing the mixture more slowly into my body.

No! Let me out of here! my inner voice screams. My outer voice submits.

Home again, I have no energy for visits or phone calls from friends. That's not me...but I must focus what little energy I have on researching how to survive, then doing it.

The Path Less Traveled

I learn I must make serious changes in my lifestyle, how I see things, and responses to stress. I find my awful experience with chemo is painfully common, however my emerging beliefs about cancer and alternative treatments are still uncommon and provocative to some.

The changes I make revitalize my health so quickly I'm amazed! It's a miracle! I find other cancer survivors/thrivers who've successfully taken this path less traveled—one out of sync with orthodox medical advice.

Is it hard? When faced with death, the changes are compelling...my journey becomes easier with the unwavering support of my family and friends who help me every step of the way. I soak up their love, advice, and financial assistance. I'm in awe of the larger network of "coaches" who appear to provide vital pieces to my "life" puzzle.

We discover an incredible counselor, the founder of The Center for the Advancement of Cancer Education (BeatCancer.org), who shows me how to tolerate chemo and regain health *without* chemo if I so choose. Since I've already started the chemo protocol, she encourages me to continue for at least a few more treatments.

"What stresses do you experience?" she asks.

"None that bother me," I reply. I pride myself on "going with the flow."

A friend reminds me of twenty-five major stresses, starting with the unexpected termination of my funding base as director of a successful university-based multicultural institute. Within two weeks, my salary, tuition for our college-age boys, and our family's health insurance are ripped away.

My father dies, then my husband's father in Jamaica passes, too, leaving us large funeral expenses. A crash totals my car and breaks my arm, our savings diminish, and more...I realize I still carry unresolved anger, resentment, and fear. I focus on reframing these emotions with gratitude and faith.

Live-it Not Die-it!

The BeatCancer.org counselor details how the "standard American diet" of meat, dairy, glutinous grain products, processed foods, chemical additives, sugars, and artificial sweeteners *wreak havoc* on us. Normally our bodies' systems eliminate waste easily when digesting healthy choices, but become overwhelmed by toxins from non-nutritious ones.

"Live-it!" declares a friend in the Rastafarian tradition of positively reworking words with negative connotations. "You're done with that 'die-it'—you're on the healthy alkaline path! Jump for joy on your rebounder!"

For years I've taken methotrexate—an immune-suppressing medication—to treat rheumatoid arthritis (RA.) Not healthy, so I stop. With *live-it*, my RA stops too!

A naturopathic doctor from 2yourhealth.us, a Philadelphia-based holistic health services center, provides colonic cleansings and delivers a juicer. My husband juices organic wheat grass or kale with ginger, carrots, apples, and celery for me to drink every morning. I'm grateful, as my body readily absorbs these healing nutrients. We blend smoothies with greens, berries, seeds, nuts, plant protein powder, and coconut milk. I complement them with lentil vegetable soup, salads, sweet potatoes, and an increasing variety of alkaline foods. Delicious!

A cousin gives me equipment to produce alkaline water. A friend, founder of The Art of Wellness Center, brings me Isotonix nutritional supplements, and a BioMat that delivers far-infrared rays to improve immune functions. She schedules me for therapeutic massages and weekly acupuncture.

"Check out Deepak Chopra's online meditations," another friend urges. I find them soothing and centering! Friends call with creative ideas, exquisite poetry, scriptures, and prayer circles, and one even sends a precious hand-made doll. Soon after my *live-it* habits take hold there's no need for medication and the chemo's debilitating side-effects disappear.

I visit an integrative doctor of osteopathy at Pennsylvania's Narberth Family Medicine for healing manipulations and intravenous vitamins. Within three months, my blood tests show that my tumor markers, lymph functions, and nutrient levels measure in the recommended ranges!

Seeing Cancer In A Positive Light

I discover that viewing cancer cells as vicious intruders is detrimental to recovery, but find it a huge challenge to see cancer as positive. I start by calling cancer cells my built-in support group, constantly reminding me to *live-it up*. Still, I plan to kill them, not a totally positive thought...

Continuing my attitude transformation, I accept cancer as a lesson liberating me from a life-draining lifestyle. I envision cancer like a low oil warning light on a car dashboard. When the dashboard light flashes, we don't disable it—rather we add oil to the car. When cancer's warning light flashes, I know my body needs a major refill of nutrition, rest, exercise, love, laughter, faith, and positive responses to stress.

I come to see cancer as a healing mechanism, my body's last defense against the build-up of overpowering toxic waste that has created an internal acidic anaerobic environment. Once that happens, *normal cells can't take it* and they mutate into cancer cells.

Writings at ener-chi.com describe how cancer cells are a survival mechanism rather than a disease, as they decrease to non-symptomatic levels when balance is restored. Cancer cells thrive on toxins and multiply *to protect me* from developing deadly acidosis. This knowledge challenges me to quickly change my ways.

"I feel *alive!*" I bubble with delight. "I can carry a whole *jug* of water now!" My excess sixty pounds melt away over four months, and I no longer crave sweets! It's fun to be a sassy size six and to dance for hours at a party!

A friend hosts a delicious *live-it* luncheon. Friends wrap me in love with touching testimonials celebrating my life. They've come from all over—even Grenada—and I overflow with happiness!

I tell my oncologist about my successful natural healing path. She admits she has no clue but encourages me to continue. In turn, I discourage her office from providing candy in the waiting room and bringing sugary fruit juices, donuts, white bread sandwiches, and sodas to chemotherapy patients. Many otherwise caring doctors aren't trained in the relationship between nutrition, exercise, and stress to disease. I want them to understand how our mental, emotional, and spiritual health intertwine with our physical health!

An Ocean Of Possibilities...

The gifts from my journey with cancer keep revealing themselves—uppermost are the healing power of faith, the love that flows through me, and *life itself.* I no longer need to *remind* myself to be grateful; I live in continuous gratitude.

Cancer pulled the rug out from under me—it stopped my workaholic self almost dead in my tracks. Cancer commanded my full attention and challenged me with choices.

Just as we water a plant's dried-out roots rather than its withered leaves—I chose to apply *live-it* treatments to the *root causes* of my cancer not the cancer itself.

My life, caught up in a swift narrow river current during most of my adult years, emerges from my cancer journey into an ocean of possibilities—for my life purpose and passions. Energized to inspire happiness, I'm grateful for opportunities to *pay it forward*.

To assist others with ways to attract abundance, I partner with *Wakeupnow*. To help the environment, I promote low cost solar energy. To provide motivation on *living life full time*, I write for *Funtimes* magazine and coach open-minded seekers to *live-it up*!

Empowered by the possibility that my voice may be the *only* one that some may really *hear*, I speak boldly, with a message resonating from my source. I joyfully proclaim *it's so good to be here* as I share my life-renewing experiences, now seen more clearly with new eyes...

ABOUT THE AUTHOR: 'Chia Cheri' created *Live-it Up!* as an energizing healthy alternative to the typical *Di-et* lifestyle that can lead to dis-ease, suffering, medical pills and bills. She specializes in coaching positive, forward thinking people to uplift themselves into more abundant lives using expertise as a *cancer thriver*, business development coach with *WakeUpNow*, university-based diversity institute director/trainer, and former healthcare executive. She is co-author with multi-millionaires of the best-selling book *The Art and Science of Success*, editor of *FunTimes* magazine celebrating the African Diaspora, and environmental advocate. She enjoys sharing her family Topaz Dream Palace Retreat in Jamaica and traveling the world.

Cheri Avery Black, MA
Human Interests Inc., President, Senior Coach and Trainer
www.Live-itup.com www.cheriaveryblack.com
chiacheri@live-itup.com
267-225-4183

About the Authors

Are you inspired by the stories in this book?
Let the authors know.

See the contact information at the end of each chapter
and reach out to them.

They'd love to hear from you!

Author Rights & Disclaimer

Each author in this book retains the copyright and all inherent
rights to her individual chapter. Their stories are printed herein
with each author's permission.

Each author is responsible for the individual opinions expressed
through her words. Powerful You! Publishing bears no
responsibility for the content of the stories by these authors.

Acknowledgements & Gratitude

OUR GRATITUDE is greater than any words we could write and yet, we'll pen them here to acknowledge those who have assisted us and continue to bring much joy and ease into our projects, our business and our lives. As we think of each of these incredible individuals, we feel blessed and honored to be among them.

To our authors, we respect you, appreciate you and love you. You've stepped forward to shine your light through your stories and you have done so with beauty, grace and courage. As your words show, you are strong, determined and resilient, and at the same time you are humble, gentle and open. You provide the perfect example for anyone facing a challenge and we're truly honored to share this journey with you. We thank you for stepping so intentionally and fully forth so that others may learn and grow from you. You are a beautiful symbol for a life well lived.

There are many lovely people on our team and we are so very grateful for their guidance, expertise, love and support! To our editor Sheri Horn Hasan who uses her intuitive guidance in asking the 'right' questions to get to the heart and essence of the authors' stories; our graphic designer Jodie Penn who artfully designs the perfect cover; and our training team, AmondaRose Igoe, Jennifer Connell, Linda Albright, and Kathy Sipple, as well as all those who contributed behind the scenes - We love each of you!

To Patricia J. Crane, Ph.D., our friend and an amazing teacher who wrote our inspired foreword - your words beckon the soul within and provide an opening for our readers.

To our friends and families, we love you more as each year passes! Your support, love and guidance continue to encourage us on our journey as we navigate the seas of our calling.

Above all, we are grateful for the many blessings and wisdom that flow to us from our spiritual connections and we are humbled by the grace that fills us each day.

With much love and deep gratitude,
Sue Urda and Kathy Fyler

About Sue Urda and Kathy Fyler

Sue and Kathy have been friends for 24 years and business partners since 1994. They have received awards and accolades for their businesses over the years and they love their latest venture into anthology book publishing where they provide a forum for women to achieve their dreams of becoming published authors.

Their pride and joy is Powerful You! Women's Network, which they claim is a gift from Spirit. They love traveling the country producing meetings and tour events to gather women for business, personal and spiritual growth. Their greatest pleasure comes through connecting with the many inspiring and extraordinary women who are a part of their network.

The strength of their partnership lies in their deep respect, love and understanding of one another as well as their complementary skills and knowledge. Kathy is a technology enthusiast and free-thinker. Sue is an author and speaker with a love of creative undertakings. Their respect, appreciation and love for each other are boundless.

Together their energies combine to feed the flames of countless women who are seeking truth, empowerment, joy, peace and connection with themselves, their own spirits and other women.

Reach Sue and Kathy:
Powerful You! Inc.
973-248-1262
info@powerfulyou.com
www.powerfulyou.com

About Patricia J. Crane, Ph.D.

Patricia's mission is to empower people worldwide with the inner resources and outer skills they need to achieve their dreams. Her company, Heart Inspired Presentations, LLC, provides workshops, training, and products to support this mission.

Patricia's own search for meaning started during a very stressful time in her life. She began practicing a simple meditation technique "just to reduce stress" and instead discovered a spiritual path and connection. She later completed a Ph.D. in social psychology with a specialty in developing wellness programs for the worksite and taught Stress Management at numerous businesses and a local university.

In the process of pursuing her own spiritual development through reading numerous books and attending workshops, she met best-selling author Louise Hay (You Can Heal Your Life) and attended Louise's first week long intensive. Patricia was later asked to join the Heal Your Life® staff for the intensives and then personally chosen by Louise to lead the powerful Love Yourself, Heal Your Life® workshop. Leading this workshop evolved into a worldwide training program for Heal Your® Life teachers, which is co-taught with her husband Rick Nichols.

During the past twenty years, Patricia has led hundreds of workshops on a variety of topics: Reducing Stress is an Inside Job, Success Strategies for Women on the Go, Creating a Prosperity Mindset, Assertiveness for Women, Creating Powerful Affirmations, Heal Your Life® trainings, and many more.

Patricia's book, Ordering From the Cosmic Kitchen: The Essential Guide to Powerful, Nourishing Affirmations, is an easy-to-read and entertaining book on how to clear the past and use affirmations and visualizations to cook up a delicious future! It is available at www.drpatriciacrane.com, Amazon, and kindle. Other products by Patricia are available on www.heartinspired.com.

Powerful You! Women's Network
Networking with a Heart

OUR MISSION is to empower women to find their inner wisdom, follow their passion and live rich, authentic lives.

Powerful You! Women's Network is founded upon the belief that women are powerful creators, passionate and compassionate leaders, and the heart and backbone of our world's businesses, homes, and communities.

Our Network welcomes all women from all walks of life. We recognize that diversity in our relationships creates opportunities.

Powerful You! creates and facilitates venues for women who desire to develop connections that will assist in growing their businesses. We aid in the creation of lasting personal relationships and provide insights and tools for women who seek balance, grace and ease in all facets of life.

Powerful You! was founded in January 2005 to gather women for business, personal and spiritual growth. Our monthly chapter meetings provide a space for collaborative and inspired networking and 'real' connections. We know that lasting relationships are built through open and meaningful conversation, so we've designed our meetings to include opportunities for, discussions, masterminds, speakers, growth, and gratitude shares.

Follow us online:

Twitter: @powerfulyou
www.facebook.com/powerfulyou
Linked In: Powerful You! Women's Network

**Join or Start a Chapter for
Business, Personal & Spiritual Growth**

powerfulyou.com

Well-Being is for Everyone

Especially, YOU!

Are You Being Called to Share Your Story?

Would You Like to Contribute to Our Next Inspiring Anthology Book?

If you are like most people, you may find it daunting to even consider writing a whole book on your own. No worries! We're here to help!

If you've always wanted to be an author, and you can see yourself partnering with others to share your story, an anthology book is the answer you've been seeking.

We provide complete and personal guidance through the writing and editing process. Our complete publishing packages include a variety of training sessions in many aspects of business growth - and you'll get books too!

We are committed to helping individuals express their voices and shine their lights into the world. Won't you join us? Become an Author with Powerful You! Publishing.

Powerful You! Publishing

Ahhh...
Well-Being

CPSIA information can be obtained at www.ICGtesting.com
Printed in the USA
LVOW12s0556200314

378083LV00001BC/1/P